A Venomous COCKTAIL

JODY VALLEY

Bella
BOOKS
2013

Copyright © 2013 by Jody Valley

Bella Books, Inc.
P.O. Box 10543
Tallahassee, FL 32302

Printed in the United States of America on acid-free paper.

First Bella Books Edition 2013

Editor: Nene Adams
Cover Designer: Linda Callaghan

ISBN: 978-1-59493-371-4

About the Author

Growing up, Jody Valley wrote poetry and short stories to bare her teenage rebellious soul—in lieu of a journal. She wanted to be either a spy or a reporter, and to never give up her skepticism. When her family frowned on her entering the field of espionage, she settled for becoming a clinical social worker—fulfilling her need to spy—and writing columns and feature stores for newspapers, as well as fighting for social justice. And now, Jody has combined her years as a journalist with her years as a clinical social worker and a social activist to write her first suspenseful mystery novel.

She lives with her partner of twenty-four years, and three dogs. Together, they have four adult children and two adorable granddaughters—with another granddaughter on the way. She does much of her writing at her cabin on a lake in northern Michigan.

Dedication

During the writing of this novel, I became a grandmother to two adorable little girls. To them I dedicate this book: Eowyn Marie Zay and Gabriella Mae Souza.

Acknowlegdments

I want to especially thank my wonderful partner, Elaine Thomason, for twenty-four great years and for her undying support in my life and writing. She also did some great editing work for me. She is truly the love of my life.

A big thanks and appreciation to my readers for their friendship, feedback and skills: To Dr. Penny Gardner, PhD—also stands for: "Pretty Happy Dyke"—for her writing and publicity expertise and always being there for me. To Mary Cook Smith, JD, for her writing and legal expertise—I certainly didn't know Michigan doesn't allow blinking beer signs in bars, as well as other legal stuff. To my daughter, Julia Zay, for her constant encouragement and for her fashion advice—"people don't wear Keds anymore," and other tidbits I would never have known or suspected. To Shirley Beckman for her writing expertise and her courage to continue to wear Keds in the face of my daughter's fashion taboos. To my son, Eric Zay, for his scientific expertise, and who is an excellent writer. To Marjorie Tursak for her initial guidance. To Marilyn Bowen for her strong arm and relaxation techniques, and her loving support.

More thanks and gratitude: To my stepdaughter Michelle Souza—who also provided feedback—and to my son-in-law Courtney Souza for the lending of their Maine Coon cat, Mr. Moxin. And to Traci Urban, my stepdaughter, and Carrie Zay, my daughter-in-law, for their love and support.

Much appreciation to all the folks at Bella Books for helping to make my novel into a book.

CHAPTER ONE

Kera

A door opened off to the side of the platform. Kera Van Brocklin watched while a young man in a dark polo shirt and matching pants emerged, rolling her father's casket on wheels across the creaky hardwood floor and depositing it in front of a marble podium. Willem Van Brocklin was making his final appearance as the mayor of Lakeside City, Michigan.

A fiftyish woman wearing a black cobbler apron and carrying a tray of makeup followed close behind. She scampered to the side of the casket, bent over, and applied cosmetics touches to his face, then quickly left. A man in a dark gray suit whipped off the Star of David from a hook on the right side of the stage, replacing it with a picture of a fair-skinned, blue-eyed Jesus. He reached behind a maroon velvet curtain blanketing the back wall, then watched as a groaning four-foot long hydraulic gold cross descended and came to a halt midway in front of the curtain.

Faux-painted marble pillars on either side of the stage framed Willem's casket where it rested on its wheeled carrier.

Two men dressed in black suits and wearing carnation boutonnières set out additional folding chairs. Kera grimaced. She would have preferred a private affair, just folks her dad had been close to. Crowds made her nervous, edgy, wanting to escape. But her sister had insisted on allowing more people to attend, saying their dad had many friends and political associates who'd want and expect to be there. They had finally compromised, agreed to try and keep the ceremony down in size by making it "by invitation only." Quite a few people had already shown up and the ceremony wasn't due to start for another forty-five minutes.

Kera's hands were getting sweaty. She rubbed them against her pants.

Kera noticed family photos displayed on a table close by. One picture showed her late mother with her dad, taken on their honeymoon in Hawaii. Just fourteen years later, her mom would be dead. She sighed. It had been difficult for her to absorb the fact of her mother's death. For several years afterward, she'd kept seeing momentary flashes of her mother everywhere, like a ghost: in the kitchen making breakfast, or knitting while sitting in her rocking chair in the living room, or putting on her makeup in the bathroom. The ghostly images had been both painful and comforting to her.

The next snapshot featured her and Dee in their high school graduation caps and gowns. Dad stood between them with his arms wrapped around "his girls." She remembered how family friends had kept remarking how much she and her sister resembled the French side of the family—their mother's people—but would quickly add that that their slender, lanky bodies were definitely inherited from their father.

Her gaze went to the next photograph. Her father stood with her twin sister, Deidre—or Dee, as she mostly called her—and Dee's husband, Don, on their wedding day. Don had soft features, giving him a pretty-boy look. He was shorter than Dee by about an inch or two—maybe he was five-foot-nine like he claimed, but she'd pegged him at no more than five-foot-eight.

She really didn't like looking at pictures of her sister's wedding day. At the time, it hadn't been the idea of her sister marrying Don that had bothered her, but that Dee was marrying a man. When would her sister "get it" that they were both gay? They had to be, because they were identical twins.

Kera shook her head.

In a third photo, Willem smiled proudly as he stood next to her. She wore her army uniform. She'd known she'd be departing the next day for Iraq. If only she had known how dramatically her life would change, and not for the better. But it wouldn't have mattered, anyway.

At that point she couldn't have turned things around, moved in another direction, because she had signed over her life to the US Army. Dee came alongside her and took her hand. "They're finished with the preparations. Do you want to go up to the casket now?" Kera nodded and walked up with her sister.

She looked down at her father's body. These past few days seemed so unreal, but death always felt that way to her. How could life just be gone, like that: snuffed out, snatched away, leaving a hole in her life? And, now, all the things she wanted to say to her father would never be spoken. She'd never be able to tell him why she'd pulled away from him when she realized she was lesbian, queer, a disappointment. No doubt distancing herself had hurt him, but she simply hadn't been able to work out how to put the pieces of her life into the picture of her father's political career, the mayor of a city staked down by its conservative, Dutch Reformed roots. She believed—more like, needed to believe—if he had known, he would have still loved her, but he probably would have thought he'd done something wrong. And even if he could have overcome his sense of guilt and failure, the city wouldn't have forgiven him.

"I'm sorry you couldn't get home in time to say goodbye to Dad." Dee put an arm around her. "But it all happened so fast. The doctor said with a stroke this massive, had he not died, he'd have been a vegetable. So I guess it was a good thing, you know, that he didn't linger." She dabbed at the tears trickling down her cheeks.

"Yeah, I guess." Kera realized her words came out without any conviction, but for her, not being able to say goodbye and tell her dad she loved him was the same kind of ending she'd had with Kelly. Death kept reaching into her world and ripping out life.

Kera looked over at Dee and saw she was crying. She put her arms around her and held her. She wished she could cry, but she had no tears. They'd gotten all used up when Kelly was killed.

Dee finally pulled out of her embrace. "I've got to get a hold of myself. But look at you, you're so strong."

"No, just numb." At least, that's how it seemed on the surface, but deeper down, her emotions swirled like an eddy.

"All in all, Dad looks pretty good, don't you think?" Dee put her hand on the shiny mahogany casket. Apparently remembering Kera hadn't seen him in over a year, she added, "These last few months, Dad wasn't looking very good. In fact, he looked terrible. He was under a lot of stress. I tried to get him to go to the doctor, but he just wouldn't go, said he was busy and would get to it."

"Dead doesn't look good, Dee, but as far as dead goes, I guess he looks okay. In my world, death comes in pieces, guts splattering—" Kera stopped. The memories pushed up, threatening to poke a hole in her battle-worn psyche. She needed to push down her demons, her monsters, but it was like trying to hold back rising puke.

"Are you okay, Kera?" Dee motioned her to sit in a chair. From her purse, she took out a small pack of tissues, pulled one out and reached over and patted Kera's forehead. "My God, Kera, you're sweating and so pale."

"I'll be okay." She certainly didn't feel okay, but that was her standard reply these days. To say anything else would lead to more questions, bringing up crap she didn't want to think about, let alone discuss.

"Well, you don't look okay. It must be so hard coming straight from the hospital to all this."

"You mean from the 'Nut Ward.'" After Kelly's death, her panic attacks, flashbacks and nightmares started, sending her stateside and into the VA hospital: more specifically, First Floor, One North, otherwise referred to—by its inhabitants—as the Nut Ward. First floor was a euphemism for garden level, no chance for jumping out of windows, no chance for permanently extinguishing her nightmares.

"Kera, don't say that. You're not crazy."

She decided to let that go. How could she explain what it'd been like being in Iraq, what it had done to her? She couldn't.

Suddenly, it felt like the focusing mechanism in her eyes had gone berserk. She blinked, trying to adjust her vision, struggling to stop the precipitous slide into her unfastened psyche. Too late. *The room faded to gray, began to move. The floor turned into roller coaster tracks. She found herself in an errant car flying off the guide rails, unattached, her landing place unknown. She wasn't taking in air. Concentrate, breathe, breathe… in and out…in and out…in and out. The wayward car found its tracks. The rails flattened out, stopped twisting and turning. The car jolted to a stop.*

Death lurked everywhere.

Too much life ripped away from her.

She couldn't absorb so much loss, any more than clay soil could absorb a hard rain.

She wasn't supposed to be sent to a war zone. The recruiter had assured—more like lied to—her. He'd said he'd been to Iraq himself, so he had to have known about the conditions there. The whole damned country was a war zone. Hell, no one knew when an innocent-looking person would walk up and explode or an IED would be underfoot, blowing-up, eradicating. No one knew when a vehicle would approach a checkpoint, spewing bullets—and fear.

No one knew when dreams would be shattered.

How could she have known she would witness Kelly stepping on an explosive, blowing her out of existence—and taking her love with her?

A deliveryman rushed in carrying two huge sprays of flowers. He placed them on either side of the casket. He was followed by a stream of other delivery people creating a seemingly endless display of flowers, covering death with vibrant colors and floral cologne. The smell sickened her.

A male voice boomed out, "Well, praise the Lord, if it's not Kera, my long lost sister-in-law, back from the war."

Kera glanced around to see Don sauntering up the aisle with a phony smile slathered on his face. How could her sister have married that phony bastard? Don had grown up in Wisconsin, but had chosen in adulthood to borrow his father's Tennessee accent, apparently hoping to make himself more appealing, more authentic, to his right-wing Christian ministry.

"Hey, Don." For Deidre's sake, she molded a minimal smile on her lips.

She noticed he'd let his dark blond hair grow out and now wore it slicked back, bunching up on his shirt collar. That must be the cool look these days, at least for up-and-coming ministers. She'd run across similar hairdos on several young, Sunday morning pastors on TV. When she was in the hospital, she'd seen these barkers of right-wing religion when she flipped through the channels trying to find something decent to watch. Sundays in the hospital were boring, no counseling sessions or therapy groups. She'd entertained herself by watching old movies and sitcom reruns.

"I'm so glad you were finally able to get here, sweetheart." Don brushed a peck by her cheek.

Kera grimaced. Don didn't like her, let alone approve of her. He saw her as a sinner, unwilling to give up her "lesbian ways," as he put it. But she didn't like him or approve of his religious convictions, the way he constantly reminded Deidre that gay people were condemned to Hell. She guessed their mutual antipathy brought pain to her sister, but she didn't know what she could do about it.

"Glad you could make it," Don went on. "Was it hard getting out of that VA hospital they put you in?"

Deidre tossed Don a disapproving look.

"Where are my manners?" Don tapped the side of his forehead with the heel of his hand, "I'm sorry about your dad. He was truly a great man and such a loss to this community."

Kera felt her body stiffen. How much longer could she make nice with Don for her sister's sake? "Geez, Don, I was selfishly thinking of Dee's and my loss, not the community's."

"Oh, yeah, certainly, that's just a given, honey. Y'all know I loved him too…I surely did." Don patted Kera's shoulder, gave Deidre a kiss and excused himself to do last-minute preparations for the service.

Kera glared at her sister. "He's not, Dee. Tell me he's not doing Dad's service." She'd abandoned Christianity in high school, but didn't have a problem with Christians as long as they didn't interfere with her life or her beliefs—but Don tried to interfere, every time he got a chance.

"How could I keep him from doing it?" Deidre's tone underscored her frustration. "Beside, he's not as bad a guy as you make him out to be. He loved Dad and cried when he died. If you want to know the truth, I think he loved and admired Dad more than his own father. I know how you feel about Don, but really, he's sensitive and a good guy, maybe a little insecure and sometimes self-righteous—I'll admit it. I'm just saying he'd be hurt if he didn't do the service, like he'd lost face. After all, he's trying to establish himself with his new church in this community. Just think about his feelings, Kera. Put yourself in his shoes."

"Lose face? That's insane!" Kera fumed.

She hated Don's control over Dee. Since their marriage, her sister hadn't been the same. Her dad didn't even go to Don's church. She didn't believe for a minute that anyone would think anything negative about Don not conducting his father-in-law's service. Hell, it would be like a doctor not operating on his family. As far as she was concerned, Don just wanted a place to grandstand, to be important, to make a great show of burying "The Mayor."

She'd never bought Don's excuse that he went into the ministry because—as he claimed—he "loved the Lord and wanted to serve Him." As far as she could see, the only person Don served was himself.

"What do you want me to do? Don's my husband. I'm very aware he has his faults, but he has his good side too. You weren't here when Dad was dying. Don was a comfort to me and had to make the arrangements. It wasn't easy. He took over and handled things when I needed him to." Deidre's eyes filled with tears. "You were in the hospital. What was I supposed to do? I didn't want to put any more stress on you than you were already dealing with. Pretty much everything was left up to me and, frankly, I was a mess myself." She swiped under her eyes with her fingers, trying to wipe away her tears. "Oh, Dee." Kera realized she needed to back off and cut Deidre some slack. She wished she could find something about Don she liked or respected and be more civil toward him. She slapped a sticky note on the back of her mind to try and find something good about Don as a gift to her sister. "I'm sorry." She took Dee's hand and squeezed it, then pulled her into a hug. "All this stuff around Dad's death must've been really hard on you, and I wasn't there when you needed me. Everything will be okay, I promise. Really." She pulled back from Dee and put out her hand.

Deidre managed a smile and offered her half of the Van Brocklin Sisters' Secret Handshake. Their handshake had been around for as long as Kera could remember. Evolving since the playpen, the handshake settled arguments, restored good feelings, promised alliance and celebrated victories.

For Kera, coming home meant she could be with her sister. That part was good, even if it meant having to deal with her asshole brother-in-law.

"Good afternoon, ladies, do you mind if I join you?" Harry Janssen, Don's friend, swaggered into the room.

Kera suppressed a sneer. She didn't know Harry very well, but he clearly expected women to turn and look at him and they did, no doubt attracted by his full head of well-coiffed, dark brown hair, crystal blue eyes and muscular build. He wore a gray, hand-tailored suit and expensive shoes. The few times they'd met, it had seemed to her that Harry and Don were handmade and special ordered for each other, a duet of religious crazies with a scheme. Harry possessed the energy and the money, and Don owned the preacher's robe, charisma and balls to pull off their plans.

Harry flung an arm over Deidre's shoulder and hers, bringing them into an unstable, neck-squeezing, three-way hug. "I thought I would watch after you since Don will be up there in the pulpit. Don't want you two ladies to sit alone."

"We aren't alone, Harry, we're together." Kera ducked and pulled out of his stranglehold hug, leaving him still attached to Deidre. Good thing she'd taken her meds this morning and seen his bear hug coming, or she might have gone off on him. As it was, her heart was beating fast and sweat began leaching through her pores.

The last time she'd seen Harry, he'd bragged that he volunteered as an assistant wrestling coach for the high school team. As much as she didn't like Harry, she had to admit that he turned out to be a good addition to the team's coaching staff, helping to bring state championships to Lakeside City Central. But certainly Harry's coaching benefited him as well by getting him more customer contacts for his real estate company, and his visibility most likely helped him get elected to the city council. His political position was probably another reason women were attracted to him—he had power. But for her, just being in his presence made her skin crawl.

"I'm sorry, Harry. My sister is tired from her trip. We're glad to have you sit with us." Deidre shot Kera their mother's "behave yourself" glance. "We don't have much in the way of family anymore. It'll be nice sitting together. Besides, you could use some company yourself, since Sylvia couldn't come."

"Yes, indeed, I'm sure missing her, as I know you are Deidre. She was so upset that she couldn't be here, but I told her I'd take good care of you."

Kera knew Sylvia was her sister's best friend. Dee had told her earlier that Sylvia had called last week about her grandmother's operation and how she'd been so sorry she had to leave town to care for her.

The organ began to play. Folks rushed to their seats. Harry led her and Deidre to the first row. She noticed Dee taking a position between her and Harry, which was more than okay with her. She wouldn't have to sit so close to his overpowering cologne and chutzpah.

Kera quickly glanced around, thankful Dee had agreed to set limits on the funeral attendance. The newspaper article she'd read had made it clear the event was just for family, friends and the city's political leaders. Had it been up to Don, she suspected he'd have rented a huge hall—hell, maybe the high school stadium—and invited the public. However, even with the effort to keep numbers down, the large room began to overflow with strangers. Gate crashers? Who'd want to crash a funeral? Morbid. Bizarre. Maybe a political thing, people wanting to feel important. Whatever their motives, she didn't appreciate all these people surrounding her. Made her panicky. She concentrated on her breathing to help calm herself.

Two ushers pushed open the accordion doors to an adjacent room. They quickly pulled folding chairs off a rack and set them out on the tiled floor for the latecomers. The organist looked up, then began replaying the hymn louder, helping cover the sliding door's unwelcome screeching and the clanking of unfolding chairs.

Kera watched as Don entered the room, darting around giving instructions to the ushers and whispering into the organist's ear.

He looked like the director of a play, moments before the first act. Apparently satisfied, he quickly left through the door in back of the room.

The organist brought the hymn she'd been playing to a close, cueing the start of the service, and then started up the processional music.

Melodic voices rose into the air as a choir wearing black robes entered from the back, walked up the aisle to the platform and onto risers located behind the podium. Don followed, wearing a dark gray robe with two black velvet stripes around the upper arms and a white clerical stole draped down on either side, adorned with large black crosses and gold fringe hanging from the edges. With his head tilted slightly upward, he carried his opened hymnal high, like an offering to God.

Kera's stomach growled. She hadn't eaten anything. She couldn't make food go down, like her throat had a knot in it. Grief picked at the thin scab over her emotions. She didn't want to lose control. Reaching into her pocket, she felt around for a small pill she'd placed there earlier that morning. She sucked up her saliva, slipped the pill into her mouth and swallowed, sending it down her dry, tight throat.

"It's so good to see y'all here today. And make no mistake about it, it is a great day," Don proclaimed. "Willem Hendrick Van Brocklin is with our Lord Jesus Christ. Amen."

A chorus of "Amens" echoed back at him.

"Jesus, right this minute, is telling Willem what a great servant he has been to our Lord." Don's voice began to rise with every word until it reached the intensity of a tent revival preacher. "Let me tell y'all why I know Willem is in Heaven with our Lord: Willem accepted the Lord Jesus Christ as his personal Lord and Savior." He took a moment to let the words rest on his audience while his gaze surveyed the listeners, including Kera. He took a breath and continued, "Willem was a wonderful family man. He raised two beautiful daughters and was a devoted husband to his wife, who has already joined our Savior, the Lord Jesus Christ. God rest her soul! She's been waiting to greet Willem in Heaven. Praise be to God!

"Let's take a minute to think about our beloved mayor, my father-in-law. Willem was an excellent mayor. In these hard economic times with all the problems in housing and the resulting loss in revenue to our fair city, he did more than keep this city afloat. In fact, he looked ahead by building new docks, a yachting marina and moorings, bringing into our city the high-end tourist trade from Chicago. He was behind the rehabilitation of our Old Fishing Village with new shops and restaurants, making it a tourist attraction that created jobs, bringing in more money to our community. Mayor Van Brocklin worked hard to get the new Water Park done for this summer. From what he told me just last week, the park is scheduled to open sometime early in August, and I'm so sorry he won't be with us on that day."

Kera heard excited murmuring in the crowd.

Don smiled and went on, "But more than all the wonderful things he has done for our community, Willem's greatness, I declare, lay in his knowing right from wrong." He paused, allowing a moment of silence, then continued, "Willem based his life on the Lord's truths. Oh, I can hear Jesus saying right now, 'Well done, my faithful servant.'" Don's arms rose in the air like an umpire signaling a touchdown.

"Amen" exploded from the crowd, jarring Kera.

Don waited for the silence to return. Stern-faced, he looked across the audience. "Willem followed God's rules, not just in his home life, but as mayor of our wonderful city."

Kera rolled her eyes at Don's long-winded sermon, squirmed in her seat and glanced at her watch. Her mind wandered: Deidre had suggested she stay at their dad's house for now and they'd get together tomorrow so they could figure out what had to be done to settle the estate. She had mixed feelings about staying at the house. Living at Dad's place would help her out financially, as well as keep the house from sitting empty. On the other hand, he wouldn't be there and would never be there again. She'd felt that kind of emptiness going home after her mother's funeral and wasn't certain she could endure it again. But she'd probably do it anyway, because she didn't have any better ideas about where to go. She hated motels and certainly wouldn't stay with her sister and Don.

Don's already impassioned words became inflamed, invading her reverie and snapping her back to the present.

"Now, y'all know there are those in our beautiful city who would threaten—no, destroy—all that our mayor tried to accomplish. There are those who would turn our city into the likes of Sodom and Gomorrah. There are those who do the Devil's work right here in our glorious city. If allowed to prevail, they will bring divine destruction upon this city we love, our city that Mayor Van Brocklin worked so hard to keep prosperous and upright.

"Both Peter and Jude make reference to and describe the sin of homosexuality as, 'ungodly, lawless, unnatural and extreme immorality.'" His fist hit the podium. "And yet," he lowered his voice to a stage whisper, "there are those out there fighting to have homosexuals added to the Civil Rights Ordinance of this city." His voice rose again. "These perverted, sinful people threaten our very existence. And don't y'all doubt it for a minute: God will have His way as He did on nine-eleven." He leaned forward over the podium and threw his clenched fist into the air. "We must fight the immorality that threatens this town! Now!"

Kera straightened up, jabbed Deidre with her elbow and whispered: "What in the hell is he doing?"

"I don't know." Deidre shrugged and held out her hands in a gesture of helplessness. "Honestly, I didn't know he was going to do this."

"In Leviticus 18:22 and 24, homosexuality is described as an 'abomination' and 'defiling.'" Don wiped his forehead with a handkerchief he'd pulled out of his pocket and continued, "This act is reprehensible and unclean. In Leviticus 20:13, it is again described as an 'abomination,' saying that they shall surely be put to death!" His fist pounded the podium once more.

A chorus of "Amens" lifted from the choir and some members of the audience. Harry voiced his agreement with the rest.

Kera turned around to see who else responded to the hateful words. About half the people there were nodding their heads in agreement. A fire burned in her stomach, sending rage into her chest. She began to shake. She leaned over to Dee and said, "That asshole. I'll kill Don, I swear."

Hearing her words, Harry glared at her. He put his finger to his lips, signaling her to be quiet, and turned his attention back to Don.

"He can't pull this shit at my father's funeral," Kera continued. "Dad didn't feel this way. He wasn't hateful."

Once again, Harry glared and held his finger to his lips, trying to shush her.

Don apparently heard the discord and looked over at them.

Deidre put a hand on Kera's back and rubbed it in an attempt to calm her, but Dee's efforts to placate her just made her angrier.

Kera got up from her seat and pushed past Deidre and Harry to get to the aisle. She hurried to the back of the room and out the exit. In the hallway, she realized she had stopped breathing again. She sucked in a few breaths and opened the huge wooden doors to the outside.

She spotted a stone bench on the funeral home's porch and sat down. The fresh summer air and the sun's warmth helped her regain a steady breathing rhythm, but her thoughts spun out of control, drenched with rage.

The sound of nearby voices jolted her out of her internal cacophony. She glanced up and found a TV camera crew on the front lawn heading her way. People stood all around on the sidewalk. A large white van with a satellite dish and the words "TV 7—News First— News Now" written on the side sat parked in front of the funeral home. The van hadn't been there when she and Deidre came. She hadn't even thought about the press showing up. Wasn't this supposed to be a private funeral, or at least somewhat private?

She was exhausted, barely able to think. She'd flown all night to arrive at eight ten in the morning. Deidre had swept her off to Dad's house to shower, get dressed and try, unsuccessfully, to eat. She'd tried to take a nap, but her mind continued to chew on itself, so she got no rest, no peace. She'd come early to the funeral home for a few last moments to be alone with her dad. Now here she was stuck trying to fathom Don's bizarre invective against gay people, delivered—of all places—at her dad's funeral. Everything seemed so unreal to her.

She wondered if she'd entered the set of some bizarre movie.

What part was she supposed to play?

Maybe it wasn't a movie, maybe she was trapped and spinning in a nightmare where Iraq and Lakeside City converged into a dump-heap of fanaticism.

Seemingly of their own accord, her hands flew up in the air, trying to hold back the invasion, but the gesture proved ineffective and too late. A woman wearing a gray suit and a bright yellow blouse stood in front of her with a microphone. A cameraman took a position nearby.

"Aren't you one of the mayor's daughters?" The reporter shoved the mic toward her.

Kera blinked, still trying to adjust to the glaring midafternoon light. Looking out across the lawn at the spectacle, she held her hand to her brow to shield her eyes against the sun. Bile made its way up her esophagus, burning as it climbed. Events were on fast forward. If only she could nail life down—just for a moment—set her feet, check a compass, learn her lines.

The reporter rephrased, "Are you Kera or Deidre?"

"Kera," she heard herself say.

"Your father was much loved by this community. I take it the service is over?" The reporter looked at the door, apparently expecting more people to emerge.

Kera steadied herself by locking onto the reporter's eyes. "It's over for me. But he's going to pay for this." she said, thrusting her thumb back at the funeral home.

She needed to find a rip, a hole in this nightmare; a place to escape. She got up from the bench, hurried down the steps and over to her dad's Buick. She glanced over her shoulder to see the camera's lens following her, like she was trapped in the crosshairs of a malevolent, psychotic force.

She got into the car, started the engine, and peeled out of the parking lot, tires screeching as she raced away, leaving black tire tracks of anger on the pavement.

CHAPTER TWO

Kera

Kera woke up, wondering where she was. Her mind was foggy, thick and polluted. The glow from a TV offered a shaft of light to the otherwise dark room.

She smelled it first, turned her head and saw, on the coffee table, the open pizza box with leftover slices and crusts, a six-pack of beer—four of the bottles empty—and a wadded up, pizza sauce-stained napkin. Her memory finally peeked through the thick haze: after leaving the funeral, she'd stopped at a grocery store, bought some beer and a boxed pizza, driven to her dad's house, ate and drank while watching some stupid TV program to distract herself so she could calm down. She'd finally fallen asleep on her dad's leather sofa.

Kera sat up and pushed off a yellow and pink afghan her mother had knitted, then reached over for the switch on a table lamp. Now oriented to place, she checked her watch for the time: ten fifty p.m. She figured she must have been sleeping for five hours or so.

She put her bare feet down on the cold hardwood floor. Her brown linen suit jacket along with the shoes and socks she'd worn to the funeral earlier that day were tossed in a heap on the floor by the sofa. She got up and went to the bathroom to pee.

Checking herself in the mirror over the sink, she noticed a pizza stain on her white blouse. She took a washcloth off the rack, wet it and rubbed the stain, but that only made it worse. She looked back up in the mirror again and stared at the barely recognizable face looking back at her. The reflection was hers, okay, but a reflection she would've hoped not to see for another thirty years or so. The image that stared back at her appeared old, wrung out, needing an injection of something or another, but she had no idea what that would be. She splashed cold water on her face, hoping to regain a little life, but it didn't work.

The beer along with her fatigue had put her to sleep which, more importantly, put her out of her anger—well, suppressed it, she supposed, but the emotion remained simmering below the surface. If Don were here, she'd likely kill him or, at minimum, beat the shit out of him.

She dried her hands and returned to the sofa. Her stomach growled. She grabbed a piece of cold pizza and one of the warm beers.

The local news program on the TV had just started. Kera saw a female reporter wearing a yellow blouse and a gray suit. Wasn't that the reporter who'd shoved the microphone in her face? She searched around, found the remote on the floor and turned up the volume.

The footage showed police directing auto and foot traffic as people emerged from the funeral service. The female TV reporter had been relegated to a place directly across the street from the funeral home. She stood talking into the camera about the mayor, his sudden illness, and how he'd be missed.

The camera moved around, scanning the scene. Kera saw what seemed like yellow crime scene tape around the lawn area, apparently to keep the crowd from trampling the grass and flower beds, and maybe to keep them at a distance from the funeral home itself.

The reporter talked about the day's events surrounding the funeral, highlighting all the dignitaries who'd attended. She turned toward a well-dressed man standing next to her—a man Kera recognized. She said, "I have with me one of our councilmen, Harry Janssen." She gave a polite smile to Harry and continued, "Councilman, I'm sure this has been a hard day for you as well. I know the mayor worked closely with you and all the council members to get many projects done."

She held out the mic to Harry, who replied, "The mayor's death is such a loss to our community." He tucked his errant tie back into his suit coat. "Mayor Van Brocklin was a good man and a great mayor. In difficult economic times, he—"

"Tell me, Councilman," the reporter pushed on, "Mayor Van Brocklin's daughter, Kera, came out of the funeral early, obviously distressed. She got in a car and left—in a big hurry, I might add. Can you tell us anything about that?"

"Well, she's recently back from Iraq, you know, and being in Iraq had to be hard on her, not to speak of having to come back home to her father's funeral. I'm sure you know she's been in a VA hospital since she returned to the States, needed some help readjusting. It must have been too much for her. That's all, really."

That bastard! Kera took a swig of warm beer. She felt like throwing the bottle through the TV set, but quickly set it on the coffee table before her momentary control broke down.

It looked to Kera like Harry was agitated and eager to halt the interview. He quickly told the reporter something about needing to get back to the family, then excused himself.

The reporter turned her attention to a thin, thirtyish woman standing on the other side of her. A breeze coming from the west blew the woman's blond shoulder-length hair into her face. She hurriedly pulled out something from her green suit jacket pocket, gathered her hair back and secured it behind her head.

The reporter brought the microphone around to the woman. "Would you tell us your name?"

"Amanda Bakker."

"Ms. Bakker, how did you know the mayor?"

"Actually, I've known the mayor since I was a kid. I was a friend to the Van Brocklin twins when I was in high school. I…"

Kera leaned toward to the TV and hit the up arrow on the volume control. She couldn't believe her eyes. *My god, that's Mandy.* She hadn't seen her since the summer between high school and college. God, that has to be…uh, shit, fifteen years ago, she estimated. Maybe longer.

She hadn't seen Mandy at the funeral home, but the fact was, she hadn't much paid attention to anyone. Before the service, she'd been too absorbed with seeing her father's body and dealing with Don and Harry and was in no shape to be social. She had planned on speaking to people after the service, but hadn't due to her premature exit.

The reporter asked, "Have you talked to the Van Brocklin sisters since the mayor's death or have any idea how they're doing?"

"I talked to Deidre for a moment. Of course, it's hard for them to lose their dad. They lost their mother so early on, like they were only eleven or twelve at the time. But I feel especially bad for Kera. Her sister told me she wasn't able to get home in time to see her father before he died. It's a tough time for both of them—"

The reporter interrupted, "Kera Van Brocklin came out of the service early and had little to say. She seemed upset with someone or something at the service. Do you know anything about that?"

"I can't speak for Kera, but I'll tell you if it wasn't for the fact that it was the twins' father, I would have absolutely gotten up and left, myself. I can't believe what went on in there. This was supposed to be a funeral, a time for honoring the mayor. But what happened in there—" Mandy gestured back toward the funeral home, "—was totally inappropriate and hateful."

The reporter's eyebrows arched. "What did happen in there?"

The expression on the reporter's face wasn't lost on Kera. The woman obviously knew she had a fish on her line. She grabbed her beer and moved over in front of the TV and sat on the floor.

Mandy's jaw was set tight. She took a deep breath and said, "The minister, Don Bledsoe—Deidre's husband, no less—used the memorial service to rail against the gay community. That man is an absolute homophobe! I can't believe he did that. And I don't believe for a minute," she sucked in more air, "he didn't understand that slamming the gay community at this service was horrendously inappropriate. It doesn't take much of a stretch of the imagination to guess that's why Kera got up and left. It was horrible and unbelievably tasteless. Really, you should have seen and heard it. I didn't talk to Kera but—"

"Do you think this has anything to do with the proposed inclusion of homosexuals in Lakeside City's Civil Rights Ordinance, the one the Council is presently considering?"

"Absolutely, but good grief, to say those things at the mayor's funeral?" Mandy turned directly toward the reporter, "Look, I'm a lesbian. Robert Davis and I have recently started an organization called LEAP—"

"LEAP?"

"Legal Equality for All People." Mandy quickly added: "It's made up of the LGBT community and our heterosexual allies—and we do have some allies in this community," she added. "But as it stands now, gay people still aren't protected in this city. For God's sake, this is 2008 and LGBT people can still be thrown out of restaurants, their homes, fired from their jobs—just because they happen to be gay or appear gay." She stopped and took a deep breath. Her large green eyes turned from the reporter to look directly into the camera and she continued, "And it's never time to be a hatemonger. That so-called man of God, Don Bledsoe, is a hatemonger, pure and simple."

"Wow, you go girl!" Kera's thoughts burst out of her mouth. She could hardly believe what she'd seen and heard. Mandy speaking out like that on TV. *And a dyke, no less.*

She leafed back in her memory, holding up Mandy against lesbian stereotypes: Mandy had been athletic, played soccer—and was pretty good at it too—but she'd dated guys and had gone with Bill the last two years of high school.

But then, Kera remembered having played the heterosexual teenager dating game as well, though sparingly. Coming out as a teenage homo would not have been a smart move for her at the time. Hell, it was a gutsy thing to do today in this ultraconservative town. Maybe it could be done in Saugatuck, Royal Oak or Ann Arbor, but not in the predominantly Dutch Reformed community of Lakeside City. She realized that Mandy dating guys really meant nothing. Still, Mandy hadn't been a kid who made her think: "baby dyke." Even seeing the woman today on TV, her gaydar wouldn't have perked up if Mandy hadn't outed herself.

Kera smiled. The girl sure had guts. Coming out like that on TV and slamming good ol' Don right where he needed it—in his self-righteous, gay-hating balls.

Impressive!

Thinking back, Kera remembered Mandy having gumption in high school too. She was the student council president in their junior and senior years, and had stood up for her classmates. Her mind flashed on an incident from their senior year: the school gym walls had been stealthily spray-painted with bright, colorful caricatures of prominent seniors. The principal hadn't seen the graffiti as valued art. He'd said if the vandal didn't reveal himself, he would cancel the class trip to Washington DC and threatened to cancel the prom as well. The artist didn't come forward, so the principal announced over the PA system that he would make good on his threats. In response, Mandy organized a group of class leaders and prominent jocks to argue that the whole senior class shouldn't be punished for the act of one student. When they emerged from the meeting with the principal, the class trip and prom were back on. Mandy had been the heroine of the day.

Kera's attention snapped back to the television when she heard the reporter goading Mandy to say more: "You said that Pastor Bledsoe is a hatemonger. Tell us what you mean by that."

"Pastor Bledsoe is trying to say if Lakeside City allows for sexual orientation and gender identity to be included as protected groups against discrimination, like race, gender, age—that sort of thing—then the city will be condemned by God. He said our lives—gay lives—are an abomination and we should be put to the death. Can you believe that? We should be put the death!" Mandy turned her face away from the camera to look directly at the reporter. "Wouldn't you call that hatemongering?"

The interview came to an end and the program switched back to the news desk.

The eleven o'clock anchorman said, "This interview was shot earlier today after Mayor Van Brocklin's funeral. We have tried to reach Pastor Don Bledsoe for comment, but he refused to speak to the media about his alleged negative comments about gays, saying he and his family were in mourning and wished to have their privacy respected. However we have spoken by phone to Harry Janssen who was at the funeral and is a friend of the Bledsoes. He's also a congregant of Pastor Bledsoe's church as well as a city councilman. Mr. Janssen said Ms. Bakker's comments were 'way overblown and out of context.'"

Kera yelled back at the TV, "Like shit they were!"

The anchorman turned to his female co-anchor. Kera recognized her as the reporter who'd interview Mandy and Harry. He asked her, "Kathy, you did the interview with both Councilman Janssen and Ms. Bakker. What was your take on what was going on inside that funeral service?"

Kathy said, "I don't know for sure, but I can tell you that this story won't be put to rest anytime soon because I tried to interview some other people who'd been in attendance, but none of them would talk to me about it. But silence won't last forever. It never does."

The male anchorman turned to the weatherman: "John, dark clouds came inland today. Is there a storm brewing?"

"You'd better believe it."

* * *

Feeling a brush against her neck, Kera yelped, sprang off the sofa, and rammed a forearm against her attacker's body.

The intruder jumped. "I was just trying to gently wake you up. I didn't mean to—"

The familiar voice stopped Kera cold. Then she saw in the dim light that it was her sister.

"Dee, don't ever touch me when I'm sleeping." Kera's hammering heart threatened to blow through her chest.

Kera was standing in front of her sister, ready for battle. They stood there staring at each other, not moving. She saw the fear in Deidre's eyes. Now she felt like some kind of monster. Dee was holding her arm close to her body, rubbing her shoulder. The sight of her sister's pain released her from the combat stance.

"Oh shit, I hurt you. Oh, god, I'm so sorry, Dee."

"No, I'm okay. I'm sorry I startled you. It's not that bad, really. I know you didn't mean to do it."

Kera saw the fright and apprehension on Dee's face and in her eyes. Since Kelly's death—at least that's when she thought it started—her reactions seemed to be taken over and controlled by some unknown force. It was scary, because she never knew when a remote control button would be pushed and she'd no longer be in charge.

"It's almost noon, time to get up—though I see you never actually made it to bed." Deidre gave her a weak smile.

Kera yawned. "The sofa worked fine, for last night, anyway." She tried to smooth out her wrinkled pants and shirt with her hands.

"Remember, we planned on going through Dad's papers and bills today to see if anything needed immediate attention." Dee went over to the heavy damask drapes that had successfully held back the morning. She tugged on the cord until the light of day pushed into the room.

Kera sat down and pulled the afghan over her shoulders and around her neck. She put her face into the softness of her mother's creation, remembering the nimble fingers and clicking knitting needles. The afghan smelled like her mother, or was she imagining it? Didn't matter because she felt her mother's presence, helping her release the power of whatever force that seemed to be controlling her.

She felt the silence hanging between her and Dee like a partition. She didn't know what to say. She looked at her sister. Dee appeared to have lost weight since she'd last seen her. The jeans looked a little too big on her. She noticed, for the first time since she returned home, that Dee had highlights in her dark auburn hair. She wondered how she'd missed that detail yesterday.

"I see you have highlights in your hair," she said. "From the sun?"

"No, from a bottle. I did it the first of June, didn't want to wait this year until they showed up from the sun. Still, it looks natural, don't you think?"

Kera nodded, though her mind had wandered as soon as the question left her mouth, so she had only a vague idea what she was agreeing to.

Deidre continued, "Sylvia told me the highlights pull out the reddish-brown tones in my eyes." She ran her fingers through her shoulder-length hair, combing it back and away from her face. "If you want, I'll do this to your hair too, even though yours is pretty short, I think it will look good on you. Don't you?"

"Ah, yeah, I guess so." Kera had picked up the thread of their conversation, but let it go again. Yesterday began coming to her in flashes, then in a full-force blast.

"Really, Kera, since we have the same color hair and eyes, it would work for you—"

Kera felt her body stiffen. What a disconnect: She and Deidre were acting as though nothing horrible had happened at their dad's funeral and were carrying on about some insignificant thing. The same thing happened when their mother died: a bad day, one to get through and not dwell on. Just put your head to the wind and move on with the business of the day. The time after her mother's funeral, Dad went back to work and she and Deidre trudged off to school under an umbrella of platitudes: they played at being little troupers by not crying over spilt milk, keeping their chins up, pushing on. Until in the dark of night, finally alone, her grief spilling out from her heart, her tears bleeding into the pillow.

Kera shook her head. Here they were again, she and her sister still not talking about what had happened, pretending there was no pain, getting on with life and being fucking troupers. It was insane. Don disrespected their father, made a mockery of his memorial service, blatantly showing contempt for her and every other gay person on earth. Dee had to be upset about that too. Didn't she? God, was Deidre really able to pretend all that shit hadn't happened?

Fire burned in her stomach. Her hand found her abdomen and held it. "Dee, we need to talk about what happened yesterday. This isn't going to be another thing that we stash in an attic."

Dee looked at her as though she didn't want to commit to understanding what was said.

"I mean it, Dee." She got up and stood face-to-face with her sister. "Do you really think you can come over here today and just pretend like Don didn't call me—and the entire gay community—an abomination? And that we deserved to be dead!" She leaned in toward her sister. "Does that bother you? Does it bother you that not only did he say those outrageous things, but he spewed that shit at our father's funeral, desecrating our father's memorial? For god's sake, don't you even care?"

Deidre pulled back. Color slid from her face, leaving a sickly pallor. Her body slumped and her gaze dropped to the floor. She looked like a shamed schoolgirl. "I'm so sorry, Kera." She turned around and sat down in a chair.

Seeing Deidre distraught, Kera backed off. She'd gotten through to her sister. Shit, she didn't want to scare her again, but she needed to talk about what had happened at the funeral. She couldn't just let it go, not this time.

She sat down on a stool close to her sister, closed her eyes, took a deep breath and opened them again. She leaned toward Deidre, her forearms resting on her thighs, lowered her voice and tried to keep it soft, non-threatening: "I'm not blaming you, Dee, for what Don did. But I'm asking: how can you stay with someone like that?"

Dee stared at her gold wedding band, turning it around and around on her finger.

Kera broke the silence. "Is that all you are going to say about it? 'I'm sorry' just doesn't cut it. I need to know you understand what Don did, how it was an insult to our father. And I need to know you care how that felt to me."

"I don't know what else I can say, Kera." Dee moved around in her chair, looking uncomfortable, pained. "I wish I could magically take all that away, but I can't. And I don't know what to do about it. I'm sure what he said had to be painful for you and I do care that he hurt you. I'm just saying—"

"And another thing, Dee, I left the service and you knew I was upset. And you never came over last night to even see how I was doing. You never even called. You weren't there for me at all." That wasn't like Dee, not being there for her. Her sister's absence of support left a black hole in her soul.

"I was so embarrassed about what Don did, but I was going to come over here anyway, but Don and I got into a—"

Kera didn't want to hear Don's name or any more about him. "'Was going to come' doesn't mean much to me. But so be it, what's done is done." She sat up straight on the stool.

Dee stared at the floor.

Kera twisted her neck to the right, then left, trying to loosen her tense muscles. "Did you happen to see the TV news media outside the funeral home?"

Deidre glanced up. "No, but I heard they were there. Don and I didn't stay very long at the church. We spoke to a few friends, but not many. Harry left to go home, then came back in and told us there were lots of people outside, including the press. He insisted we leave through the back door. He didn't want us having the stress of dealing with the news media."

"Did you watch the news last night?"

"No."

"Well, if you had watched, you would've seen Mandy Bakker being interviewed, right after Harry was interviewed."

Dee covered her mouth with her hand. "What did they say?"

"The short and not-so-sweet of it was that Mandy Bakker—did you see her at the service?"

Dee nodded. "I spoke to her briefly yesterday."

"She talked about Don slamming the gay community—which by the way, if you didn't know, Mandy's a lesbian." Kera flashed a quick half-smile, then dropped her grin and went on. "She told the reporter she hadn't wanted to disrespect our father; otherwise she would've left the service because of what Don did. Harry, on the other hand, lied his fucking head off by telling the press I was 'tired from being in Iraq' and implied I was some kind of lunatic because I was in a VA hospital to 'adjust,' I think he said, and I was upset because of Dad's death and that's why I left early." She stopped there. She wanted to say more but figured that was probably enough for now. She'd wait for Dee to absorb what she'd recounted.

Dee got up and went into the bathroom. She soon returned, wiping her tears and blowing her nose. When she sat back down in her chair, she winced in pain.

"What's wrong?" Kera asked, recalling she had noticed her sister looking pained when she first sat down, but had passed the expression off as an emotional thing. But now it appeared more like Dee was physically hurt. *Oh, god, did I injure her even more than I thought?*

"Nothing."

"What's wrong, Dee?" Her response had come too fast. Kera didn't believe her.

"Nothing, I told you." Dee turned her eyes away from Kera.

"Nothing, shit!" Kera stood and looked down at Dee in the chair. "It looks like you're in pain, right here on your left side. Did I hurt you there?"

She bent over and gently touched Dee where she guessed the injury had occurred. She replayed where she'd accidentally struck her sister. Her shoulder...the right one, not on the left side. That blow shouldn't be causing her pain there.

"I'm okay, Kera, really." Deidre didn't flinched when touched.

"No, you're not." Kera wasn't fooled.

"Yes I am, now leave me alone."

"I will not! Are you going to show me?"

Deidre didn't move.

Kera knew her sister too well. "Are you going to stand and pull up your blouse for me to see, Dee? Or am I going to have to pull it up myself? It's your choice."

Deidre sighed and got up. She raised her blouse, but only a little. She moaned when she tried to raise it higher.

Kera realized Dee couldn't get her arms up any further. She pulled the blouse up higher. A mass of bruises covered her sister's ribs on both sides and on her back. "What the hell happened to you?"

* * *

Kera rummaged through her dad's rolltop desk, trying to find bills and whatever else that might need attention. She hated her dad's office. The room was dreary, even more so than the rest of the house. The door to his office had always been kept closed—known by her and her sister as a "Keep Out" zone. Her dad had told them he did much of his city business at home to be there for her and her sister, but city business was private, so they and their friends needed to stay out. She smiled at the thought. She, Dee and their friends couldn't have been less interested at peeking at his "city business."

Kera sneezed. She believed mildew lurked in these dark places. The staleness of the air testified to its lack of exposure to the rest of the world. She opened the curtains and sneezed again from the shedding dust as the drapes opened, then pushed up the windows to let in fresh air.

She struggled to keep her mind on task. The image of Dee's bruised ribs kept invading her consciousness. When she had asked her sister how she got the bruises, Dee told her she had fallen off her bicycle while riding with her biking group on the Fourth of July, insisting she hadn't stayed in shape over the winter and the ride had been her first long trip of the year. According to Dee, the injury was merely a matter of her getting too tired and not paying attention, causing her to run into a tree and fall off the bike.

Kera didn't believe her. Dee couldn't lie to her. Neither one of them could fool the other. She didn't know why her sister even tried. It was insulting. Secondly, she was no paramedic, but Dee's bruises just didn't add up to falling off a bike. The injury looked more like someone had beaten the shit out of her. Besides, she remembered, Dee didn't appear to be in any physical pain during the funeral, and the supposed bicycle accident was almost two weeks ago. And the bruises were too fresh. When she'd confronted Dee on her story, pointing out the inconsistencies and obvious lie, Dee had grabbed her purse and left, telling her she didn't have to put up with being called a liar.

So now, she was left to go through her dad's papers by herself. She found a few bills, but nothing that had to be paid immediately. She realized she would need to call her dad's lawyer so she could get access to his accounts to take care of things.

Looking through the desk and having to deal with all his affairs cemented in the fact that he'd never again go into his office, never sit at this desk. An unbearable heaviness weighed down on her, like having a field of grief, cut and baled, then strapped on her back.

She sucked in a deep breath and kept sifting through the papers, sorting by categories. If only she could go upstairs to her bedroom, get under the covers, sleep, escape life. Wrong. There would only be nightmares waiting for her there.

She came across a letter from Dr. Jeffrey Stevens of the local United Church of Christ advocating for the inclusion of LGBT people into the city's Civil Right's Ordinance. She guessed Mandy was right about some het allies in this town. Amazing. She stuffed the letter back into the envelope and tossed it in the miscellaneous pile.

An unopened envelope addressed to her dad with Deidre's name and return address on it puzzled her. Why hadn't Dad opened it? She realized it was posted a few days before her dad suffered his stoke. He'd probably just tossed his mail on the desk and hadn't noticed the letter from Dee. He was known for putting off the task of dealing with his mail. She stared at the envelope. She would give it back to Dee the next time she saw her. The contents weren't any of her business.

She tossed the envelope aside and went through more papers until she pretty much had them all categorized.

She looked back at Dee's letter to Dad, picked it up and tapped the envelope against the end of his desk, laid it down, and went to get a glass of water. When she returned, she picked up the envelope from Dee and held it up to the light. It looked like a letter. She couldn't understand why on earth her sister would write to Dad.

She put the envelope down. Her curiosity was killing her, so she picked it up again, ripped it open and read the letter inside:

Dad,

I'm sorry I was short with you on the phone yesterday. I wasn't myself. You don't deserve to have a daughter speak to you like that. And you're right, I've been distant with you. I owe you an explanation.

I've so wanted to have a marriage like you and Mom had, but I don't know if I ever will. I love Don, but just don't know what to do right now.

I have to tell you why I've been "distant," as you said. Three weeks ago I had a miscarriage. I was two and half months pregnant. You know how much I've wanted a baby, and now it's gone. The reason I lost the baby is painful as well. Don pushed me into a wall, then kicked me when I fell. The next morning, I miscarried. I feel so angry with Don that I swear I could kill him, as he killed our baby. I hate feeling this angry. I never thought I could be this upset and feel such utter loss.

Don has gotten upset and hit me several other times, but never like this last time. He is always so disappointed with himself afterward and tells me he's sorry and won't do it again. I know he is under a great deal of pressure because of leaving his old church and starting this new one. Only God knows why, but I still love him. I'm going to try to keep our marriage together, at least for now. I'm hoping after he feels more settled in his church, he'll return to his old self.

Please don't talk to him about what I have told you. I really mean it, please don't! It would humiliate him, make him mad, and make this worse for me. He has promised me he can overcome his outbursts. I just ask that you pray and support him. Please pray for me as well. I'm trying to get over my anger at him right now and be understanding through this difficult time.

I love you,

Deidre

PS: Dad, I don't want to keep bugging you, but please make a doctor's appointment. As I keep telling you, you don't look well to me, and I know you've been under a lot of stress yourself.

Kera sat back in the desk chair. Why hadn't she sensed her sister's anguish? That wasn't normal. Was she too absorbed in herself to pick up on Dee's distress? Was it because she had been in too much pain herself and couldn't take on another ounce of hurt? Could life's pain become so relentless that there was a point when more pain simply had no room to exist, no more ability to be perceived by the body or psyche, a kind of spilling over? It seemed that way for her.

She reread the letter, not wanting to believe what she knew was true, confirming her worst fears. Those bruises she'd seen on her sister this morning could only mean one thing: Deidre had been beaten up again by Don.

That fucking bastard!

CHAPTER THREE

Kera

Kera drove up to and parked in front of the Turtle River LGBT Community Center on the corner of Holland and Dunes Drive. The community center was housed in an old, two-story, rectangular building with a false front. She remembered years ago, this location had been a mom-and-pop corner store with an attached barbershop with family quarters upstairs.

She'd been around when members of the LGBT community bought the building, it was crumbling in on itself. With their limited funds and lots of volunteer labor—several carpenters included—they'd remodeled it and given the outside the look of a poor man's painted lady with light purple clapboard, dark purple window frames and a cotton candy-pink door, making the nickname for the place, "The Pink Door."

Above the doorway, a rainbow flag flew from a pole jutting from the side of the building. She recalled the fun she and a group had had while painting the inside, all in muted rainbow colors.

Kera opened the pink door. The last time she'd been at the center was when she'd been on leave from the army, right after her military police training. The director of the center convinced her that the LGBT community could benefit from her skills in self-defense, given her military police training and the black belt in martial arts she'd earned in college.

She began thinking about the time she'd gotten into martial arts at Michigan State University. She'd achieved a second-degree black belt in tae kwon do. During that time she'd also joined the Army ROTC at MSU to help with college expenses. Her father was a public servant, and though her family lived a comfortable middle-class lifestyle, he would have had to get a second mortgage on the house with both her and Dee in college. Her sister had been a great student in high school, so she'd received some scholarship money. Kera hadn't applied herself, making mostly Bs and Cs. At the time she'd figured if she did the ROTC thing, it'd make up for her lack of foresight in high school.

Kera shook herself out of the past and stepped inside the building. The smell of fresh paint greeted her. Clear plastic draped the furniture that was shoved to the middle of the lounge. Tarps lined the perimeter.

Two women in clothes splattered with paint rolled a fresh coat of green onto the walls. They turned and waved at her, then yelled out condolences about her father's death, followed by requests for more self-defense classes.

Kera nodded, found a smile to offer and gave them a thumbs-up, though she felt like shit, had nothing to give, and vaguely wondered if there was any weed to be had in this place. She figured she could use a few hits to mellow out, but better not, she reconsidered. She needed her anger to keep her going.

Both painters had been in her self-defense class, but she couldn't remember their names. She tried to recall. Ah, Carina and…shit… what's her name…oh, Penny, that's it, Penny. Remembering names was hard, but she was working on improving her memory, or had been working on it before she had so much other shit to work on, like getting her sanity back. A staggering goal, she feared, but hopefully attainable.

Kera picked her way through the lounge, trying to avoid getting paint on her clothes, and headed back through the hallway to the coffee shop. She inched herself around a guy standing on a ladder who was repairing a problem on the ceiling. Spotting a table stacked with brochures, pamphlets, and other gay-related materials, she reached down and grabbed a copy of the latest *Lesbian Connection*.

She'd called Mandy to thank her for speaking out to the press on television about Don's tirade against gays. After chatting on the phone and trying to catch up on the years since they had last seen each other, Mandy had suggested they get together at the Pink Door for a cup of coffee.

The door to the coffee shop was open, Kera walked in.

"Hey Kera," Mandy got up from a table, walked over and gave her a hug. "Wow, you look in great condition."

Kera wondered how Mandy could think she was in great shape when she felt like such a mess of a person? If Mandy could peek into her mind, she'd scream and run. But apparently, her outward presentation belied her inner turmoil, or maybe Mandy was pretending not to see.

Kera's hands moved to her waist, smoothing and tucking her yellow button-down shirt into her khakis. She'd noticed many people kept their shirts out and guessed it was the latest fad, but she was too soon out of the military to see the new style as anything other than a shirt that needed to be tucked in.

Mandy must have read her misgivings. "Okay, maybe you're a little worn and frayed around your emotional edges, but physically, well, you're fit, girl." She grinned and motioned for Kera to sit down. "Can I buy you a coffee?"

"Sure, make it regular and black. Where I've been, fancy coffees were not on the menu. My system probably couldn't handle that frilly stuff anymore." Kera sat down.

Mandy came back with coffee and two brownies: "These brownies are absolutely to die for. They make them right here. I don't want to spoil your great figure or upset your system, but chocolate does wonders for the soul, especially good chocolate. And we know that your soul could use some TLC." She gave one of the brownies to her.

Kera blew on her hot coffee to cool it. "So on the phone, you told me you were practicing law. Somehow that doesn't surprise me. You were more of a rule follower than I was."

"Yes, but you probably had more fun than I did. I was a real straight arrow, too much so."

"I don't think straight applies to you." Kera gave Mandy a wry smile. "You turned out okay. When did you come out?"

"In college, my junior year."

"What about Bill, your high school heartthrob?" Kera sipped her coffee.

"Really, he wasn't that much of a throb, no guy ever was, that's what got me thinking…then Karen Langley got me feeling." Mandy grinned. "What about you?"

"I hardly dated at all in college. Was virtually nun-like." Kera stopped, remembering one woman, Shelly, whom she'd been involved with.

It wasn't like they had dated or anything. No one knew about their nighttime meet-ups. Shelly even had a boyfriend at the time. It had been mostly a sexual thing, both of them trying to accept their sexuality and having first-time experiences with each other. For her, it had less to do with love than lust. She figured that was true for Shelly as well, because when they graduated, they went their separate ways, never looking back or at least never communicating again. She wondered where Shelly had gone and how her life was turning out.

She shook off the recollection and went on, "Actually, I pretty much knew who I was in high school, but didn't want to deal with it, trying to be the mayor's daughter and all—at least not disgrace him completely. I told Dee and a friend of mine, but that's all. I gave poor Dad enough difficulty in high school not being the student I should have been, and way too often teetering on the edge of getting into trouble." She stopped, smiled. "Uh, let me say that again. As you know I did get into trouble, but luckily not the real serious stuff. Though at times, for sure, I was dangerously close." She pushed aside the memories of her rebellious teenage years, the YouTube clips that had bubbled up and played in her head.

Mandy nodded knowingly.

Kera continued, "I made another bad life decision by doing the ROTC thing and ending up in the military, not a good choice for a queer. But the worst part, I learned I wasn't cut out to watch my friends getting killed." She felt herself flashing back to Iraq, seeing death, smelling death.

Mandy's voice pulled her to the present. "That must have been horrible. I can't even imagine how bad that had to be."

Since returning from Iraq, Kera's emotions slid on black ice, hard to identify, but nevertheless sending her off track and into places she didn't want to go, like flashbacks. She'd never done well with emotions. Her VA therapist had worked to bust through, get to them, expose them and lessen the sting. No luck, so far, except for pissing her off. Shit, the therapist did that well.

However, the compassion in Mandy's eyes threatened to bust through, chip away, expose. Kera took a deep breath and changed the subject. "The military wasn't all bad. A woman named Kelly yanked me out of my closet and set a fire in me. I couldn't deny myself a minute longer." Remembering Kelly's smile flashed warmth throughout her body.

Mandy raised her eyebrows, "And where is Kelly now?"

The warmth left, replaced by a cold metal blade skewering her heart. She hesitated and finally said, "In pieces…some six feet under… bits of her are mixed into the dirt of Iraq." She swallowed hard and took another sip of coffee to wash the brownie—and the pain—down. "Mandy, we need to push the escape key on this topic. I can't deal with it, okay?"

"I'm sorry, I didn't mean to—"

"No problem. I shouldn't have brought her name up." Kera put down her coffee and quickly redirected the conversation: "So what about you? I mean, is Karen still in the picture?"

"No, we parted ways after graduation, too. We were growing apart. Graduation was a good excuse to call it quits. To tell the truth, we weren't good for each other." Mandy brushed a few stray crumbs off the table.

"And now, anyone special in your life?" Kera asked.

"On and off stuff. Haven't found anyone I thought was long-term material, for me at least." Mandy picked up her napkin and wiped her mouth. "Besides, I stay incredibly busy with my work—"

"What kind of a lawyer are you anyway?"

"I work for Lakeside City Legal Aid." Mandy tossed back her head and laughed. "That's why I drive an old VW. Wealth is definitely not in my future."

"What've you been doing besides keeping poor people out of jail?"

"Well, LEAP is keeping me real busy right now. In fact, I wanted to talk to you about that, maybe something you'd be—"

Boom!

Kera hurled herself to the floor and scrambled under the adjoining table, her hands over her head, bracing herself. She was sliding back to the war zone:

An IED exploding, gunshots crisscrossing, coming close, hitting—
Carcasses blowing apart: legs, arms, fingers—
Sand in her mouth, eyes, abrading her face, stinging, choking—
Objects flying, rolling, crashing—
Feet racing, bodies falling—
Voices shouting, screaming, crying, pleading—
Blood splattering, flowing, trickling—
Remnants of life—
Stench of death.

Her heart pounded. Sweat dripped from her face. Arms pulled her up into a sitting position. The sight of Mandy's face tugged her back to Lakeside City.

CHAPTER FOUR

Don

Don Bledsoe looked around his new church office, took a deep breath and slowly let it out. He still had boxes to unpack but little room left for their contents. More boxes from his food drive for the homeless were piled in the corner.

When he'd left his previous church, he'd brought with him his special ministry to the street people of the city, both the supplies and his passionate commitment. There hadn't been any argument from the senior pastor about Don's right to take his budding project away with him, as it had been his baby from the start.

He planned on expanding his outreach to the homeless by getting more involvement from the folks who had faithfully followed him to his new church. He hoped to get his parishioners committed to making warm, home-cooked dinners and distributing them daily.

He made a mental note to look at the kitchen and see if anything needed to be done to make it ready for preparing all those meals. For now, he needed to finish getting his office together.

In his previous church, his office had been about twice as big. After three years there, he'd collected lots of books, papers and just random stuff. He concluded that if he put the remaining boxes in his home basement, he'd probably not miss anything. It'd be one more thing he could cross off his to-do list.

Having made that decision, he could move on to more important things, like looking over the agenda for tonight's church board meeting.

Don heard the back door of the makeshift church close. He looked at his watch: six twenty p.m., too early for the board members to be arriving. The meeting didn't start until seven o'clock. Maybe it was Lilly Potter, his secretary. She only worked in the mornings, but she sometimes came back to check on things or do extra work for him, especially since things were in such disarray.

His church had only rented this location for now—not what he thought of as a proper building for his congregation, but it would have to do since the building search committee hadn't found anything else and they'd stalled out on the search.

However, his good friend and church board president, Harry Janssen had stepped in and come up with the idea of an old fraternity house, abandoned two years ago by the TKE fraternity. He was thankful Harry was a realtor and able to find them a building to rent. He realized the huge old house wasn't in the best part of town. Vanderwill College had pretty much migrated to the south and abandoned some of the older buildings or used them as warehouses. But as Harry had explained to him, the place had potential for a makeshift church, at least until the congregation could raise money, find the right land and build their new church. Harry had handled the whole matter by talking to the landlord and convincing the guy to spring for some money necessary for the remodeling.

Don felt certain God had sent Harry to him.

He'd met Harry five years ago when the man started coming to the Second Reformed Church where Don acted as the assistant pastor. He and Harry hit it off right away. When he started having a conflict with the head pastor and members of the congregation, Harry had suggested—and he'd agreed—that he leave and start his own independent church so he'd be free from interference by denominational authority.

He would be the one in authority.

His church would be a place where his interpretations of the Gospel and its relevance for today would be appreciated and unquestioned. Finally, he wouldn't have to try and fit his beliefs into anyone else's ideas of how to understand Holy Scripture. He knew his followers were devoted to him. Now that he had his own church, he could bring them along. His dream had come true. He was free to preach The Word and grow a congregation, thanks, in a large part, to Harry.

"Don, how's it going?" Harry stood at the doorway of his office. "I see you're getting settled in."

At the sound of Harry's voice, he turned around. "Oh, it's you. I thought I heard Lilly downstairs. I didn't hear you come up. Must have been too absorbed in thought. Yes, I'm finally getting my things arranged, at least mostly so." He signaled for Harry to have a seat across from his desk. "I think I've stuffed as much as I can in this place. The rest will go back home for now."

Harry walked over to the desk and picked up the picture of Deidre. "That's a great picture of your wife, but then, she's a beautiful woman. You wouldn't have to work hard to get a good picture of her."

"Yup, I'm a lucky man in so many ways." Don adjusted his desk calendar. "Say, have you looked around? The remodeling is coming right along. Praise the Lord we're being able to do this, knocking down walls, combining rooms and all. We have some church folks coming in on Saturday to paint."

"Well, you know, the landlord will make out on all this remodeling when he goes to sell or rent the place out again. This old place was constructed in the thirties and has seen better days. Thousands of college guys have lived here and if these old walls could talk, well—"

"Speaking of what college guys could have been up to—that reminds me, I've been thinking we'll surely need to have a dedication ceremony for the church this fall when the remodeling is done. We need to cast out any ol' demons and call in the Holy Spirit." Don grinned. "Harry, maybe you ought to be part of the dedication. You know, give a talk."

"No, Don, the spotlight is not my thing. I'll run the business end and leave the talking and preaching up to you. As you know, my friend, I'm not good at public speaking. Makes me a nervous wreck. Remember that time I was supposed to address the statewide Realtor's Convention? I could barely sleep the week before. I got through it, but it wasn't my shining hour, believe me. I couldn't be talked into it again. Now you, you're the charisma guy. Words flow out of you like liquid velvet. But when necessary, you can make words sting like lemon juice on a cut finger. No, I'm strictly a background guy."

"And a great one at that, an incredible support to me."

Don did appreciate all of Harry's support. Harry had become a good friend, a mentor, and had encouraged him to make this big move to start his own church.

Without Harry, he wouldn't have been able to do it, to realize his dreams, to fulfill God's plan for him. Surely the Good Lord had sent

Harry to him. He was determined to live up to both their expectations by bringing the Lord Jesus Christ to people and stamping out sin. He was determined to make God and Harry proud of him. He surely would.

"You deserve the support, Don. But hey, speaking of the dedication service this fall, we can't forget to leave some time in our schedules for hunting. I'm already itching to go deer hunting." Harry put up his arms and wrapped them around his imaginary rifle, tucked it into his left shoulder, put his finger on the trigger and took aim as he peered down the scope at his imaginary prey. "I can see a big buck as we speak. How about you, Don, are you ready for the hunt?"

"That's a given, Harry, I will be so ready for some relaxation. I think we can rent the same cabin we had last year. I'll give the guy a call, but I'm pretty certain it's available. It's time we made our arrangements."

Harry walked over to the only window in the office. "Last week I was looking at new rifles, thinking of getting me another one. While I was shopping around, I found some great new boots, a new jacket, gutting knife and new long johns." He turned around. "Damn, I was cold last year. I won't be this year, though, thanks to the new under gear I bought. It wicks so when you sweat, it pulls away the moisture from you body. It's made from some space-age material. You ought to get some."

"Where did you find it?"

"At Thomas Outfitters." Harry sat down in the chair across from the desk.

"I'll check it out. I certainly need something warmer too. I thought I'd freeze my butt off last year. You know, that day it was below zero and the sun never peeked out all day." Don put his hands behind his head and tipped back in his chair. "Not to change the subject, but what did you think of the article in the *Lakeside City Journal?*"

Harry furrowed his brow. "Oh, you're referring to what that Amanda what's-her-name said? The one who talked to the TV reporter, too?"

"Yeah, the newspaper reporter called me because of what Amanda said about the funeral service. Supposedly, I hurt the feelings of homosexuals or something of that nature. She asked if I wanted to comment. I told the reporter I had no comment, that my family was in mourning and I'd appreciate their respecting my privacy. But I've been thinking about it ever since. Maybe I should have talked to her. The article was too one-sided, all about what that woman had to say and about why the addition to the ordinance was 'necessary' for homosexuals." Don picked up a pen and began tapping it on the edge of his desk. "We got to get our act together. The Lord is counting on us, Harry."

Harry nodded in agreement. "When I was at our last city council meeting, we decided to put the ordinance on the agenda for one of the Wednesdays of this month, to allow the public to speak about it, then we'll be voting. We need to get the community up in arms about this matter. We don't have much time, you know. The meeting is coming up fast, think it is on…let me see, Wednesday the what?" He pulled out his cell phone to check the date: "July…oops, how did I get ahead to 2009? Let me back up to 2008. Okay, let's see, today is the seventeenth. The vote will take place on Wednesday, the twenty-third of this month. Wow, time is flying. We only have six days! We are behind the curve on this one. We've got to get going." Harry put the phone back in his pocket.

"Yes, indeed." Don took out his pocket calendar and flipped through it.

"Speaking of this issue, I haven't officially put the ordinance matter on the church board agenda. We should talk about it after we adjourn tonight's meeting, have a special unrecorded meeting. It's important we don't have any written records of our church board looking… well, you know, political." Harry added, "It wouldn't look good for me as a councilman or for our church, for that matter, because being perceived as political runs a risk of losing our tax exempt status, and we sure don't want that to happen."

"Good thinking, Harry." Don looked at his watch, got up and walked around his desk. "Think we'd better get down to the boardroom now. We have a big night planned." He put his hand on Harry's shoulder. "Let's get to work."

* * *

After the board meeting, Don plopped down on the faded red plaid sofa—with lumpy cushions—in his office and glanced around the room. The furniture fit the ambiance of the building, old and make-do, but that would change when he got his new church. His thoughts turned to the board meeting.

Sam Zander, the church treasurer, had reported that the building fund was growing slowly, but the membership was increasing nicely and the influx would soon positively affect the building fund. They'd also made the final decision on the new church name, the name that Don had pushed for: "The Church of God's True Words."

The new church name reflected his commitment to God's truth. He would draw new people into the fold through his preaching of that truth.

Many people told him he was magnetic. He could feel the magnetism when he had people on the edge of their chairs. Preaching was a high for him, like he'd achieved a state of grace where God's words flowed out of him with the force and purity of water surging down a remote mountain river in springtime. He was grateful God had bestowed the truth on him, along with the gift of speaking it. After each of his sermons, he got down on his knees to give thanks to God for allowing him to be His representative on earth. Was there any greater honor or responsibility? Not in his opinion, but he worried at times if he was up to the task.

Exhausted, Don looked at the clock on the wall. Ten twenty-five p.m. He'd been up since five thirty in the morning.

He thought the meeting about preventing the proposed change in the Civil Rights Ordinance had gone pretty well. The plan was for him to continue preaching the evils of homosexuality to the congregation, but not directly mention anything regarding the city council, the ordinance, or the plans he and Harry had made.

One of the newer board members, Dave Reilly, had reported he already had several church members who had gone ahead and established a group of concerned citizens against the proposed change in the ordinance. They'd named their organization Citizens Against Perversion or CAP. Dave had said many church members were committed to the group, but there were also people unconnected to their church who'd signed up as well.

Don was pleased with the participants who were not affiliated since he and Harry didn't want their church seen as the instigators or the main force behind CAP. They'd been late getting the opposition going, but now things were really moving fast.

So far, he'd heard the group already planned several protests events. However, he preferred to think of their protests as educational events. That's why the CAP folks would carry signs speaking of God's will, God's commandments, and God's wrath to those who turned away from Him.

He'd have to talk to Dave about the campaign's focus. First try and change the hearts and minds of the sinners by letting them know God's laws and commandments. Of course, if they failed to get their message across, they'd need to make sure the city didn't legitimize the sinful lives of homosexuals.

Don reflected on what Harry had made clear at the meeting: he was not to be connected to the group in any way since he served on the city council and needed to appear neutral on the issue.

But of course, everyone there—except maybe Jimmy Johnson, the board secretary—knew Harry wasn't neutral. Harry became enraged when Jimmy suggested the church not get involved in this particular city issue. After Jimmy spoke up, Harry berated him, letting him know that homosexuals were perverts and would contaminate the moral fiber of Lakeside City. Don was proud of Harry for setting Jimmy straight.

Yes, he thought to himself, Harry was someone he could count on. His friend was a true comrade in the fight against evil.

Sam had concluded the meeting by telling everyone that some remodeling and building funds could be "diverted" to the cause for some of the startup costs. After that, money would be raised through fundraisers and donations.

A tap on the door startled Don, bringing him out of his reverie. He sat up straight and looked at the opening door.

"Don, do you have a minute?"

Don relaxed. "Sure, Sam, take a seat." He pointed to a worn black vinyl chair across from the sofa. "What can I do for you?"

Don admired Sam for his great mind for figures. The man was in the mortgage lending business and had been with the same company since he'd left college. Sam told him a couple of weeks ago he'd gotten his twenty-year pin.

It amazed him that Sam was in the business world at all because Sam wasn't well put-together. The man dressed in all the right kind of clothes, but he was overweight and wore suits clearly too tight for him, and they appeared as though he'd slept in them. His shirt was often pulled out from his waistband, and his tie knot couldn't come together because his neck spilled over his too-tight collar like overflowing dough.

He remembered Deidre had once said that every time she saw Sam, she wanted to go over to him and fix him, like a mother might before her son's recital.

Sam set his church papers on an end table and sat down on the edge of the chair. He appeared to be gathering his thoughts.

Don noticed the man seemed anxious about something. He bent forward, resting his forearms on his thighs and clasping his hands. "What's wrong Sam?"

"I've got myself into a mess, Don."

"What kind of a mess?"

Beads of sweat formed on Sam's forehead. He fidgeted in his seat like a kid waiting his turn for a flu shot. "I'm in financial trouble. You see, I got laid off last week. I know you're aware of all the problems in the housing market these days. Well, as you may know, it's become a problem in the mortgage business as well—"

"Yes, I'm aware of the problems in housing, just horrible. I'm so sorry you've lost your job because of it. But in your favor, you are a real talented guy. Surely you will find something else. And you know, the Lord is with you. I'll put you on our prayer chain. And you'll get unemployment, right?"

"I'll get it, but it won't be nearly enough to get me through this, and…well, it's more than just that, I have a lot of debt." Sam flushed. The beads of sweat combined into drops and started running down his face. "I don't know how to say this any other way, so I'll just say it. I have big gambling debts." Sam took his eyes off him and looked down.

Don pulled back. "I declare, I don't believe that, Sam, a smart business guy like you…our church treasurer and a deacon, no less. How could you do that to the Lord Jesus Christ, our church, and to your family? I just can't believe you'd get into something like that. You're one of the Lord's best men."

"I'm so ashamed." Sam stared at his hands. "I know I have sinned and God is punishing me for it. But now it's hurting my family and I swear by all that's holy, if God gets me out of this mess, I'll never gamble again."

Don saw the man was contrite. He needed to let up on him, let him know about God's love and forgiveness. "Sam, the Lord loves you, but I'm concerned the Devil has gotten a hold on you. You're going to need to fight hard, really hard, to pull his grip off from you. You'll need to get down on your knees day and night to keep that Devil at bay. You know, Sam, I get down on my knees too. We all have to fight off the outstretched hand of the Devil. The good news is that God wants us to win these battles. You set yourself straight with God and He will be there for you. That's just a given. I'll be right with you on this, praying for you. Indeed, I will be. And I'll be praying for your whole family."

Sam raised his head. "There is something more you could do, Don. I'm going to be needing money fast. My gambling bill is coming due. I was wondering…well, as you know, uh, I gave the building fund twelve thousand dollars. You have to know I hate asking and God knows I don't want things to be this way, but if I could just get that money back, it would get me out of this pickle I'm in. I would pay it back when I get—"

"Now Sam, taking money from the Lord is not going to get you back into His good graces or release you from the grip of the Devil. That's exactly the wrong thing to do." Don felt panicky. If he returned the money to Sam, would others find a reason to ask for their contributions back, too?

Not only that, but starting a new church, getting people to come along with him, and having them invest in his venture had taken so much from him already. Dealing with it all left him stressed and exhausted. To get this far, then have to take a step back... No, he couldn't do it. Money was tight. God had put a lot of responsibility on him and he was finally seeing some of the fruits of his labor.

And he'd be letting God down.

"I just can't let that happen, Sam. I can't give you that money back. Lots of people are counting on it. And frankly, it's just not part of the Lord's plan."

Sam's face went from flushed to sunburn red. He grabbed his church papers and stood up, his hands shaking. He glared. The veins on his neck bulged as if they might burst through his skin. His voice grew loud. "Look Don, these people I owe this money to, they're not nice people. I can't wait any longer. I have to have that money back. Now!"

Don was startled by Sam's lightning-fast morph from a penitent sinner to an angry, demanding madman. The transformation seemed so out of character. He realized, right then, that Sam's gambling and his unreasonable demands had to be truly coming from the Devil himself—Sam had to be possessed.

Don looked at the enraged man and said, "If I let you have the money back, then I would have to return it to others when they wanted a new car, needed to pay a heating bill, you name it. Pretty soon, God wouldn't have His church." He stood to gain equal footing with Sam. "These are difficult times for us all. But I'll tell you, Sam, God needs this money. He needs this church to guide the people of our city. You were at the meeting tonight. You know what's happening in our community."

Don felt his face burn and his heart pound. How dare Sam give money to God, then ask for it back. He couldn't let Sam have the twelve thousand dollars. He wouldn't let it slip through his fingers so easily. God had entrusted him to fight the Devil and preach His Word. He wouldn't, couldn't, let God down.

"So you are not going to give me the money back?" Sam's arms hung stiffly at his sides, his fists clenched.

"That's what I'm saying. I've been entrusted to carry out the Lord's will—you need to understand that. It's not about me, Sam, it's about what the Lord has asked of me." Don glanced over and saw Harry standing in the doorway, watching them. Fearing what Sam might do next, he was relieved to see his friend. He yelled out, "Hi Harry, come on in."

"Hey, Don, what's happening here? I heard loud voices, thought I'd come to check things out."

Sam looked around and saw Harry coming through the doorway. He glared at Harry and back at Don.

Buoyed by the two-to-one situation, Don turned back to Sam and said, "I think it is time for you to leave, Sam, and I think it is time for you to give up the financial position on the board." He realized Sam's work as the treasurer on the board could put the man in great temptation. "The Devil is still with you. He surely is. I truly hope you can overcome this situation, and I'll surely be praying for you." He put his hand on Sam's back and escorted him to the door.

Sam didn't resist Don's efforts to get him out of the office, but he shook off the guiding hand and continued out the door. Turning, he glared, shook his finger, and snarled, "Believe me, Don, you're going to regret this!"

CHAPTER FIVE

Don

Don poured his first cup of morning coffee and took the mug to his study and sat down at his desk.

When he and Deidre had bought their house a year ago, he'd promised her they would only stay there a few years. He knew Deidre didn't really like their fifties ranch-style house. She would have preferred an old Victorian, but the ranch was in their budget range. Maybe someday, when things were better financially, he could buy a house Deidre loved. In the meantime, he had converted an extra bedroom into his study. The other bedroom remained a guest room until someday when they needed the space for a nursery.

The thought of a baby gave him a sick feeling inside. Deidre's miscarriage was his fault. He'd tried to make it up to her, but he knew there was really no atoning for what he had done. She hadn't forgiven him, neither had God, nor had he forgiven himself. He worked hard not to let his anger get the best of him, but like his father, he didn't often succeed.

Don prayed—more like implored—God to give him restraint and patience. He didn't understand why it'd gotten more difficult, not less, for him to control his temper. And now, because of his failure, he'd lost his baby.

He begged God to take away his despicable sexual urges, but so far his prayers fell flat on God's ears. He hated those dirty, sinful thoughts, always having to beat down those horrifying feelings that led to fantasies, which led to...

He didn't want to think about it. Maybe—well, no doubt that's why God wouldn't let him have his baby. He didn't deserve children. If Deidre ever knew what went on inside his head and how he relieved himself of those sordid urges, she'd leave him.

He feared—no, knew—these intrusions of vile thoughts and impulses came from the Devil himself. He'd been told by other preachers what could happen when someone preached God's truth, as he did. He knew a messenger of the Lord was surely vulnerable to the clutches of Satan. And indeed, if Satan did have claws in him, God might well refuse to hear his prayers.

He knew he would have to do something really big, something that would prove to God he was no longer in the grips of Satan.

He had a strategy.

He was certain his plan would let God know he was clearly back in the fold and clearly deserving His grace. His plan was already in the works. He was leading the attack against homosexuals. He would either convert them or drive them out of Lakeside City. He had to succeed, both for the sake of the city's citizens and for the salvation of his own soul.

Deidre's head peeked through the study's doorway. "Want some breakfast?"

His wife's question jerked him out of his mind's fretful churning. "Yes, surely. Now you mention it, I smell the bacon cooking. You're up early, don't you have today off?"

"Yes, I do, but I just couldn't sleep, so I thought I'd get up." Deidre yawned. "It will be ready in just a few minutes."

"I'll be right along."

Deidre had worked full-time as a social worker at the hospital, but after they married, she'd cut her hours. He hated to admit it, but he was glad he'd agreed—caved in would be a better way of putting it—on her working part-time instead of insisting on her quitting altogether.

In his way of thinking, a minister's wife needed to be an example of a Christian woman's role: stay home and tend the family. But as an assistant minister at Second Reformed Church, he hadn't been paid all that well. Now he'd started a new congregation and money was tight, he was grateful for Deidre's paycheck.

He got up from his desk and headed into the kitchen for his breakfast.

Don dragged his chair out from the small table in the breakfast nook and sat down. He looked at the ring on the third finger of his right hand: black onyx with small diamonds forming a cross. Harry had given the ring to him shortly after they'd formed the new church. At the time, Harry had said the ring was meant to remind him he was truly God's messenger. Since then, every morning, he had a habit of rubbing his fingers across the diamonds, feeling the shape of the cross which served as an inspiration to keep Jesus and his mission in his heart and in his work. He'd vowed to God he'd never remove the ring from his hand.

Deidre brought over plates of scrambled eggs, hash browns, bacon and toast. She went back for the coffeepot and placed it on a hot pad in the center of the table, then took her seat. "How did the board meeting go last night?" She picked up her fork and dug into her eggs.

Don swallowed a mouthful of bacon. "Went fine."

He had no intentions of telling her about the clandestine meeting that took place after the board was dismissed. She didn't need to know about the plan to gear up for the fight against including homosexuals in the city's Civil Rights Ordinance. That would just stir things up again.

He couldn't believe his bad luck, having a queer sister-in-law. The fact that Deidre was heterosexual should be proof to everyone that homosexuality was a moral issue not genetic, as queers claimed. If they were truly born into that condition, he judged, wouldn't Deidre be as queer as her identical twin? It was obvious to him that homosexuality was clearly a choice to go against God's law.

He and Deidre fought about her sister's immorality because his wife was willful and stuck up for her sister. He'd warned her on many occasions to keep her wrongheadedness about this issue to herself and to pray she be granted God's help in seeing her sister's sin. If only Deidre could receive God's truth, she'd be able to save her sister. He couldn't understand why she wouldn't want to do that?

Then there was the funeral for her father, he knew he shouldn't be agitating over the service, but he couldn't help himself. All he could think about was how Deidre had gotten upset with him about the eulogy he'd given. He'd made it clear that homosexuality was an abomination. She didn't understand the funeral was a perfect time for Kera to hear God's words and come to understand that Willem wouldn't have approved. He'd also used the opportunity to let the public know he didn't endorse his sister-in-law's lifestyle.

But once again, an argument with Deidre had led to his anger getting out of control, exactly what he'd been trying to avoid. When they'd gotten home from the funeral, Deidre's badgering made him lose his temper. He'd truly tried to control himself, but it felt like trying to hold back a tornado. If she'd just listened and tried to understand, but she didn't. When the rage subsided, he'd realized the damage he had done to her and he knew he had failed, once again. But God surely had to understand that Deidre bore some responsibility, too, didn't she? After all, he reasoned, her ignorance and bullheadedness tried him. No, more like baited him.

Now Deidre sat in front of him She'd made his favorite breakfast and was acting sweet. Maybe she finally did understand she'd pushed him too far. Or maybe, more than likely, she was being nice to make him feel guilty.

Deidre interrupted his thoughts. "How are things progressing with the building fund?" Deidre lifted her cup and blew on the coffee.

"Sam said it was coming along nicely." He picked up his cloth napkin which had fallen on the floor, shook it, and put it back on his lap.

"Speaking of Sam, how's he doing? His wife told me they were worried about his job."

"He lost his job. In fact, he had the nerve to ask me to return the money he'd donated to the building fund. Can you imagine that? He wanted the money back that he'd given to the Lord." Don spread jam on his toast.

Deidre set her fork down on her plate and stared at him. "So you're not going to give the money to him?"

"Give it back?" Don scowled. "It's not his money anymore. Like I said, he gave it to God." He scooped up the rest of his eggs and shoveled them into his mouth. He felt his anger rising and his heart beating faster.

"Don, the man is out of work. He has a family. A building isn't what's important. People are important. Certainly you understand and believe that."

"The building is important, Deidre. It's God's house. It's a place for people to worship and learn about His commandments and a place to save their souls. You just have a hard time getting that, don't you? Try looking at the big picture for once! Besides, Sam's been foolish with his money." Don felt his face getting hot and his body tensing, constricting like a snake. "Sam lost lots of money gambling. That's a sin, Deidre. God has no sympathy for him, nor do I, for that matter. Enough said."

"I thought God was forgiving." Deidre pushed away her plate. "I know the building is important to you, Don, but I'm just saying it seems to me that God is more interested in people than any random church. And Sam has a wife and kids. Do you think God should punish them as well?"

Don grabbed his napkin from his lap, stood up and slapped it onto his plate. "Random church, is it?" He glared at her. "Is that what you think of my work, creating a random church? What is wrong with you anyway? You—"

"I didn't mean that, Don. I just—"

"Even Harry agrees with me. He came into the office when Sam was actually threatening me about not giving his money back." Don stepped over to where Deidre sat and stood over her. "Who are you to tell me what's important to God?" Every cell of his body felt ready to explode.

Deidre didn't say anything, just stared at him. Her eyes seemed to be accusing, judging, baiting him.

His fists kept clenching, knotting, releasing. He watched her expression turn fearful. She ought to be scared. She'd just insulted his life's mission, as well as tried to tell him what God wanted. Turmoil brewed inside him. He tried to keep his emotions in check, but he might just as well have tried to hold back a charging bull.

"Remember, I'm the pastor, here," he shouted. "You are the pastor's wife. That's it, and don't you forget it." As if by its own volition, his arm drew up to his shoulder, cocked, then his fist slammed into Deidre's face.

Deidre yelled and clutched her nose. Blood gushed, pouring down her face, running down her hand and arm.

He grabbed his napkin off his plate and threw it at her.

She put the white napkin to her nose. Blood immediately soaked through the cloth and dripped on the table.

He stood frozen, witnessing the aftermath of his anger, but his rage didn't abate. In fact, he felt angrier. Not just at Deidre, but at God.

Why had God forsaken him?

Where was He when he needed Him?

Why hadn't He stopped him from hitting his wife?

Don didn't know what to do with his rage, but he knew he needed to get out of the kitchen, away from Deidre.

He hurried to his study.

Don sat with his elbows on his desk and his hands supporting his head, staring down at nothing in particular. He thought about when he'd lost his temper and struck Deidre before, the blows had landed in places on her body where people wouldn't see the marks, the evidence.

Even when Deidre lost the baby, no one could tell, but now they would see everything. Her nose was probably broken, but if not, the punch would leave visible bruises.

He moaned. Why couldn't he control himself? Lately, his anger and his urges were getting more frequent—far too frequent and more intense.

His foot tapped, keeping rhythm with the thumping beat of his heart. To his horror, he felt the hardening between his legs.

He raised his head and glanced at a framed picture of himself standing behind his Sunday school kids on the last day of his ministry at his previous church. He reached over and turned the picture over so their eyes couldn't accuse him.

Where were his controls, his resolve?

He begged and pleaded to God for mercy.

He commanded his penis to go down, but it didn't respond. His erection only grew more demanding.

Tears filled his eyes and rolled down his cheeks.

Defeated. Beaten. Worse yet, ignored by God.

He grabbed his keys, got in his car and drove off to find relief.

CHAPTER SIX

Kera

Kera pulled a hot blueberry bagel out of the toaster, dropped it on her plate, and blew on her fingers before opening the refrigerator and finding the cream cheese.

She was thinking about her flashback fiasco in the coffee shop at the Pink Door. Besides upsetting, the incident was damned embarrassing. She hated her skittishness, or was it mental fragility? No, she didn't like those words. They sounded craven, weak, like she was breakable. Maybe mentally impaired was accurate.

Crap, there were no pretty words for her fucked-up head. People were going to think she was a total "nut case." *Yeah, those would be the words.*

Mandy had been great about it. Even so, Kera felt like a fool, especially since the noise that startled her had come from the guy fixing the ceiling in the hallway.

She'd been told a stray dog—a German shepherd-rottweiler mix—had gotten into the building through a door left open for deliveries. The young mutt had run down the hall and crashed headlong into the ladder, spilling the worker. Both man and dog came out of the collision okay, certainly much better than she had fared.

Kera's cell phone played "The Stars and Stripes Forever." She looked at the caller ID. Deidre's name popped up on the screen. She made a mental note to change the ring tone. "Hey, Dee, what's up?"

"Kera, can you come over? I need to get to the hospital." Besides upset, Deidre's voice sounded weird, like she was breathing through her mouth.

"What's wrong?" Kera felt her heart start racing, bringing her out of her morning mental fog.

"I don't want to go to the hospital where I work. Can you take me to Grand Rapids? Or maybe we could just go to an urgent care center around here. I need a ride. I can't drive."

"What happened?"

"Please, Kera, just come. I think my nose is broken and I can't stop the bleeding. I'll tell you about it when you get here. Please hurry."

"Sit down, hold your head forward and pinch your nostrils together."

"I thought I was supposed to hold my head back."

"No, no, don't do that, you'll just swallow your blood." Kera had learned basic first aid in the military.

"Hurry, Kera, I feel dizzy."

"Okay, sit down and hold on. I'll be there in five." Kera threw her bagel in the sink and grabbed her car keys off the counter.

She got to Deidre's house in four minutes. She knocked on the door and tried the doorknob. When the door opened, she yelled, "Dee, where are you?"

No response.

"Deidre!"

She didn't see her sister in the living room, so she rushed to the bathroom and found Dee sitting on the toilet seat with her head forward and a bloodstained washcloth under her nose. Blood was splattered all over the sink and floor, as well as dripping down her arms and onto her blouse.

"My god, what happened to you?" Kera pulled the washcloth down a little so she could see her sister's face.

"Don hit me." Dee's tears dripped down and mixed with the blood, making the red less intense.

"Where is he? Where's that bastard!"

"He left...I don't know where."

"That son-of-a-bitch!" Kera wished the asshole was still there so she could personally wring his fucking neck. She grabbed a hand towel off the rack to supplement the already blood-saturated washcloth, took Deidre's free arm and helped her up. "Come on, let's get you to a doctor."

After they finished at the urgent care facility, Dee wanted to return to her own home. *Not going to happen.* She made it clear Dee had two choices: the battered women's shelter or their dad's house with her.

Dee had been indignant at the suggestion of the battered women's shelter, claiming she was not an abused woman. But she backed down, at least somewhat, when Kera reminded her of all the bruises on her ribs and back.

The capper came when she let her sister know she'd found the letter to their dad explaining Don's abuse as the reason for the miscarriage. Dee relented begrudgingly and finally agreed to stay with her.

In the kitchen, Kera pulled an ice cube tray from the refrigerator's freezer compartment. She crushed some cubes and filled the ice bag, took it to Deidre who sat in a recliner in the living room. She placed the bag gently over the bridge of Deidre's nose with instructions to keep her head elevated as the doctor ordered.

According to the X-ray, Deidre's nose was broken, but the bone was not displaced and wouldn't require further medical intervention. Nevertheless, Kera could see colorful bruises were on the way.

When the doctor had asked how the injury happened, Dee had pulled a lie out of her back pocket. Kera's first inclination had been to insist Dee tell the truth. She figured her sister needed to hear herself say the words, admit Don was an abusive bastard. But she'd decided her sister was in enough distress. She'd backed off, not contradicting her. She'd save the confrontation for later.

Kera pulled up a wooden rocker near Dee's chair, picked up the ice bag from off her sister's nose, looked at the damage and put it back. "What a son-of-bitch you have for a husband!"

Dee didn't respond. She just closed her eyes.

Kera pulled her cell phone out of her pocket and punched in Don's phone number. She looked at her sister and said, "I'm going to let Don know you're here and he's to stay the fuck away."

Don didn't answer.

She left a message, "Don, this is Kera. I took Deidre to the doctor after you got done breaking her nose. She'll be staying with me. Do not come over here or I'll call the cops. Better yet, I'll shoot you myself. I mean it, Don. Stay the fuck away from my sister!" She put her phone back in her pocket.

"My God, Kera, you shouldn't have said a thing like that or even thought it." Deidre grimaced when she tried to adjust the recliner back a little.

Kera decided not to respond to Dee's disapproval.

The threat that had exploded out of her mouth came back to her, reverberating in her head. She wondered if she could really kill Don. As far as she was concerned, beating up her sister felt no different than if Don had done it to her. No, actually, she figured hurting her sister was somehow worse.

Could she kill someone in anger, someone outside a war zone, someone that Uncle Sam hadn't okayed for death?

She recalled in military training, she'd worried she wouldn't be able to shoot in a real situation. Like maybe she'd freeze and end up dead herself. Hell, she'd never killed anything in her life before, except mosquitoes and flies. She'd even avoided ants on the sidewalks and hand-carried spiders out of the house.

She'd feared she might find herself in Iraq, staring down the barrel of her gun at another human being in a case of kill or be killed and not be able to pull the trigger. She'd even had nightmares about it.

She flashed back to a sweltering hot, dry day in Iraq, the first time she'd been called on to pull the trigger.

She was just coming on duty at the checkpoint. Two Iraqi men drove up to the barrier. Two on-duty MPs walked up to the old truck to check them out. The GIs were probably dead tired and more than ready to be relieved, and they'd let down their guard. When she approached behind the MPs, she saw a third guy in the back of the truck rising into view. He held a gun pointed at the American soldiers—a case of kill or let her comrades be killed. To her relief, her training kicked in. She'd fired without hesitation. To be more accurate, she'd sprayed bullets into the truck, killing them all.

She was a killer, no doubt about it. Those weren't the only deaths she'd been responsible for over there.

She shook off other memories popping up like ducks in a carnival shooting gallery, not wanting to think about how many times she'd killed enemy combatants. How much easier would it be to kill Don, a man she hated? She was afraid of the answer, afraid to go down that dark tunnel to the inner chaos of her mind.

She felt shaky, unsteady, on the verge returning to Iraq through her memories. She reached in her pocket and fumbled around for a tranquilizer she'd put there that morning. She grabbed a glass of water, popped her pill and drained the glass. Wiping her mouth with the back of her hand, she forced her thoughts back to her sister and said, "For god's sake, Dee, why do you put up with him? You've never tolerated that sort of shit from any guy before. And when did he turn into such a fanatic?" She didn't wait for an answer. At that moment, she didn't really care, because in her opinion there could be no justification for staying with someone like Don. "He was always a religious nut—at least I always thought so—but I didn't think he was so narrow-minded, so high on hate for gay people. How can you stand that?"

Dee didn't move or answer the question.

She pushed further. "What kind of hold does Don have on you?"

Dee finally lifted the ice bag off her face and raised her head. Her eyes and nose were red, puffy, and had continued swelling since they'd come home. She hesitated and finally said, "I know that this doesn't excuse him, but Don was beaten by his father when he was a kid. He really hates himself after he's lost his temper. He really does, Kera. Don't look at me like that. You don't know."

Kera knew her expression reflected skepticism and anger, but she couldn't do anything about the way she felt. As far as she was concerned, Don was an asshole, period.

"Honestly, Kera, he doesn't want to be like his dad. He tells me how sorry he is and wants to change—and he didn't used to be that way. Honest." Dee let her head fall back and rest against the back of the recliner. "I swear, he was a real sweet, loving guy when I married him. And, I've been trying to figure it out, myself." She tried to clear her throat. "Damn, the blood and mucus make it so I can hardly breathe. It's so gross." She grabbed some more tissues from the side table and continued, "It seems to me he started to get all rigid and weird about his religion around the time he met Harry Janssen. As best as I can put it together, Harry is kind of like a father figure to Don." She stopped, gently dabbed around her nose, and went on. "I know Harry's not all that much older—about forty-three, I think, and Don's thirty-five— but I really believe Don sees him that way. Don wouldn't admit it, but I think Harry is the supportive male figure in his life he didn't have growing up. Harry is a father figure kind of guy. I know the high school wrestlers see him that way. I've gone to a few wrestling matches with Harry's wife, Sylvia, and you could see those kids idolized Harry. They even call him 'Pop.'"

"So does Harry-the-Pop know that Don's being abusive to you?" Kera picked up her glass, realized it was empty but decided not to go and get a refill. She set the glass back down. She didn't want to interrupt her sister now that she was finally addressing the topic of Don and their relationship.

"No, and I know Don would be very upset if Harry knew. As I said, he looks up to Harry and wants his approval." Dee reapplied the ice bag. "Even though Harry's a big man, I know he's not one to strike a woman. There are lots of reasons why I believe he wouldn't be violent. If for no other reason, hitting a woman or someone weaker than himself would be so against his image. You know, he's the swoop-in-and-save the underdog or damsel-in-distress kind of guy. That's Harry."

"Does Harry get off on this father figure stuff? I mean, in Don's case, does he know how Don feels about him?" Kera adjusted the afghan she'd pulled over Dee's legs. She was surprised her sister was being so open about Don, though mostly excusing his behavior. Deidre always defended Don whenever she was critical of him.

"Well, Harry must be aware that he can influence Don. Like I said before, Don didn't used to be so narrow-minded in his religious beliefs. Gosh, if he had been, I wouldn't have married him. Of course, early on I didn't know Harry that well, but as he and Don got closer, I could see Harry's influence on him. And believe me, Kera, if you ever listen to Harry's religious beliefs, you'd think you were listening to Don. As I think of it now, it's sort of like Don has become Harry's puppet. Don loves the spotlight and Harry loves to hear his beliefs come out of Don's mouth." Deidre sighed and took a deep breath. She flinched. "Every place on my face hurts."

Kera stood up. "I can see why. Your whole face is puffing up, except maybe your chin." She looked at her watch. "It's time to take the ice off, for now." She lifted the bag from her sister's face and set it on the floor. "We'll put it back on in a little bit. The doctor said only fifteen minutes at a time."

Kera thought she had interrogated her sister enough. She was glad she had asked the questions and relieved that Dee was finally straight with her.

Kera had begun to wonder about her sister. She and Dee had always told each other everything, or almost everything, and even if they didn't agree—which most of the time they did—they stood up for each other. So when Deidre ignored Don's tirade against gays at their dad's funeral and also lied about Don's abuse, she'd felt totally thrown under the bus.

Now she understood. Dee was dealing with an abusive man and she'd been scared. Still, she wished her sister had confided in her before. Maybe she could have prevented all this from happening. Of course, being in Iraq, she wouldn't have been able to help, but she was home and things would be different now.

"I'm going to make some phone calls, then go and get some stuff for your mucus problem." Kera slipped a pillow under Dee's head. "See if you can sleep or at least rest. If Don has the nerve to show up here, don't go to the door, don't let him in, don't talk to him. Got it?"

Deidre nodded unconvincingly.

"You promise me, Dee." Kera gave her sister a stern look.

"I promise." Deidre sighed.

CHAPTER SEVEN

Deidre

Deidre woke with the sun streaming into her room. Still groggy, she watched tiny dust particles in the air floating in a sunbeam, taking her back to a simpler time when her mother would be down in the kitchen and the smells of breakfast wafted up the stairs to her room—the same room she now occupied.

She basked in the warmth of the memory, but the present quickly poked through the past, bringing a truckload of pain with it. She vaguely remembered Kera helping her to bed. She turned her head to check the time—Good God, even moving her head was painful. The clock read eleven ten a.m. She couldn't believe she had slept in so long. Must be the medication the doctor gave her making her sleep this late.

Her nose throbbed. She looked on the nightstand for her pills, but the bottle wasn't there. The pills must be still by the recliner where she'd sat last night.

She got up, slipped on her clothes, and went into the bathroom to check her face. The area around her eyes and nose was still puffed up and becoming black and blue. Bad, but not as bad as she feared. Kera had done a good job of helping her ice it.

Still, the damage was hard to look at, not just because of the physical wound, but because it reminded her how much her life had veered off track and into a ravine.

She hated the questions about her life seeping into her head. No, actually, more like the answers—the ones she knew she should choose—that bothered her, unsettled her, and would undoubtedly shake her footing, but that was too much to think about right now.

She looked away, grabbed a washcloth, wet it and held it against her face. The warmth of the wet cloth felt good. Then, she combed her hair and tried to put on makeup to cover the damage, but touching her face was painful. What she really needed to do was get to her pain medication.

Having done all she could, she went downstairs to find the bottle of pills. She spotted them on the table by the recliner and dumped out the prescribed dosage into her hand. She checked the intensity of her pain and added another tablet. She popped them into her mouth, washing them down with last night's water. Hopefully the pills would soon get rid of or, at least, dull the pain coming from her face. She would have to figure out a way not to think about the mental pain—something she'd gotten pretty adept at in the last few months.

In the kitchen, she found brewed coffee and saw a note from Kera on the table.

Dee,
Hope you slept well last night. Remember, I have to go to Battle Creek today to the VA hospital to check in there. I'm going to meet Mandy at the gay bar at six thirty tonight. I'll have something to eat there so will home late. See you if you're still up, otherwise, see you in the morning. I brought you some chicken soup you like from Resnick's Deli—it's in the fridge with some other stuff I picked up. If you need anything, give me a call. I have my cell on me. Please rest! Tomorrow morning, let's grab some bagels and go to the beach to sit and soak up the spirit of the lake, like we used to—that is, if you're feeling like it. It's been a long time since I've been there. I think it would be good for us both.
Love ya Big Sister,
Kera

Deidre thought about how Kera often called her, "Big Sister." Beating Kera out of their mother's womb was probably the last brave and adventuresome thing she had done. She was more like her mother: a peacekeeper, a caretaker, a follower of the path laid out for her—or at least what she thought was laid out for her.

Maybe that's why she stayed with Don. She didn't know how to leave the path. She pondered the thought. Why wasn't she more like Kera? Damn, her sister wouldn't put up with someone like him. Kera was the risk taker, the one who stuck her neck out and looked in all directions, the one who went where she needed to go.

Actually, Kera pretty much found her own way in life. She possessed a free spirit, not one for tagging along on someone else's trail.

Deidre figured she could use some of that same spirit now.

The same quality she admired also worried her. Kera didn't seem to understand the stress she caused her. She might have—did—make a questionable choice in a husband, but Kera often made capricious and sometimes weird life choices, like her spiritual beliefs. Good grief, whatever is out there—odd or strange, or both—Kera was bound to find it and become part of it.

Except for the military, that choice seemed oddly mainstream— not for their family, particularly—but a mainstream choice for Kera. Of course, she knew Kera had joined the military to pay for college, but still, look what her service in Iraq got her—PTSD and off to the VA hospital today.

Maybe she should have ridden along with Kera. She knew how stressed and edgy her sister had become. Unfortunately, last night she'd been in too much pain to think about anything else, but now she felt her anxiety level building.

Thinking about the past, she realized ever since their mother died, she'd felt as though she had to watch after Kera like a surrogate Mom.

Kera's deployment to Iraq had been a nightmare for her. She could feel Kera's emotional and physical distress—and vice versa—which had always been the case even when they weren't in direct communication with each other.

When Kera was wounded, she'd felt the pain, right at the spot of the wound. When Kera's girlfriend Kelly died, she'd suffered her sister's grief. However, sometimes, like in the case of Kelly's death, the signals between her and Kera got mixed up, like wrong synapses firing, or maybe the communication between them became like a gossip chain ending with distorted details leading to wrong conclusions.

When Kelly had died, she'd misunderstood the intense grief Kera felt at the loss of her lover. She'd thought Kera had been killed and became distraught, mentally paralyzed, and barely able to sleep or eat until she got a call a week later from Kera.

Damn, she needed to stop worrying about Kera so much. She had enough on her plate, but she was not unaware of the fact that spending her time worrying about her sister meant she avoided her own problems.

Deidre smelled the coffee Kera had made for her. She went to the cupboard, got a mug and filled it. Spotting fresh bagels Kera had apparently picked up at Resnick's, she popped one in the toaster.

She heard a knock at the door. She decided not to answer, not wanting to deal with anyone, especially given her puffy, bruised face. Probably one of those Save-the-Great-Lakes guys looking for a contribution. She'd given money to them on many occasions. She could forgo a donation this time.

When the knocking didn't stop, she decided maybe she'd better check. She tiptoed to the living room door and peered through the peephole.

Good God, it's Don, damn him. She saw the drapes were closed and figured he wouldn't know if she was in the house or not.

He knocked on the door again and yelled, "Deidre, I know you're in there. Please answer the door. I just want to talk to you."

Deidre peeked at him again. He had a bandage on his face.

"Deidre, please…please let me in, honey. I just want to talk to you and explain. I'm so sorry. Please Deidre."

Don sounded like a puppy begging, whining to come in from the cold. She couldn't stand to hear his pleading, sounding so sad, so pitiful. The more he went on with his begging, her feelings went from being sorry for him to finding his behavior disgusting, child-like, manipulative. She watched, waiting for him to give up, but he didn't seem inclined to go away anytime soon. It looked like she was going to have to tell him to leave.

She took a deep breath and opened the door, but kept the locked screen door between them.

Don looked horrible. His face was bruised with a bandage under his right eye. She wanted to ask him how he'd gotten hurt, but why *should* she ask him? Wasn't the point supposed to be about her getting hurt, not him?

She felt confused, conflicted, not sure what she should do or feel, like an eggbeater had scrambled her brain and all her emotions together. She wasn't able to identify the individual ingredients or parse them so she'd know how to feel or what to do.

From somewhere deep inside her head—certainly not her heart—came a demand for her to be strong, not give in, not play into whatever game he was up to this time. She straightened her shoulders. "What do you want, Don?"

"Can I come in? I just want to talk to you." Don put his hand on the screen door latch and pulled. The door wiggled, but didn't open.

Deidre checked to make sure the door was locked tightly. Her heart raced.

He pulled on the latch, again, his eyes pleading with her.

"No, Don, if you have anything to say, just say it right here. I'm not letting you in." Her words sounded stronger to her than she actually felt.

Don winced. "If I could just come in and sit down. I'm really in pain, honey."

"Me too, Don, thanks to you. So say whatever you are going to say because I'm closing this door in three minutes." She didn't know if she could stand by the three-minute promise, but at least her warning set a goal in her mind.

"Look, I don't want to make a scene for everyone to see." Don tugged the latch again.

Deidre shook her head, "Give me a break, Don. That was a really lame attempt to get me to let you inside. We're not in the city, as you well know. I suppose if you yell loud enough, someone could hear you, but you're well aware of the fact that no neighbors can see us from here." She laughed without amusement. "You are going to have to do a lot better. Better yet, you need to accept you are not coming in here."

"Okay, okay. I just want to tell you how sorry I am. Really, Deidre. I'll never lay my hand on you again, as God is my witness." Don held up his right hand to signify his pledge. "I just—"

"I've heard your promises before, Don. Why would things be different this time?"

Hearing the words come out of her mouth, Deidre suddenly realized she sounded like she was counseling a victim of domestic abuse at the hospital. Kera had been right about her. She hadn't wanted to see. Like most battered women, she'd made excuses for Don. How could this have happened to her? She felt stupid, embarrassed, ashamed.

Even worse, she had to admit to herself that she'd been so out of touch with her own life.

"Because Deidre," Don's voice broke into her thoughts, "I know God has spoken to me and I've really changed this time. I promise I will never even raise my voice to you again, let alone strike you in anger. Please, Deidre take me back. Come home."

Oh, God, maybe he can change, maybe…

As a social worker, she had to believe people could change. Otherwise, she had no business in that line of work. Her fingers found their way back to the door lock.

"Could you just come out on the porch and talk to me out here?" He backed away to allow for the door to be opened.

Deidre's hand jerked off the lock. It was as if Kera had reached around from behind her and yanked her hand back. She knew if she'd been in more conscious control of herself, the door would be open right now and she be on the porch with her husband. "No, Don, I...I need to have this door between us."

Don let out a heavy sigh.

"What happened to you, anyway?" That was an automatic caring response she'd wished she hadn't allowed out of her mouth. She knew the question would open the floodgates to Don's travails, woes, stresses, excuses.

"Well, God spoke to me through some teenage thugs. I was beaten and robbed by them last night, just as I was coming out of the church. I went to the emergency room to get patched up. Look, honey, I have stitches." Don pointed at the bandage under his eye. "One of them hit me here." He moved his hand down to his ribs. "I got punched good right here, too. Good God, it felt like the kid had something hard attached to his knuckles. My ribs are really bruised and they're killing me right now—I guess it's time for more pills." He shook his head, "I got to tell you, I went down hard and I don't remember much else."

"So God sent thugs to beat you up, is that what you are saying?"

Don nodded.

"That doesn't make a lot of sense to me, Don. And your three minutes is ticking down."

Deidre realized the "three minutes is ticking down" phrase came from Kera's lingo. Maybe her sister *was* behind her, whispering in her ear. At any rate, Kera would be proud of her. Speaking those defiant words made her feel more powerful, more in control. *Maybe that's why Kera is brave, more forceful in the world. It's her words, or maybe her words come from her power...*She'd have to give that matter more thought.

"Well, I see it like this, Deidre," Don interrupted her contemplation. "God works in mysterious ways, and I guess He just thought I wouldn't get His message unless He gave me some of the same medicine I gave to you. He surely impressed me this time." Don shook his head.

"Well, I can't say I feel sorry for you, if that's what you want."

"I understand that, honey, that would be a given. God wouldn't want you to feel sorry for me. I deserved it. God's made that real clear to me."

"Did you call the police?"

"No, this was a gift from God. It was God's doing. The thugs were just His messengers, a message I really needed, Deidre. Only the Lord could have gotten it through my thick skull." Don whimpered a chuckle. "Besides, I only had about twenty-five bucks on me, so they didn't get that much money."

She mulled over the "gift from God" explanation—that was certainly a new one from Don. She had to give him credit for creativity, making lemonade out of lemons. He got robbed and beaten up, then tried to turn the mugging into a key to her heart, or at least into her sympathy.

"Deidre, I prayed a lot last night. God said He wanted you to come back to me now that I'm healed."

A scared, desperate little boy pushing his brand of God-talk nonsense stood in front of her, trying to fast talk his way out of another mess he had made for himself. She realized it was all over for her. She had no more respect for her husband. Oprah would have called it her "Ah-ha" moment. There was no going back to Don. She could only wonder why she had swallowed his bait these past months and why she had stayed hooked to him for so long.

"Well, Don, that's not what God told me. He told me to stay away from you, forever. He said I don't need to put up with your abuse and your feeble excuses any longer." She couldn't stand the sight of him for one more minute. She closed the front door.

Don knocked several times as Deidre walked to the kitchen, working hard to ignore his pleas. She sat down at the kitchen table and held her head in her hands, covering her ears, trying to block the sound of his continued pounding on the door. Finally, the knocking stopped. She so wanted to hang on to her enlightenment, her resolve, her "Ah-ha" moment. She wasn't going to feel sorry for Don anymore. She just wasn't. He could go to Hell!

Her hands fisted, but her anger at him made her feel guilty.

CHAPTER EIGHT

Kera

The new car smell validated the low reading on the car's odometer: five thousand plus miles.

Kera was enjoying driving her dad's new Buick Le Sabre. It was comfortable and easy to drive, especially on long trips like going to Battle Creek and back today, but the Buick was definitely an older person's car—a granny car. If anyone she knew spotted her in it, her reputation would be ruined.

When she was ready to buy a vehicle, she wanted something that could be also used for off-the-road travel, exploring and camping. Probably a Jeep Wrangler. Besides its versatility, a Jeep was a dyke magnet—not that she was ready to date, but someday, hopefully.

She checked the speedometer: eighty-five mph. She tapped the brakes, got down to seventy-five. She didn't want risk getting stopped, especially since she had plenty of time to make it back to Lakeside City for dinner with Mandy. She set the cruise control.

Cruise control. What a concept. Too bad she couldn't set cruise control on her brain, slow or at least control the spinning memories—no, more like horror films—that plagued her. She supposed what she really needed was an OFF button.

Her time at the VA hospital had gone pretty well. She'd been set up with a VA counselor in Grand Rapids—closer to Lakeside City—along with refills on her meds. Since she'd come home, she'd been stretching out her supply by cutting the pills in half; maybe that's why she'd had that table-dive reaction to the sudden noise at the Pink Door. Then again, she might have had a meltdown anyway. Who knew these days?

Maybe she could score a little weed somewhere to smooth her out.

It was evident to her that her baseline for tolerating the world had certainly changed, like there was the pre-Iraq and the post-Iraq self. Her pre-Iraq self had been pretty easy-going. The post-Iraq self felt like a bunch of tangled, frayed wires ready to ignite, whenever or wherever. She had to count on her meds to quickly bind her emotions, wrapping her anger tightly to keep her from going off, exploding.

She'd called Deidre just before she'd left the hospital. She'd been a bit nervous about leaving Deidre at the house without being there, but her sister had sounded good and said she found the soup and was watching old movies on TV.

Kera forgot to ask if Don had called, but Deidre would have told her if he had…wouldn't she? That bastard hopefully took her threat seriously and stayed the hell away. He better have.

A road sign for Lakeside City indicated five miles to go.

Kera mulled over her conversations with Mandy. When she'd called Mandy last night to learn about the LGBT community's plans to counteract the religious right, Mandy had asked her to go out, have drinks, grab some food, and talk about LEAP's strategy. She didn't know how to read the invitation. Mandy could have suggested they get together for coffee, or she could've just given her a time for a LEAP meeting since the members met regularly. But Mandy had said for "drinks and food."

Okay, she pondered, she and Mandy were long-lost school friends—a valid reason to have dinner together. But on Saturday night? Wasn't that date night? Friday night wouldn't have been so questionable because it was an after-work, on-the-prowl kind of night. If Mandy had said Friday night, she would have taken the invitation to mean: I'll tell you about LEAP and then we'll scope out the women. Or Mandy could have asked her to go to Sunday brunch. Now that wouldn't mean anything other than getting together as old high school friends and catching up.

So, was this a date or not?

Did this mean more than she was ready for?

Kera's all-of-a-sudden clammy hands slipped on the steering wheel. She dried them off on her slacks. She had to admit, Mandy was attractive. Damn attractive. But she wasn't ready for dating, or love, and certainly not commitment—but maybe sex.

She smiled. She couldn't remember the last time she felt a smile on her face.

* * *

The Out-and-About bar was located on the corner of Tulip Street and the Blue Star Highway. She parked her car in an adjacent lot and walked over to the bar. A light breeze blowing in from the lake felt soft and refreshing in the otherwise warm, humid July night.

The gray stone building looked like a small castle, both inside and out. Kera had been in the bar several times when she'd been home on leave. She pulled open the large wooden door and entered. She stood there for a moment waiting for her eyes to fully adjust to the low lighting.

She liked the interior's gay-style medieval motif: On one wall, dyke knights wearing leather jackets and armor helmets rode horses whose legs were actually motorcycles wheels. The knights charged with swords thrust forward. On another wall, a chorus line of buxom male dancers wore medieval dresses hiked up to their waists, showing off their legs and exposing well-endowed male appendages—bulging and threatening to spring from their strained underpinnings.

A voice yelled out, "Over here."

She saw Mandy sitting at the bar, waving her over.

Mandy got off the stool and gave her a hug. "Hey, glad you're back safely. How was your trip?" She patted the barstool next to hers. "Before you tell me, let's get you a drink." She signaled to the female bartender, dressed in Renaissance peasant, to come over.

Kera slid onto the stool and looked over at the draft beer spigots and said, "How about a Bell's Ale, on tap."

The bartender nodded and grabbed a mug.

"Are you hungry? They're serving out on the patio tonight." Mandy pushed her dish of beer nuts over closer to Kera.

"No, not yet, these will do for now." Kera grabbed a handful of beer nuts. "How about you?"

"I'm fine, I can wait to eat. How did your day go?"

"Got stuff done. Got new meds. Filled out a bunch of papers and got a shrink. That's it in a nutshell."

The bartender handed her a mug of ale. She took a long draw, delighting in the cold brew rolling over her tongue and down her throat. She hadn't had her favorite ale in a long time. She wiped her lips with the back of her hand, set the mug down on the bar, muffled her burp, picked her mug up again and drained it. She nodded to the bartender to bring another.

She felt her facial muscles releasing and her lips turning up on the edges.

A second smile.

Being here with Mandy felt...what was it? She wasn't sure but it felt good, that she knew. It was a kind of soothing, softening, or comforting...something that made her feel loose. Or was it the ale on an empty stomach?

She couldn't hold on to the calm respite: An internal warning appeared, like words running along the bottom of the screen on CNN: Relaxing brings death. Warmth brings loss. It felt like every cell in her body was scrambling to the blaring of an internal alarm. It was as though red lights were flashing, a loudspeaker was blurting: "Alert! Alert!" Then gates clanged shut. Lockdown.

Her muscles now constricted. She was back in control.

She took a breath and said, "So Mandy, tell me about your organization. I think that's where we left off on the phone last night."

Mandy told her about LEAP, and why it had been formed. She wanted Kera to become a member of the queer group in their fight to include LGBT people in the city's Civil Rights Ordinance. Mandy thought it would be good for the cause to have her join the group and to "come out" to the greater community of Lakeside City. She believed it would be a plus for the movement, being she was the daughter of the late mayor—the "beloved" mayor, as Mandy had put it.

"You know, Kera, you are quite the celeb in the gay community. It would be good, too, for the morale of our folks if you became part of our group and joined the fight."

Kera listened, elbows on the bar, staring at the lit Budweiser sign on the wall. She listened to Mandy, getting the gist, but she felt like Mandy wanted to pull her into something she didn't need or want. Hadn't she put in enough time fighting a war?

When Mandy stopped, Kera took a sip of ale and looked her directly in her eyes. "So, you asked me to dinner to get me to make a big coming out to the community, lend my name—or more like my notoriety—to the cause. I have to say, I'm feeling a bit used here."

Mandy pulled back, as if Kera had just thrown a punch at her. "Well, I guess having grown up with you, I felt like...oh, shit, I'm sorry. Really, Kera, I thought this could be good for you. It'd be a way to counteract the damage your asshole brother-in-law has done to our LGBT community, as well as to you. I know you're pissed at him too."

Kera realized she'd gone too far. "I didn't mean to come off so hostile. I'm sorry. I seem to be on such a short fuse these days. The shrink said that's part of the PTSD stuff, but I don't want to make excuses for myself…it's still inexcusable, as my mother would say." She managed a meek smile.

Mandy's expression softened. She flushed. "That's only one reason I asked you here tonight. Actually, LEAP was the easier topic to bring up. The other reason was that, well…I just wanted to…damn, I'm really stumbling around with this." She looked over at the bartender standing close by, raised her glass. "I could use another pinot, please."

The bartender nodded and took away the empty wineglass.

Mandy turned back to her. "I just thought we could be, ah… oh shit, I wanted this to be more of…well, kind of a date, and though I truly think it is a good idea, I more or less used the LEAP thing as an excuse to see you. There, I said it."

Kera felt her mouth open, but nothing came out. She'd worried that Mandy might be thinking of their getting together as a date, hoping their friendship would turn into something more. She couldn't think what to say without hurting Mandy's feelings.

She wished she wanted to date, wanted a relationship, or could even have one again, but she didn't think a relationship—even dating—was in the realm of possibilities for her, not at this point in her life. Being here with Mandy felt good. However, the pain of Kelly's death had devastated her, emptied her, allowing for the ghost of what-might-have-been—and anger for Kelly not being there—to come in and occupy her. There was no space for anyone else.

Her therapist kept telling her she needed to acknowledge her pain and recognize her sadness, allow herself to grieve, let the tears come so she could heal and move on. According to her shrink, her unexpressed sadness had morphed into anger spilling into her life like poison polluting a river. As she saw it, the trick was to keep her pain—the sadness—from turning into anger. Problem was, she couldn't get in touch with her sadness. It was like she'd lost it somewhere along the way, making her incapable of crying. Besides, she had to admit, anger was easier. Anger had energy to it and seemed to rub out her pain, at least momentarily.

What was she supposed to do with her love for Kelly? Pack it away in a box and stash it in the attic of her heart? What was she supposed to do with the memories, the good ones, the horrifying ones? Is it possible to put good pictures in a memory scrapbook and leave out the bad ones?

She and Kelly had met in the army ten months before Iraq and were deployed together. Before Kelly, she had never felt that kind of love and intensity of feeling. It was as if her life had gone from black and white to full color, from discordant to melodic, from taking one day at a time to embracing existence, and wanting to get up every day, even in a war zone.

Then in a flash, Kelly was gone. Kera had been twenty feet from Kelly when she died—no, "died" was too pretty a word. Kelly had been blown up, shattered. Ugly words were required for the horrific images, smells, and sounds burned into her senses, smoldering and festering, consuming her.

And she hadn't been able to save her.

"Kera, I'm feeling really uncomfortable right now." Mandy's voice broke through her reverie. "Will you please say something like 'you're too ugly for me bitch,' or 'shove off,' or anything, really. Just not silence."

The bartender put down a fresh glass of wine in front of Mandy.

"Shit, I'm sorry. I don't mean to be an ass." Kera reached out and touched Mandy's arm. "I'm flattered. I really am, Mandy. I want to be a friend…and I find you very attractive. I like you a lot. It's just that I'm not in any shape to date or for anything serious right now. Hell, maybe never. I'm just way too fucked up—"

A voice from behind, yelled, "Hey, Mandy how's it going?" A guy walked over and slung an arm around Mandy's shoulder. "I hope I'm not interfering or interrupting anything."

Mandy turned around on her barstool. "Hey, good to see you Kevin, what brings you out, tonight?"

Kera sighed, relieved. Maybe there was a god. But maybe she shouldn't get carried away with just one example of being saved. However, she did feel grateful to this guy Kevin for breaking in at that very moment.

Kevin waved over the bartender then turned back to Mandy. "Being it's Saturday night and I didn't have anything much to do, I thought I'd crawl out of my closet to see what's happening."

Mandy got off her barstool, put her hand on Kera's shoulder and asked, "Kevin, do you know Kera Van Brocklin?"

Kevin extended his hand to her. "Hi Kera, I'm Kevin McNeil. I'm not sure we've met before, but I've certainly heard of you and I've met your sister, Deidre."

Kera estimated that Mandy was about an inch shorter than her, so comparing Mandy and Kevin's heights, she figured Kevin stood at least 6'6," maybe even taller if he stood up straight. He was lanky with long arms and legs. His nose was long and V-shaped at the end, looking like it was pointing at his mouth. He had a thick crop of unruly black hair with large ears protruding through the overgrowth. She figured his mother had been kind by not naming him Ichabod.

Kera reached out and shook his hand. "How do you know my sister?"

"I work with—or I should say, for—Harry Janssen. Need I say more?" Kevin turned to the bartender and ordered a Grey Goose gimlet.

"No, I guess that says it all, except how can you work for a jerk like him?" Kera grabbed her mug off the bar and took a swig of ale. "I wouldn't have thought he'd want a queer working for him."

"It's a love/hate thing. The Janssen Group—that's our real estate group, obviously named after you-know-who—benefits from having a gay agent. I pretty much get most of the LGBT business in this town. That makes him money and Harry loves money." Kevin held up his right hand and rubbed two fingers against his thumb.

Kera noticed his hand and fingers were as long and thin as the rest of his body. Were his knuckles bloody? Hmm, she thought, maybe she was carrying the Sleepy Hollow theme too far. Probably just seeing things. These days, she didn't trust her perceptions all that much.

"Okay," Kera said, "that explains why Harry wants you, but why do you want to be around him? Can't do much for your self-esteem."

"Maybe it's because I get off on annoying him." Kevin smiled then turned thoughtful. "That's probably why I stay, but when I first started out in real estate, I was so closeted, I didn't think I would ever come out to anyone, anywhere, at any time. So it didn't matter who I worked for, since I supposed almost anyone in the business wouldn't like who I am. Over the years, I got a little pride in myself, that's when I came out to Harry. That was probably....oh, maybe two years ago. I thought Harry should appreciate all the business we were getting from the gay community." He grinned. "Besides, I wanted to challenge the damned bigot. I wanted him to come face-to-face with his principles, you know, his love of money versus allowing a queer on his team. For him, it's got to hurt, especially knowing money won out. Actually, I think he pretty much suspected I was gay, but he didn't want to deal with it, so he hadn't said anything to me. It was his version of 'Don't Ask, Don't Tell.'"

"Got ya." Kera smirked. She and Kelly had dealt with the military's homophobia and it hadn't been easy. But she knew she'd take those difficult and uncertain days back in a flash if she could get Kelly back, too.

"Kevin, looks like your drink is here. Grab it and join us at that table over there, it'll be easier to talk." Mandy pointed at a small round table in the corner. "Have you eaten? Kera and I are about to order some food."

"Sure, sounds great." Kevin took his drink off the bar and followed them.

Kevin made a show of gallantly pulling out the chairs for them, then sat down. He waved to a young male waiter. "Hey, can we see what's on the bill of fare tonight?"

The waiter nodded and left. Kevin's eyes trailed the young man as he went to get the menus. "Hot."

Kera saw Kevin tracking the waiter. "I take it you're single."

Mandy jumped in. "Kevin is a hit-and-run kind of guy. Relationships aren't for him. Right, Kevin?"

"That's right, forever single." Kevin held up his gimlet in a toast. "Here's to singleness and sex without commitment." He lowered his drink and looked at Kera. "Relationships are too open, too out there. It would complicate my business."

"How so?" Kera scooted her chair closer to the table.

"Well, it's one thing to have people think you might be gay but quite another thing to have a partner on your arm." Kevin glanced at a guy just coming into the bar. He threw both arms up in the air and started singing in a stage whisper, "Looking for love in all the wrong places, looking for love in too many faces..."

Mandy took a menu from the waiter who'd just come back to their table. "Come on, Kevin, if we don't let hets see us as couples, they'll never get used to seeing us together."

Kevin turned to Mandy, "I admire your spirit and your guts, and I leave that job to you and your wonderful activism. But for me, having been in the service, my sense of well-being has been battered and bruised in that fight."

Kera nodded in agreement. "Yeah, getting through the military in one piece has only a little to do with the foreign enemy." She felt a sudden kinship with this guy.

"Speaking of battered and bruised..." Mandy took one of Kevin's hands. "How did you get your knuckles and hands so banged up?" She grabbed his other hand. "Look, you're bleeding."

Kera looked over at Kevin's hands. Damn, it wasn't her overactive imagination. She'd seen blood on his knuckles. Maybe there was hope for her yet.

Kevin said to Mandy, "Got into a little scuffle, that's all." He chuckled. "But as they say, you should have seen the other guy."

Mandy gave him a stern look. "Really, Kevin, I don't need the business of keeping you out of jail."

Kevin grinned. "Okay, Mother Mandy. Hmm, looks like I need to put some more salve on my knuckles. I've got some here in my pocket, somewhere." He flinched as he fished in his pants pockets looking for his salve. He finally found it and said. "These damned cuts keep breaking open on me. Guess I need to wash them off before I put this stuff on." He got up from his chair.

Kera watched him as he headed toward the men's bathroom door, which sported a sign showing a dancing condom declaring, "Don't be a silly, Billy."

"Kevin's a good guy," Mandy explained to her when they were alone, "but he's so afraid of being gay, he doesn't let himself have relationships. The problem is, one day he's going to get caught when he's going out to McFarland Park to have one of his little sexual trysts. I'm scared for him. Three years ago, the police put some men out there as gay decoys and trapped some guys. I defended two of them. All the men who got caught having sex out there—with the exception of one guy who killed himself because of his humiliation—left town because they were either fired or laid off. One guy was told he was being let go because of downsizing. They knew they could never get work in Lakeside City again."

Kera shook her head.

"You know, Kevin has some real anger issues," Mandy continued. "He puts on this air of a laid-back kind of guy, but as you can see, he got himself into something. And I've seen him lose it. Once he—" She saw Kevin returning to the table and changed the subject. After he sat down, she said, "Kera, you probably don't know this, but Kevin was in the Green Berets."

Kera raised an eyebrow. "Green Berets, huh? Cool. When did you get out?"

"About four, almost five years ago. I was forced out."

"'Don't Ask, Don't Tell?'" Kera took a sip from her mug.

"Yep." Kevin looked down at the table. His thumb and forefinger flicked a book of matches off the table and onto the floor.

Mandy watched the matchbook sail to the floor, then turned back to Kevin and said, "Kera was in the army, an MP—"

Suddenly, loud angry voices came from the bar's open front door.

Kera looked toward the ruckus. People in the bar went to the doorway to see what was happening, while others started escaping out the back.

She got up with Mandy and Kevin and hustled over to the other side of the room near the door. There were too many people blocking the doorway for her to see what was going on. Kevin motioned her and Mandy to go with him to a window where they could get a better view.

Kera saw people with signs marching back and forth in front of the bar. One man was dressed like Jesus, dragging a large wooden cross and encircled by other protestors. The signs proclaimed: God hates homosexuals! Homosexuals are Going to Hell! Repent Now! Many signs simply read: Citizens Against Perversion. Other signs referenced different passages of the Bible.

Bar patrons poured out onto the sidewalk, yelling for the demonstrators to leave, to get away from their bar. Protesters responded by yelling out Bible verses and promises of damnation.

A short, burly guy charged out the door, shaking his fist at the protesters.

Kera couldn't hear what he was saying to them. She cracked open the window and turned to Mandy. "Who's that guy?"

"That's Vinny Belsito. He's the guy who was fixing the light on the ceiling at the Pink Door and fell off the ladder when the dog came running in. You know, when you—"

"Okay, okay, got it." Kera didn't like being reminded of the flashback at the Community Center. It embarrassed her.

Kevin looked over at her, "Hey, I heard about your nosedive under the table—Vinny told me," Kevin said with a wry smile. "Shit, you don't need to feel bad about it. You should have seen me when I first came back from overseas. I was jumpy as hell. I'm doing a lot better, but it still affects me." He turned back to the window.

Kera was grateful that at least Kevin wasn't seeing her as a total kook. Still, she hoped news of the incident wouldn't spread through the community. But really, how could it not. To think otherwise was delusional. She turned her attention back to what was happening outside and saw Vinny yelling and shaking his fist at the protesters.

Mandy shook her head. "That Vinny's a real hell-raiser, even when he's not provoked. He won't make things better out there, I'm sure of that. Confronting those bigots, like that, isn't the way to help our cause. Really, it will only hurt it."

Kera watched as Vinny got closer to the group carrying the signs. The crowd from the bar closed in on the members of the Jesus parade, trying to move them off the sidewalk and into the street. She thought that she recognized two of the men holding signs. She didn't know their names, but she was sure she had seen them at her dad's funeral. No doubt they attended Don's church. *Figures!*

Don's words from the funeral service came back to her. Hearing his voice and his words reverberating inside her head reignited her rage. She could feel herself become jittery, agitated, starting to come uncorked.

Looking across the street, she saw men piling out of cars. They headed over to several queens and started taunting them, loudly threatening to remove their male identity from between their legs. About six or so other guys—all carrying clubs—came charging up the street toward the mêlée. Two of the queens started beating on "Jesus" with their purses, bringing the sign holders into the fray.

Unable to watch or contain herself for even one more second, Kera bolted for the door.

From behind, she heard Kevin yelled out to her, "Wait up Kera, I'm coming with you."

* * *

"Thanks for bailing me out, and so fast, no less. You must have connections at the jail. Everyone else who was arrested is still in there. I sort of feel guilty, walking out while they're stuck in that place—but not bad enough." Kera flashed Mandy a guilty smile. "It's not like I want to go back." She opened the car door and got into Mandy's silver Volkswagen.

Mandy pulled out from the Lakeside City jail's parking lot. "You're lucky I had a friend on duty tonight."

"I know you don't agree with what I did. I really appreciate you getting my ass out of there." Kera found a small, half-eaten bag of chips on the rear seat of the car. "Mind if I—"

"Have at 'em. They've been in there a while so they may not be too fresh."

Kera was starving. She hadn't eaten any dinner, not to mention all the energy it had taken out of her to fight those assholes. She thought about how upset her father would have been with her—more like horrified, pissed, and publicly embarrassed—to have to retrieve her from jail.

Death had spared him.

Her mind floated off to another time when her father—and especially her mother—had been really upset with her. That incident also involved her being in the public eye.

She and her friend, Janet, had taken out her father's motorboat. Her dad's rule was that they were to stay on the Turtle River, not to venture out onto Lake Michigan. Her parents feared the sudden dangerous changes of weather the lake was known for. Her adolescent mind judged the rule: stupid. She'd figured she could handle the boat as well as her dad could—even he had admitted that—and he drove the boat out onto the lake.

One day out on the lake, the weather changed fast. She and Janet tried to get back to the river. The wind created swells higher than she had ever seen. She'd turned the boat into the waves to keep from capsizing.

She remembered the bottom of the boat rising up with each breaker, then slapping down on the water between the whitecaps. She'd felt like she was riding a bucking bronco. Her boat took on some water, but mostly waves rushed over the deck and back into the lake. A wild ride, exhilarating, filling her with pure bliss.

She never wore a life jacket unless, of course, her mom and dad were around. But when she was out of sight of her parents, she shed the cumbersome annoyance. Mom and Dad didn't understand that a life jacket wasn't cool, and besides, it was too confining. Having the bulky thing on ruined her ability to feel the freedom of flying across the lake. To her, wearing the life jacket was the equivalent of wearing a helmet on a motorcycle—she didn't do that either. The wind flying through her hair was half the joy of riding down the highway or zipping across the lake. Helmets and life jackets got in the way of a good time.

Her craft hurdled the waves. Sprays of cool water blasted her body. She'd felt alive.

Suddenly, she saw a flash of bright green in the water, then it disappeared. When the green color bobbed up, again, she saw a woman—wearing a green blouse—in a small boat. It was clear that woman was in trouble. The small vessel looked as though it might overturn at any time.

Kera slowed her boat, maneuvering in the direction of the endangered woman. As she got closer, she saw the panic on the face of a middle-aged woman who started yelling to her. Kera couldn't hear her over the noise from the wind but she could read her lips: "Help! Help! Please help me!"

Just as Janet was about to throw out a rope for the woman to grab, the little boat tipped over, throwing the woman into the raging water.

At first, she couldn't see the woman. Maybe she was under the boat, but wherever she was, she was without a life jacket.

The woman appeared again, struggling to keep her head above water, fighting to stay afloat. Coughing, she thrashed, sank, scratched her way to the surface, then sank back under the water.

Kera searched the lake trying to see the woman, hoping she'd come up again. Then she spotted her in the water. The woman's head was tilted back, barely above the water. She wasn't struggling anymore. No more fight in her. She could only grab for air.

Kera knew she had just seconds to get to the woman, because soon she'd go under for the last time.

As she was diving into the lake, she saw her slipping under again. Kera swam up to the surface, but couldn't find her. She fought her way through the water to where she thought she'd last seen her, then jackknifed her body and pushed herself down under the water, searching for the bright green blouse.

Her air was running thin when she finally found the drowning woman. She took hold of the woman and pulled her to the surface.

Janet threw out a life ring buoy. She grabbed it, got the woman on, and towed her to the boat.

Unfortunately, the closest place to bring her boat ashore was the city dock where a camera crew from the TV stations had set up, reporting on the intensity of the storm. A reporter spotted the rescue scene and filmed it—quite a news story in and of itself, but when the reporter realized one of the mayor's daughters had saved the woman, the story became headline material.

That headline cost her boating privileges for the entire summer, even though she received an award from the US Coast Guard for her bravery—her mother called it her "foolhardiness." Her father had said she'd embarrassed him publicly. Though people might have seen her as a hero, he believed they would think he and her mother were neglectful parents for allowing her out on the lake in a storm.

"Really, Kera, I'm just saying." Mandy's voice startled her, brought her back to the car and her stale chips and Mandy's reproof. "You jumping into that fight and staying there long enough to get arrested wasn't good on so many levels. But I'll shut up. I guess you don't need me to chastise you. Besides, I'm quite certain it wouldn't do any good."

Kera didn't respond. She was thinking about how she'd flown out the bar door and into the fray—a knee-jerk reaction. It was like she possessed no control over herself, at least not when it came to people like her asshole, religious right, wife-abusing brother-in-law. She'd seen Don's face on everyone one of those—

Mandy broke her train of thought: "You must be hungry. I know I am. Want to stop somewhere and grab a bite? In trying to get you out of jail, I haven't eaten anything, either."

"Hey, I'm sorry about that. Sure, I am hungry too, but if you don't mind, let's get something at a drive-through so we can eat in the car. I'm feeling exposed, working on notorious. First, I'm caught on tape screeching out of the funeral service like I'm in a get away car after a bank heist. Then tonight, reporters take my picture as I'm hauled off to jail." Kera wadded up the empty chip bag and tossed it on the backseat.

Mandy drove into a Wendy's drive-through. They got their food and parked in the back of the restaurant.

"How are you going to feel tomorrow morning when your picture is on the front page of *The Journal*?" Mandy took a bite of her cheeseburger.

"Depends on whether or not they got my good side." Kera gave Mandy a wry smile, trying to look unconcerned, and kept munching on her fries.

She did wonder why she hadn't split sooner, got her ass out of there before the cops came. She pondered a moment and realized how damned good it'd felt to have a place to vent her anger.

At the time, she hadn't thought about the cops showing up. Even if she had, she wasn't sure she would have left. She hated to admit it, wouldn't admit it to Mandy, but she'd enjoyed punching and kicking those people. So much so, she hadn't felt any pain from the punches landing on her—not then, anyway. Like her body had numbed, deadened, gone somewhere else—physically, that is. Out on the street in front of the bar, her anger was in control, surging through her veins like an electrical current. No one at the scene—certainly not her—had yanked the plug until the cops showed up and grabbed her.

"You got yourself a couple of cuts and maybe a bruise forming on your face." Mandy turned the rearview mirror so Kera could see herself.

Kera bent forward to look into the mirror, trying to determine the damage. "Geez, I thought I was getting all the punches in. Guess I needed to bob and weave a little bit more."

Mandy shook her head.

"By the way, whatever happened to Kevin?" Kera asked, putting her empty food wrappers into the Wendy's bag.

"He called me on my cell phone to see if you were okay. He was relieved he'd gotten out of there before the police arrived. If his picture had gotten in the paper, it would have outed him and ruined his career here." Mandy hesitated. "I guess I shouldn't tell you this, but he mentioned…well, actually praised, your fighting abilities." She flashed an admiring smile. "I have to say I was impressed myself. You did some serious shit-kicking." She quickly dropped the smile and assumed a stern look, "Not that I approve of your actions, either as a lawyer or an activist. I—"

"Oh, shit, what time is it?" Kera looked at her wristwatch. "Geez, it's already almost ten. I need to call Dee. She's going to be really upset if she sees the eleven o'clock news." She grimaced. "Damn, I just don't feel like dealing with her tonight. She can be so like my mother."

Kera thought about when she and her sister were kids. Dee always stepped in—interfered would be a better word—to make sure she was "being good and following the rules." Having Dee along nagging at her was like taking her mother everywhere she went. She loved her sister, dearly, but she just had to escape Dee at times, to hang out with friends who weren't monitoring her. Friends like Janet Cooley, who enjoyed adventure and had a bit of a wild side, too.

"Do you want to stay over at my house tonight?" Mandy asked. "You sure could use to have your banged-up face attended to. And I'm just the girl to do it." She grinned. "After all, I took first aid in high school. I think that would qualify me for most everything—except surgery, maybe."

Kera laughed. She thought a minute. "Well, if I did, I would still have to call Dee. But I guess that would be better than the alternative."

"If you want, I could call her and tell her you were really tired. It's not like I'd be lying. I'll let her know you're okay but went to bed, and staying over was my idea."

Kera didn't respond. She wasn't sure it was a good idea for her to spend the night with Mandy. Would Mandy expect to sleep with her? Have sex?

Mandy must have read her mind. "Don't worry, I have two bedrooms, you'll have your own space. What do you say?"

"Yeah, okay, but Dee needs to know what happened because it's going to make the news and she might be watching the TV and—"

"I'll explain it to her and you can avoid—until tomorrow anyway— her mothering thing."

"Okay, but I need to pick up the Buick, it's still at the bar."

"If you don't mind, let's pick up your car in the morning, I'm exhausted." Mandy put the key into the ignition and started the car.

"Okay, the car will be there tomorrow, and it's the coward's way out not going home tonight, but I'm out of juice." Kera sucked up the last drops of Pepsi from the bottom of her paper cup. "Got some pajamas for me?"

"No problem."

* * *

"Oh, shit!" Kera bolted up out of sleep, grabbed the large furry something that had landed on her head.

Before she even made it out of bed, she threw the night invader against the wall. Its shriek splintered the night's silence. She dropped to the floor, fingers of both hands laced together, protecting the back of her head.

The bedroom door burst open. She glanced up to see a Maine Coon cat madly making a run for it, screeching as it flew through the opened doorway.

She sat up, her heart pounding, sweat dripping.

Light coming in from the doorway silhouetted a woman. "Kelly?" She reached out toward the shadowed figure.

A voice broke through her mirage. "No, Kera, it's Mandy."

Reality began to seep in, like sewer sludge oozing up from a clogged drain: *Kelly is dead.*

"What happened?" Mandy sat down on the floor next to her.

Kera rubbed her forehead. "I don't know. Well, I guess I do know now. A monster cat jumped on my head. I was sleeping and...all I know is I was under attack, or thought I was."

"Oh, Kera, I'm sorry. I didn't realize Mr. Moxin was in here. He must have been sleeping under the bed or in the closet when you closed the door last night. Here, let me help you up." Mandy got up and held out a hand to her.

Kera stood, shaking, then sat down on the bed, still breathing hard, her heart racing.

Mandy went into the bathroom and brought back a hand towel. She sat down beside her. "It must have been awful in Iraq." She patted the sweat from her face. "I'm so sorry you had to experience all that."

"I can't seem to stop shaking." Kera crossed her arms around her midsection, trying to hold herself together and feeling if she didn't, she'd break into a thousand pieces.

"Here, why don't you lie back down."

"I don't know if I can sleep now. I keep seeing things...I can't get them out of my mind. My shaking won't stop."

"Why don't I hold you, would you let me do that?"

Kera had reactions like this many times before with no one there for her. It'd be nice to have someone hold her, but it made her feel weak to accept Mandy's offer of comfort. She wished she could just pull herself together, get on with her life—whatever that meant. She couldn't look into Mandy's eyes, couldn't say yes, but she felt her head nodding.

Mandy crawled into bed with her, took her in her arms and held her close.

They lay together quietly. Mandy gently ran fingers through her hair. She was beginning to understand why cats purred. Mr. Moxin would be jealous of her right now, if he could see her snuggled up to Mandy—in his place. She looked over at the clock. She'd only been in bed a short time. God, this was going to be a long night. She knew how long nights could be. She'd endured plenty of them. But the rhythmic stroking of her head began to calm her, drawing away painful pictures and thoughts, leaving her feeling like she was existing in a…a…what? A void. That was it. But it wasn't scary. In fact, her sense of nothingness calmed her. She wouldn't mind staying there:

A peaceful waiting room—for death.

Her breathing slowed, her shaking stopped.

She floated in serenity.

* * *

Kera popped awake. She looked over at Mandy sleeping next to her and then glanced over at the clock on the nightstand. Shit, only a little after midnight. She closed her eyelids, only to find bodies exploding as she drifted into a nightmare.

So much for the void and its serenity.

She couldn't still her mind or body. She got up and went into the living room, turned on the TV and flipped channels until she came to a rerun of *Frasier*. She watched for a while but couldn't get into the sitcom. Her restlessness demanded she do something, move, go somewhere and try to calm herself. She tiptoed back into the bedroom, retrieved her clothes, and got dressed.

Damn, she didn't have her own car. It was at the bar.

She saw Mandy's keys to the VW on the end table next to the sofa. Hell, it was only ten minutes to the beach. She figured she wouldn't be gone long. She'd be back way before Mandy got up.

She reached for the keys.

* * *

Kera sat behind the VW's steering wheel in the parking lot of McFarland Park overlooking Lake Michigan. The moon was full, giving off a stream of light that danced across the lake. She counted seven cars in the parking lot—not that many, really, given this was Saturday night at the gay boys' rendezvous spot.

She wondered if this was a normal night's trade these days. Maybe she should've gone down further on the beach to be alone, but hell, the guys sure weren't going to bother her. They were busy, hooking up and going off into the dunes. Kind of sad. She figured they were either scared to be out in the world or stuck in a marriage they thought they had to have and this place was their outlet. Maybe, she considered, some might like the thrill of it all.

She looked at the cars. Some were empty, but others had someone inside, no doubt waiting for a connection. She noticed a car with two guys, probably doing the small talk thing before heading into the dunes.

The anonymity...hmm, she mulled the concept over, maybe she could get into sex without commitment or emotional ties. The problem was, as she saw it, most women were into all the emotional and commitment stuff. In the end—whenever and however that came—a relationship would only bring more pain.

Still, maybe she could take a page from the guy's book, hook up and leave before emotions had a chance to enter into it, but women didn't do parks. Not their style. They brought sex to their dens instead of taking it to a neutral spot. Sex in a den conjured up a whole different meaning.

She'd have to watch out for those honey traps.

Kera got out of the car and walked to the beach. She took off her shoes and splashed in the shallow, warm water, each step settling on hard-packed, rippled sand.

A man and woman walked past her along the shoreline, holding hands.

Damn them. That's what she'd planned to do with Kelly: walk hand in hand along the Lake Michigan shore. She grabbed the phantom hand—held out to her by her own desire—and walked along with Kelly's ghost.

For a while, the walk felt good, almost real, a dream come true, but too soon Kelly's ghost faded away, disappearing into emptiness.

Anger rushed into her, filling the vacuum—anger for her loss, now directed at something tangible: the het couple. Didn't those hets know that the area was considered the gay beach? Damn them. They had almost every other beach in the world. Why tread on what little the gay community could think of as their own space? She wanted to scream at them.

Get off...Get out of here!

She took in a deep breath. Don't go there, she told herself. Turn away from the anger, breathe in the serenity and be with the lake. That's what she had come to do, like she'd done growing up, and especially after her mother died.

She sat down, breathed in and out, in and out...focusing, listening to the sounds of the water splashing on the shore, quieting her. Her spirit leaned into the waves, and now she bobbed in its rhythm: a peaceful journey.

That was better. Her heart rate slowed. Her anger subsided.

The pulse of the lake connected her to the rhythm of the earth, bringing into her a feeling of oneness. In her mind's eye, her soul floated and seemed to sprout silver threads, drifting out, like from a sphere, connecting her to a universal harmony.

The void filled with good stuff.

A car door slammed, jarring her back to the present.

Still, she felt better, her anger diminished, leaving her memory free to drift in time to a good place, to when she was about thirteen and having a sleepover at Janet's house.

She and her friend had snuck out of the house at midnight to go to the lake, though further down the beach from where she sat now. They'd brought their sleeping bags and gone up into the sand dunes, smoked cigarettes and drank cheap wine. They told each other their secrets. She shared that she was gay and Janet had kept her secret. She wondered, where was Janet now? How was her life turning out? The last she knew—after graduation from high school—Janet had taken off for Montana to visit her aunt for the summer and would decide what she wanted to do with her life after she returned home.

What she remembered most about that night—sleeping in the dunes with her friend—was their childhood impatience for independence, along with a belief that great things would happen when they took over steering their own lives. But for her, being behind the wheel of freedom and choice hadn't turn out to be all it was cracked up to be.

Neither was life.

A breeze came up, chilling her. Kera grabbed her shoes and went back to the car. She got into the VW. She knew she should return to

Mandy's but she didn't think she could sleep there. Even if she could, she'd probably be bombarded by nightmares.

She picked up her cell phone to call Mandy, but thought better of waking her. She looked at the time on her cell: 1:20 a.m. Better sleep might be had here by the lake where she felt calm. Just for an hour or two, then she'd go back to Mandy's.

Having made that decision, she pushed the seat back, then tilted it down as far as it would go and closed her eyes.

A closing car door woke her. She heard another slam. She couldn't remember where she was until the cramped quarters of the Volkswagen oriented her. She pulled the back of her seat up and stretched her legs.

One other vehicle besides hers was still in the parking lot, but it was leaving. She looked down at her watch, but it wasn't on her wrist. She supposed it must have come off during the fight at the bar. Last week, she'd noticed the clasp on her watchband was weak. She should have gotten a new one. She'd meant to.

She wiggled around looking for her cell phone. She knew she should be getting back before Mandy woke up and wondered where she was. She noticed her phone had fallen on the floor, so she reached down, picked it up, and checked the time—3:51 a.m. She sat back a moment, still drowsy, then released her seat to the reclining position again. Couldn't hurt to rest for a few more minutes.

A cry of a gull woke her. She popped up her seat, rubbed her eyes and looked around. No other cars in the parking lot. She needed to get out of there before she fell asleep a third time. She put the key in the ignition and drove out. As she left the parking lot, she noticed a Mercedes parked down the street. She'd seen several Mercedes, like that one, when she was at the gay bar. She figured he didn't want his car to be seen at McFarland Park. Made sense.

A reddish twilight glowed over the lake, reflecting in the water. The light made her recall the old mariner's warning her father used to recite on mornings like this one: "Red skies at night, sailor's delight. Red skies in the morning, sailors take warning."

CHAPTER NINE

Don

Don spit out a piece of the eraser from the top of his pencil. He'd almost bitten it down to the metal trying to figure out exactly what he wanted and needed to say. He couldn't seem to get his Sunday morning sermon on the sin and perversion of homosexuality written the way he wanted. Something was missing.

He believed his sermon required something new, something sensational, to inspire his congregation to continue the fight against the homosexuals—without, of course, his actually having to mention the ordinance. Not that he needed to get every word in place because he never read or followed a sermon script, but he liked to have his ideas thought out, with a few notes so he could bring himself back to the topic if he happened to stray too far.

He blamed Deidre for not being able to think right. How could she forsake him, especially at this time in his life? God had given him a mission. Didn't she realize that? Perhaps God was testing him. Surely that had to be it. God wouldn't give him more than he could handle. He'd preached the same message many times, but he was beginning to wonder if God had overestimated his strength.

Maybe God had chosen the wrong man for the job.

Maybe this was his Gethsemane.

He hadn't been able to work at home because the house haunted him, played back memories he didn't want to think about, so he'd decided to try his church office. Besides, he hoped he'd be more inspired in God's house and wouldn't think about what he had done to his wife.

Her bloody face flashed before him.

He took in a deep breath, squeezed his eyelids shut and reopened them, banishing her image, or at least fading it out, so he could get back to his calling.

He had brought his Sunday clothes and shaving kit with him in case he decided to remain overnight. He could sleep here on the sofa and get ready for church services in the morning, before anyone showed up. Since the building had been a frat house, it had showers. He'd checked them out. Not all that clean and had mildew around the edges, but they'd work.

He wondered what people would say when Deidre wasn't at church tomorrow. He needed to come up with a good reason for her absence.

He got up from his desk and paced back and forth. Deidre's car was still in their driveway. So he couldn't say she'd gone out of town for her work. The solution finally came to him: he'd say she had flown out somewhere. But where? He didn't have an idea where she'd go, so he gave up that possibility.

Good God. He started worrying Deidre might show up at church tomorrow morning with her broken nose. She wouldn't do that, would she? No, not unless she wanted to humiliate him. He pulled out his handkerchief and sopped up the moisture accumulating on his face and neck.

He put his hand on his rib cage. The touch barely hurt. The medication the doctor had given him worked well, especially since he had decided to double the dose.

When he began thinking of his story about the teenage thugs and how he'd gotten beaten up and robbed by them, a revelation came to him: the thugs would be gay. Yes, that's it. These gay thugs beat him up for speaking out against homosexuals, then took his money to boot. That made gays look bad and made him a martyr.

Wow. That was the perfect angle for his sermon, something to rile up the congregation. And God would certainly understand his little white lie was for His cause. Surely, the Lord would approve. He smiled to himself.

But now he needed to figure out why Deidre wouldn't be in church tomorrow morning. He figured he could say she broke her nose when she got up in the night, didn't turn on the light and ran into the edge of an open door. He had done the same thing when he was a little kid. Didn't break his nose but he'd sure ended up with two black eyes and a banged-up nose. It could have happened to Deidre, too.

The more he thought about it, the more it seemed like that was what did happen. He could visualize it, clear as day. He grabbed a white tablet off his desk and jotted a note to tell Deidre how she got her broken nose. As mad as she was at him, she'd surely stick by him and accept his version of events.

He needed to get Deidre away from her sister's influence so she'd see the light and come home. Having Kera home from the army was a real burden for him. Maybe Kera wasn't planning on staying in Lakeside City. He hoped she'd leave after their father's estate was settled. She would be nothing but trouble for him if she planned on staying. Clearly, she had too much influence on Deidre. He'd have to pray about that situation. God would need to show him the way.

The phone rang.

Don looked at his watch: a little after midnight. Good God, he wondered, who'd be calling at a time like this? Maybe it was an emergency.

"Hello, this is the Church of God's True Words, Pastor Don speaking."

He was just starting to get used to using the new church's name. He liked the sound of it. Thank the Lord, Jimmy Johnson's name suggestion had finally gone down in defeat.

Jimmy had wanted to name the church, "Church of Jesus by the Lake." The guy liked the image of Jesus standing by Lake Michigan, ready to walk on water, and thought a mural of Jesus stepping onto the water would be great, like the steps of faith into rugged waters, "akin to the struggle our congregation had in leaving the old church," he'd said at the meeting.

It amazed Don how many votes Jimmy got for the name and concept, but the proposed name didn't convey the message he wanted: true words. Furthermore, the church was a little over a half-mile from the lake, not beside the lake, as he had pointed out to the board.

"Hi, Don," Harry responded. "What are you doing there so late? Don't you ever stop working?" Before Don could answer, he went on: "I've been trying to call you at home all night, I finally decided to try the church. Sorry to bother you so late, but Sylvia and I got concerned when neither you nor Deidre answered, and I needed to tell you about—"

"Deidre probably went to bed early. She wasn't feeling so good. I'm sure you haven't heard, she broke her nose the other night, bumped right into an open door. Poor thing didn't turn the light on. Besides hurting, she's pretty embarrassed about it." Don believed he'd gotten the story out quite convincingly, though his heart pounded.

"Oh, I'm sorry, Don, give her my best. I'm sure she's in some real pain."

"The doc gave her pain medication, but it still hurts." Don realized he'd better tell Harry his story of how he was robbed; otherwise, his friend would wonder why he'd waited until Sunday at church to let him know. "For that matter, I'm in a bit of pain myself."

"What's wrong? Hope nothing serious."

"Well, I'll be okay, but last night I was mugged right out here by the church—young thugs, teenagers. They couldn't have been out of high school yet, I'd say. And get this: they were queers. They beat me up, said it was because I preached against them. Then they took my money."

"You're kidding me! That was a terrible thing to have happen to you. What did the police have to say about it?"

Don hadn't anticipated the question, nor had he thought his story through. If he'd been attacked as he said, he would have called the police, and he certainly wasn't about to tell Harry that it was God's doing, as he had told his wife. "Uh, no...I don't know why but I didn't call the police. I—"

"Are you okay? Did you see a doctor?"

Relieved to move on, Don said, "Yeah, don't worry, I got medical attention. I have some pretty sore ribs, a few cuts—one needed stitches—but basically, I'm just a bit battered and bruised, I'd say. The doc gave me some pain meds, so I'm not hurting much. Really, I'm doing fine." He'd had all he could handle for the moment with his made-up story. He wanted to move on. "By the way, why did you call me?"

"Oh, yeah, more bad news, I'm sorry to say. I've been trying to get a hold of you because I got a call from the city council president about what happened tonight at the gay bar. Remember, I told you our group was going to protest there tonight?"

"Yes, certainly, what happened?"

Harry's voice rose. "The queers came out of the bar, yelling and screaming, and attacked our folks."

"Good Lord." Don was shocked. How could peaceful protesting turn into violence? That wasn't what he'd wanted to happen.

Harry went on, "Well, it was John's place as council president to call an emergency meeting about the incident, so of course I went. He's worried about all the ruckus going on around town regarding this ordinance stuff. From what John told us, the protesters—our folks— were minding their own business, just peacefully demonstrating like they'd talked about at the CAP meeting. Then for no good reason at all, they were attacked by the patrons—the queers—in the bar, who ran out and assaulted them. I'll tell you what, Don, starting this fight with our folks will be bad press for them. That's for sure."

"Oh, my…were any of our folks hurt?"

"Yes, a couple of our people were taken to the hospital, don't know who yet. Apparently, a few people were arrested, but reports are sketchy. I didn't catch the TV news, but I've been trying to get more information. Fortunately, I heard no one was seriously hurt, but wanted you to know about it, especially since our congregation will be upset about it tomorrow at church."

"They surely will."

"Frankly Don, I'm really sorry some of our folks got hurt, but the good news here is that, as I said, it will be really bad PR for those who want the ordinance changed. Attacking peaceful protesters will show the citizens of our community who they're trying to give special privileges to. In a way, it couldn't have been better for us—you know, all the negative publicity this incident will bring."

"Yes, I can see that but I'm worried about our folks. That had to be so scary for them. Maybe I should go over to the hospital, tonight… but then, that might not be a good idea because we don't want to risk people knowing we're involved in any way. So maybe I shouldn't go after all."

"Right."

"But Harry, somehow we need to be there for them."

"Tell you what, I'll call someone from the church board to go over to the hospital and minister to them. How's that? I'd go myself, but that wouldn't look good either, with me being on the city council and all."

"How about Jimmy Johnson? He has the gift of ministering to people. I've seen him work with folks who are upset and—"

"No, no, Don, remember he was against our involvement in the ordinance altogether. He got upset at the board meeting the other night when we were discussing it. Remember? I had to come down on him pretty hard."

"Oh, yeah, you're right about Jimmy's attitude, now that you mention it."

"By the way," Harry said, "Dave told me he thinks Jimmy's son is gay. In fact, one of our folks at the protest said they thought they saw Jimmy's son at the gay bar."

"Oh, I surely hope not. And I pray for Jimmy's sake that his son didn't stray off the path of righteousness because Jimmy would have to make some difficult choices, wouldn't he?" Don didn't like putting it that way, but if anyone in the congregation decided to condone homosexuality, especially if it involved one of their kids, he would have to tell him or her to leave the flock. It would be painful, for him, but he would do it. He sure would!

"Well, whoever you get to go to the hospital, have him let our congregants know how upset I am about what's happened to them and I will be visiting with them as soon as I can."

"No problem." Harry cleared his throat. "Oh, by the way, before I forget, I bumped into Rich Harmon earlier today. He stopped me when I was pulling out at the post office. He happened to see my new hunting gear in the car. We got to talking, and he asked if he could tag along on the hunting trip this fall. I told him it was okay, if you were okay with it. I promised to call Rich tomorrow to let him know for sure. His wife wants to go on a fall cruise and he needs to make sure the time won't conflict with our hunting trip."

"Sure, it will be fun having him along. Rich is a good guy."

"Okay, I'll let him know."

"Come to think of it, does Rich happen to have a vehicle we could use?" Don asked. "As you know, I keep taking my car in to get it fixed because it constantly stalls out on me. I don't know why the garage guys can't seem to figure it out, but I don't trust my car anymore, even if they claim—once again—that it's fixed. Don't want us to break down out in the boonies. Wouldn't mind having this loaner I got—it's a Subaru Forester. It'd be great for hunting instead of my old clunker, but—"

"I don't think I'm willing to take mine," Harry chuckled. "Don't want to be messing up my shiny new car."

"No, you're right about that, it's an expensive vehicle, but a truck would be good, if we could get our hands on one." Getting tired, Don rubbed his eyes.

"Last year, George's truck worked out great for bringing back our kill, but since he won't be going this year... I'll tell you what, I'll ask

Rich if he happens to still own that old Ford truck. That would be ideal."

"Didn't know he had a truck. That'd be great"

"Well, Don, guess I'll let you go so you can finish up and get home. And hey, you really should tell the police about getting mugged, especially given all the other stuff that's going on around here. The authorities need to know what those queers are up to."

"Yeah, well, we'll see." Don grimaced. He really didn't want to report the supposed beating by gay kids. He worried the story he was spinning could get out by way of the news media. He didn't believe the guy who'd beaten him up wanted publicity, either, but he didn't want to take a chance on being branded a liar.

"Don, you need to get home and get some rest. I can hear you yawning." Harry laughed.

"I'm thinking I might just stay here tonight. I don't want to wake Deidre. I brought some clean clothes. I can shower and get dressed in the morning right here."

"Okay, but don't let the oil burn too late, you've got a big sermon tomorrow. Need to hit the hay myself. See you in the morning."

"Good night, Harry."

* * *

Don plopped down on the sofa. He had forgotten to bring his pajamas, but he didn't mind. If someone showed up, he wouldn't want to greet that person in his nightwear.

He closed his eyes and tried to calm his mind. In the light of day, he was confident, mostly confident, that he could handle what was on his plate, but when he tried to fall asleep, all his doubts busted through his barbed wire defenses, followed by uncertainty and fear.

Would Deidre forgive him, support him, come back to him?

Would people buy his cover-up stories?

Could he lead his church and carry out God's plans?

But most of all, he needed to conquer his sin. He had to stop the feelings, the cravings—all coming from the Devil.

In his mind's eye, he held up a shield with a cross on it. There. If he could keep that image up, the Devil couldn't get hold of him. He'd be able to protect himself if he could just cement that picture in his head. But with his doubts came desire and the incessant cravings creeping through his shield like marauding ghosts.

He got off the sofa, went down on his knees and implored his God to help him, but in spite of his pleas, the swelling between his legs grew. *Go away, go away.* He snapped at his penis with his thumb and forefinger, but it got harder and more demanding.

He wept and implored God, but no answer came to him.

He got up from his knees and like an addict in search of his dealer, grabbed the keys to the Subaru and rushed out of the church.

Don tried to get himself to stop, turn around, go back to the sanctity of the church. He'd been in this state before—too many times; in fact, the latest incident just yesterday—begging himself not to go, failing to overcome the sin, imploring God to intervene. As in the past, he didn't have the strength to fight temptation on his own. And like the past, God had forsaken him once again.

He thought about how his sinful acts led to God denying him a baby. He understood, for surely he hadn't hit his wife that hard, not enough to cause the miscarriage. If he had gotten a little too rough, it was God's doing, God's way of taking the baby from him. He'd been God's instrument.

If Deidre found out what monster lived inside him, how it came out, she'd despise him and would never, never want him back.

He was unrighteous...morally repugnant...the scum of the earth. Letting his God-given mission, his church and his family down. His soul was in eternal jeopardy.

Ruination would be his fate.

But he couldn't turn his vehicle around and go back to the church. A dark force was dragging him, bringing him down, sucking him under. He had no control, no power—a captive, taken along for the journey.

Don pulled into the parking lot of McFarland Park and turned off the engine. He saw only one car, an old VW, parked in the lot, but the vehicle seemed unoccupied. He decided the driver must be up in the sand dunes.

Maybe he'd climb up there himself and see.

Rib pain broke through his double dose of Vicodin, warning him that maybe the guy up in the dunes was the guy who'd beaten him up yesterday. He'd better not head up there without knowing who might be there.

He decided to wait for someone else to show up in the parking lot. That way, he could check out the guy first.

Don sorted through his duffel bag. He'd brought store-bought glasses, a wig, cap, and a fake mustache and beard. He decided against the beard. And he'd make sure the mustache was better adhered than it'd been yesterday, when it had fallen off and gotten him recognized and beaten up.

He didn't know how he could possibly let himself come here again tonight. Why didn't getting beaten—and being in pain—stop his urges? He was stupid, an idiot, too weak to pull away from the Devil's hold on him. His disgust for his sinfulness nauseated him, but not enough. He couldn't leave. Sexual relief trumped his mission, his resolve, his self-respect.

His only consolation—if he had any—was that he knew he wasn't a queer. He was not one of those perverts. He sinned, yes, but he wasn't a homosexual. He was sure of that. It was just that he had visitations from the Devil. The proof was that his urges had gotten so much worse since he started his campaign to rid the city of those perverts. That surely had to be the reason.

"Oh," he moaned aloud, "if someone would show up so I can get this over with."

In his rearview mirror, he saw a set of headlights entering the parking lot. The car stopped, pulled back out again and drove slowly down the street. He couldn't see the car or where it went, but a few minutes later, someone walked into the parking lot from the direction the car had gone.

Don understood the guy didn't want his car seen in this place. In the past he'd left his car out on the street too. However, tonight he had a loaner, so nobody would recognize this vehicle.

He could barely see the man coming toward his Subaru. The night was too dark, no streetlights on the beach and the clouds had just moved in, fading the moon and stars. From what he could make out, he didn't think this guy was the one who'd beaten him, but he couldn't be sure because the attack had happened too fast. Fact was, he probably wouldn't know his attacker if he saw him on the street.

He heard gravel crunching under heavy footsteps coming closer.

Don pushed the unlock button on his vehicle's door.

The guy got into the backseat, directly behind him.

Don still couldn't see the guy's face in the mirror. There was so little light and the brim of the stranger's cap was pulled down, hiding his face. He wondered why the guy hadn't come around and gotten into the passenger's seat. Strange.

He reached over to disengage his seat belt so he could turn around, but before he could release the belt, an arm wrapped around his neck, pulling him against his headrest and pressing on his windpipe, making him gag.

Cold metal pierced the left side of his throat. Pain ripped through him.

Using both hands, he grabbed the strong arm around his neck, but he couldn't budge his attacker. He tried to force his body forward, but the seat belt held him in place.

Oh, God, he was trapped. He tried to yell, but only gagging sounds came out.

Don fumbled around, feeling for the seat buckle. His fumbling hand found the release button. He tried pushing it, but his fingers were sweaty, maybe bloody too, and the angle was bad. He couldn't push squarely down to release the belt.

"Who are you?…Why?… If it's money…" he managed to speak in a whisper, but even then, his words came out crushed, gravelly, weak.

The cold metal pushed in further. A hot gush of blood ran down his neck, soaking his shoulder and chest. He felt warm breath near his ear and heard the attacker's heavy breathing. He gasped, "Don't have…money…on me…but can…"

He couldn't understand why the guy wasn't talking, wasn't saying something to him. *If he doesn't want my money, why does he want to kill me? Oh, God, why did I come here? Deidre will find out, and the community, my church…I'll be ruined. I have failed Thee. Please forgive me, I promise…I promise…*

His chest convulsed. Only a trickle of air made its way into his lungs. Again, he tried to pull against the arm squeezing his throat, choking him. His hands went limp and fell to his lap.

The attacker whispered in his ear, but the words seemed scrambled, unintelligible.

Help me, Lord Jesus…I'll never…I'll live a life of righteousness, I'll never…

The metal sliced downward.

Searing pain ripped through him.

Blood gushed, warm.

He kept hoping for help, hanging on, struggling against death, though mostly in his head since his body couldn't help him any longer.

Hope fled. His life flickered like an ember.

Death reached out and took him in.

CHAPTER TEN

Kera

Kera screeched. She'd turned the cold water knob too far and received an icy blast from the showerhead.

From the bedroom, Mandy yelled to her, "I forgot to tell you it's hard to adjust the shower's water temperature. You need to turn those knobs ever so slightly or you'll overcorrect."

"Fine time to tell me," Kera yelled back.

After Kera had returned from the lake, she'd slipped back in bed with Mandy and fallen asleep. When she woke up a few hours later, her foggy brain struggled to figure out where she was and why she was in bed with Mandy. Last night came back to her: the cat attack, Mandy holding her, and her trip out to the lake to calm herself. She was grateful she'd returned from the beach before Mandy woke up.

Kera wrapped a towel around her body, tucked the edges together and walked into the bedroom. "It's all yours. That shower felt wonderful, except for the sudden onslaught from the Arctic." She smiled.

"Sorry about that."

"How about I put on some coffee before I get dressed? That is, if you tell me where things are."

"Great, the coffee's in the cupboard that's under the coffeepot." Mandy headed for the shower.

Kera went to the kitchen, made coffee and brought two mugs into the bedroom. She set one on the nightstand on Mandy's side and got back into bed holding the other. She still felt groggy, and needed a caffeine fix. Coffee first, dress later.

Eventually, Mandy emerged from the bathroom with a towel wrapped around her head. She tied together her yellow terrycloth bathrobe.

"I put your coffee on your nightstand," Kera pointed out. "As I remember, you take it black, right?"

"You got it." Mandy took her hairbrush off the dresser, removed the towel from her head and began brushing out her hair. She sat down on the edge of the bed, grabbed her coffee and took a sip. "Ah, yes, life is better with a shower and fresh coffee." She moved onto the bed and rested against the headboard.

Kera rubbed her shoulder with her free hand. "Geez, I'm feeling a little sore from my workout yesterday."

"Workout? Is that what you call the brawl you got into at the bar?" Mandy laughed. "I can imagine you are feeling some pain today. Here," she motioned to her, "let me see if I can rub out some of that pain in your shoulder. Why don't you turn over and lie down on your stomach."

"That would be great. And as long as you're at it, I've got a little pain in my back too." Kera flipped over. Actually, she felt pain in a lot of places on her body. Certainly, some of her hurting came from the bar brawl, but some, she figured, came from holding her muscles so tight due to tension.

"I'm thinking the pain might be everywhere," Mandy said, pulling down Kera's towel, "given how active you were last night."

"You're right about that." Kera watched Mandy reach into the nightstand and take out a bottle of massage oil. She felt Mandy perching over her, straddling her body. Soon, firm hands flowed over her back, rubbing away her soreness. "Oh, that's so wonderful. You're really good at this." Her whole body began to relax. "I love the smell of the oil."

"It's lavender." Mandy's hands worked their way from Kera's shoulders down to the small of her back. "I need to take my bathrobe off, I'm getting way too warm. Will you have a problem with a naked woman rubbing you?"

"Not a problem. Anything to keep my masseuse happy." Kera rested her forehead on her crossed arms. She raised her head slightly to add, "I can't see anything, anyway, unless you get me a hand mirror." She snickered.

"What was that last comment?" Mandy's tone had a smile in it.

"Nothing much, just an observation—or not—excuse the pun." Kera heard herself giggle—a strange, distant, long-ago sound.

Mandy picked up on her joke and laughed. "Sorry, but I don't happen to have my mirror nearby."

Mandy's oiled, scented hands glided over her, moving up and back and sideways, zigzagging slowly, over and over again. She moaned with pleasure.

"I see—or should I say, hear, that I'm doing some good."

"Oh, yeah." Kera felt her tense muscles starting to release.

"Let me know if I start pressing down too hard."

"It's just right."

Kera knew Kelly's hands just by touch. Mandy's hands were different, smaller, more delicate. She told herself that if she didn't stop thinking about and comparing Kelly's hands to Mandy's, she'd end up feeling guilty for somehow betraying Kelly by allowing another woman's hands to soothe her this way. She needed to get over Kelly's death, let her go. She was tired of the pain.

She felt tears coming into her eyes. The warm, feminine contact with Mandy was penetrating her emotional armor. She didn't think she could handle the exposure, nor did she want to try. She commanded her feelings to shut down, go away, but in doing so, sensual pleasure slipped in to fill the emptiness.

Mandy's warmth moved over her.

Her towel had slipped down to her legs with the movement—or had it been pushed down that far in the beginning? Was she wrong, or were the healing hands changing their mission, asking for something in return?

Her skin tingled as her senses shifted into overdrive. She struggled to find the brakes and get back in control. She'd better pull back, slow down…oh, god, she didn't think she could, not now. Damn, did Mandy want this too? What would it mean? How would sex change things between them? Here she lay in Mandy's den—the emotional place. Right where she'd decided she didn't want to be.

Shit, who cares!

Her juices were flowing. The dam had burst. She'd deal with the consequences later. Mandy would have to understand that what was happening right now was strictly physical, nothing emotional, for her anyway.

She reached back and touched Mandy's leg, gently stroking, hoping to receive a clear invitation.

Mandy rolled off, pulling Kera closer to her.

Oh god, yes, she'd been invited. Their bodies came together, their thighs and breasts gently touching. Mandy's skin was as smooth as silk. Mandy's lips were soft and melted against her mouth. The sensation filled her, excited her and made her need more.

"The Stars and Stripes Forever" blared out.

"Shit." Kera pulled out of the kiss and bounced off the bed like she'd been caught by her sergeant in boot camp. She looked over at the source of John Philip Sousa's unwanted serenade and grabbed her cell phone off the nightstand. "I've got to remember to get rid of that damned ring tone."

"Don't answer it…whoever it is can wait." Mandy sat up and patted the bed beside her, beckoning Kera to come back to her.

Kera glanced at the caller ID, then looked at Mandy. "It's Dee. I'm sorry, but I have to answer this, something's wrong. I can feel it."

"I'm feeling something myself." Mandy groaned, laying back down on the bed and rolling over.

"Hey, Dee, are you okay?"

Deidre responded, "No, Kera, please come to Dad's. The police are here. Don's dead…he's been murdered, it's terrible, I—"

"Oh, my god, how'd that happen?"

"Please just come, hurry."

"Hold on, Dee, I'll be right there." Kera grabbed her clothes from the chair and started dressing.

"What's wrong?" Mandy sat up.

"Don's dead, murdered. I don't know how it happened. Dee just said I needed to come to Dad's. The police are there."

"I'd better come too. She should have an attorney present." Mandy got up and started putting on her clothes.

"Mandy, she didn't kill Don. She wouldn't do—"

"I didn't mean to say she did." Mandy struggled to get her sports bra over her head. "But she should have a lawyer with her anyway."

Kera zipped up her pants. She mulled over Mandy's words. Maybe Deidre was a suspect, so maybe Mandy should be there. After all, Deidre was an abused woman, whether or not she liked admitting it. Domestic violence wouldn't look good to the cops. She'd better tell Mandy.

"I don't think I told you, but Deidre is staying with me because Don beat her up and broke her nose. It wasn't the first time either. I was going to tell you about it last night at the bar, but things sort of, well, went in another direction and—"

"That's all the more reason I need to be there. You cannot believe how the police will jump on the first person who might look guilty or have a motive, and they seldom look around for anyone else." Mandy stopped talking as she pulled her blouse over her head. "And they always suspect the spouse. I can guarantee you that much." She grabbed her pants and sat down to put them on. "And if she's been beaten by him, hell, they'll hold on to the idea that she's guilty like a dog clutching a steak bone."

"Come on, let's go." Kera picked up Mandy's keys—she'd put them on her nightstand when she'd come home from the lake.

Mandy glanced up from putting on shoes and saw her take the keys, making her wish she'd put them back where she had found them, out in the living room. She realized it was too late for explanations now. She tossed Mandy the keys.

Mandy shot her a questioning look.

"I'll tell you later. We need to get to Dee."

* * *

The detective looked at Kera, then Deidre and back to Kera. "You girls certainly do look alike—even with your sister's broken nose. Oh, I'm sorry," he held out his hand, "I'm Detective Brown, LCPD."

Kera nodded. She and Deidre were used to the comment. She tried to let go of her annoyance over him calling them "girls." No sense pissing off the guy who might be thinking her sister was a killer.

She went over to the leather sofa where Deidre sat, tears running down her cheeks. She put her arms around her sister and whispered in her ear, "Mandy is going to be your lawyer right now. She doesn't want you to say anything unless she says so. She'll do the talking."

Dee's face questioned her words. She gave Dee her "trust-me-I'll-tell-you-later" glance.

Mandy put down her purse and greeted the detective. She acted as if she knew him from other cases. "Hi, Detective Brown, I'll be representing Mrs. Bledsoe. What's going on here?"

The detective led Mandy into the kitchen. Kera noticed two uniformed policemen searching around the house, while a third officer went outside.

"But I have nothing to hide," Dee whispered to Kera.

"Doesn't matter, I'll explain later." Kera fished for a tissue in her pockets, found one, and wiped Dee's wet eyes. "Can you tell me what happened?"

"The detective told me they found Don's body in a vehicle in the church parking lot." Dee started crying again. "Oh, Kera, he was stabbed to death."

"When?"

"Late last night. Well, actually, they think it was sometime real early this morning, they're not sure exactly…goodness, today is Sunday. Who will they get to preach the sermon?"

Kera thought Dee's question was weird. The man was dead and her sister worried about who'd take care of his obligations. Come to think of it, Dee would fret about it. That was her nature.

Dee continued, "Apparently, a police vehicle was cruising the area and Don's car—his loaner vehicle, that is—was spotted in the church parking lot. The officer knew there usually wasn't a vehicle in the lot, especially at that time of morning." She wiped her nose. "Oh, it's just so horrible. I can't believe this is happening."

"When did the cops get here?" Kera gently rubbed her sister's back.

"About an hour and a half ago, maybe longer. I don't know. The detective told me what happened, then asked about my broken nose, so I told him. He asked me why Don had stitches over his eye, so I told him about the gang of kids attacking him. After I told him, he called the station about Don's attack, but Don hadn't reported it. I could have told the detective that, but then I would have had to tell him Don thought that the attack was from God, so he didn't really blame the gang, and that would be why he wouldn't have called the police."

Kera shook her head. Now the cops were going to wonder if they were dealing with a couple who'd thrown punches at each other and the wife ended up killing the husband, or had someone else do it for her. Hell, they might even begin to consider she had murdered her sister's husband, or had a part in it. Shit. She mulled over the idea and decided not bring up the possibility to Dee, not right now. Her sister didn't need anything else upsetting her.

Dee went on, "Then the detective asked if they could look around. I said I had nothing to hide, that's when I called you."

Mandy and Detective Brown came into the living room and sat down.

Detective Brown furrowed his brow, glanced at some notes he had taken, then looked up at Deidre. "Ms. Bakker told me she's your lawyer, is that—"

"Detective, can I see you a minute?" One of the uniformed officers entered the room and signaled the detective to follow him.

When the detective was out of the room, Mandy turned to Deidre, "In cases like this, the spouse is a suspect pretty much automatically.

Detective Brown told me you let him in and said he could search your dad's premises. Is that right?"

"Yes, like I told Kera, I have nothing to hide."

"That's okay," Mandy said.

Kera read Mandy's expression and knew her sister's answer wasn't actually okay. She would have objected to the cops searching the place without a warrant. She should have come home last night and she'd have been here when the cops came.

Mandy continued, "I just don't want you to talk directly to the police anymore. I'll do your talking for now, okay?"

"Okay." Deidre blew her nose.

"You have an added reason to be suspected, Deidre, because you're a battered wife. I don't, for a minute, believe you killed Don, but I need to know where you were and what you did last night. I know you didn't answer your phone when I called to tell you Kera was staying overnight with me."

"I didn't go anywhere. Last night, I went to bed early, read a little and fell asleep."

"Did you talk to anyone on the phone or see anyone last night?"

"No. Like I told the detective, I look so horrible, I didn't want anyone to see me. I didn't have my cell phone in the bedroom, so when you called, Mandy, I didn't hear it. I listened to your message when I got up this morning." Dee looked at Kera and raised her eyebrows.

Kera knew what Dee thought about Mandy and her being together last night. She shook off the look, turned to Mandy and asked, "After talking to the detective, what do you think is going to happen? Do you think that he'll—?"

Detective Brown reentered the room with a letter and an envelope in his hand. "Mrs. Bledsoe, we found this letter in the rolltop desk. It seems it was written by you and sent to your late father." He showed the piece of paper to Deidre. "Look at that signature, is it yours?"

Deidre look at it, and nodded.

Kera turned toward Mandy and mouthed the word, "Fuck."

* * *

Mandy sat at the Van Brocklin kitchen table with Kera and Deidre. "Okay, here's what's happening: The detective wanted to arrest Deidre," Mandy said, "and I talked to him a while, emphasizing that he had only circumstantial evidence, that she's the daughter of the beloved mayor who just died, and how would it look to arrest the wife of a murdered minister—a woman in mourning? Blah, blah, blah.

You know, there's a lot of politics in this case working in your favor, Deidre…right now anyway."

Deidre stared ahead, not responding to Mandy.

Kera reached for Dee's hand. "Dee, tell me what's going on with you. Talk to me."

Dee sat there not moving with her gaze fixed on the window across from her.

Kera thought her sister looked as though she'd been turned to stone. "Please say something, Dee, what are you thinking?" She patted Dee's icy hand, trying to get a response from her.

Dee's eyes turned slowly toward her. "I don't know what I'm thinking. I can't absorb all these horrible things. Dad is gone. Now Don. My world doesn't feel real. It's like someone else's life and somehow, I've gotten misplaced in it."

Kera felt no loss at Don being gone, but she could feel the pain coming from her sister like a jagged vibration. She and Deidre were like conjoined twins connected by the same emotional and physical pain system. "Yeah, for sure, it's a lot to absorb, Dee. Right now, you need to lean on me, at least until you get your bearings. I'm going to take care of you, don't worry. I'm here for you now."

Mandy took Deidre's other hand. "Is it okay if Kera steps in for you until you feel like you are ready? You don't have to worry. We won't do anything big or important without you being involved or without your approval. It'd be just until you're feeling a bit better. Kera and I will work together to get you through this situation. I'll still want to talk to you about things you might know or that might be important, but that conversation can wait for now."

Deidre nodded and stood, using the table edge for support. "That's fine. Kera can stand in for me. I need to lie down. I'm exhausted. Stuff keeps swirling around and I can't put it together."

Kera watched her sister leave. Dee was like a zombie. She would have to keep herself together to deal with the murder and everything else. That would be quite a task, she figured, since she and her sister were like two barely functioning motors on a twin-engine plane flying over the Rockies.

Mandy interrupted her thoughts, "We'll talk later, Kera. I'm going, now. I need to get in touch with some people and do some checking around. But I'll be getting back with you. I know you want to be with your sister."

"Yeah, I do." Kera got up from the table. "Thanks Mandy. I really appreciate you coming here with me."

"No problem." Mandy headed toward the door.

CHAPTER ELEVEN

Kera

Kera drove out of town on Turtle River Drive. Having grown up around here—their house was on this street—she'd driven this route many times. The street turned into Turtle River Road when it crossed over from the city to the countryside, changing from paved to dirt and becoming narrow and heavily lined with deciduous and evergreen trees.

She rolled down the car windows to allow air to blow on her face. Humidity was high, intensifying the sweet aroma from wildflowers poking up along the side of the road. The heat—in the high eighties—might have been unbearable except for the breeze coming off the lake.

The road paralleled the river as it snaked inland, past her father's house. She slowed. For a moment, she thought she saw her father standing by the road, waving at her. She blinked her eyes and he was gone, but she was left feeling like a rock had settled in the pit of her stomach. She shook off the image, or at least tried to, and sped toward Moran Brady's house.

Moran had come into her life when she'd been a sophomore in high school. She remembered that year as the time in her life when she could no longer relate to her Christian upbringing.

Her first foray out of Christianity took her into existentialism. She'd read Kafka, Dostoyevsky, Camus and a few other authors who confirmed her suspicions that she was pretty much fucked for having been born. She felt alien to life itself, or maybe more like she was on a wild flying trapeze with frayed ropes, tumbling meaninglessly through the abyss of the universe without a net. Existentialists didn't use nets. They didn't have any. As probable as the dark theory of the universe seemed to her, she'd found it too damn depressing. She'd wanted and hoped for something more sympathetic to her existence.

Abandoning the vendors of dreariness, she'd discovered and moved into her Buddhist period—albeit short-lived. She finally realized she was a bit too ADD for Buddhism, although she agreed with the concepts. Unfortunately, the practice of meditation took more attention than she could muster. Moreover, she found it a contradiction to have to focus hard to think about nothing or at least that's how it seemed to her. The nothingness she was supposed to achieve—if she'd even gotten close to it—had seemed like a return visit to the black hole of existentialism, the ultimate in nothingness.

She'd shelved her search and had about given up when it seemed some force—destiny, fate, random chance—had responded to her spiritual quest by tossing Moran into her life. She remembered their first meeting like it was yesterday.

She and Moran had met one afternoon when she'd been canoeing down the Turtle River by herself. On that particular day, she happened to look up and saw a blue heron flying overhead. About a minute later, a bald eagle. She knew it was unusual to see two very territorial birds in such a short time period. She'd become so engrossed in watching the birds in flight, she hadn't paid attention to a large dead tree that had fallen in the river.

One of the huge branches smacked her, tipping her canoe over and dumping her into the water. When she surfaced from under her canoe, she saw an old woman sitting on the fallen tree's huge roots. At first, she thought she might be seeing things. She rubbed the water out of her eyes.

The old woman stared at her with an amused smile. She had mostly gray hair with a smattering of red, worn parted in the middle and hanging down like a mop in loose spiral tendrils. The diminutive but sturdy looking old lady stood, easily balancing herself on the root structure. Her long dress must have followed her out of the sixties. Hiking boots and a Detroit Tigers' baseball cap completed her outfit. A small leather pouch hung from her neck.

Smiling, the old woman stepped down from her perch and held out a hand. "I'm Moran, and that's my tree you smacked into." Moran chortled, pointing to a branch. "But I don't suppose you did any damage to our planet, since that branch is in process of becoming part of the earth again. So, how did you fare?"

"I'm okay, mostly wet and embarrassed," she'd answered, taking the offered hand and letting Moran help her out of the water.

"Ah, I saw what took your attention away. Those are magnificent creatures, now, aren't they? Worthy of your attention…or at least some of it." Moran chuckled again. "Come on, grab your canoe, pull it up right here." She pointed to a spot on land. "I'll help you with getting those clothes dried and we can have some tea while we're waiting." She nodded at her house, only a few yards up from the river.

At the time, Kera thought, she had no idea how important meeting Moran would be to her. In accepting the invitation and following Moran to her house, she found a friend, mentor, shaman and mother figure—exactly what she needed. Most of all, she found a connection to the universe. Not a safety net so much as a feeling of being a part of something, not alien to it.

Whenever she had problems or felt disconnected, she sought out Moran. She was certain she'd never needed the old woman's wisdom and warmth more than she needed it now.

Kera drove to Moran's place, a 1908 Folk Victorian house suffering from weathered wood—here and there, she caught glimpses of old gray paint—listing porch steps, and a guaranteed-to-last thirty-year roof in what must be its fortieth-plus year.

She hadn't seen Moran since her last leave from the army. As she turned her car into the driveway, Moran came out to greet her, walking slowly. The old lady never let the world push her any faster than she needed to go.

When Kera was a teenager, she'd thought Moran was old, but when they met, Moran had just retired from teaching at the local college. She'd been in her sixties at the time. Now, she guessed, Moran had to be pushing eighty.

When she'd called last night, Moran hadn't even heard of her dad's death. Moran didn't get a newspaper, didn't own a TV and only listened sparingly to NPR on the radio. In keeping with her philosophy, Moran believed staying current with the daily news was useless because life pretty much spiraled around, up or down. In the end, she believed things pretty much remained as always. She'd say it was a waste of her time and energy getting all snagged up in the constantly changing details of the same old stuff. If she needed to know something, she'd find out, sooner or later.

Kera pulled up and stopped the car right in front of Moran, who stood in the driveway. Moran's arms were spread wide, inviting her to fill them. She jumped out of the car and hurried into Moran's hug.

Inside the house, Kera glanced around at the kitchen and living room. Everything seemed unchanged since she first stepped into the house years ago: same table and chairs, furniture, drapes. If anything had changed, she couldn't discern it.

She felt good to have something seemingly locked down, unmoving, unchanging. Just what she needed: a moment in time where life seemed not to have moved on, except for a few more wrinkles on Moran's face. Being in this house with this woman stabilized her like a balancing pole steadied a tightrope walker.

She and Moran sat down together on the sofa. She told her friend about Kelly, Iraq, her PTSD, her pending medical discharge, her father's death, Don's murder and Deidre's mess.

"When we talked briefly last night, I sensed an intense negative energy, and now, my goodness, I'm hearing a tornado has swept through your life." Moran patted her hand.

"I don't want my negativity to contaminate you."

Moran winked. "Well then, when I do my work with you, I'll wear a surgical mask and gloves."

Kera chuckled. "Maybe you should."

"Now, dear." Moran cleared her throat, assuming a more serious tone. "I know we have a lot of work to do. You've accumulated so many invasions, your body and spirit are overwhelmed. As you know, each negative experience or thought that comes your way lodges in you and poisons your spirit. We need to pluck them out."

"If you take them out, I don't know if anything of the original me would be left. I don't feel hope and I don't see a good tomorrow. I need to believe in life as something I want again. But even more importantly, I need to help Dee out of the mess she's in. I have to get the old me back for that to happen." She felt something welling up inside of her, maybe fear. She couldn't be certain. She took a deep breath.

Moran shook her head knowingly and explained, "When I remove an invasion, like say, your emotional wounds from the killings in war, or bad thoughts and words from other people, or whatever negativity lodged in your body, you will then have room to nurture back the good stuff which hasn't really ever left. It's just been overwhelmed, scorched, like trees in a forest fire. But be assured, the seeds of your being are still there, waiting to spring to life again. We need to remove the debris, allow your soul to recover."

Kera nodded. Moran had worked with her before dealing with invasions and she'd experienced the cleansing process. She'd gone through this healing to help get past her mother's death and move on. But this time? She wasn't so sure, so much had happened to her—

Moran's voice broke through her doubt. "All right, let's get on with it. We've some serious healing to do, but first, I need to get the sage and do some smudging."

Moran got up, went to her altar near the fireplace and picked up a bundle of white sage. Striking a match, she held the flame to the sage until it began smoking.

She asked Kera to come and sit in one of two chairs facing each other. She walked around the perimeter of the room, waving the smoking sage in the air, around Kera and herself. She held the sage bundle in one hand, shaking a rattle in the other. She slowly twirled around, arms gliding through the air, smoke from the sage wrapping around her, enveloping her as she invited the spirit world's attendance. She put the sage down in a clay dish on the altar along with the rattle, and then took a buffalo drum off the wall and started beating it in rhythm.

Kera closed her eyes. Her breathing started to slow down and become deeper. Her tension cracked and loosened to the drumbeat.

The shaman's words merged into a chant and moved in rhythm with the beating of the drum, bringing Kera's spirit drifting along for the ride into the world of her knowing, her healing, her hope:

She felt herself floating in a boat on calm waters, bobbing to the pulse of the sea. A fresh, cleansing breeze blew through her. Another place, another time.

The drumming stopped, only soft chanting now.

Warmth hovered, extracting negative energy—

Winged pain flew out and up like bubbles, popping in the rays of the sun. The heat from a warm beam of light soothed, mended...

Gravity let go of her.

She rose and floated in space, a drifting flotsam of throbbing memories gliding by her like painted ghosts. She reached out, her hands grabbing ravaged particles of the past, accumulating them in her palms, touching, pondering, reviewing...

She blew the pieces from her hand. The bits of life drifted off and returned, reforming in different shapes and faded colors, sprinkling down on her like soft rain...

The beat of the drum started up, faster and faster...

Releasing her.

Gravity took hold, bringing her back down gently to the boat.

The jumbled, merged sounds of the chanting, separated, then coalesced into phrases of distinguishable words, transporting her back to the room.

She opened her eyes.

"How are you doing, Kera?"

Moran sat, bent forward, hands flat on her thighs, looking intently into her eyes. "My spirits and I took out bad energy, made room for the good to return."

Kera rubbed her hands together, regaining sensation that had left during her voyage through inner space. "I feel...uh...lighter."

Moran nodded and sat back, waiting.

Meeting her shaman's soft gaze, Kera felt a rupture in her emotions, like water bursting through a crack in a dam and into her eyes. It didn't feel to her like she was crying. More like, involuntary tears streaming down her cheeks as the words tumbled out. "When my friends started dying in Iraq, I felt like life was slipping through my fingers. I couldn't hold on to anything. I couldn't save my comrades—one day there, next day gone, a nightmare splattered in blood and guts. Then when Kelly was gone, I felt empty until anger poured into me, like a gully washer." She took a breath and sat back.

Moran handed her some tissues and spoke slowly and softly. "Your pain from so much loss created a crater in you. The emptiness of that crater became a place to store your anger. Your feelings of helplessness stirred that anger into a toxin that's been poisoning your spirit."

Kera realized how trapped she'd felt in her unbearable memories of Iraq, of Kelly's death. "But Moran, I feel like I'm living in my memories, a chain circle of nightmares I can't escape."

"Those painful memories, nightmares, are yours."

"But I don't want them!"

"You have to own them, my dear, accept them, not run from them." Moran put a hand gently on her leg. "They have wisdom to impart, if you'll listen and glean meaning and understanding from them. Then the memories will fade, stop stinging, lose their power, and find their rightful place in your life."

Kera thought about Moran's words. "Gee, I think I was doing that in the boat—in my journey—when you were working on me. My memories were floating by me and I was grabbing them, examining them. It was all strangely calming for me."

Moran nodded, a knowing smile on her face.

She stared at the old woman's bony, wrinkled hands. These were the hands that had pulled her—so early in life—out of desperation and into the emotional safety she'd needed. "But until then, where do

I find the hope things will get better? Where do I find the strength to go on and do what I need to do?"

"It's all in your rucksack, my dear, along with the love so many people have given you, even if they're no longer on this earth. Their love remains for you and within you."

Kera wanted to believe. Moran wouldn't tell her such things if they weren't true. Moran had helped her cope with life in the past and always—

"But I must tell you." Moran bent forward and looked directly into her eyes again. "When I was communicating with my spirit teacher, she told me to tell you to be careful. You are in danger."

"Your spirit teacher probably meant Deidre is in danger. You know how everyone gets us mixed up. Your spirit teacher must have too."

"No, dear, she clearly meant you."

CHAPTER TWELVE

Kera

Kera waited until evening to pull into the parking lot of Don's church. She parked the car away from the street and close to the building, not wanting to be easily noticed. She'd come there to find out what went on in the neighborhood after dark.

She thought about her meeting with Mandy yesterday morning.

She'd related to Mandy what Dee had told her about Don being beaten up and robbed by teenagers outside his church. Mandy called her friend, Elena Armstrong in the DA's office, to confirm there had been no report of Don's alleged attack.

She and Mandy believed it was odd Don didn't report the attack, even though he had felt he was "being punished by God," because Don was a real crime-and-punishment sort of a guy. Mandy told her that second to homosexuals, Don was known for raging against what he called, "thieves, thugs and women of the night."

Kera had gone on the Internet to check out crime statistics in Lakeside City. She'd noticed the old section of the campus wasn't a high crime spot and definitely not a teenage hangout area. The police spent most of their time answering calls out at the Old Fishing Village. The next busiest crime area was a run-down neighborhood on the west side of the city. The mall came in third, an area most reporting problems with teenagers.

She grabbed her flashlight, got out of the car and looked around. The parking lot was on one side of the old frat house, now serving as a church. On the other side, across the street, stood remnants of abandoned tennis courts in decay—posts without nets and broken concrete sprouting weeds through the cracks. Behind the church, a neglected baseball diamond that hadn't seen a game in years.

Farther on, she spotted some old buildings and decided to walk down to them.

One building had been the college's old library. She walked onto the porch, flashed her light in the window and peered inside. The building seemed to be used for storing old desks, bookcases and chairs. Nothing much else from what she could tell. She tried the door. Locked. She went around checking other entrances, finding the side and back doors locked as well.

Next door was the original building for chemistry labs. Like the old library, the building had its name engraved above the main door: Vanderwill College Chemistry Laboratory, 1901. She peeked in a side window. The structure appeared pretty much the same as the last—an old building with old stuff inside.

The buildings looked untouched by vandals. No broken windows, no signs of forced entry, just benign neglect as far as she could see. There didn't seem to be anything of interest to tempt anyone, other than an antiques dealer perhaps, in the market for old college furniture. Nothing suggested gang activity in the area. No graffiti and no groups hanging out. Furthermore, she didn't see much litter, the kind of droppings one might expect in a neighborhood where young people hung out.

Kera walked down the street to a neighborhood of older homes where lights were on and cars parked in driveways. She spotted a guy coming out of a house. By the light of the streetlamp, she gauged him to be in his late twenties, maybe early thirties. He was putting something into his car.

She stopped. "Beautiful night, just look at those stars."

The guy looked up. "Sure is."

"I was just wondering, are these houses around here mostly occupied by students?" She hoped he'd answer her question before he started wondering why she—a stranger—was walking around the neighborhood at night.

"Yup."

"Ah, my husband and I were thinking of moving here in the fall. How's the neighborhood, anyway? Is it safe, do you think?" *My god, now he has to think I'm nuts, standing here late at night asking about the safety of the neighborhood. So much for making it up as you go along.*

"Oh, yeah, my wife and I feel very safe here...well, at least we did." He closed the car door and walked over to her. "Usually it's quiet, not much going on, but early Sunday morning cop cars were at the frat house—I mean church—over there." He pointed. "I got up to feed the baby—it was my turn." He smiled. "And that's when I saw them out the window. Cops all over the damned place, red lights flashing, ambulance, the works. The next day in the newspaper, I read that the minister of the church was murdered. Glad I'm graduating in August and we're getting out of here." He stopped, thought a minute, then said, "But really, that's the most excitement we've had since we moved in here. The only excitement, actually."

"You don't have gangs or teenagers prowling around here?"

"Nope, never seen any. Since I'm a student, I'm at home a lot, all times of the day and night. Hey, I'd better get back inside. My wife's gone and I'm on baby duty."

The guy turned and headed toward the house. He stopped and turned around to look at her. Kera figured the question of her being out there late at night had just registered in his brain. She quickly headed back to her vehicle.

She sat in her car, trying to put the pieces together.

Mandy had told her the police reported Don's car parked in the far corner of the church's parking lot when they found him early Sunday morning. Harry told the police Don had been working there late that night—a Saturday night.

There would have been few, if any, cars in the lot when he went to the church. Why would he park his vehicle way back there, a longer walk without much light from the street? Don wasn't particularly into exercise. She guessed he could have come to church in the light of day and not have thought he'd be leaving in the dark, but still, most people would park closer to the door.

Don's body was found in the passenger's seat. Why would he have gotten into the car on that side? Unless he'd been looking for something in his glove compartment and planned on returning to the church.

She was putting her flashlight back under her seat when she thought she saw a shadowy movement out of the corner of her eye.

She looked up. Nothing.

She looked to either side. Still nothing. She decided she must have been imagining things.

Suddenly, in the rearview mirror, she caught the silhouette of a man. He was close, too close.

Her heart pounded.

Shit, where was the lock button for the damned doors?

A man's face appeared in her window.

She recognized it: Harry Janssen. She rolled down the window. "Jesus Christ, Harry, you scared the living shit out of me."

"My dear, such language, taking the Lord's name in vain and right here next to the church. And for goodness's sake, what are you doing here?"

"Well, what the hell are you doing here?" Kera opened the door and got out of the car.

"I'm the president of the church board, in case you didn't know, and we've just lost our minister. Maybe that will give you a clue as to why I'm here. There's lots of work to be done. My own duties as president and now I have to figure out what needs to be taken care of regarding Don's obligations."

"I suppose so. Do you know when the funeral service will be?"

"I don't know for sure. The coroner said he didn't know when they'd release Don's body, all depends on when they get done. You know, they're doing an autopsy and running some tests. They always do that in homicide cases, but when I asked about Thursday or Friday, he thought it could be possible. The board and I discussed the matter and decided the sooner, the better. People need closure."

Kera nodded, though she thought that was an overly optimistic estimate on the part of the coroner, but she didn't say that to Harry.

"I've got to plan the service. The board wanted someone who really knew Don personally, so the task fell to me, though I'm not good at this kind of thing. I've never done anything like it, but Lilly, Don's secretary, said she'd help me. It's so unbelievable. I can't believe he's gone. He is—was—my best friend. We had so many plans. I don't know what I'm going to do without him." Harry took a handkerchief out of his pocket, wiped his eyes and blew his nose. "I'm sorry. I've been a mess since I found out."

"No need to apologize, Harry." Kera wouldn't shed tears for Don. She guessed it was good Harry and her sister could.

She conceded to herself that Don had done some good things in the past. At least, she used to see some good in him before he got right-winged in his thinking and became abusive to his wife. Hell, no one was all bad.

He'd gotten a house funded and built for runaway kids, and he cared for the elderly, visiting them in their homes. He'd once told her it was wrong to call the elderly "shut-ins." Don figured the aged were "shut out" by a world that didn't want to bother with them. She thought his observation had been pretty insightful.

At his last church, he'd even put his words to work. He'd gotten several vans that could handle wheelchairs, designating them for use by elderly and people with disabilities, so they could be brought to church or transported during the week to other places they needed to go.

Her problem was, the good stuff Don did had been sullied by his abusiveness toward her sister and his intolerance for gay people. So, tears for him had to come from somewhere else, not from her.

"Will you please thank Sylvia for me for watching after my sister?" She'd been relieved when Dee had consented to stay with Sylvia so she could be free to look for Don's killer.

"Certainly," Harry assured. "Thank goodness, Sylvia got back from her grandmother's place on Saturday. I know she's a comfort to Deidre." He scratched his head, "Now, why did you say you came out here tonight?"

"I didn't say, but Dee told me Don had been beaten up and robbed here by teenage boys. I was checking out the area to see if I could find anything that might suggest who killed Don."

"Isn't that a job for the police? Could be dangerous for you to be out here, especially at night." Harry pulled out his phone: "I need to call Sylvia. All this has been so distressing."

Kera could see the stress on Harry's face. The guy appeared really shook up by Don's death and he'd been tapped to do the service. She wouldn't want to be put in that kind of a position.

Harry punched in a number. "I don't have my car with me," he said to Kera while waiting for a response. "Sylvia said she'd pick me up, hope she didn't forget and go to bed. She turns off her phone at night. Really, Kera, you should be more careful, being out here at this time of night."

"I can take care of myself, Harry. My concern is that the police, right now, seem to be focused on my sister as a suspect. I can't just sit back and—"

"No, you're kidding. That's ridiculous. Why in the world would they think Deidre would do such a thing?"

"Because Don was physically abusive to her."

Harry didn't seem to hear her answer. "Damn it, where's Sylvia?" He glared at his phone as though the device were culpable for his wife not answering his call. He shoved it in his pocket.

"Harry, if you want a ride home. I'm going that way." She signaled for him to get into her car.

Geez, why was she feeling sorry for Harry? But, she considered, he had to bury his friend and didn't feel capable of doing the service, and now his wife wasn't responding to his call to come get him. Certainly she could muster some compassion for the man.

"Okay, it's not far, less than a mile. I could walk it, but I'm really tired. God knows when, or if, Sylvia will answer her phone." Harry got into the passenger side. "Uh, what did you say about Don? I'm sorry, I was trying to call Sylvia and I didn't hear you."

"I said Don physically abused Dee." Kera started the engine and pulled out of the church parking lot.

"Kera, you'd better not be spreading lies about Don. He wasn't an abusive person, and I guarantee he never would hurt Deidre in any way. I don't know where you ever got a crazy idea like that."

Okay, that pissed her off. "I know you and he were good friends, Harry, and it's hard for you to believe, but you might just as well know that Don is the one who broke Dee's nose."

Harry stared at her, an incredulous look painted on his face.

He started to respond, but Kera cut him off, "Did you know he beat her the night of Dad's funeral? And before that, he beat her so bad that she lost a baby. She was a couple of months pregnant."

Harry blurted, "I don't believe you, not for one moment. Deidre broke her nose running into a door in the night. Don told me about that. And…and losing a baby, that's an out-and-out lie designed to make Don look like a monster, to publicly disparage him. I won't allow anyone to defame him like that. Do you hear me!"

Kera's first inclination—what she really ached to do—was stop the car and push Harry out, but instead she took a deep breath. Shit, the guy was an asshole, but what the hell, she shouldn't have laid the facts on him like she did. She needed to keep reminding herself the poor jerk was trying to plan a funeral service for his best friend. "I'm sorry, Harry. I shouldn't have told you that, at least not tonight."

"You shouldn't have said that at all. It's a pack of lies, Kera, a damned pack of lies!" Harry stared straight ahead, his jaws and fists clenched.

She pulled up to the curb in front of his house.

He got out, turned toward her and shook his finger at her. "You'd better not spread falsehoods about Don. I'm warning you. You can be sued for spreading those kinds of vicious lies. And will be, I promise you."

That did it for her. "Fuck you, Harry! You'd better move away from this car fast, or I'll back up, take aim, and run over your sorry ass."

CHAPTER THIRTEEN

Kera

Kera sat on one of the steps leading to Lakeside City Hall. She was early. She'd promised Mandy she would be at the city council meeting this evening and on her way, she'd stopped by a coffee shop and bought a grande café mocha that she'd decided would serve as her dinner and dessert.

She removed the lid from her coffee and licked whipped cream off the top.

"Hey, Kera."

She looked up to see a man heading her way. The sun behind him cast his figure in shadow, so she couldn't make out his face, but the extremely tall, lanky body with protruding ears gave him away—Kevin McNeil.

"Hey, can I share the steps with you?" he asked. "I need to give Mandy these papers for a real estate closing coming up for one of her clients. She told me she'd be here tonight."

"Have a seat." Kera patted the cement next to her. "I'm waiting for Mandy myself. I promised her I would speak at the city council meeting tonight, for whatever that's worth." She smirked.

"Sweet. I think your presence will be worth a lot. People really loved your dad. He was a great guy."

"I don't know. Given all that's happened since then—me getting arrested, Don's murder—who knows how things will all play out? The focus might become more about me and less about Dad."

"Speaking of Don's death, I haven't heard anything about his funeral—not that I care—but someone in the office was asking about it." Kevin sat down.

"The last I heard, they're planning the service to be either Thursday or Friday morning, but I'd not bet on it being that soon. Anyway, whenever it happens, Dee and Harry will be keeping it low key."

"I suppose you'll be going to support Deidre."

"Yeah, that's the reason and the only reason."

Kevin frowned. "The paper said Deidre was—the paper actually said, 'claimed to be'—abused by Don. Is that true?"

Kera nodded. "She was battered and I've seen the results of Don's abuse. Right now, she's sporting a broken nose from the bastard."

"Wow, I wonder if my boss knew. Of course, he probably thinks wife beating is okay, given his religious beliefs."

"I don't know about that. When I first told Harry that Don punched my sister in her face and broke her nose, he looked startled, like he didn't know about it. And then he denied Don would do such a thing. He didn't just think Don wasn't guilty, I got a strong sense from him that he wouldn't approve of hitting a woman, and Dee thinks the same thing."

"Really, that's refreshing, but hard to believe."

Kera continued, "Harry said that Don told him that she had—get this—run into a door in the middle of the night. That, of course, would be Don's made-up version of how she got her broken nose," she scoffed. "Harry still believes Don's story, in spite of what I told him. Don was not only a wife beater, but a damned liar. I've been wondering if Harry's wife ever told him the truth, or if they even communicate, because Sylvia must have known about—"

"Well, if it isn't my fighting buddies." Vinny Belsito, a guy she recognized from the Pink Door, bounced up the steps two at a time and stood in front of Kevin. He was a short, dark-haired, stocky guy with tattoos starting at his wrists and spreading up both arms and into his sleeveless T-shirt.

Kevin yelled out, "Hey, Maryland, how's it going?"

"Doing okay." Vinny looked over at Kera. "I'm Vinny Belsito." He extended his hand.

"Yeah, I know who you are, but hadn't heard you called, 'Maryland.'"

"Oh," Kevin explained, "Maryland is a nickname."

"How do you come by that handle, Vinny?" Kera moved over a little in case Vinny wanted to sit down, but he remained standing.

"Pretty easy, I'm originally from Maryland. There's another Vinny in the community, but he was first on the scene. I guess around here, if you have the same first name as another person, you get a second tag to go by."

"Got ya."

Vinny continued, "Hey, Kera, I got to say, you're some kind of a bad-ass fighter." He threw up his right hand to Kera for a high-five slap. "When you were out there ass kicking with me, I didn't know who you were, so I had to check around to find out. Where did you learn to do that stuff?"

"Tae kwon do."

"Yeah, and she just got out of the army. Military police, weren't you?" Kevin shot Kera an admiring look.

Kera nodded.

"I'd have you in my gang, anytime." Vinny grinned, giving her a wink. He pulled a toothpick out of his shirt pocket and put it in his mouth.

"Well, before you sign me up, you have to remember that I throw myself under tables, like when someone falls off a ladder. That's how cool I am." Kera decided making a joke of her PTSD might help cover up her embarrassment.

"Hey, I'm sorry. That dog running through the hallway caught me and my ladder unaware, but still, I should have been quieter going down." Vinny laughed. "I only found out it was you I'd spooked when the woman who runs the coffee shop told me about it the next day."

"Hey, Vinny, getting political tonight, are you?" Kevin asked.

"Yup, I'm going, but frankly, I don't believe much in talk. I'm a take action kind of guy. In fact, they should make an action figure out of me."

Kera thought Vinny sounded half serious about his remark. Come to think of it, she could sort of see him as an action figure, not like the bigger than life ones on kid's programs or in comic books, but a short, battery charged, stocky version.

"Hey, good to meet ya, Kera. I think I'll go in and try to get a front row seat for the freak show."

"Oh, Vinny, before you go," Kevin said, "I inherited an old rifle from my grandfather. I want to get an estimate on its value. Could I bring that out to your shop, maybe sometime tomorrow?"

"Sure, I'll be there all day."

"Sweet. I'll try to get out there around lunchtime."

Vinny hopped up the steps and disappeared into the building.

"What exactly does Vinny do?" Kera asked.

"He owns a gun and knife shop just outside of town. He has a great collection of old guns. If you want to know anything about firearms, Vinny's your guy. He's not there a lot because he goes around the country buying and selling." Kevin glanced at his watch and got up. "Well, I can't wait any longer for Mandy. I have an appointment I need to get to. Would you mind giving this to her?" He held out an envelope.

"Sure, be glad to. I guess that means you're not staying for the meeting."

"Nope, I don't like getting involved in these things or even being seen at them. Bad for me and my business. I can't afford to lose my cool, like how I did the other night at the bar. Oops, I'd better get out of here fast, the TV guys have shown up. Don't need any stray coverage coming my way." Kevin rushed down the steps and out of her sight.

Kera noticed several TV vans in the street, looked like from Grand Rapids, Lansing and Detroit. Reporters were interviewing some of the people gathered outside the city hall.

A journalist from the state's LGBT newspaper, *Between the Lines*, was also there, interviewing and taking pictures. Tonight's council meeting was a bigger deal than she'd imagined.

For the most part, she found it pretty easy to tell who was for or against the ordinance change.

A few folks carried signs they'd have to leave outside the building. She'd heard the local newspaper and TV stations had spread the word about what would be allowed into and tolerated at the meeting.

The gays and their allies held rainbow flags of all sizes and some signs that caught her eye: "Straight but not Narrow," "God Loves Us All, Quakers for LGBT Civil Rights," "Gay and Straight—Together, UUs of East Lansing—A Welcoming Congregation, Lansing Area Human Rights (LAHR)."

"Hmm," Kera murmured softly to herself. "Mandy will like that this fight is bringing in people from other parts of the state."

She continued studying the crowd. The opposition wore crosses on their lapels or around their necks and displayed homemade signs with Bible passages declaring God's hatred of homosexuality. She wondered how could that be possible. *A god creates us, then hates us. Well now, that sucks.* She smirked.

Her train of thought kept chugging on. Did people think about the centuries of Muslims and Christians soaking the earth with each other's blood, all in the name of God? And didn't they ever wonder about, say, the Irish—both sides sporting their version of a Christian God? How did that work for them? Certainly puzzling. No, more like confounding. But in a way, she felt envious of believers. She'd like to feel that sure about something...anything. Round and round her thoughts twirled like a skater on ice. Thin ice. Knowing there was no good place to fall—

Kera heard a car door slam, pulling her out of her mind-spin. Harry Janssen drove into a councilman's reserved parking spot, got out of his car and headed to the back of the building. She had gone through the same entrance with her father many times. A wave of sadness washed over her.

The doors opened. People and camera crews started flooding inside. She needed to stay on the steps until everyone else got in. Crowds weren't good for her, made her jittery, edgy, wanting to get away.

One of the reporters spotted her and headed toward her. To avoid him, she decided to run over to the coffee shop and get a refill. She figured he wouldn't follow her since he'd want to find a good place for himself at the meeting.

When she got across the street, she turned and saw him go in the city building.

Returning to City Hall, Kera stopped at the door. She didn't know what had happened to Mandy. They were supposed to meet here. She finally decided to go inside and find a place to sit before all the seats were taken.

In the front of the room, members of the city council sat at a semi-circular table. Kera saw Harry intently talking to a councilwoman who didn't seem to agree with him. She guessed he was trying to do some last-minute arm-twisting. The mayor's chair was vacant, but a nameplate remained in front of the seat. A pang of grief shot through her. She hadn't prepared herself for seeing her dad's empty chair there—and certainly not his nameplate.

The rest of the room was reserved for the public seating area, with church-like benches, every row descending one step until the last row was situated on the same level as the council members. A dais with a microphone was centered in front of the first row, meant for citizens to address the council.

Looking around she realized every seat was taken. She should have gotten there earlier. Spotting the speaker's list, she went over and signed up Mandy and herself.

Just as she resigned herself to standing, two women with large Christian cross pendants dangling around their necks got up and moved to the dais, lining up to speak. They undoubtedly hadn't felt the need to attend a council meeting before, or they would've known they'd be asked to sit down and wait for an invitation by the President of the Council if they wanted to speak.

She was glad the seats were on the aisle, which would make it possible for her to be in the crowded room. She hurried over and grabbed their chairs, took off her suit jacket and placed it on the other chair for Mandy.

Earlier, Kera had worried that coming to the city council meeting would stir up her ire, like Don's rampage against gays at her dad's funeral, but so far, her rage was supplanted by fear for her sister's welfare, consuming her, gnawing on her.

How in hell was she going to find Don's killer?

Kera glanced up at a clock on the wall. Damn, the meeting had been going on for over an hour, still no Mandy. What had happened to her? She was a leader of LEAP. It was critical for her to attend this meeting. Mandy had already missed her turn to speak, although her co-leader Robert had filled in for her, but still, she should be there. When her name was called, she made her case to the council. She claimed her father would have been in favor of including the LGBT community in the ordinance. Cheers went up for her statement—the gay community was there in force.

After she finished speaking, Harry Janssen asked pointedly, "How can you know your father's opinion on the matter?"

The bastard had apparently heard—probably from Don, she figured—that she hadn't told her father she was gay. "Dad was not hateful," she shot back. "He'd want to protect people from discrimination."

Having spoken her mind, she returned to her seat, wondering how her father might have taken the news that she was a lesbian. Was it better to assume he would have loved and accepted her, or to have told him and possibly been disappointed and hurt by him? She'd never have an answer. Her opportunity to know for certain had passed. She suspected the question would live with her the rest of her life, like a nagging ache.

Kera's thoughts flipped to Mandy, who wasn't the type of person to blow off her responsibilities. Not her style—especially when it came to an event like this. Hopefully, nothing had happened to her.

She wished the council meeting would come to an end soon, but a long line of people still waited for their turn to speak. She felt like her anxiety meds were about to run their course and she didn't have any more on her.

Her mind swirled back to her default worry: Don's murder. Who could have done it? Who had a motive besides Dee? She guessed everyone in the whole LGBT community would've wished him dead. So where to start? Who else outside of the gay community? Maybe Dee would have some ideas.

She heard a ringtone from the council's table. Harry fished in his suit coat pocket and retrieved his cell phone. Everything stopped as the council members and the audience watched Harry answer his call. He turned away from his mic and said something inaudible into the phone. He got up, excused himself, and left the room.

Kera felt a new pang of anxiety. Ordinarily, Harry leaving a room would be a reason to celebrate, but something about the situation felt off to her.

The council president resumed calling the night's speakers. "Rev. Stevens...let's see." He looked down at his paper. "From the United Church of Christ. You've indicated you want to speak for the inclusion of gays into the ordinance. Would you please approach?..."

Kera kept an eye on the council members. She wondered how many of them would either have the inclination or courage to vote for the ordinance change. Some of them didn't even appear to listen to the speakers. Probably tired or their minds were already made up. She had to admit that for the most part, people were pretty much saying the same basic things over and over. However, as her father would've said, city council meetings offered a chance for folks to vent their anger and fears.

She glanced at the dwindling line. She was tired and worried. When would the monotonous meeting finish so she could find out what happened to Mandy? Her back hurt from the hard wooden seat. It couldn't be much longer, but maybe she should—

"Mr. Willis, please approach the council. I believe you're next to speak." The council president's voice interrupted her thoughts.

"Thank you. I'm Nathan Willis. Reverend Don Bledsoe was my pastor—God rest his soul." Nathan was a short, balding man leaning on a cane. He sported a large cross fashioned from nails on a twine necklace dangling from his neck down to his midsection. He continued, "I'm here to tell you if we allow homosexuals to be recognized in the law, we let them know their sinful lifestyles are okay and we all know they are not okay. God says it. I believe it!"

He emphasized his conviction with a firm nod and a tug on his cross, pulling the pendant out in front of him and waving it from side to side for everyone to see. He flashed a self-satisfied smile, turned and walked back to his seat.

Kera shook her head. She couldn't believe some of the arguments people used to keep gays from legal protections. But others clapped and cheered.

"Please, no applause. This is a meeting, not a show." The council president pounded his gavel and called out: "Ms. Jackson...is Ms. Jackson here?"

"Yes, sir." A hand shot up.

"You're next to speak, madam. Come on down to the dais, please."

A heavyset woman in a yellow, purple and red floral dress and a large matching purple hat with yellow and red flowers around the brim got up from her seat. Kera thought the dress looked like it'd fit her about thirty banana splits ago.

Balanced on purple pumps, Mrs. Jackson squeezed down the row of attendees until she reached the aisle and went from there to the dais to the tune of her clinking bracelets. She plopped her basket weave purse down on the podium, opened it and searched for something inside. When it didn't seem to appear, she frowned. She glanced over at a wooden table by the side of the dais. Taking her purse, she moved over to the table, turning her purse over and dumping out the contents. The council's proceedings came to a halt when her keys, tubes of lipstick, mascara, powder cases, combs, tweezers, a metal nail file, and other unidentifiable items clattered on the table. A handful of coins fell on the floor and rolled in all directions.

Kera was ready to get up and help, but two men in the audience beat her to it. They scrambled around to fetch the purse's wayward contents, returning the items to Mrs. Jackson, who seemed not to notice the commotion and snickering in the room.

Finally, she let out a sound of victory, pulled out a piece of paper and stepped up to the podium. "Hello, your honors," she said, looking straight ahead at the council members, "I'm Millie Jackson and I've lived in Lakeside City all my life. I believe I have a right to say something about this matter." She put her crinkled paper on the dais and smoothed it out with her hands. "I am for this addition to the

Civil Rights Ordinance," she read, "because homosexual people aren't called gay for nothing. They are happy people and love to go to parties. We need more gaiety in the world because things are in such bad shape. And they are all so creative." She glanced up, departing from her prepared presentation, and added, "I just love Elton John and his songs, and he wears such beautiful outfits too. And that Ellen girl—I can't remember her last name, but she's the one on TV—dances in the audience. Well, anyway, she loves her mother and gives her free tickets to her show. So that's why I'm for the ordinance and that's all I got to say."

Ms. Jackson turned back toward the bench, put her items back into her purse, snapped it shut, placed the handle on her arm and returned to her seat.

Well, Kera thought to herself, can't say much for that argument, either, but at least Mrs. Jackson was entertaining and on the correct side of the issue.

The council president referenced his speaker's list and read out loud, "Jesus of Nazareth?" He looked up sheepishly. "Okay, who put this name on here?" He glanced around at his fellow councilpersons, as though one of them was pulling a prank on him.

"Here I am." A guy dressed like Jesus stood up.

Kera had seen the Jesus impersonator in his white tunic and sandals outside earlier and on the night of the brawl at the Out-and-About. Apparently, he had been required to leave his huge cross with the signs outside, but he had his Bible. When he got to the dais, he opened it and started reading passages.

"Please sir, would you give us your name?" The president looked tired.

"I'm Jesus of Nazareth."

Someone in the room yelled, "I thought only citizens of Lakeside City got to talk. This guy is from Nazareth."

Laughter and applause erupted. Kera laughed with the rest of the audience. She noticed even some on the council couldn't keep a straight face.

"Please, everyone," the president broke in. He held up one hand, gesturing for calm. "Look, Mr. Who-ever-you-are, everyone is supposed to give his name, his real name."

"My name isn't important. I'm just the Lord's messenger," the Jesus-man protested.

The president paused. He turned to his colleagues, covered his mic with his hand—though everyone could hear him anyway—and said, "I'm not going to argue this one. The next thing you know, it'll be reported in the paper tomorrow that I'm against Jesus. I'm making this the last speaker for tonight."

The council members nodded. Kera thought they looked weary as well.

"Okay, get on with it," the president snapped. "We don't have much time left and the council has other things to get to this evening."

God's apparent courier went back to reading from the Old Testament of the Bible, about the sin of homosexuality.

When he got to the end of his second passage, the President interrupted the recitation and asked him to speak his mind, not read his Bible.

"I don't have a mind," he said.

Laughter broke out again. A guy from the crowd yelled out, "That's your problem, fella!"

The bearded man in white turned toward the attendees and shouted, "You are all going to Hell!"

Jesus' followers chimed in, "Amen."

Kera had dreaded coming to the meeting tonight, but she was beginning to be glad she did. She hadn't laughed so much in a long time.

The president banged his gavel. "We'll have order in here or we'll clear everyone out. That's a warning and a promise."

The crowd quieted.

The Jesus impersonator said, "I meant to say that what matters is not what I think or what is in my mind, but what does matter is what the Lord commands of us. Our Lord, Jesus Christ wants us to—"

Kera wondered if the Jesus-guy knew that the real Jesus never mentioned anything about homosexuality being a sin. But then, she figured pointing that out to him would be like flushing words down a toilet.

The president set down his pen. "Quite frankly, we've heard a lot tonight about what Jesus wants us to do, sir. I don't think you can add much more."

He turned to the secretary and asked her if they still had a quorum, given the absence of Harry Janssen. The woman indicated they did, since they only needed nine members present—excluding the president.

"Okay. In that case," the president said, "I promised a vote on this ordinance tonight and we're going to have it."

Voices grew soft and finally hushed except for a few scattered coughs.

The president rustled a few papers. He looked around at the council members and said, "All those in favor of adding LGBT people to the Civil Right Ordinance of the City of Lakeside indicate by raising your hand:"

Kera realized she was holding her breath. It seemed to her everyone else in the room was doing the same.

Three hands went up, then another...then another. A collective gasp sounded throughout the chambers.

"All those opposed."

Four hands shot up.

The president proclaimed, "Five for, and four against. The inclusion of LGBT people into the Civil Rights Ordinance passes."

A cacophonous roar came up from the crowd, filling the room.

The Jesus impersonator raised his Bible and bellowed, "God will be punishing us! The Lord will—"

The president pounded his gavel, then stood up, continuing to hammer the table. "Let's have order...let's have order in here. I understand some of you are upset by this decision. If you are unhappy about the vote, you have recourse. There's a petition process—"

Kera didn't wait to hear any more. She left the building. On her way out, she hadn't spotted Mandy. Maybe she'd come in late and had to stand in the back with the other latecomers, so had already left. Kera looked around but didn't see her. Where in the hell was she?

She saw Vinny coming out of the door and making his way over to her. "Hey, did I tell you it would be a zoo in there, or what?"

"Yeah, Vinny, you were right about that, but things really worked out well. I don't think many people thought the ordinance would pass...and it wouldn't have, if Harry Janssen hadn't been called out of the meeting. What a stroke of luck for us. Mandy, if she ever shows up, is going to—"

"Janssen wasn't for it?" Vinny plopped down on a step.

"No, absolutely not," Kera said, "and had he been here, it would've been a five to five vote. The president would have had to break the tie. I don't think he would have allowed it to pass. From what I've heard, it wasn't so much a personal problem for him, more like he worried about what might happen to the city if it did pass."

Vinny looked bored by her explanation. Not surprising, given what Mandy had told her and what she'd seen of him in action. He didn't appear much into politics, just knowing when to show up for a fight. He had undoubtedly hung around the meeting in case he was needed to bust heads.

He stood up. "Did you hear the guy who said Don was a goddamned martyr? He wanted a statue of Don," Vinny sneered. "Can you believe that shit? Don Bledsoe deserved just what he got, I mean, he—"

"Yeah, sure, Vinny." Kera pulled out her cell phone. "I don't understand why Mandy didn't show. I'd like to give her a call, but I don't seem to have her number in my contacts." She checked her incoming calls list. "Oh, I think this might be it. Sorry, Vinny, I need to see if I can get a better signal somewhere else. Nice seeing you."

Through the crowd Kera heard a voice calling her name. She stopped and surveyed the crowd and saw Mandy.

Mandy rushed toward her. "Kera, I'm sorry I didn't get here and I didn't get a chance to call you, but—"

"Yeah, sorry you couldn't make it to the meeting. Great news, as I'm sure you can tell by the crowd—"

"Kera, I just got back from the police station. The cops came to arrest Deidre."

CHAPTER FOURTEEN

Deidre

Deidre looked at Lake Michigan through the bay windows in Sylvia Janssen's sunroom. Dark, frightening clouds threatened on the horizon. The whitecaps on the lake had scared off most boaters. She noticed a small craft bobbing in the water, perhaps one of those fishing boats folks chartered from the docks down at the Old Fishing Village. The vessel labored toward shore, waves belting its starboard side, impeding the small craft's inland course.

She turned away from the window.

Sylvia's twelve-room home on the high dunes was done in an upscale cottage decor. Deidre thought the interior was nice, and all accomplished without the help of a decorator. That had impressed her. She wished she had that kind of talent.

The sunroom was her favorite place. She and Sylvia had spent many hours here planning church events or just gabbing. Those were happier days. She sat down in a white wicker chair, took a deep breath and slowly let it out.

Sylvia had been a great support to her when Kera was deployed to Iraq. Whenever her worry for her sister got out of control, she'd call Sylvia. Unlike Don, Sylvia hadn't told her to pray about it, which always felt like useless advice since she was already praying and it didn't help. She'd finally stopped seeking comfort from Don about her concerns and called Sylvia instead. And unlike Don, Sylvia didn't make disparaging remarks regarding her sister's sexual orientation.

Sylvia came into the room carrying a pot of tea and a plate of cookies on a tray. She placed the tray on the glass-topped, wicker coffee table. "Are you sure you don't want some dinner?"

"No, there is something about being frisked, handcuffed and hauled off to the police station that ruined my appetite."

"I can't believe you were almost arrested. That is so ridiculous. You wouldn't hurt a mouse and that's a fact. I remember getting a live mouse trap for you so you could catch that critter and release it out in a field." Sylvia put sugar in her cup. "All this is crazy, just crazy." She stirred her tea with a spoon.

"That's not how the cops and assistant DA saw it. I was in the process of being arrested, when suddenly I was told I was being let go. Just like that! Thank God. Later Mandy told me if I'd been charged with first-degree murder in this state, I wouldn't be able to get bail." Deidre broke her cookie apart and put a small piece in her mouth.

"That must have been so horrible. I didn't know what to do when the police came here and took you away. I felt helpless. It was so awful…and for you, good Lord, it must have been one of the worst moments of your life."

Deidre nodded. She'd been scared to death and she was still scared. Reality had finally settled in: the police thought she would actually kill her husband.

In the beginning, she'd been in shock over Don's murder and hadn't really grasped that the police really thought she'd killed him. But it's one thing to say and/or write in a letter that you feel like killing someone, but quite another thing to actually do it. Didn't they understand? She looked at her hands. Her fingers were trembling.

"Thank God, I finally got my wits about me a few minutes after they took you away and got a hold of Harry at the council meeting. He usually turns off his cell phone during those meeting, but luckily he forgot and left it on—"

"Yes, he told me he left the meeting and came right after you called him." Deidre took a sip of her tea. "Then Mandy showed up shortly thereafter. Mandy and Harry put pressure on—I'm not sure who— but they convinced the powers-that-be that arresting me wouldn't be politically smart, the police had a very weak case, and besides, I wasn't going anywhere, meaning I wouldn't leave town. Harry vouched for me and told them I was and would continue to stay with you. His support no doubt helped. I have to say, Harry must have a lot of pull in the community."

Sylvia added, "And you were lucky Mandy got there so fast."

"I can't tell you how much I appreciate Harry and Mandy for all they did to keep me from jail. Later, Mandy said the assistant DA's decision to hold me—the former mayor's daughter—would have been a politically chancy thing to do and that fact plays to my favor for now, but she didn't know for how long."

Harry walked into the room. "I want you to know the board and I have come up with an idea, and if you agree, we'll go ahead with it. First, let me back up and fill you in, the coroner says it might be quite a while yet before he releases Don's body. I guess I misunderstood and thought it could be sooner. So, given that fact and knowing folks need closure, the board and I came up with the plan of having a memorial service. When Don's body is ready, we'll have a short graveside service—only for family and close friends. I know this is really late notice, but if you agree, I have a team of people ready to make phone calls to members of the congregation."

"So, you were thinking tomorrow or Friday?"

"Tomorrow is a better day given some other things that are scheduled at the church."

"That's such short notice." Thinking about the service for Don made it hard for her to breathe.

"It is, but at least everyone knew it was going to be tomorrow or Friday, and we probably wouldn't know until the very last minute."

Deidre took in a deep breath and let out a sigh. "Okay, guess it really doesn't matter."

"And as we discussed," he put his hand on her shoulder, "we're only letting church members and your sister know about the time and day since it's a private service. The public won't be there and you'll have lots of support." Harry thought a second, then said, "Deidre, I contacted Don's elderly aunt in Oregon a few days ago. She said she wouldn't be able to make it due to her health. That was really all he had in the way of family, right?"

Deidre nodded, then remembered Don had a cousin somewhere in Wisconsin, but they'd been estranged for years. She didn't see any reason to contact him.

Harry's cell phone rang. He pulled it out of his suit coat pocket and answered. "Yes, she's right here." He handed the phone to her. "It's your sister."

Deidre walked into the Janssen's kitchen. "Hi, Kera."

Kera answered, "I've been trying to call you, but you've not been answering your phone, so I decided to called Harry."

"I'm sorry I—"

"Not a problem, I'm just glad I got ahold of you. Mandy told me they'd tried to arrest you. I wished I had known, Dee—I'd have been down to the jail in a flash. But actually, Mandy said it was really better I wasn't there. She's probably right. I might have come unglued. Are you okay?"

"I'm scared, Kera. I don't understand why this is happening to me. It's just all so unreal."

"I know, but we'll get through it, I promise. Mandy and I are going to find out who killed Don."

"How on earth are you going to be able to do that?"

"I don't know, but we'll do it, I promise. Speaking of Don, do you have any idea who might have wanted to kill him?"

"No, not really...uh, maybe the guys who robbed him. I don't know why they'd want to kill him. You'd think if they wanted to do that, they'd done it that night. But who knows?"

"Well, try to think about it, okay? See if you can come up with anyone else who might have a motive."

"I'll try but—"

"Do you want me to come over tonight? I will, if you want me to."

"No, I'll be okay here." Deidre didn't feel okay, but nothing could really be done about that. There really wasn't anything Kera could do that Sylvia couldn't.

"You could come back and stay here with me at Dad's house. But really, if you feel okay there, it's probably better for you to stay with Sylvia. I'm going to be busy working with Mandy."

"You're right, it will be better for me to be here with Sylvia and Harry, at least for a while. In fact—come to think of it—Harry told the DA I'd stay with them, so I really do need to be here. But please keep in touch, Kera, I worry about you."

"All right, I guess you do need to hang out there. I'll give you a call—"

"Oh, Kera, before you go, we've decided to have a memorial service tomorrow instead of waiting for Don's body to be released, since he was told it could be quite a while yet before that happens. Will you be able to come?"

"Yes, of course I will."

Deidre ended the call. She walked back into the sunroom and handed Harry his cell. "Thanks, Harry." She sat down.

Sylvia got up and excused herself to go into the kitchen to make more tea.

"How are you doing?" Harry put his phone into his pocket.

"Other than being scared as hell, I have no idea. All I know right now is that I'm so tired I can hardly think. I feel like I'm being pulled down underwater and I have no strength to fight."

"Don't worry, they'll find out you didn't do it, and we are one hundred percent behind you." Harry patted her shoulder, shaking his head, "I can't believe Don's gone. He was my best friend and I was probably the last person to talk to him before he died. Good God, if I'd only known—"

"You were? When was that?" Deidre took a sip of tea. Her mouth had been so dry the last few days. She couldn't seem to get enough liquids.

"I talked to him late Saturday night. Sylvia and I were playing cards...our gin rummy night, as we call it. I called him, tried to get a hold of him at the house, but neither you nor Don answered. I needed to let him know several of our parishioners had gotten hurt that night at the CAP demonstration."

"What demonstration?"

"It was, uh, a demonstration that—" Harry hesitated and finally said, "it happened at the gay bar. It was supposed to be peaceful, but to make a long story short, they were attacked by the qu...uh, homosexuals and taken to the hospital."

Deidre cringed. Harry was hardly any better than Don when it came to gay people, but she was in short supply of help and needed all the support she could get. Besides, how many battles could she fight? She wasn't doing very well fighting for herself, let alone—

"The city council president called me about it," Harry continued, interrupting her thoughts, "he was concerned about the safety of our citizens. That's when I started calling around trying to find Don because of the involvement of...well, a few of our folks." He cleared his throat. "I thought Don might want to call on them, being their pastor and all. I finally thought to call the church. Don was busy, there, working on his sermon. Of course, Don was upset that some of the people from the church had gotten hurt. He told me he was going to visit them after church on Sunday." He pulled out a white handkerchief from his pocket, "I can't believe he's gone...I'm going to miss him so much. He was a wonderful guy."

Sylvia reentered the room, holding the freshly filled teapot. "Harry, I know you don't want to face the facts, but Don had his faults too." She turned to Deidre. "Harry and I had a...well, disagreement Saturday night. I told him Don had anger issues and he had been physically abusive to you in the past and had broken your nose. I'm sorry, dear, I know telling him broke your confidence, but I just finally had to say something. Harry had fallen for Don's explanation of you bumping into a door in the night. Despite what I say, he still doesn't believe Don would abuse you." She glared at her husband, "Do you Harry?"

"Now, Sylvia, I don't think we need to bring all this up with Deidre right now. He's my best friend...well, was."

"I'm bringing it up because you go on and on about how Don was such a great guy—not that there weren't some good things about him, there certainly were. But how do you think it makes Deidre feel when you say all that about Don when she's in pain over the broken nose he gave her, as well a broken heart from a husband who abused her. And she's now dealing with his death, not to mention she's been accused of his murder as well! For God's sake, Harry, stop just thinking about yourself and your loss. Put yourself in Deidre's shoes."

Harry turned to Deidre. "I'm sorry. I do know you're hurting too." He wadded up his handkerchief and put it back into his pocket.

Harry's apology felt halfhearted and off the point to her, but Deidre could at least see, somewhat, where he was coming from and how hard Don's death must be for him, as well as how difficult it must be for him to acknowledge Don's abusiveness. After all, she had been in denial herself—her head in the sand, more like quicksand—for so long.

But as she made her excuses for Harry, she realized she really didn't feel any compassion for him. The proof of Don's handiwork was right there in front of him: her broken nose. And he didn't believe her. Even worse, he didn't believe his own wife.

She glanced at Sylvia. She could tell Sylvia wasn't impressed by Harry's apology.

Harry said, "I need to go to an emergency board meeting early tomorrow morning, before Don's funeral, so I've got to get to bed. We have to start looking for a new pastor. People are going to need spiritual help with everything that's happened, here. I've heard there's an assistant pastor in Muskegon who might be willing to come, at least temporarily. Anyway, I need to get my church board on this as soon as possible and go over my notes for the service, and...and I don't know what else."

Harry turned to Deidre. "I'm so sorry, I hope my mentioning a new pastor didn't upset you. Believe me, a guy like Don can never be replaced. He was one hell of a guy. I hope you finally understand that."

She just stared at him, wishing she could stuff a rag in his mouth.

He continued. "It's important to hire someone as soon as possible. I can't help people through this tragedy on my own and I don't have it in me to try. As a matter of fact, I really don't have it in me to do Don's service, at all, but I can't avoid it. Anyway, there's a whole congregation that needs a pastor who can—"

Sylvia sneered, "You don't get it at all, do you Harry?"

He ignored her remark.

"Yeah, fine, Harry." Deidre looked away, avoiding Harry's eyes. She'd pretty much had it with him, too. She was sorry she'd even tried to make excuses for him. All she wanted was for him go, get out of her sight.

Sylvia looked at Harry in disgust, turned and left the room.

Deidre suddenly remembered the phone conversation with her sister. She needed to endure him for another few minutes. "Harry, before you go, Kera asked me if there was anyone who might want to kill Don. Do you have any ideas about that?"

"Hmm." Harry pulled on his chin as though he had a beard. "That's a good question, but can't say as I do. No one specifically. People loved him..." Then, his eyebrows went up and he looked thoughtful.

"Did you think of someone?"

"Well, I know one thing: you are not a person who could kill Don or anyone for that matter. I hate to say it, don't want to be insensitive, but it seems to me your sister, as explosive as she is—" Harry didn't finish the sentence.

Deidre believed he let his words dangle there like bait. The expression on his face appeared to be questioning whether she'd rise to it or move on. Anger made its way to the tip of her tongue, but she said in a slow, staccato rhythm, as calmly as she could, "Don't ever say that again, Harry, or I—"

"Well, you know, at your dad's funeral, she said she wanted to kill Don, right in the middle of the service."

"She didn't say that." But as soon as the words were out of her mouth, she remembered Kera had said exactly that.

"You heard her, and she did say it. I'm not lying. Don't you remember? And the police asked me about—" Harry stopped and seemed to reconsider. "Well, certainly, lots of homosexuals would probably be willing to kill—"

Deidre felt a crack in her tolerance widening and threatening to burst, allowing years of unexpressed anger to spew out like lava. She'd had her arms wrapped around herself, holding her together, keeping her in one piece. Now she let her arms drop. "Harry," her face burned, "you can think whatever you want about my sister's sexual orientation, but I can't tolerate your thinking she's a killer, or that she'd even think about killing Don. I don't care what she said at Dad's funeral. It was just talk, her anger coming out like my anger came out in my letter. Damn it, just forget that I asked!"

Harry left the room.

Deidre heard him mumble something about Kera's learning to kill in the war. If she didn't need Harry on her side, she'd...well, she didn't know what she'd do.

CHAPTER FIFTEEN

Kera

Kera opened the door and entered Lakeside City Legal Aid. The ambiance screamed poverty. The building was located on the outskirts of the downtown in a former gas station that had undergone a makeover of sorts.

The scattered wooden chairs and desks were vintage fifties—probably from an old school—and adorned with nicks, scratches and thin varnish. The orange and brown tiled floor was chipped, cracked and offered foot-worn paths leading here and there and sometimes, nowhere in particular. Paper clips, rubber bands and punched-out paper holes dotted the floor. She saw three lawyers' desks, made private only by the small spaces separating them and an occasional plastic plant, necessitating an unspoken rule: mind your own business.

Clients waited in a row of chairs across from the receptionist's desk. A baby cried. Kera turned her head and saw the mother trying unsuccessfully to calm her discontented offspring. Meanwhile, a young boy fired a pencil torpedo launched by a rubber band. The yellow wood and lead missile ended its flight, barely missing a little girl playing on the floor. The boy's mother jumped up from her chair and grabbed his arm, yanking him back to his seat.

A harried-looking receptionist seemed to pay no attention to her arrival. Looking toward the back of the room, she spotted Mandy at her desk.

Mandy held a phone receiver between her ear and shoulder. She glanced up and motioned her over. She hung up the phone and shoved her yellow tablet to the side. "Glad you found me. So how did Don's service go this morning? I've been thinking about you and your sister. God, when it rains, it pours. I can only imagine how hard it was for the both of you."

"It went okay, about what you'd expect. Let's say, we got through it...Oh, by the way, Detective Brown was there, keeping an eye on us."

"Figures."

Kera didn't want to talk about Don's memorial anymore. She'd had about all she could take of Don and Harry for the day. She needed to change the subject. "Cool digs you have here."

"Yup, serving the poor brings with it all the benefits of deprivation."

"Unfortunately, Deidre will fit in well here, financially speaking, as an impoverished widow and part-time social worker." Kera pulled out a container of mints, popped one into her mouth, and offered the package to Mandy.

"Thanks." Mandy took a mint. "You're right, her financial standing certainly qualifies her to use our services. I can spend my work time on her case without feeling guilty." She thumbed through the pages of her notepad. "I wanted to let you know I talked today with Elena Armstrong in the DA's office—she's an assistant DA and a friend of mine." She looked at Kera, flushing lightly pink. "Uh, well, and my ex-lover. I only tell you that in the spirit of full disclosure."

"Good networking skills." Kera snickered.

"Glad you appreciate my sordid past." Mandy's lip curled up in a half-smile. "Anyway, I was digging for information about Deidre's case. I wanted to know what the police thought they had on her. Elena, of course, mentioned Deidre's letter, you know, the one she wrote to your father—"

"Yeah, sure wish I had gotten rid of that letter after I read it." Kera's shoulders tightened. "That letter was a signed statement from Deidre about Don abusing her and killing her baby. A double whammy for motive. Oh, yeah, and not to mention she said she'd like to kill him as well."

Mandy tapped her pen against her desk. "After sending the letter, she suffered further abuse from Don—a beating, a broken nose—and the timing's way too close to Don's murder. Plus, she has no alibi. On the other hand, the police have no witnesses, no murder weapon, and no corroborative evidence."

Kera slowly twisted her head to the left, then right. Her neck cracked like a rusty, out-of-use crank. She thought she should seek out a good masseuse. She brought herself back to the matter at hand and asked, "What do they know about the killing? I heard from the paper he was stabbed. Could Elena tell you anything else?"

"Elena said the homicide detectives working the case were being closed mouthed, partly because they don't want any information leaking out and partly because they haven't gotten the autopsy results. She found out Don's body had been in the driver's side of the vehicle when he was killed. Presumably, he was transferred to the passenger's side by the killer."

"What?" Kera scooted her chair closer to Mandy's desk.

Mandy continued, "They have no clue why Don was killed, then moved over to the other seat. Not as yet anyway." She glanced at her pad. "They have the vehicle now and are going over it with a fine-toothed comb. The car was a loaner vehicle or maybe a rental. Not sure of the make, one of those four-wheel drive types. Apparently, Don had been having trouble with his own car, so he'd left it with a mechanic." She pushed her chair back and stretched her arms behind her head, locking her fingers together. "That's pretty much all I have."

Kera frowned. "Okay, now as I see it, we need to find out who killed Don since the police think they already know and won't be working that hard to find someone other than Dee. I think the obvious choice is someone in the gay community, unless I can find someone else in Don's life with a reason to kill him." She sat back in her chair, crossing one leg over the other. "Mandy, you know the members of LEAP. Do you know anyone who might want to kill Don? Has anyone made threats? He's been such an enemy to our community."

"Not really." Mandy shook her head. "I can't think of anyone."

"What do you think of Vinny—the guy who fell off the ladder at the Pink Door? He sure raises red flags for me. When I was at the council meeting last night, I got weird vibes from him, plus I learned about his thing for guns and knives. And he sure blows up easy—but then, so do I." Kera gave Mandy a sheepish look. "But still, I wonder where Vinny was when Don was killed."

"Good question."

"I think I'll look into Vinny. I know he plays pool in the Out-and-About during their Thursday night tournaments, so hopefully, he'll be there tonight."

"Good idea."

Kera bent over to loosen her left sandal strap, which was digging into her skin.

"Talking about alibis, I need to tell you the cops aren't just looking at Deidre." Mandy hesitated, then continued, "According to the scuttlebutt at the DA's office, they're interested in you as well, perhaps thinking both of you are involved in Don's death. Someone told them about you threatening to kill Don at your dad's service."

"What?" Kera popped up from adjusting her sandal. She thought back. Yeah, she'd threatened Don, true, but Dee wouldn't have said anything to the cops. On further reflection, she realized Harry had heard her, too, and that fucker would blab. She bet he couldn't wait to get to the police to tell them about her. "I was pissed, Mandy, angry with what he did at my dad's funeral. That's all."

Mandy didn't say anything, just kept looking at her.

The prolonged silence felt accusing. She stood. "By the expression on your face, I wonder if you think I, or for that matter, Dee, had something to do with Don's death."

"Calm yourself and sit down. I'm telling you what is being considered by the DA's office, what Elena heard, not what I think. They're going to want to know if you have an alibi for the night of Don's murder."

Kera sat down, trying to recall the time frame around Don's death. She'd gone out and fought the protesters, was arrested, then went back to Mandy's house.

Mandy was with her the whole time. Why was she asking her about an alibi? Then it dawned on her. She had left Mandy's place in the night because she couldn't sleep. A little after midnight, she estimated. She didn't return until dawn, but she had gotten back in bed before Mandy even knew she was gone…unless Mandy woke up and realized she wasn't there. If that had been the case, Mandy would probably have stayed up waiting for her because she'd be worried… Then, it came to her, the next morning, when she and Mandy were leaving to go over to her dad's house because the cops were with Deidre, Mandy had seen her take the keys off the nightstand on her side of the bed. She and Mandy hadn't yet discussed why the keys were there, instead of where Mandy had left them in her living room.

Kera cleared her throat. "I guess you want to know about your car keys, huh?"

"That would be a good start."

"Okay, I fell asleep, but I kept waking up. Couldn't stay asleep. I finally decided to get up and watch TV, but there wasn't anything interesting on and besides, I was just too restless. I thought about the lake, how it's always been calming to me, but I remembered my car was still back at the bar. I saw your keys and…well, I took them and drove your car out to the lake shortly after midnight, I'd say. I'm sorry I took your car. I guess, technically, I stole your car, but that's where I went that night."

"I don't consider your actions theft, nor do I care that you did it." Mandy leaned in closer. "I don't suppose anyone saw you there at that time of night?"

"Well, maybe, sort of. I went to McFarland Park. There were cars out there for sure, but I didn't really see anyone. At least, no one I knew."

"Were you seen by anyone else?"

"There was a couple walking on the beach—a het couple. At the time, I figured they were out-of-towners, probably from one of those rental cabins up the beach. I was sitting in the sand as they walked by. Even if they saw me, I'm sure they wouldn't remember me, or would have even seen me well enough to recognize me. Shit, I don't think I could identify them. And as far as anyone in the parking lot, a few guys sat in their cars, but I didn't get a good look at them and I doubt they noticed me. As you know, they had other things on their minds."

"What time did you come back to my place?" Mandy was taking notes.

"The sun was just about to come up, whatever time that was."

"You stayed out on the beach that long?"

"No, it got a bit cool, so I went back to the car. I fell asleep. I was in that really drowsy, gooey state, you know, where you keep waking up but can't really get awake, so you let yourself be pulled back down. That kept happening. Finally, I woke and realized I'd pretty much spent the night there. I worried you might have gotten up and wondered where I—and your car—had gone."

"Looks like nobody saw you during the time Don was killed." Mandy stared straight at her. "That's not good."

"Yeah, I guess so, but Mandy, I swear I had absolutely nothing to do with Don's death."

Kera searched Mandy's face for a sign indicating she believed her. Maybe Mandy was trying to believe her, but she didn't appear convinced.

"No one saw you, Kera—that's a problem." Mandy bit her lip.

Kera got up from her chair and glared. "You don't believe me, do you? You think because I got into that fight with those religious-right nuts, I can't control myself, therefore I would murder Don.

Well, you're wrong. I didn't kill him, and Deidre didn't kill Don, and together, we didn't kill Don!"

She got up to leave.

Mandy said. "I do believe you, Kera, but you need to get a lawyer. I won't be able to defend you because, being you were at my house that night and I know you left, I could, would, be called as witness if you were on trial."

Kera turned back and stared at her. Mandy was right about not being able to defend her, but that was the least of it as far as she was concerned. She was sure that Mandy didn't believe her. That's what stuck in her craw.

CHAPTER SIXTEEN

Kera

Kera sat on the barstool at the Out-and-About, thinking about her afternoon of driving around and trying to cool down from her anger at Mandy.

When she'd finally felt a modicum of composure, she'd gone to see Deidre at Sylvia Janssen's house. She'd wanted to see how her sister was doing after going through Don's memorial that morning. She thought her sister's nose and face had still looked pretty bad, but a lot of the swelling had gone down thanks, as Dee claimed, to her insistence on applying ice.

Sylvia had left to do her volunteer work at the historical museum, so she and Dee sat in the sunroom and talked.

Dee told her that she was mostly numb when it came to Don's memorial service, and was much more upset about the headlines and pictures in the newspaper. The paper had run pictures of Dee when the police took her in, planning to arrest her for the murder of her husband, and then another picture as she came out of the police station after the DA had stepped in and decided to release her.

Her sister told her she'd tried to take a nap, but couldn't get the newspaper pictures out of her head, in spite of Sylvia rubbing her back, trying to relax her. Kera was grateful for Sylvia and Harry, fully backing Dee and encouraging her to stay with them regardless of the bad publicity that was undoubtedly costing Harry, both in his political life and real estate business.

Dee had also told her she'd called her boss at the hospital and had been placed on paid leave, at least for the time being. It was a relief to her not to have to go into work and face her co-workers.

Kera didn't tell her sister about Mandy saying that the cops were now suspicious of her, as well; or that Mandy seemed to think that Kera was capable of killing Don—or maybe even in cahoots with Deidre. Dee didn't need to know all that right now. She figured, why upset her even more.

The other thing preying on Deidre's mind concerned Don's abusiveness and why she'd put up with it for as long as she had. She remained upset with herself for making excuses for him all that time, for thinking his violence would stop as suddenly as it had started. She'd felt embarrassed about her behavior and wondered how she could have become so inured to the abuse. Especially distressing to her was that she hadn't done more to defend Kera against Don's tirades about her sexual orientation.

The more Deidre talked about her problems, the more Kera felt that her sister sounded better, maybe stronger, more resolved, definitely getting her head turned around and seeing her husband for who he'd been. Don's death seemed to have freed Dee to look at herself, as well as what had happened in her relationship with him.

When Sylvia returned from the museum, she'd asked her to stay for dinner. Kera declined. Besides not wanting to be around Harry, she had already planned to come here to the bar for dinner, and wait and see if Vinny showed up for the Thursday night pool tournament. If he showed, she planned on entering the competition as well. She'd played a lot of pool in college and in the military and could hustle with the best of them. Hopefully she'd get to talk to Vinny and see if she could find out where he'd gone after their clash with the protestors.

The bartender brought her a menu. She scanned it for something healthy. She was trying to get back to her former lifestyle. In Iraq, the troops had been fed high carb, high fat foods, probably to give them more energy, but not fit for someone trying to live a long and healthy life. Although, she concluded, that might not be a big factor if she ended up in jail for Don's murder.

She glanced down the menu items and spotted a walnut, cherry and chicken dinner salad. Sounded good to her until she realized the chicken was poached. Poached? Who in hell would do such a thing to chicken? Yuck, had to be slimy white meat. Nasty.

"What can I get you?" The female bartender swiped a rag across the bar, caught some crumbs, dragging them along until they fell to the floor.

"Ah, just give me a cheeseburger and fries and a side salad...and a Bell's Ale, on tap."

The bartender smiled. "You got it," then went to the kitchen door and yelled out Kera's order and came back. "Hey, I don't want to stick my nose in where it doesn't belong, but I just want to say I'm sorry about your sister being arrested and all."

Kera put the menu down. "Actually, she wasn't arrested. I know it was confusing in the story the paper ran. An assistant DA was about to arrest Dee, but apparently the DA stepped in and stopped it, guess he thought better of it. In fact, the DA has taken over the case—anyway, that's what the radio reported."

"That must be a relief." The bartender put the menu under the bar.

"To a degree, they still suspect her, but they don't have enough evidence to hold her. She didn't kill her husband and I need to help her prove it...by the way, how do you know my sister?"

"Last year when I was in the hospital, I didn't have a job, a place to live, nothing. Deidre busted her butt to help me. She's not the type of woman who would kill someone, that's for sure. The cops are barking up the wrong tree if you ask me."

Kera glanced at the woman's nametag. "Thanks, Allison, I appreciate that. And you're right, Dee would never hurt anyone, let alone kill a person."

"Hey, just call me Ally. If I can ever be of any help, let me know. I'd like a chance to give back to her. She's a wonderful woman."

"Thanks again, Ally, I don't know what it would be...hey, come to think of it, there's something you could do."

"Just name it. Oh, just a second, let me grab your drink for you." Ally took a mug, filled it from the tap and brought it to her. "Here you go. Now, how do you think I could help?"

Kera sipped foam off the top of the mug and wiped her mouth with the bar napkin. "If you were to hear anything—like say, someone overly enthusiastic about Don's death, or someone saying something you thought sounded strange or suspicious, you know, anything that might be connected to the murder—you could let me know."

"Yeah, you bet. I'll keep my eyes and ears open. So do you figure the killer is someone from our community?" Ally reached under the bar, brought up a few more napkins and set them next to her.

"I don't know, but it's a possibility. Don was no friend."

"That's true...Hey, let me check on your food." Ally went to the kitchen and returned with a plate of food that she set down on the bar in front of her and returned to washing glasses.

Kera picked at her cheeseburger and fries, ignoring the salad.

She'd bought a newspaper and began scanning the pages for any news on Don's death. She found a column in the local news section written by the local crime reporter, Daniel Williams. He quoted Detective Brown saying the police were quite sure Don was not murdered in the church parking lot, but killed somewhere else and his body transported to the church, most likely by the murderer. Brown went on to point out Deidre, the battered wife, remained their prime suspect.

Kera put down the paper, picked up her burger, and took another bite. Whoever killed Don sure had to feel grateful he was a wife abuser because that fact certainly kept the police looking Dee's way. The cops probably figured she and Dee worked together to put an end to the abuse. What the police didn't understand—or didn't care about—was that Dee could never hurt anything or anyone.

As for her, she'd experienced all the death she could handle for one lifetime—though if anyone could drive her to murder, it would be someone like Don, someone who'd physically—and emotionally—abused her sister.

Kera thought about Mandy's implying that she might be Don's killer. At least, that was what Mandy seemed to be saying to her when she was asking about her alibi. But to be fair, Mandy really didn't know her very well anymore. They hadn't seen each other in years. A lot of life had happened between high school and now. For one, she'd come home from Iraq with blood on her hands. Mandy wouldn't be that far off thinking she could have come uncorked and found killing easy, or at least a viable method of getting Don away from her sister.

The more she considered the matter, the more she understood how Mandy might even wonder—like the authorities—about the possibility of the Van Brocklin sisters conspiring and carrying out a plan to murder Don. Yeah, she had to admit, if she were in Mandy's position, she'd probably think the same thing. Well that was scary thought. She swallowed hard and took another drink of her ale.

Kera fidgeted with her food, moving the fries around her plate. Getting the cops to look elsewhere was going be like trying to push a river in the opposite direction. She hoped keeping Mandy on her side wouldn't be such a challenge.

So, far she'd disregarded all Mandy's attempts to reach her on her cell phone. Mandy had called four times. Each time, she didn't answer.

She hadn't even listened to her voice mails or read her texts. Maybe, she should do that now. She pulled out her cell.

A voice behind her yelled, "Kera, what's up?"

Kera twisted around on the barstool. "Hey Vinny. Here for the pool tournament tonight?"

"You bet. What about you?"

"I thought I'd give it a whirl. Haven't played in some time. I'm no doubt rusty." Kera tucked her cell back into her pocket.

"Man, you sound like a hustler." Vinny sat down on the stool next to her and ordered a Bud.

"No, Vinny, I just dabble." She gave him a wink.

"Really, Kera, how good are you? I'm looking for a partner and if you're any good, I want you with me, not against me."

Kera smiled. "Well, Vinny, I come with no guarantees, but I've won a few bucks at the game. And you?" She didn't really care how well he played, she just wanted the opportunity to talk to him, but didn't want to appear overly eager.

"I can hold my own." Vinny tossed her a confident grin. "Would you like to give a partnership a try?"

"Why not...when do they get started?"

"Strictly on gay time. But it should be starting soon. It's past seven. Hey, looks like things are moving now. Let's go." Vinny popped off his barstool and hurried over to where people were signing up for the tournament.

Kera bit into a cold fry and pushed her plate away. She grabbed her ale and joined Vinny. "Are we all set to play?" She put her mug on a table.

"Good to go. We'll be starting by playing those two dykes over there by the wall." Vinny pointed. "I've played them before."

"Are they any good?"

"Oh yeah, they're good. They always team up. Maybe they're a couple, not sure. The one with the black pants and red shirt, she's something else. She can run a table like no one I've ever seen. But if she loses her concentration, she'll blow a gift-from-God shot. Hey, they're coming over. It's time to rumble."

* * *

Kera and Vinny sat at a table. They'd won four games and waited for their next challenge.

Kera thought about how right Mandy had been in her description of Vinny. She had described him as needy, a loose cannon, ready to fight at a moment's notice. In their last game she'd had to calm him down when he thought an opponent was cheating, but after his tirade against the supposed cheater, he ended up buying the guy a beer. Clearly, Vinny had a hard time fitting in and making friends, but desperately kept trying.

She wondered if murdering Don might make Vinny feel like a hero to the gay community, even if he didn't tell anyone about the killing. No, she concluded, he'd have to tell someone to make Don's death worthwhile and for him to feel important, even if he only confessed to one other person.

If he did kill Don, she was determined to be that one person.

"You're pretty good, Vinny." She patted him on the back.

"You're pretty good, yourself. I've been taking notes," Vinny looked like a schoolboy who'd just been given a gold star. He added, "You seem to play a notch above whoever we play."

Kera shot him a grin. "You think so, do you?"

"I think you are a hustler." He tossed back an admiring smile.

"Perhaps some people inspire me to better myself." Kera had been slowly sipping her drink. She needed to stay clear-headed, keep her edge.

"Yeah, like those phony Christian assholes the other night. They sure inspired me." Vinny made a fist and punched at the air.

Ah, that was the opening she had been waiting for, now to take advantage by rummaging around in the man's head. Playing pool together certainly helped her bond with him and gain his trust. But up until this moment, she hadn't seen a natural opportunity to pry into what he did after the fight on the night Don was killed.

"Man, that was some night, Vinny. We sure gave it to those bastards." Kera laid on a little butch by slugging down the last of her ale, slamming the mug down on the table, and putting her feet up on an adjoining chair. "Yup, we showed them what coming around our place with their signs would get them, but they deserved more than just a beating. They deserved what Don got—a heavenly reward." She drew her arm across her mouth, wiping the last of her ale from her lips.

Tipping his head to the side, Vinny regarded her like he was trying to figure her out.

Would he step out on a limb?

She could only hope he was buying her act.

He finally said, "I'm sure you're happy to see that pig out of your family, huh, Kera?"

"Yup. In fact, I'd like to give the killer a reward, that's what I would like. I'd give 'em a medal and my eternal gratitude…and hell, all my money if I had any." She signaled Ally to bring another drink.

Vinny seemed to be studying her, staring intently, like she were a specimen under a microscope.

She moved on with her bravado. "Sort of wish I'd done the job myself. I could have, you know. I took out a few in Iraq. Don't suppose it would feel much different. Maybe better, given who he was. Killing in Iraq wasn't personal, but with Don, I'd have personal satisfaction, maybe even some glory from folks around here."

"You think?" Vinny looked at her, his eyebrows raised.

"Oh yeah, for sure. Maybe a parade." She laughed at her exaggeration. Vinny chuckled along with her, but never took his eyes off hers. She felt like she had him on the line, the hook in his mouth. Now to reel him in.

Vinny looked thoughtful, but after a moment, seemed to shake off whatever he'd been considering. She decided she needed to give him a little more line.

Kera grabbed the fresh mug from Ally. "You know, Vinny, there's no way my sister would've left that asshole. She had a severe case of battered wife syndrome. I think that's what they call it. Strange stuff, how a woman will stay with the bastard no matter how bad she's being treated." She glanced at Vinny, checking his reaction.

"I understand what you're saying. I really do, Kera."

"Call me, Ker, Vinny, that's what my close friends in the military called me," she lied. "I see us now as solders in the fight against the religious right." She slapped Vinny on the back.

She worked to draw Vinny in and give him comfort—albeit counterfeit comfort. She'd started to feel like a worm, manipulating him that way. Here was a guy, needy for friends, wanting to belong, and she was playing him. She hoped her spirit guides would understand her actions were for the greater good. If it turned out he had no part in killing Don, she'd have to make it up to him.

Vinny smiled. "Thanks, Kera—I mean, Ker."

Ally came by, wiping tables.

"Hey, Ally, looks like Vinny needs a fresh beer. He's almost out, would you bring my partner another one on me."

"Gee, thanks, Ker."

"Hey, anything for my pool buddy and soldier-in-arms." She raised her mug, clinked it against Vinny's bottle, and then offered him a fist bump.

God, could she lay it on any thicker and not totally hate herself? But she had to believe it was for a good cause. The end justified the means, right? She had no time to work out the ethics, but it didn't matter. Right now, what did matter was keeping Dee and herself out of prison for something neither one of them had done.

She and Vinny sat quietly for a while, watching the pool game.

He finally said, "You got arrested at the fight Saturday night. How was that?"

"Ah, wasn't anything, Mandy got me out fast. Speaking of arrests, where did you end up that night, anyway? I sure know it wasn't in jail with me." Kera laughed, trying to make her question sound off-the-cuff and not important.

Vinny smirked. "Had some business I needed to take care of. I—"

"Do you mind if I join you?" A familiar voice came from behind Kera.

Kera turned around and saw Mandy. "Uh…sure." She pushed out a chair with her foot. "Have a seat." She'd wanted to talk to Mandy about their meeting that morning, but the woman's timing couldn't have been worse.

Vinny got up from his chair. "Hey, Mandy, good to see you." He turned to Kera. "Ker, I think I'll go catch some practice with Hal over there. Let me know when we're up."

Mandy sat down. "I've been trying to get hold of you. I'm sorry if I gave you the wrong impression, I know you think—"

"No, no. I'm sorry I got so defensive this morning. Really, I can see how you might think I would kill Don. Shit, under the right circumstances, I probably could, but I didn't."

"Kera, I don't think you killed Don. I was only trying to say that you don't have an alibi. That's a problem. But it doesn't mean I believe you killed him."

"Yeah, but you'll probably be in the minority soon given the police are suspecting me too. Hell, maybe you already are."

"That's why we got to find out who actually committed the murder." Mandy flagged down the waiter and ordered a glass of pinot.

"Speaking of Don's murder," Kera said, "I came here tonight to check out Vinny. He's a hothead and as far as I'm concerned, totally capable of knocking off Don. Vinny says some scary stuff. In fact, tonight, with a bit of encouragement from me, he's been running off at the mouth about Don."

"Oh, really, what did he say?"

"Well, I was going on about how I thought Don got what he deserved, egging Vinny on, making him think that whoever killed Don would be some kind of fucking hero. He was going along with me. Just as you walked up, it seemed like he was close to telling me what he was doing after the fight Saturday night. He said he was 'taking care of business.' Shit, I know that could mean anything, but it was how he said it—his tone, his look, added to how he appeared while I was talking about Don's death. Certainly nothing that would hold up in court. Just a feeling."

Mandy grimaced. "Looks like I showed up a little too soon. He might have said something more concrete."

"Maybe, but who knows? He and I will be playing those dykes over there." Kera pointed out her competition. "I'll have another chance at him."

"Good. By the way, do you know the name of the man who was sitting at the table there?" Mandy pointed to one of the tables close by.

"What man?"

"The man who just got up and went to the bathroom. He looks a little familiar, but I can't place him. He was reading a paper, *Between the Lines*, I think. He has sandy, short hair, stocky build, stands about five feet eleven inches, or just under six feet anyway."

"I don't know. I was vaguely aware of someone sitting there, but didn't really pay much attention. I didn't take note of him when he got up."

"Oh, well, probably just someone I've seen around the community." Mandy chuckled. "Always looking to recruit new members for LEAP."

"Can't help you there. Here comes Vinny, looks like we're up again." Kera stood.

"Wish I could stay and watch, but I need to get home to Mr. Moxin. I forgot to put more food out for him this morning. I bet he's real pissed at me." Mandy scooted back her chair.

Kera grabbed the cue stick she'd leaned against a chair. "Yeah, I've learned my lesson about pissing off that cat." She waved goodbye to Mandy and headed toward Vinny and the waiting championship game.

Mandy headed for the door then turned toward Kera and yelled back, "Hey, be careful and stay out of trouble, okay?" She opened the door to leave.

Kera nodded, hoping she could.

CHAPTER SEVENTEEN

Kera

Kera lay in bed twisting and turning, unable to relax enough to fall asleep. She'd spent all day tending to a few urgent matters—at least the city council president thought they were urgent—regarding some papers her dad had in his home office. Finding them had been no easy task since she had to go through all his file cabinets as well as his desk. She'd spent pretty much the whole day trying to track down the material the president needed, finally getting them to the council president's office just before he left for the weekend.

She'd slept in, hung over from having stayed at the bar too long and drinking too much after the tournament. She hadn't planned on staying, but Vinny insisted because they'd won the tournament and he wanted to celebrate. But still, she couldn't believe her Friday had gone by so fast.

Now she was in bed stewing. She'd been so busy all day and had little opportunity to think much about the pool tournament last night and her time trying to get information from Vinny. But now, her mind wouldn't shut down. That's all she could think about.

After Mandy had left, Vinny had resisted answering any more questions. Instead, he'd colored in his action-figure image with tales of the fight, crowing about his encounter with a paunchy, bald guy who'd hidden outside behind the partially opened door of the bar, looking "scared as shit" and holding a sign that read: "God Hates Queers—I Do Too." Vinny bragged about running up to the guy and demanding he speak those written words out loud and to his face. According to Mr. Action Figure, the guy had started mumbling incoherently. Vinny said he couldn't tolerate "the coward's" groveling. He'd slammed his fist into the guy's stomach, causing him to jackknife and fall. Before "the flab" hit the ground, he'd delivered a karate chop to the back of the man's neck.

The guy had begged him to stop. At that point, Vinny said he'd told the guy if he wanted to be spared, he'd better come up with some cash—big bucks to buy his absolution, as Vinny described it, to pay him to forfeit his moment of pulverizing pleasure. The guy had handed over his wallet containing a mere eleven dollars.

For Vinny, taking so little money to halt a beating was a gross insult, so he'd beaten "the crap out of him." In going through the guy's wallet, he saw the man's driver license. His victim's name was Sam, but Vinny couldn't remember the surname other than it started with a Z.

Unfortunately, "Sam" had been Vinny's father's name. He hated his father, so he'd thrown Sam's wallet back at him and sprinkled the eleven dollars over the man's doubled-up body.

After that, as Vinny had recounted, "I gave him one last swift kick to his kidneys, then headed over to 'Jesus,' my next victim."

Kera told Vinny that "Sam" was undoubtedly Sam Zander, whose house and Vinny's businesses were only about a block apart from each other on the highway. She'd known this because Deidre had pointed out Sam's house to her one day. That bit of information had served to infuriate Vinny further. He didn't like the idea of being so close to that "piece of garbage."

Vinny's ranting convinced her how scary he was. He possessed a mercurial nature, a penchant for violence and bravado. She figured the guy probably believed his machismo was pretty much all he had to bring to the table. And if she was right about that, was killing Don the offering he'd laid on the LGBT altar? She'd have to keep working on him.

Her thoughts kept spinning. She had an image in her mind of a spinning roulette wheel, the ball landing on Don in a coffin. He would never again hurt her sister. Shit, that might not be true if she didn't find his killer. Don's trip to the grave could send Dee—and probably her—to jail.

Kera's thoughts rolled back to Vinny. She wished she didn't think he'd killed Don. She'd discovered a likeable side to him, maybe because he was pitiable, an underdog. She was a sucker for the down and outers, but she had to remember Vinny had motive, explosiveness, and might think killing Don would turn him from an underdog into a superhero of the gay world. Plus, he was the only suspect she had.

She found it strange that Vinny had gone to Don's Thursday morning service—she'd forgotten to tell Mandy that he'd been there. She didn't bring it up to him Thursday night at the tournament because she was trying to work on his whereabouts the night Don was killed—and he never brought it up either. Come to think of it, how in hell did he even find out about the memorial service and the time? Maybe she'd said something about it, but she didn't remember doing that. Well, obviously, he and Don hadn't been friends or even acquaintances. Maybe his presence was like a pyromaniac's need to watch the fire and enjoy the blaze and devastation. Guess he could have gotten the information out of an unwitting church member.

Hearing Harry's voice break on several occasions, it'd been obvious to her how hard it was for him to conduct the service. The church had been packed with the congregation, as expected. The eerie and unnerving part for her was hearing the police outside the building. Apparently, the cops had expected more violence, or at least felt the need to prepare for the possibility. Periodically, loudspeakers blurted out code words from police radios—startling, disrespecting the solemnity, and infusing the room with apprehension. Had they thought Don's killer would come and try to murder someone else? Or had they been expecting demonstrations from the LGBT community?

Kera and Sylvia had situated themselves on either side of Dee, holding her hands throughout the service. Her sister didn't cry. She'd remained as emotionless as a zombie, or perhaps stuck on automatic pilot.

When they'd gotten up to leave, Kera turned around and saw Detective Brown still there, sitting in the back. She'd seen him coming in before they sat down, and noticed him watching them throughout the service. She was sure his presence was not due to sympathy for the family. He'd been there to watch, to observe.

Mandy was right. Detective Brown was focusing on Deidre—and probably her—the way a bird dog locks onto a pheasant. It was up to her to find the real person who'd murdered Don.

Her thoughts continued whirling and swirling, playing and replaying the events of the past few days. She was exhausted, but not sleepy. She reached for her container of sleeping pills.

The doorbell rang.

Kera put the unopened bottle of sleeping pills on the nightstand. She looked at the clock: twelve forty-three a.m. Were the cops coming back for something they'd forgotten? Or maybe looking for Dee, or her? It'd be just like them to disrespect a person's sleeping hours. Whoever it was had picked a lousy time to show up.

She made her way down the stairs in the dark, got to the door and peered through the peephole. The porch light wasn't on, making it difficult to see. She could only make out one person standing there. Looked like a woman to her. A female cop? She thought about returning upstairs to bed, hoping the person would go away, but her curiosity got the better of her, causing her to unlatch and open the door.

"I should have called, I know." Mandy stood there, swiping her fingers through her wind-blown hair, combing it back from her face. "I tried to give you a call before coming over, but you didn't answer."

Kera felt her anxiety kick in. "Is there anything wrong?"

"No, no, I just wanted to talk to you. I know I could have waited until tomorrow, but—"

"No problem. Come on in. You'll have to excuse my clothes, I was in bed, as you can see." Kera glanced down at her blue and white striped pajama bottoms and blue T-shirt. She stepped aside, allowing Mandy to enter.

"I'm sorry. I shouldn't have come so late."

Kera's eyes took in every inch of Mandy as she walked into the foyer. God, the woman was beautiful. Her sleek body modeled a navy blue suit with an emerald green blouse, emphasizing her stunning green eyes.

She wondered why Mandy was here at this time of night, since she said there wasn't really anything wrong. "Are you sure there's nothing wrong?"

"No, really. I've learned a few things, thought you might want to hear, but nothing—"

"Well, that good. " Kera rubbed her brow. "Hey, I'm glad to see you. I couldn't fall asleep anyway."

"Oh good, I didn't wake you. God, I just got out of the office. So much paperwork, I'll never catch up."

Kera guided Mandy into the den.

"Wow, I haven't seen this place in years, looks pretty much like when I last saw it. Let me think...I'm pretty sure it was at your graduation party."

Kera motioned Mandy to the sofa.

"I remember you had quite a spread that day. It was, in fact, the first time I had ever eaten snails." Mandy laughed. "I thought they were quite a treat. Whose idea was it to have snails?" She sat down.

"Mine, sort of a random selection on my part. Dad said that Dee and I could have anything we wanted for the buffet. I wasn't really into the menu that much, so Dee took care of it. I guess at some point, I decided to throw in my two cents. I do know I'd had them at some fancy affair Dad took me to—can't remember exactly what it was—but that's where I got a taste for snails. I still can't believe Dad let me have them. It must have cost him plenty. Want a glass of wine?"

"Sure, if you'll imbibe with me. Do you have red?" Mandy put her purse on the floor beside her.

"Yup, even got some pinot. Dad used to drink it." Kera went into the kitchen and came back to the den with two glasses, a bottle and a corkscrew. "I guess I'll change things up a little and have a glass of this stuff with you."

Mandy looked at the bottle, "Wow, that's more expensive than the pinot I drink."

"What were you going to tell me?" Kera popped the cork, poured out two glasses, gave one to Mandy, and sat down beside her.

"Deidre called me earlier this evening. She said she remembered something that might help us." Mandy took a quick sip of her wine.

"What's that?"

Mandy put her glass down on the coffee table. "Well, apparently, Sam Zander—the church treasurer—threatened Don. You know Sam, right?"

"Yeah, sort of. Not personally, but Dee has talked about him. So when did he threaten Don, and why?"

"On the Thursday before Don was killed. After a church board meeting, Sam asked Don to let him have his money back, the money he'd donated to the new church's building fund. Don refused. Sam became hostile and threatening. Deidre said Don told her about the incident the next morning. That's when she got into that fight with him and he ended up breaking her nose."

"Hmm, Dee and I never discussed what set Don off. So that was it. It was hard enough that day, getting her medical attention and trying to persuade Dee to look at what was going on between her and Don. I didn't even think to ask what instigated their fight that time. I probably figured it didn't matter."

"Deidre said she told Don he should give Sam his money back."

"Why did she think that?"

"Because Sam lost his job and was having money problems. Deidre felt sorry for his wife and kids."

Kera couldn't understand. "Don was an asshole, but not that way. I can't see him refusing to help someone out in a situation like that."

"According to Deidre, Don was mad at Sam because he'd lost a lot of money gambling and he needed the money to pay off his gambling debts—not money to feed his kids. Don got all riled up about Sam being a sinner and told Sam that God was punishing him for those sins—"

"Now that sounds like Don."

"Apparently, Harry was there at the time."

"I wonder why Harry never mentioned the incident to me." Kera took a drink of her wine. "I haven't tasted this stuff in quite a while. Not too bad."

"Deidre told me Harry had forgotten about it too. She said he's had so much on his plate with planning Don's memorial, the church stuff, his work, and his city council duties that the incident escaped his memory. But when Deidre remembered about Sam and brought it up to Harry, he verified that Sam had indeed threatened Don."

"Well, now, that's very interesting. Seems I have two people with motives. I wonder if Sam has an alibi. More importantly, I wonder how I can find out. Not like I can chum up to him like I'm doing with Vinny." Kera smirked. "Hmm, maybe I'll just have to get at the truth by beating the shit out of Sam."

"Kera!" Mandy put down her glass. "Don't you dare! All we need is for you to be charged with assault and—"

Kera threw up her hands defensively in front of her face. "I'm kidding, I'm kidding, honest. But it's so hard to get a person to talk to you when you don't have a badge. I'll have to try to weasel a confession out of him somehow."

"Speaking of confessing, did you get much more from Vinny? You know, after I blundered in and ruined things for you?"

"No, he bragged about his exploits beating up protesters and other testosterone-charged activities. He did tell me about his joy in throwing a few blows at Sam Zander. Sam was there that night at the bar, carrying a nasty sign that really set Vinny off, so he threw a few punches Sam's way. I, of all people, don't blame him for doing that." Kera flashed a smile and then turned serious. "Vinny's so volatile and I think he really enjoys violence. Oh yeah, I forgot to tell you he somehow found out the time of the memorial service and showed up.

I'm not sure why in hell he was there, unless he came thinking he'd see the body, his handiwork—not knowing the service had turned into a memorial and the body wouldn't be there."

"You mean like people who set fires?"

"Exactly, and frankly, even with this new info about Sam, I still think Vinny could have killed Don, but I'm certainly going look into Sam threatening Don." She scratched her head. "Gambling debts, huh, those are not nice people Sam's dealing with. He has to be feeling really desperate—"

"Yes, I'm sure he is. There's another interesting—actually, very interesting—tidbit Deidre mentioned."

"What?"

"I guess right after Sam made his threats, Don canned him from his job as church treasurer." Mandy picked up her wineglass.

"I can understand why."

Mandy went on, "But as Deidre pointed out to me, Sam most likely still has access to church funds. With all that's gone on, I bet there was no time or thought regarding changing signature names on church bank accounts. A good question would be, now that Don is dead, has Sam suddenly come up with the money he needed?" She sat back, hiked up her suit skirt a bit and kicked off her shoes, pulling her legs up on the sofa.

"That's interesting. Treasurer, you say." Kera rubbed her forehead. "I didn't know that. You're right, it's an excellent question. With Don out of the way, Sam could solve his financial problems with a little fancy bookwork." Following Mandy's lead, she leaned back on the sofa, taking note of Mandy's hiked skirt.

"I asked Deidre how he was qualified to take care of the books. She said he was in banking. Mortgages, I think."

"The situation gets more and more interesting. I'm beginning to feel some hope here. I wonder if we should give our info to the cops, try to guide their noses in another direction." Kera reconsidered her suggestion. She didn't trust them. "No, come to think of it, I don't think so. I'll look into Sam myself, see if I can dig up something."

"I agree. As I said before, when the police in this town get locked onto a suspect—or suspects—it would take a crowbar to pry them off. And frankly, according to Elena, the DA is not looking beyond you and Deidre."

Kera added more wine to their glasses.

"Are you trying to get me drunk? More wine could put me out." Mandy rested her head on the back of the sofa and closed her eyes. "Oh, it feels good to relax."

Kera was beginning to feel a glow from the wine. The tension gripping her shoulder muscles began letting go, leaving her with a rush of warmth coursing through her body. She didn't know whether it was Mandy or the wine or both giving her this feeling of being in the right place at the right time with the right person, riding along on a wave of contentment. She couldn't believe she felt this way with everything going on in her life. She thought the goddesses must have granted her a moment of reprieve.

She laid her head back, took a deep breath, and let it out slowly, trying to recall when she'd last felt this way. She remembered the time before she left for Iraq, when she and Kelly had spent two weeks on Isle Royale in Lake Superior. Isle Royale was a mystical place for her, a place where good things happened in her life and she'd wanted to share it with Kelly.

She and Dee had first gone there with their parents when they were little. Then, when she was in high school, she'd convinced her dad to let her go by herself. Hiking the trails and camping out made her feel part of and connected to something bigger than herself. In her senior year, she and Moran took a trip up there together. The shaman woman had taught her how to communicate with the land in a way she hadn't experienced before. Moran could touch a tree, a rock or plant and feel the warmth of its life force. As she hiked the trails, she claimed the earth sent up an energy and joy that propelled her for miles with little fatigue. Moran led the way, stopping only when a tree, plant or rock spirit called out to her.

Kera's thoughts floated back to the last day at Isle Royale when she and Kelly had hiked to her favorite spot on the island. She'd been saving this place for their last hike of the trip. They'd sat down to look out over Lake Superior. The day had been warm with a slight breeze from the lake cooling their faces. They'd watched gulls fly over the water, diving for fish. She'd put her arm around Kelly and kissed her, taken hold of Kelly's hand and told her she wanted to spend the rest of her life with her—

She jerked herself out of her reminiscences. Most memories of Kelly started out nice, but ended up stinging like a nest of angry bees. She took a deep breath and blocked the pictures by forcing herself into the present, sitting next to Mandy. She needed to move on before she lost the good feeling she'd had.

Mandy looked at her intently. "Are you all right?"

Kera reached for Mandy's hand. "Yes, of course." She looked into Mandy's large green eyes and said, "Now, where were we the other night when we were so rudely interrupted?"

"I believe we were in my bed." Mandy smiled and moved closer, cuddling up to her.

"I believe there's a bed upstairs, but what do you say we snuggle in front of the fireplace on Dad's bearskin rug—it's very comfy."

Mandy nodded, still smiling.

"I'll put a match to the logs. I set up everything for a fire the other night, but didn't light it, so it's ready to go." Kera got up, went over and grabbed the matches on the mantel. She squatted down to light the fire.

Mandy followed and knelt down behind her, putting arms around her.

She felt Mandy's warm lips moving around the back of her neck and Mandy's fingers moving under her T-shirt. Chills of pleasure ran through her body.

The fire grew higher, casting a warm glow.

Mandy lay down on her back, pulling Kera over her. "My, this rug is soft to lie on and you feel delightful on top."

Kera's lips found Mandy's and melted into them. She reached up and ran her fingers through Mandy's silky hair, while her lips and tongue found Mandy's neck, kissing and tasting her. She was desperate for more. Straddling Mandy's legs, she gently pulled her upright and whispered, "Let's see how the rug will feel to you on your bare skin."

She unbuttoned Mandy's blouse, took it off, and ran her hands slowly over Mandy's shoulders and down her arms. Her skin was smooth, soft like the petals of a tulip. Piece by piece, Kera unwrapped her gift, unveiling slowly and carefully as if she were trying to save the wrapping paper.

She lowered Mandy back down to the rug. Hovering over her, she placed her hands on Mandy's breasts, cupping and savoring. Her hands drifted down and over Mandy's belly, hips and thighs, taking in the body's beauty: toned, curvy, inviting.

Kera whispered in Mandy's ear, "How does the bear rug feel without your clothes on?"

"Wonderful, but it would even feel better with your naked body on top of me. I'd be the meat in a pleasure sandwich—bear rug as the bottom slice and bare Kera as the top slice." Mandy giggled.

Kera took off her clothes and straddled Mandy. "Yum, you do look delicious, like a buffet set out for a princess." She bent and met Mandy's mouth with hers, then moved her lips down further, exploring, pleasuring, relishing. She alternated between Mandy's lips, neck and breasts as she discovered new textures and flavors.

Mandy's fingers ran through her hair, guiding her head and setting the pace.

Kera moved downward, her body in rhythm with Mandy's, dancing to the connection. She circled and moved into the area of Mandy's pleasure, finding her destination, gently tasting, caressing, massaging and penetrating.

Mandy's hips and thighs rose to envelop her like flames. The sounds of bliss from Mandy merged and intensified in Kera, kindling her passion and blazing through every vein like fire ripping through a parched forest. She moved to the center of Mandy's exhilaration, unleashing and bursting the tension into ecstasy.

With Mandy's explosion of joy came release for her as well.

CHAPTER EIGHTEEN

Kera

Kera pulled the car out of the driveway and pushed the button to roll the window down, letting in the morning's fresh smells of plants sprinkled with dew. She sucked in a deep breath. The fragrant air took her back to her times with Moran.

Years ago, she would get up early, jump in her canoe and paddle to Moran's place. It didn't seem to matter how early she got there, Moran would be ready and waiting on a log by the river with her backpack. In the canoe, they would journey further up the river to watch the wildlife come down to drink. She remembered how the deer would look up and watch the canoe drifting closer and closer. Moran would intone in a quiet voice. The wide-eyed creatures would gaze back at her, appearing mesmerized by her vocalizations. Moran alternated her chanting with moments of silence and listening—later revealing what the deer had communicated back to her. On one occasion Moran told her that an elder deer had conveyed a message meant for her, saying she needed to—

A dog darted across the street right in front of her car. She slammed on the brakes, reflexively, jarring her from her reverie and into Iraq: *gunfire, people scrambling, blood splattering, screaming—*

A car horn blasted behind her, yanking her back to Lakeside City.

She pulled the car off the road, focused on her breathing and wiped the sweat from her brow. The black Labrador continued on seemingly unfazed by his near encounter with death. But for Kera, a phantom stench of death surged through her, like sludge, like miasma, like the ghost of death past.

She gripped the stirring wheel, squeezing it, commanding herself to breathe, to move out of her memories and stay in the now. She took a few deep breaths, got herself together, almost together, and pulled out onto the road.

She was headed over to see Sam Zander. She had to find out if Sam had anything to do with killing Don. She didn't have much of a plan—actually, no plan at all. She'd have to follow her instincts, play it by ear.

Before Mandy left that morning, she'd suggested starting a conversation with Sam by telling him she was visiting on Deidre's behalf, making it appear that Deidre was concerned about Sam and his family. Kera supposed it would be as good an opening as any. But since Sam was angry with Don for not giving his money back, would he be angry at Dee too, being she was his wife, assuming she'd agreed with her husband? If that were true, he probably wouldn't be willing to talk to her.

She began to wonder how effective she was, playing it by ear—that seemed to be what she was doing with Mandy, as well. Maybe, with Mandy, it was more like playing it by lust…or was she using Mandy as a comfort, a distraction from her reality? Maybe. Being with her did have that effect.

That was a distressing thought.

She wanted to think of herself as strong, independent, not needing anyone, because she'd learned one of life's laws: if she needed someone, she'd lose them like Mom, Dad and Kelly. Hell, she might even be putting Mandy's life in jeopardy by even being around her, by allowing Mandy to become important to her. She needed to keep telling herself she didn't need Mandy, she didn't need anyone.

Well, she did need her sister. No way she could hide her need for Dee from the shadowy forces that controlled such things—she'd have to run harder and faster than Fate. Her sister's life was in danger of being ruined. If she didn't act, Dee could end up in jail for the rest of her life. She couldn't—goddamn it, she wouldn't—let Dee go away too.

She pressed down on the accelerator.

* * *

Kera turned off the highway and into Sam's dirt driveway, parking the Buick beside a blue Ford Focus. She walked up to Sam's house and looked around for a doorbell. Seeing none, she knocked on the front door.

Sam's home was an old schoolhouse converted to residential use, but kept its roots by being painted schoolhouse red. The house still sported the old roof bell, long ago retired from calling kids to class. A mailbox in the shape of a miniature yellow school bus sat on a post near the street. The landscaping looked like it had once been done professionally but now suffered from neglect.

Getting no answer, Kera knocked harder. The car parked in the driveway didn't necessarily mean anyone was home, but she thought she'd walk around to the backyard, just in case anyone was out there and couldn't hear her knocking.

In the back of the house, she found a white privacy fence surrounding the yard. She opened the unlocked gate and went through, noting a wooden deck, an unoccupied swing set and an empty kiddie pool in the deserted yard. She quietly slipped onto the deck cluttered with abandoned toys, an open gas grill with sticky barbeque tongs in a dirty pan on the grate, and a green plastic overflowing trash can.

She made her way to the sliding glass patio door. The curtains were half open and the door slightly ajar. She moved to a spot where the curtains on the inside of the door would hide her from the view of anyone inside.

Peering into the open crack of the door, she saw Sam sitting in a blue overstuffed chair, staring at a darkened TV set. He was barefoot and wore dark sweatpants and a white T-shirt that didn't quite make it over his paunch. Morning light shone in, revealing his disheveled hair and several days' growth of whiskers. Fast-food sacks, paper wrappers and cups were strewn around the room.

Kera knocked on the glass to get his attention. He didn't move or acknowledge hearing her. Through the crack in the door, she said, "Can I come in, Sam?"

Sam turned his head, squinted at her.

"I knocked on the front door, but guess you didn't hear me." Kera slid open the patio door and stepped in. "I came to see how you're doing."

Sam blinked hard. "Oh, Deidre, I couldn't make you out. The sun's too bright behind you."

Kera moved closer to him. "I'm Kera, not Deidre. But Deidre sent me to come and see how you're doing. She's worried about you and your family. May I sit down?"

Before Sam could say no, she sat in a chair. Sam had some cuts and bruises on his face. She figured she knew where those came from—his encounter with Vinny.

"You can tell your sister I'm okay," he sneered, "that is, if you consider losing my wife and children an okay thing." He grabbed his side and grimaced.

She guessed she knew where the pain in his side had come from as well, but she wasn't about to bring up bad memories. "What happened to your family, Sam?"

"My wife went home to her parents and took my kids."

"I'm sorry, that must feel horrible." Kera bent forward a little in her chair, trying to conjure a look of caring and concern. In spite of her dislike for the man, she felt a little bad for him. He looked like shit, had lost his job, maybe his family, and was in financial trouble, big-time.

"How would you know how I feel? Your kind, they don't have wives and kids."

Kera bit her lip. Just when she'd started to feel for the guy, he had to show his stripes. For his sake and hers, she decided to let go of his last comment. "Well, I can see a guy who looks down in the dumps. When did they leave?"

"Two days ago. I don't have the means to support them. They'll be better off without me, anyway."

Kera noticed his right hand tucked down at his side, fidgeting with something. Her instincts told her he had a gun there. How long had Sam been sitting there, trying to get the courage to kill himself? She figured he wouldn't hesitate to kill her first, if she didn't play things right. "Sam, just because things are down now doesn't mean they'll always be that way. There are others who've been down and have been able to turn their lives around. You can make things right. Just takes time."

Sam pulled out a pistol. "This is what's going to make things right for my family and get me out of my misery. I've already made the decision. There's no turning back now." He put the muzzle to his right temple.

"Now Sam, talk to me a while. Why do you think killing yourself will help anything? I really want to know. Hell, maybe I can help."

She was aware most people who threatened to commit suicide were ambivalent and would welcome a shred of hope, a reason not to pull the trigger. Frankly, she didn't care if Sam lived or died, but she needed to know if he had anything to do with Don's death.

"There is no help for me, things have gone too far...way too far." Sam lowered the gun to his lap, but he held fast to it and his finger remained on the trigger.

Watching him put down the pistol confirmed her belief that he wanted to talk. She softened her voice. "How so, Sam?"

She needed to keep him talking and wanted him to feel he had someone to sympathize with his side of life—everyone needed a shoulder to cry on, someone to understand. Even if he remained committed to doing himself in, he'd take the chance to let someone know his anguish. Meanwhile, maybe she could figure out a way to get the gun from him.

"I told you, I can't support my family. A man is nothing if he can't take care of his own. I lost my job and I owe lots of money to...well, people." Sam kept glancing down at the gun in his lap.

"Sam, a guy with your education and experience will find another job."

"I'm not young anymore. In this economy I'm a real has-been." He looked up at her. "I can't make the house payments. I've even gone to the bank to try and work something out, but I'm underwater with it and they weren't willing to help me. I'll soon lose it altogether." He rubbed his left hand across his forehead. "There won't even be a home for my family to come back to." His voice rose. "Can't you understand that? It's all over for me. There's just too much stuff that's gone down. My wife will be better off as a widow. She'll be free to marry someone else who can take care of her and the kids."

The information from Sam—that he had no money—made her believe he hadn't embezzled from the church coffers and probably hadn't intended to. It still didn't answer the question of whether or not he killed Don.

She needed to keep him talking. "I'm sorry Don didn't give back the money you gave to the building fund. Deidre told me about it. Did you know she was very upset with Don for not returning it to you?"

"No, I didn't know that. Deidre is a good woman."

"Yes, she is, I'm proud she's my sister. And did you know she is the number one suspect in Don's death?"

"Oh? No, I didn't." He seemed to be thinking about it, then asked, "Why's that?"

"She wrote a letter to my dad. In it, she said she was so upset with Don that she could kill him. She didn't mean it, of course. Just one of those marital moments when you're really pissed." She didn't think it would be especially helpful for her to go on about Don's abusive behavior and Dee losing her baby.

Sam didn't respond. He just kept staring at his gun.

Kera tiptoed toward her next subject. She felt like she was on borrowed time with Sam, not knowing what might set him off next, or how long she could keep him from putting the gun to his head and pulling the trigger. But she wanted to revisit the money issue between him and Don. "I understand the money you wanted back from the church was truly yours. Don should have returned it to you, knowing your circumstances. He was being a real jerk, given what you are going through. You must have been really pissed at him."

Sam got the point. "If you are asking me if I killed Don, I didn't."

"Okay, I believe you. But just to clear your name, where were you Saturday night when Don was killed? The police will want to know."

Sam glared at her. She realized his despondency had flipped over into anger. He shook his finger at her. "Listen, you bitch dyke, you have no right coming in my home and trying to blame me for Don's death. That's what you are doing here, isn't it? It's not that Deidre sent you."

Kera almost laughed, but she controlled herself. She wondered if he'd meant "butch" or "bitch." Either word, she guessed, probably worked for him. She shook off his comment and focused back on her mission. "I'm not blaming you, Sam. I'm merely asking you something the police will want to know."

"Well, you are not the police and I don't have to tell you where I was that night." Sam stood up. He held the gun in his right hand, now pointing it at her.

Kera lowered her voice. "Hey, Sam, settle down. I was just asking a question. You told me you didn't do it, so I believe you. Deidre never said you were the kind of guy who lied, so I'll take your word for it." Dee had never said anything to her regarding Sam's character, but invoking her sister's name was the only way she knew to try to de-escalate the guy.

But it didn't work.

Sam raised the gun higher, now aiming at her head. "You know, I wouldn't be in this position if it weren't for you queers."

How in the hell did he make his way to that conclusion?

"Uh, how's that?" She figured she probably didn't really want to know, but she needed to keep him talking and she also needed to move the conversation to a place that didn't seem to require his pointing a gun at either one of them.

Sam apparently had everything worked out. "God's wrath has come down on us, all because of you people. God is angry and He wants His true followers to purge our country of your kind. I'd be doing God's work if I got rid of you before I kill myself."

Kera put her hand up and out in front of herself. "Now Sam, I don't think you are a killer, no matter what you think of me or other gay people."

Sam hissed back, "You're an abomination. I know the Lord would be happy to be rid of you all."

Behind the patio door curtain, Kera noticed the shadowy figure of a man on the deck outside. Sam clearly couldn't see him. She had no idea who it could be, but any distraction right now might help, unless it was someone coming to collect the money for Sam's gambling debts. If so, she could be in even more trouble.

The shadowed figure moved soundlessly to the patio door opening and froze.

Kera focused back on Sam. The gun in his hand wobbled. Sam used his other hand to try to stabilize his aim. Unfortunately, he stood close enough to her so no matter how badly he shook, if he pulled the trigger he was bound to hit her.

"Look, Sam, do you want your kids to live with knowing their dad was a killer? Is that the legacy you want to leave them with? Think about it. Killing me won't solve any of your problems. It will just make things worse." Kera glanced around the room, trying to spot an escape route.

She glanced toward the patio door again. At that moment, the shadow moved into the opening of the door. With the intense morning sun shining behind the intruder, she couldn't make out his face.

"That's where you are totally wrong." Beads of sweat dripped from Sam's face. "If I kill you, I will be a hero in the view of my church and the Lord. At least I'll have done something right. Then I'll kill myself and the Lord will take me in. I'll have redeemed myself."

Oh, god, now he'd found a cause, something honorable, something heroic, something to die for. She's been dragged into his death legacy plans. She needed a counterplan fast. She estimated approximately four feet between Sam and herself. If she wanted to take Sam down, she'd have to distract him, get his aim to move off her, then move in quickly and take control of the gun. Hopefully, she'd still be able to deal with the man at the patio door.

Before she could put her plan into effect, the shadowy figure flew through the door opening, grabbed Sam around his chest and pulled him backward, causing them both to fall on the floor. Sam's gun fired several times.

Kera noticed blood oozing from her left shoulder. One of the shots had hit her, though she didn't feel any pain.

She looked at Sam, flailing like a portly sea turtle—minus shell—tipped over on his back and piled on top of his assailant. Squashed underneath Sam, the trapped attacker moaned, squirmed and thrashed, trying to free himself from his behemoth prey.

Suddenly, the attacker's hand—gripping a knife—found Sam's neck and stabbed into it. Blood gushed. Sam rolled to his side, grabbing at his throat, gurgling and gagging. His blood poured out and puddled on the tiled floor.

Kera snatched Sam's gun and aimed at the two men.

The intruder sat up. "Kera, don't shoot! It's me, Vinny."

"Good god, Vinny, I thought you were some goon coming for Sam to collect on his gambling debts. What the hell are you doing here?" Kera lowered the gun and wiped sweat off her forehead with her shirtsleeve.

"I'd just pulled into my shop parking lot when I saw your car drive by, slow down and turn into Sam's place. I got curious and worried for you. Not a good idea to go to the house of right-wingers without backup, Ker. Since I was just a stone's throw away, I hiked on over and climbed the back fence. When I didn't see you, I decided to explore. Good thing I did, huh?"

Kera nodded. "Yeah, guess I can't argue with that."

Vinny got up. "You've been hit, Kera."

"I'm okay, it's not that bad. I don't think the bullet is in me, probably just grazed my shoulder." She grabbed a wad of tissues, pressed the makeshift bandage to the wound. She bent over and felt Sam's neck, checking for a pulse. "Goddamn, he's dead, Vinny, looks like you got his jugular."

"Holy fuck! I say we get the hell out of here." Vinny grabbed his knife off the floor.

"Jesus, Vinny, we should call the police. You had cause for killing him. If we leave, we'll both look guilty as shit."

She knew when the police came she'd be arrested. The incident would be the last straw. What were the chances the cops would believe Sam had been killed in self-defense, and she had nothing to do with it? Zero to none, she figured. And, how would she ever get to the bottom of Don's murder sitting in jail? Wouldn't happen! She couldn't take that chance. If she wasn't free to find Don's killer, she and her sister would be hung out to dry with no one to fight for them.

"But Ker, the cops are going to—"

"You really should stay, Vinny, and tell them what happened. When I can, I'll back you up, but right now, I need to leave. They'll arrest me and I need to help my sister. I really hate leaving you here like this. I'll send a letter to the cops and tell them what happened, and when I can, I'll talk to them personally. I promise."

"Hey, I'm getting out of here too. It's really better if I'm not a part of this situation either, believe me. This is a bad scene, man. I'm not hanging around."

Kera knew the cops would look for her because her damned car was out in the driveway and no doubt someone will have seen it there. Vinny had come in through the back. Probably nobody had seen him, but Vinny was—justifiably or not—the one who put the knife in Sam's throat.

She didn't plan on taking the rap for him. If he thought he could weasel out of his responsibility, he was dead wrong. Didn't he understand leaving wouldn't stop her from eventually telling the cops who stabbed Sam? Of course, she couldn't count on them believing her. She sucked in a deep breath. Maybe Vinny just wasn't thinking clearly, wasn't considering the implications for her if he left.

Or maybe he was.

She knew nothing about him and his past. Running a gun and knife shop called for a clean police record, but for all she knew, he could have been in legal trouble elsewhere, left, and then assumed a new identity here. It wouldn't surprise her. Or maybe he just hadn't ever been caught at doing anything illegal.

Vinny ran into the bathroom and came out with a towel. "Hey, we'd better get rid of any fingerprints or anything that would pin us to his death—"

So that's Vinny's plan. He'd erase his presence from the house. He had to know she didn't have that luxury with her car sitting in the driveway.

Not going to happen! She was not about to let him take the towel and remove himself from the murder scene. If Vinny's fingerprints weren't left here, she'd be screwed. It'd look like she'd been here alone and killed Sam. Vinny wouldn't have to admit he'd ever been in Sam's house. He'd undoubtedly leave his DNA, but the cops would have no reason to look his way, and knowing the mindset of Detective Brown and the DA, they would think she was lying if she told them differently, and not bother to investigate this scene any further than her involvement.

She had to come up with something quick. An idea hit her. "Hey, Vinny, I think I hear someone coming," she lied. "Whoever it is must have heard the gunshots. Let's get out of here, hurry." She grabbed Vinny's arm, making his towel drop to the floor, and pulled him to the patio door.

She and Vinny ran to the gate leading to the front yard so she could get her car. Through the narrow gaps in the fence boards, she saw someone approaching from the other side, damn it. She backed off and peeked through a small hole in the fence, seeing a stocky man with light brown hair heading right for them. The man looked a little familiar but she couldn't place him.

She turned to Vinny and put her finger to her lips. "Shhh, a guy's coming."

Together, they ran to the fence on the other side of the house adjoining a small wooded area next to the highway and climbed over it.

Vinny said in a hushed tone, "Let's head over to my shop."

They took off running again and made it to Vinny's shop and went inside.

He got out his first-aid kit to treat her bullet wound. Kera took off her shirt so Vinny could apply antiseptic to her wound. He reached in the first-aid kit and got out bandages. "Looks like it's pretty much done bleeding. I don't think that guy saw us leaving Sam's place, do you?"

"No, I don't and I didn't see anyone other than him coming up to the gate. I think I've seen that guy somewhere...but maybe not, probably just a neighbor who heard the shots. The poor guy, he's in for a bad afternoon, walking in there and finding Sam dead like that. It won't take long for the police to show up." She finally started feeling the pain from the bullet wound to go with the antiseptic's sting. "That's enough of that shit, let's get to the bandage." She held the pad as Vinny taped it to her shoulder.

"How's that." He pressed down on the tape.

"Looks good, Vinny. Say, did anyone see you going into the backyard when you came over to Sam's?"

"I don't think so, but I can't be sure. I cut through the woods to his backyard fence. Someone might have seen me leave my car at the shop and cross over to the woods, but I don't think so. Sure hope not."

"Well, the cops are going to know I was there, especially since I had to leave my dad's car sitting in the damned driveway. I'm totally screwed. God, could I have left a bigger calling card?" Kera shook her head. She'd have to hide out somewhere, but where could she go?

"I think it's time to get out of Dodge for a while, at least until I know what's going down." Vinny put on a clean shirt he'd grabbed out of a closet. He rolled up his bloody one and shoved it in a plastic grocery sack. He handed Kera a fresh T-shirt. "Here, I keep a few spares on hand. You can't put your bloody one back on. I'll put your stained clothes in the sack with mine and get rid of them both."

She took the clean one and gave him hers. "I got to figure out a place to go myself."

"You can come with me, Ker."

"No, Vinny, I need to hang around here."

"Why? You've left your calling card, they'll be after you."

"My sister needs me." She started to say, to figure out who killed Don, but thought better of it because she couldn't be certain he wasn't the killer. She watched him as he tied the plastic bag containing the bloodied shirts. She thought about how Vinny had been quick to slit Sam's throat. All he really would have needed to do was get the gun away—

Several emergency vehicles flew past the shop, sirens blaring.

It was time to get out of there.

CHAPTER NINETEEN

Deidre

Deidre's heard her cell phone ringing in the bottom of her purse. She rummaged around trying to find it before the ringing stopped. She finally found her phone and saw the caller was Mandy, so she answered.

"Can you talk?" Mandy sounded serious.

"Uh…yes."

"I need you to be alone so no one can hear our conversation."

"I think Harry and Sylvia must have gone to church, but they could be home any time." Deidre looked out the window. "The rain seems to have stopped, so let me go down to the beach."

She opened the door of the sunroom and went outside, then descended the long wooden stairs hugging the cliff, leading down to the beach. She had counted them, one hundred and twelve in all, with a landing and resting bench at step number fifty-five.

For the last few days, she'd been using the stairs for a cardio workout. Her legs were sore from the exercise, but if she was going to fight for herself, she needed to get mentally strong. For her, challenging herself physically was as much a mental thing as physical. Harry had offered her his bike to ride for exercise, knowing how much she loved riding. But biking wasn't as much of a challenge as the steps and besides, she feared being out on the road might leave her vulnerable to the press. For now, she'd stick to the stairs.

She stopped at the landing and put the phone to her ear. "I can talk now."

"Okay, but you might want to sit down." Mandy's voice sounded grave.

"Oh dear, what's going on?" Deidre grabbed the railing and sat down on the little bench.

"Have you heard from Kera, yesterday or today?"

"Oh, God, no. What now? I've been feeling so anxious, I just knew something horrible was going on."

"You didn't hear from the police? I'd thought they'd be at your place—I mean Harry's—looking for her, or at least asking you about her."

Deidre thought back to last night. She'd been sick—nerves, she was sure—and was throwing up a lot, until she finally fell asleep. "For God's sake, Mandy, what happened?"

"Well, Kera drove out to Sam's place yesterday. She was followed by an undercover cop who'd apparently been tailing her—in fact, I think I might have seen him at the gay bar the other night when I was there talking to her. Anyway, the cop waited outside in his car while Kera went into Sam's house. After a while he heard gunshots and went into the house and found Sam dead—and Kera gone. Kera must have left Sam's place on foot, apparently out the back way. No one has seen her since and now the cops are looking for her."

"Oh, my God, I can't believe it. Why did she go to Sam's?" Deidre could hardly breathe, like she had been kicked in the stomach.

"I told Kera Friday night about Sam threatening Don. She told me Saturday morning—uh, I stayed the night with her." Mandy cleared her throat. "Anyway, she said she was going to Sam's to check things out."

Deidre groaned. Her nightmare was getting worse. Oh God, what had Kera done?

Mandy continued, "I was concerned about her going there, of course, but I honestly wasn't all that worried. Kera can take care of herself. Damn it, she wasn't going there to kill him, just trying to get some information from Sam, I can guarantee you. If nothing else, her killing Sam would certainly be counterproductive." She stopped for a moment and then said, "That was a weird thing to say, I know, about killing a person, but it's true nonetheless, because Kera's trying to prove someone other than you or she killed Don. Why would she want to kill Sam?" She answered herself. "She wouldn't. It doesn't make any sense."

Deidre took note when she heard, "stayed the night," but filed it away for later. She was too worried about Kera's physical safety to be concerned—at this point—about her sister getting into a relationship she obviously wasn't ready for. "So Kera told you she was going out to Sam's, but as you said, certainly not to shoot him. Oh my God, I wish she hadn't done that. Something must have gone wrong, horribly wrong."

"I don't have all the information yet, but as I said, Kera told me she intended to check out his alibi. I don't know if the police have put much together about what happened yet, but apparently, the cop outside heard gunshots and that's why he decided to go into Sam's house. But the strange thing is, Sam didn't die of a gunshot wound. He died from having his throat cut. I don't know what to make of that. I'm having a hard time putting it together, but—"

"Oh, God!" Deidre's brain ran a red distress message across her nervous system: That's how Don died—a knife slitting his throat.

Deidre placed her elbows on her thighs, holding her head in her hands. She felt mentally paralyzed, like her brain had been tasered. Suddenly, her breakfast made its way up to her throat. She stood and heaved her egg omelet and toast over the stairway rail.

When the retching ended, she sat back down. "Mandy, tell me Kera had nothing to do with Sam's death or Don's. I know Iraq changed her, but she wouldn't...please tell me she wouldn't—"

"I know it looks bad, really bad, but hang in there. I don't...well, I don't want to believe Kera could do that kind of thing either. Look, at this point, we have no idea what went on at Sam's, but we have to believe she didn't kill him in cold blood, no matter how bad things look for her right now."

"Kera couldn't have done such a horrible thing. It's not in her, any more than it's in me. I don't care how emotionally injured she is." Deidre felt tears dripping down her cheeks. She pulled up the collar of her blouse to wipe her eyes. "Oh, Mandy, things are piling up against her...and me too. Besides you, Harry and Sylvia, we have no one supporting or helping us. The police will think it's an open-and-shut case. As Kera used to say: 'We've just been flushed down the toilet.'"

"I know things are looking bad, right now, but—"

Deidre interrupted, "Mandy, I wonder why the police didn't come to talk to me." She thought a moment, then said, "Maybe it was because I was sick and Harry and Sylvia knew Kera hadn't been over here. And Sylvia was with me all day, so she would know I hadn't heard from her…but still, why didn't they wake me this morning before they went to church? Guess they were trying to protect me, but still."

"I hate to dump everything on you like this, but I need to tell you something more. It's all going to come out soon and better you hear the news from me."

Deidre heard Mandy take a deep breath. Oh, God, how much more horror could she take?

Mandy went on, "The police now think Don was killed at the gay beach, then transported back to the church. They're saying he was murdered in the driver's seat, dragged over to the passenger's side, and apparently, the killer drove his body to the church. They found a wig, fake mustache and non-prescription eyeglasses either on Don or in his car, I'm not sure which."

Deidre tried to think about what that meant, but couldn't sort it out. Why would Don be at the gay beach? Had the murderer been in disguise? Made Don drive out to the beach, killed him, then drove him back to the church? But why? And who? She mulled over the facts, but nothing made sense to her.

Mandy was quiet on her end for a bit. At last, she said, "Another thing: my car was seen that night at the gay beach parking lot—"

Deidre interrupted. "What do you mean, your car was seen there?"

"I didn't drive it there. Kera did."

"What? I don't get it."

"Kera was at McFarland Park the night Don died. Remember, she stayed at my place that night."

"But why would she have your—"

"She told me later she couldn't sleep, so she took my car to the gay beach—she didn't have hers—while I was asleep. Kera said she'd wanted to sit on the beach and listen to the waves so she could calm herself. According to her, after sitting there a while, she got back in the car and was planning on returning to my place, but she was feeling really tired. She decided to sleep in the car for a while, but as things turned out, she pretty much spent the night there. She didn't get back to my place until early morning."

Deidre felt a second round of her omelet coming up. "Just a minute, Mandy, I—" She stood and dumped the rest of her breakfast over the rail. Her throat burned and her stomach felt like a food blender on high. She put her cell phone to her ear and heard Mandy speaking.

"Deidre, are you okay?"

"Not really…well, yeah, I'm okay…sort of."

"Oh, shit, I should have come over to talk to you in person. You shouldn't be alone now."

"Sorry, Mandy. My stomach doesn't deal well with stress." Deidre put her hand on her belly. The burning had started there, but she felt the acid blaze all the way up her esophagus.

"I'm at my office, I'll be over to pick you up in a few minutes."

"That'd be good, but I don't want to go back up to the house. Harry and Sylvia might have returned or will soon. I'll walk down the beach to the public access road and meet you there."

"Got ya. See you in about fifteen. I'm on my way out the door."

After Mandy ended the call, Deidre continued down the stairs. She pushed Kera's number on her speed dial. Kera didn't answer. The voice mail came on. She waited for the after-message beep. "Kera, this is Dee, I'm so worried about you, please call me as soon as you can."

She started walking on the beach toward the public access area. She stopped, took off her sandals and hiked along the shoreline near the water's edge where the sand was wet and hard-packed. The water lapped her feet, cooling them, but she wished she had something to cool down her racing mind. She couldn't hold one thought in her head for more than a moment without it being trampled on by the invasion of other thoughts, swirling in and confusing her.

Why had Don been at the gay beach parking lot? Had he strayed so far from any kind of mental health that he had taken to stalking gays? She didn't think he'd be out there to try and "cure" them. But if he were doing either one of those things, he certainly could have gotten himself in trouble.

The painful knowledge that Kera had been out there at exactly the same time pierced into her mind like the stab of a dull needle. "God," she murmured under her breath, "Kera was at the gay beach at the time of Don's death and now she's been placed at Sam's death too."

She decided she could allow herself to be ninety-five percent sure that Kera didn't do it. The five percent of doubt came from her fear that something as traumatic as Kera's experiences in Iraq might have changed her sister more than she'd thought.

The war might have pushed Kera over the edge, damaging her so badly she'd lost her ability to control her anger and frustration. Maybe Iraq had trained her to believe that killing settled things. Maybe killing had been put in her game book as a way of taking care of problems when they got too bad.

These thoughts were too painful, overwhelming her. She needed to switch to the positive ninety-five percent.

Kera had hated serving in Iraq. Deidre could read between the lines of her sister's correspondence. Kera didn't get off on war. In fact,

Kera really never mentioned anything much about killing. At one point, her sister had told her she didn't want to talk about it. What did that mean? Certainly Kera hated death. Didn't she? God, did she just slip back into her doubt? Apparently there was a little more than five percent of concern but she wasn't about to reevaluate. The process was too upsetting.

Deidre wondered how certain Mandy felt about Kera's innocence. Mandy didn't really know Kera like she did. But Kera and Mandy were obviously getting to know one another. How involved were they? She knew they were together on at least two nights.

Her mind flitted around like a moth on speed. Where was Kera? How come Kera hadn't called her? Kera must know she'd be upset, not knowing where she was, being left in the dark.

Two people getting their throats cut and Kera was at both places. What a horrible, ghoulish way to kill someone. She tried to stop herself from picturing it, but her mind seemed bent on terrorizing her by presenting her with images of how the murders could have happened. If she hadn't already lost her breakfast, more would have followed. As it was, she bent over, but nothing came out except a deep retching sound and remnants of hope.

She sat down in the sand, laid back and shaded her eyes from the sun, trying to focus on the gulls flying overhead. She needed some relief, if only for a few minutes, from the snake pit her life had slipped into. It was as though some all-powerful, demented editor had spliced in a big piece of someone else's misfortune into hers and Kera's life stories.

Deidre heard her name called. She sat up and saw Mandy walking down the shore toward her. She waved her over. "Hi, I'm sorry, but I am a little weak-kneed right now. I needed to rest for a while."

"No problem. I figured you'd be close by." Mandy sat down beside her. "You really look pale."

"I don't feel so well. Like I said, my mental condition expresses itself, physically—always has." She put her hand on her stomach. "I just can't understand why Kera hasn't called me. This is unlike her, really unlike her. After I talked to you, I tried to call her cell phone. She didn't answer, but I left her a voice mail to call me back. I don't suppose you have any idea where she is? Have you tried to call her yet?"

"Yes, I've tried to reach her, but she didn't answer my call either. I haven't a clue where she is or where she'd go. I keep hoping she'll call you or me." Mandy unscrewed the top from a bottle of water and took a drink. She pulled out another bottle from her purse and offered it to Deidre. "Here, I brought one for you and some medicine to settle your stomach." She rummaged around the bottom of her purse. "I take these sometimes when my stomach is upset. Thought they might help you."

"Thanks." Deidre shook out a couple of pills and downed them. "How did you get all this information about Sam's death? It wasn't in the morning papers." She screwed the cap on the bottle.

"I have some connections with the police and the District Attorney's office. Unfortunately, pretty much everything I've told you will be splattered all over tonight's news. They have every cop available looking for Kera. The press is all over this case and pretty soon reporters will be on you like ants on honey. At this point, it wouldn't be good for you to talk to them. You need some time to get your wits about you."

Deidre rolled her eyes, took a breath and let it out. "And how am I going to achieve that?" For the life of her, she couldn't picture herself having her "wits" about her, let alone finding the strength to talk to the press.

"You will," Mandy assured her. "I want you to feel stronger and surer of yourself when you eventually speak to reporters. I'll help you with what to say when the time comes. I'll be right by your side. We've been lucky, so far, Harry has kept them off you, but I don't know how long he'll be able to keep it up."

"I don't think I should ask Harry to shield me any longer. He's put his political career and business in jeopardy by being involved with me and letting me stay there. I need to leave soon. It's not fair to him or Sylvia. In fact, I think my presence at their home is causing friction between them. Harry is in such a sensitive situation being on the council, the church president, and his business. Me staying in their home is taking a toll on them and their relationship. They're good friends and I don't want to cause them more problems."

Mandy raised her eyebrows. "What about you assuring the DA you'd stay there with them? It wasn't a condition of your release, in any way, but—"

"I can't worry about that right now and I doubt he'll find out, really, but whatever. I've got to get out of there." Deidre was at her wit's end. Somehow, she thought, worrying about a promise to the DA was at the bottom of her list of things concerning her, besides, it wasn't any kind of legal commitment she'd made to him.

Mandy brushed some hair from her eyes. "Where could you go? I would have you come and stay with me, but I'm expecting the press to be all over me, too, given I'm the lawyer."

"I don't know. I can't just take off somewhere. I need to be around here for Kera, even if I don't know where she is. At this moment, I can't say what I'll do. I'll have to think about it, I guess."

Deidre stretched out on the sand. She crossed her arms over her eyes to keep the sun out, wishing she knew how to keep the world out, at least long enough for her to find her sister. Thoughts of Don being at the gay beach came back to her. "Mandy, you didn't say how the police figured out Don was killed at the gay park."

"Someone saw his vehicle there. A guy came forward after the photo of Don's car—or loaner vehicle, I should say—was pictured in the newspaper. When the police went to investigate, they found tire tracks matching the vehicle. They also found Kera's watch in the sand somewhere on the beach—a watch Kelly had given to her. Kera's and Kelly's names were engraved on the back, so it was easily identifiable. They couldn't figure out how Kera got to the beach that night until they talked to me and found out she had taken my car. I can't tell you how much I hated having to give them the information, but what else could I say?"

Deidre took her arms off her eyes and turned her head toward Mandy. She saw the woman searching her face, undoubtedly looking for a sign of absolution from her. "I don't blame you. Like you said, what else could you have told them?"

"I know, but it made me feel like I was helping the police incriminate Kera—and of course, I was."

"I understand. I really do. You had to tell them the truth." Deidre got to her feet. "I need to get back to figuring out where I'm going, but before I can go anywhere, I have to get back to Sylvia's and get my stuff. I want to be out of there before they come back from church. Hopefully, I'm not too late. With any luck, they'll have gotten involved with church stuff, or gone to brunch with some of their church friends. They sometimes do that. If I'm still there, I know Sylvia will try and keep me from leaving."

"Do you have any ideas where you could go?"

"Not at the moment. I'll try to figure that out as I pack. I need to be someplace where Kera could find me if she tried. Good thing I finally went home and got my car the other day." Deidre bent over and grabbed her sandals. "Thanks for coming and for the pills." She turned toward the Janssen's house and started walking back.

"Be careful and stay in touch," Mandy yelled after her. "You know the police will be watching you, expecting Kera to show up—or hoping you'll lead them to her."

CHAPTER TWENTY

Kera

Yuck. Kera ran into a cobweb—a sticky, massive one, clinging to her face like cotton candy. She used her wet shirtsleeve to wipe the spider's dwelling off her face—at least most of it. Without a window, light was sparse, only narrow streams of daylight seeped through small cracks between the wall planks of the old shed.

It had started to rain after she'd left Vinny's. Without a vehicle, she'd hoofed it, trying not to look like someone leaving the scene of a crime—like she was doing—and staying out of view of roaming cop cars until she reached her current sanctuary. Her clothes were soaked, along with the rest of her. Her hair dripped and her shoes squished when she walked. Inside the shed, she heard water dripping from a leak in the roof, each drop pinging as it splashed on the hull of an overturned metal canoe resting on cinderblocks.

For hours, she'd been sitting on the floor of the shed, periodically getting up to stretch her legs. The wait for nightfall seemed endless, but she needed the cover of darkness to conceal her planned escape up the river.

She checked the time on her cell phone because she'd lost her watch, but had no idea where or when. If she ever got out of this mess, she'd look for it. The watch was precious to her because it was a gift from Kelly.

The shed was clearly home to a family of mice, probably several families given the number she'd heard scurrying around. She figured she must be considered part of the décor by now as the mice felt free to scamper over her legs and up her back. She wasn't as bothered by them as much as she was by the spiders that found her appealing. She itched from the snacks they'd made of her.

Kera hoped Jim wouldn't need anything from the shed anytime soon, or notice the padlock was missing. His shed was the best—actually only—place she'd thought of to hide until sundown.

In her high school years, she'd worked summers for Jim's Canoe Livery. Fortunately, Jim still hid the key to the rickety shed in the same old place. Even back then, he rarely opened the shed, only using it for storing worn-out things his wife claimed needed to be thrown away, but he couldn't bear to discard.

Kera heard people speaking outside. She sat down from her stretch and listened, recognizing Jim's voice immediately.

"Nope, haven't seen her," Jim said. "In fact, I'd say I haven't seen her since she went off to Iraq…no, let me think, maybe it was sometime when she was home from college. Gosh darn, to be truthful, I just couldn't exactly tell ya. I mean, I could have seen Deidre and thought it was Kera, never really could tell them girls apart. They was both good workers, though, I can tell you that much."

She heard footsteps coming closer to the shed and stopping just short of the door.

Another male voice said, "Well, thanks anyway. Here, Jim, would you call this number if you happen to see her?"

"It says here you're a detective. What you want with Kera?"

"Oh, just need to talk to her."

She held her breath. Were they going to open the shed or not? She tried to decide if she should move over and get under the upturned tipped-over canoe. The problem was, she'd risked making noise if she tripped over or kicked something.

"Hey, by the way, what's in that old shed there?" Kera suddenly realized the voice belonged to Detective Brown.

"Good stuff. My wife call's it junk, though." Jim laughed. His voice and laughter were gravelly, probably from his years of smoking.

"Do you mind if I take a peek?"

"Sure enough, I don't go in here much, but you're welcome to take a gander."

Kera slipped beneath the canoe just as she heard the tug on the shed's door. *Wow, that was close.* She almost hadn't made it under in time.

"I don't know what happened to the lock I had on here. Just old things I save in this place, but mostly spiders, mice and probably a snake or two." Jim chuckled. "Heck, you can't never trust these kids today. They can't remember nothing, especially putting things back or locking things up like they're supposed to. Someone probably put that lock in their pocket and forgot to put it back on the door. Kids, they don't pay attention, but what ya gonna do?"

The door creaked open, bringing a blast of light into the shed.

"You can look in, but I'll tell you what, you won't find anyone in there. Ain't fit for humans."

"I think you're right about that. Looks like you store mostly cobwebs in there," Brown chuckled.

Kera heard things being moved around.

"Well, well, would you look at that old paint can anchor," Brown said. "My dad filled a paint can with cement like that when I was a kid. We used it for our swimming raft we had out in the lake. I haven't thought about that raft in some time. We kids had a great time with it in the summer."

"Yup, never know when I'll need that again—you can always use an anchor, living on the water. And that old canoe back there, she leaks like a sieve, but the metal could come in handy someday. In fact, I hear scrap metal is goin' for a pretty penny these days, especially aluminum." Jim coughed and spat. "Lots of unique valuables in here if you can get past the spider's work to get to 'em."

"Okay, I guess I've seen enough."

The door slammed shut.

"I'm going to have to buy a new lock, I guess." She heard Jim say as he moved off. "I'm sure no one around here will know where it went."

* * *

The night had grown dark enough to take off and hopefully not be seen.

Kera tied her tennis shoes to the belt loops of her jeans and slipped into the river. She wished she could take off her jeans. It'd sure make swimming a lot easier, but then she wouldn't have any pants when she got out on land. She'd just have to deal with it. The water was warmer than she'd thought, but she remembered water always felt warmer at night because of the cooler air temperature.

She was relieved to be out of the shed and on her way up the river. She had eaten the peanut butter and jam sandwich and apple Vinny had given her earlier, though she was still hungry. Luckily, he kept a supply of food at his shop.

She figured she had a little over five miles to go upstream to get to Moran's house, if she could make it that far. Her shoulder hurt a lot and she had to swim against the current, but there'd be places she could pull out and rest.

Could she get there without being seen? Though Jim's Canoe Livery was closed now, there would most likely be a few private boats out on the river. She knew as she made her way farther inland from the lake, people could see the river from their big bay windows, or might be outside taking in the cooling breeze.

Maybe when she got to her dad's place, she could get her old canoe and take it the rest of the way if no one was around, especially cops. They'd probably be watching the house—not a good idea to stop there. She told herself to be patient. She couldn't afford to make a mistake and end up in jail.

She'd been moving upstream for about an hour—in and out of the water—when she heard the engines, then she saw flickers of light bouncing off the water around her. She turned onto her back to get a better view. The lights of several motorboats perforated the night, threatening to reveal her. She was more vulnerable now she was out in the middle of the river on her way to the other side. She'd been moving back and forth, depending on which bank provided more cover for her. The motorboats must have pulled out from the canal she'd passed about ten minutes back.

She now saw three speedboats swerving left and right over the middle of the river like a pack of water-skimmers injected with caffeine.

Kera calculated she probably didn't have time to make it to either bank to avoid the onslaught. On the other hand, staying in one place, treading water, and hoping for the best was a crapshoot. She kept swimming in the direction she had been heading, pushing herself hard. She heard voices laughing and yelling, sounding like a flotilla of teenage partiers.

In her experience, kids in boats didn't pay attention. They tended to be reckless and didn't look out for others on the water—not that she could be easily seen in the dark. People piloting the crafts wouldn't even be thinking about someone swimming at this time of night, especially without some kind of floatation device.

She'd been part of the party scene when she was a teen. The thought brought back the memory of Shawn Simmons, a good friend of hers. He'd died one night during a party held at his house, not far from here on the river. His parents had left for the weekend. Shawn had declared it was party time at the Simmons' home. After numerous kegs, shared by about fifty kids—herself included—Shawn and some guys decided to take out his dad's boat.

What exactly happened that night was never made clear. She'd heard two different stories. In the first, Shawn had decided to do a flip-dive into the water from the deck of the boat while it was still moving and hit his head on the side of the vessel, apparently knocking him out as he splashed to his death. In the other version of the story, Shawn and his friend, David Langdon, had gotten into an argument that turned physical. David punched Shawn, sending him overboard.

The police got the first story, but later, the second story emerged from several of the guys who had been on the boat at the time.

They never found Shawn's body. She kept having an eerie feeling that she might see him or bump into him on the river, as though after all these years, his body would be still whole, and his eyes would stare at her. Ridiculous. She kept reminding herself the river wasn't the icy water of Lake Superior where bodies were known to be preserved. Still, she couldn't shake the feeling, even now, and every time any part of her body hit something solid in the water, she was creeped out.

The engines grew louder and the streams of light brighter, locking on to her path. It was time. She took a deep breath, dove down, looking for refuge in the depth of the water. Pushing down, deeper and deeper, searching for the bottom, she found a rock lodged on the river's floor. She grabbed it, hung on, anchoring herself.

Vibrations came from the boat motors overhead. Damn, directly over her in fact. Why didn't those kids go home? It was raining, for god's sake. Apparently, they didn't care. At that age, she probably wouldn't have cared either.

She tried to will the boats to move on, wondering how long she could hang there holding her breath.

Her hands slid off the slippery rock and she started floating upward. She pushed herself down again, finding and gripping the slick anchor.

Her lungs screamed. Any second, she'd have to let out the stale air she held in her lungs. If she didn't surface for fresh air, the water would fill her up, just like the river had taken Shawn years ago.

She had to get to the air, soon. Were the boats leaving? She thought so, or was she just hoping? No matter, she needed oxygen regardless of what awaited her.

She released her grip, swam up and broke through the water's surface, blowing out air like a breaching whale, then sucking in fresh.

The stern of the last boat was visible about ten feet from her position. She heard the kids continuing their raucous party. The other boats were well on their way, headed in another direction. Hopefully, they wouldn't circle around and come back, rejoining the last boat.

Just when she thought the nearby boat would never leave, it's engine revved and it soared out after the others, carrying the loud party down river.

Exhausted, Kera flipped over so she could float on her back and rest her arms and aching shoulder. She paddled with her feet to the river's bank and pulled herself out of the river, water pouring off her as she stepped ashore.

She ran her hands up and down her arms, trying to warm herself from the cool night air, Her clothes sucked up against her body, skintight and seemingly vacuum-sealed. She had been running on automatic, not feeling, moving in survival mode. She sat down on a rock, cuddling herself with her arms tucked around her midsection.

The horror of her life came at her in a whirlpool of fear. Her shivering turned to trembling. No meds on her, nothing to stop the moving pictures haunting her mind or the future that threatened her, nothing to take the edge off her runaway life with no off-ramp in sight.

She was just waiting for the crash.

An owl hooted close by. She listened. *Imagining things, no doubt… no, there it was again.* If it were an owl, that would be a good sign—for her, anyway, or at least it always had been. In some Native American cultures, the owl was a bad sign portending death. But the owl was Moran's power animal and had come to her several times in the past when she'd needed help. Was the bird here to help her this time?

Once, when she'd been hiking and inadvertently about to come between a mother bear and her two cubs, an owl had appeared on a branch right in front of her. The sight of the magnificent bird stopped her in her tracks. While she'd stood quietly observing the bird, she caught sight of a mother bear crossing the path about twenty feet ahead of her. The bear was heading for her cubs who were playing on the other side of the trail. Had Kera kept walking, she would have found herself between the cubs and their mother, a place no one should ever be.

Another time, she only heard an owl, but never saw it. She still didn't even know if Iraq had owls. Nonetheless, that night she'd decided to divert her platoon from their chosen path to a secondary route based solely on her interpretation of the owl's cry. She'd heard it as a warning about the road. Her decision to change the route proved to be the right one. She learned later that the next platoon, taking the planned route she'd abandoned, had been ambushed and only two soldiers had survived.

The owl hooted again.

Yes, she was almost certain she'd heard it.

She couldn't see anything, but she heard a fluttering noise like the bird had just moved closer to her.

Was she imagining things? Maybe she was hallucinating from fatigue.

The rain had stopped, but the clouds hid the glow from the stars. She was too far upriver for any light from the city and there weren't any homes on this section of the river. She turned her head toward the spot where she thought she'd heard the owl.

A strange, warm, soothing breath of air gently blew over, in and through her as if she were porous, calming her body and spirit, allowing her to stop shaking. She suddenly felt infused with new resolve and fresh life.

It was owl's doing, she was sure.

She inhaled the last drop of the owl's energy and slipped back into the water.

She figured she had a little over five miles to go upstream to get to Moran's house. The thought of trying to get her old canoe came to her again. The canoe was certainly ready to go. She had planned on going for a ride in "Sadie" the day she took Dee to emergency care. Damn, if she could just get the canoe without being seen, her trip to Moran's would be easier. She told herself to be careful. She didn't want to do something stupid.

Exhaustion could give birth to bad decisions.

* * *

The clouds finally moved on, releasing light from the night sky.

Kera saw Sadie's sleek, dark figure waiting on the bank. Seeing her beloved canoe was akin to having a chocolate ice cream cone dangled in front of her, but she feared the consequences of trying to grab it.

She swam through the cattails, moving slowly while trying to get a better view of her dad's house. She felt like she was coming home from long ago.

There had been many good times for her family on the long, glassed-in porch on the riverside of the home. In summer, the windows stayed open, allowing the breezes to cool them. Her memory echoed with the laughter of her mother, aunt and grandmother as they sat on the glider swapping recipes and telling family stories. She saw her dad, uncle and grandfather playing horseshoes and heard the ringing of the U-shaped iron crashing into the metal post.

She saw Dee and their cousins from Pennsylvania doing cartwheels under the spray of a water sprinkler. She felt herself running out the screened door to join them and heard her mother yelling, "Don't let the door slam!" Mother's plea had come too late. It most always did. The screened door slammed back on its frame.

For the first time since her father's death, she understood the house and memories were just hers and Dee's now. There was no longer any Mother, Father, or for that matter, no other family members to validate, add to, or correct their recollections. Her grandparents had died in their midsixties. Her aunt—her mother's sister—was killed in an auto accident two years before her mother died. Her uncle remarried a woman from England, moved there and took her cousins with him. Who knew what became of them? Her family had been torn apart and scattered—dead and alive. Other than Dee, the only pieces of the family remaining for her were sensory imprints.

Kera took in a deep breath and blew it out. Her memories vanished, propelling the door-slamming girl of her recollection into the woman, running from the cops while trying to clear her and her sister's names. She needed to concentrate on survival and on what was left of her family, as well as getting back its honor and integrity, like gluing back the broken pieces of a priceless family heirloom.

After she spent about ten minutes not seeing any movement around the house, Kera climbed the bank and went into the high weeds. Still nothing, no movement or signs of life. She crept around the perimeter of the property, staying out of sight by using the heavily treed areas around the house for cover.

The door to a small screened porch on the side of the house stood slightly ajar. Was someone in there or had she forgotten to close it tightly? When she'd first come home, she'd noticed the door needed repair since it wouldn't stay shut without engaging the lock. But she thought she'd pulled the door closed and locked it. Maybe not. She was so preoccupied these days, she could have easily forgotten.

There didn't seem to be any lights on in the house, which looked empty. The door from the inside porch to the kitchen appeared closed. She knew that door was locked, or at least she knew she had locked it before leaving last time.

Kera decided to go around to the roadside and check there. The long driveway wound around in the shape of an S so the house couldn't be seen from the road. She slunk from tree to tree, stopping at each to make sure she hadn't been noticed.

Creeping around her property this way took her back to her army basic training, but she felt naked without a weapon. She remembered her father had a deer-hunting rifle, probably still downstairs in the case. She tried to think where he kept the key. Oh, yeah, in his desk drawer. She remembered seeing the key when she'd been going through his papers. That was when she'd found Dee's incriminating letter to Dad. If she could only go back in time, she would destroy that letter, damn it. But how in hell could she have guessed what was about to come down on her and Dee?

Her mind flipped back to the rifle. She decided she really didn't need a weapon, not right now anyway. What she most needed was Sadie, her beloved canoe, her ticket—or at least her fighting chance—to get to a safe place.

She spotted a car parked out on the road about one house down. The car was positioned so the driver had a view of any comings and goings to the house.

She inched nearer to the car, hunching down as she reached the high weeds near the road's edge. A man sat in the driver's side of the unmarked car. The cops were waiting for her all right, but they were apparently expecting her via road, not river. They probably thought no one would try to swim upriver against the current. They didn't know her. Hell, going against the current was beginning to be a fucking metaphor for her life. She didn't see anyone else, but she needed to be careful, not get complacent. The police may have placed lookouts along the riverbanks.

Kera observed the car's driver. She guessed she'd been keeping an eye on his car about ten minutes and was fairly certain he was just monitoring the place, checking to see if anyone might show up. How long had he been there before she saw him? She figured if he wanted to search the house, he would have done it already.

She decided she'd chance getting Sadie and take her out on the river. She was exhausted, cold, and her shoulder hurt from having to swim for so long. Hell, without the canoe, she might not make it.

Slipping out of the weeds, she found the cover of the trees and made her way back toward the house. Her stomach growled from hunger. All she'd had to eat that whole day was a bagel for breakfast, a sandwich and an apple. Her swim up the river to her house left her feeling starved. If she could just sneak into the house to get something to eat, that would hold her over until she got to Moran's.

She didn't think she could get in through the small side porch. Though the screened door was open, the main door from the porch into the kitchen part of the house would be locked and she didn't have the key. She didn't want to go in the roadside door in case the guy did get out of the car and walked up the driveway. That left her the side door by the garage on the opposite side of the house—well hidden from view by the trees and couldn't be seen from the driveway. She made her way over and unlocked the door and stepped in onto the stair landing that was halfway between the basement and the main floor hallway.

She noticed a flashlight sitting on the ledge leading down to the basement. She grabbed it and switched it on. Spotting an old rag hanging from the stair rail, she put it over the head of the flashlight to dull the illumination.

She climbed up the steps from the landing to the hallway, and from there crept into the dining room. Her foot kicked an empty beer bottle, startling her as it rolled across the hardwood floor. She stopped, took a breath, then picked it up and set it on the dining table before moving into the kitchen.

She tried to remember what food she could quickly grab and be on her way. There wasn't much in the house because she hadn't done a complete grocery shopping, only picked up things here and there. When she opened the refrigerator, the light came on. She hadn't ever realized how bright the light was. She quickly unscrewed the bulb, then searched the fridge with her flashlight: ketchup, mustard, salad dressings, A-1 Sauce, rotten lettuce, dried up oranges, beer, slice of dried out pizza. That was about it. Nothing edible. Her eyes retraced their scan, hoping she'd overlooked something. She considered taking a swig of ketchup, but she wasn't that desperate.

Kera opened the pantry door. At that exact moment, she heard a noise from the direction of the small, screened porch. Someone was there. The door had been left open, she'd seen that from the outside, but hadn't bothered to check it out before hitting the refrigerator.

Dumb, Dumb, Dumb!

Why hadn't she just grabbed her canoe and gotten the hell out of this place?

Ducking down, she slipped through the house, made her way to her dad's study, got to his desk and retrieved the key to his gun case. She moved back to the hallway, making her way down the stairs to the basement. The shells were right where they had always been kept under the gun cabinet. She removed the rifle from the case, loaded it and returned upstairs to the kitchen.

She moved to the door leading out to the screened porch and put her ear to the solid core door. The only way to check for intruders on that porch was for her to either open the door or sneak around the outside of the house and look in through the screen. But if she went outdoors, she didn't know who might be there. Someone could be waiting for her.

She heard more noises, a soft shuffling sound from the porch that seemed to come from close to the door.

Kera put her hand on the doorknob and pushed the door open, the stock of the rifle under her arm and her finger on the trigger. She moved the barrel left and right as she moved through the doorway. The sound came from the left, behind the far side of a utility closet her father had built for her mother's garden tools.

Not wanting to turn on the light or even use the flashlight for fear of alerting the man in the car—or anyone else who might be lurking out there—Kera swung the rifle around, pointing it where she thought she'd heard the sound, thinking whoever had broken into her house must be crouched down in the corner.

"Come out of there or I'll start shooting." Kera was mostly bluffing. The last thing she wanted to do was blast the night with the sound of a gunshot. If it came to defending herself, more than likely she'd take the butt of the rifle and pummel whoever was on the other side of the closet before running for the river. The relatively small area meant not more than one person could be hiding there.

She warned, "You've got five seconds to show your face before I—"

A furry dark mass flew out from behind the closet, dashed through the open screen door, down the steps and into the night, leaving remnants of bird suet in its wake.

A damned fucking raccoon. A big one at that. She was glad her army buddies weren't there to see her threatening a poor raccoon with a rifle.

She let the barrel of the gun drop down and wiped her forehead with her arm.

She went to the kitchen, but wasn't feeling that hungry anymore. She needed to get the hell out of there. On the kitchen counter, she spied an unopened box of Zone bars she had bought. She grabbed the box, laid the rifle on the table, found her boat paddle propped up in the corner of the porch and ran for the river.

She pushed her canoe out into the water, jumped in, and headed for Moran's place.

As she paddled along, relieved to be back on her way, Kera was thinking about Moran. The old woman got overlooked by the citizens of Lakeside City, or maybe just forgotten—that'd be the best scenario.

After retiring from teaching at the college, Moran had retreated to her house and ten acres of land. She had never been exactly in the midst of the Lakeside City's social life. She didn't fit in to the Dutch Reformed scene. The only people who paid much attention to her were the out-of-towners who came in search of a shaman. She had quite a reputation in the shaman community as a spiritual healer. People traveled great distances to see her, but in Lakeside City, she went unnoticed except when she rode her bicycle, toting groceries in the back and front baskets.

Kera knew Moran wasn't seen as someone special, not like she saw her, but more of a town oddity, around for so long the locals ignored her. Moran was part of the hometown landscape like the old fire station museum, or the town's Statue of the Lost Sailor, or the gulls perched on top of dock posts.

She didn't like having to call on Moran for help, putting the woman in any kind of jeopardy by staying with her, but she was short on options.

Fortunately, Moran was pretty isolated from the community and her place was not easily seen from her neighbors' houses. The way Kera figured it, no one should notice her there. Moran most likely wouldn't know—and she wasn't about to tell her—that the cops were after her, at least not until she was ready to leave. To her knowledge, Moran never read newspapers, didn't own a TV, and only occasionally listened to the radio, so she could plead complete ignorance if need be.

Still, Kera would need to get out of there as soon as possible. She didn't like Moran being put in the position of hiding a fugitive, whether she knew it or not.

Oh, god, a fugitive. That's what she was, wasn't she?

CHAPTER TWENTY-ONE

Deidre

Deidre knew she was being followed. In her rearview mirror, she saw a car pull out as she left the driveway and follow her down the road. The car tailed her all the way to the Out-and-About bar. She wasn't exactly surprised she was being followed, but it was unnerving.

She felt desperate. She had to find Kera. She wasn't expecting her to be at the gay bar—certainly Kera would know not to show up at the Out-And-About. However, someone there might have an idea of her whereabouts.

She wondered if the police had planted someone inside the bar? Surely their department didn't have a large enough staff to be following her, as well as placing undercover cops everywhere she or her sister might go. After all, this wasn't Detroit or Chicago. She was probably just being overly paranoid.

The cop following her would probably peek into the bar and see that her sister wasn't there. Then, he'd hang out until she returned to her car, hoping she'd lead him to Kera. And that was going to be a problem: finding Kera without leading the cop straight to her.

But she was getting ahead of herself. First, she needed some idea of how to go about locating Kera. Right now, she didn't have a clue.

The bar wouldn't be that busy on a Monday night, but she had to start looking somewhere. Sitting by herself in her house and trying to think of places Kera might have gone wasn't getting her anywhere.

For her, having to stay in the home she'd shared with Don seemed like inhabiting another world, in another time, another state of awareness; a place where she had withered and worse, lost her way. Getting out of the environment and searching for her sister helped her emotionally, even if she didn't know exactly what to do.

She thought about the terrifying mess she and Kera were in. Would life ever be the same again? Of course not, how could it be? What a predicament. She didn't want to go back to the way things were, but she was scared of going forward. She sighed.

Kera was the brave one, not her. But, she reminded herself, they had the same identical genes, so she must have it in her to be brave too. However, if she were to assume everything was identical between them, she'd have to believe they had identical genes for their sexual orientation as well. Apparently not. Ever since Kera came out about her sexuality, the lingering question remained wedged between them like a cruel joke. The medical profession pronounced them monozygotic—and they looked like physical duplicates. From the "same cookie cutter," their mother used to say.

Whose life was a lie? She thought she knew the answer. So did Kera.

In fact, that's what they'd been asking each other ever since Kera came out. At the time she'd accused her sister of being rebellious, wanting to shock people. In time, she finally came to realize if that were true, if she truly was trying to upset others, Kera wouldn't have kept her sexuality a secret from almost everyone for so long.

Kera, on the other hand, had suspicions about her "supposed heterosexuality." Kera had accused her of "acting straight," because she was a pleaser and a peacemaker and couldn't handle admitting to herself that she was, in fact, gay. Kera used to accuse her of squeezing herself into heterosexuality, like cramming her feet into too-small shoes. Later, Kera had added that she'd taken Don and his version of Christianity to bind her there. Kera really knew how to piss her off.

Deidre pulled her thoughts back to the present; she needed to concentrate on finding Kera. She couldn't believe Kera would go to Sam's house with the idea of killing him. No, something had to have gone horribly wrong.

Though Kera was no longer a Christian, that didn't make her a bad person even if Don had thought otherwise. Deidre knew Kera was a truly moral and spiritual person. Her sister hated killing. She talked to plants, even trees. Kera used to walk around ants on sidewalks. She remembered when she was a kid, Kera would find baby birds fallen from their nests and nurse them back to health. She used to call her sister Saint Frances of the Riverside. That kind of background surely didn't make someone who'd up and kill another person.

Except maybe Kera had changed in Iraq.

Kera didn't really talk to her about what'd happened over there. She never wrote about it in her letters—what few there were—and avoided war stories in her e-mails and phone calls home.

Deidre knew Kera had killed. She didn't know how she knew, she just knew—identical twins know. For certain, she could tell how traumatized Kera had become, no doubt because of her experiences there. Who wouldn't be?

Oh, crap, she realized she'd flipped her position, making a case for Kera's possible character transformation and describing someone capable of killing thanks to war. Well, if Iraq had changed Kera, she still would support her sister and fight for her. Sam's death would not come between them, no doubt about that. Damn that stupid war! Who could be part of it without being disfigured, one way or another? And now the war had left its scar on the one person she loved most.

She pulled into the bar's parking lot. The stone castle-type building somewhat intimidated her. The interior was probably dark and damp, like places where scary movies were filmed, but the bar was also a "gay place." Kera being gay was one thing, but to be in a room full of gay people…she'd never experienced that before. She knew she was being ridiculous, probably homophobic. Didn't homophobia mean fear of gays? She needed to get a grip, as Kera would say, and get on with it.

The car following her had passed by the parking lot and pulled over to the curb about a half a block ahead of her. She took a deep breath and got out of her car.

As she walked inside, the female bartender dressed in period garb looked up at her and yelled, "Hey, Kera."

Deidre walked over to the bar. "I'm not Kera. I'm Deidre, her sister."

"Oh. Can't tell you guys apart, especially since I'm not expecting you in this place. But I do know you. And you know me. Don't you remember? I'm Ally, Ally Davis. You helped me when I was in the hospital last year, I—"

"Oh, yes, I do remember you. I thought you looked familiar. We found you that apartment over on Maple. How are you doing?" Deidre pulled out a barstool and sat down. Seeing someone she knew made her feel better.

"Doing fine. I really appreciated all you did for me when I was getting out of the hospital. You went above and beyond for me." Ally cocked her head. "Boy, oh, boy, what happened to your nose? I didn't notice at first. The light's so dim in here."

"I broke it. My nose is actually looking a little better now." She didn't feel like going into how the injury happened. "If you don't mind, though, I'd rather not talk about that at the moment."

"No problem." Ally wiped off the bar counter with her rag. "I'm sorry to hear about the trouble you and your sister have been going through. I want you both to know I don't believe a word of the stuff they're saying against you in the papers. Nobody in here believes it, or at least nobody I've heard of. You and your sister got a lot of support around here."

"That's good to hear. We need all the support we can get. Speaking of that, I came here because I'm looking for Kera. By any chance, have you seen her?"

"Not recently. Let me think…oh, yeah, the last time I saw her was last Thursday night when she and Vinny were playing pool."

Deidre sighed. "I've got to find her before the police do. I just know she didn't kill Sam Zander. I don't know what happened between Sam and her, but she's not a killer." Her stomach churned.

"Who's this Sam Zander, anyway? I read about the murder, but—"

"He attended Don's church."

"Why in hell do they think your sister killed that guy?"

"Because she was at his home on Saturday, the day he was killed."

"Holy shit! The paper didn't say anything about Kera being there, just that the cops were looking for someone 'of interest,' I think they said."

"Ally, she didn't kill him. I know it looks bad, but Kera isn't a killer. I know her. Something must have gone wrong, terribly wrong. I need to find out what happened. For some reason, Kera took off from Sam's house and no one has seen her since. Now the police are looking for her."

"Can I get you a drink on the house? Seems to me like you could use one."

"Thank you for the offer, but I need to keep a clear head. I'll take a Diet Pepsi. I need caffeine, not alcohol." Deidre plopped her purse on the bar.

"Coming up." Ally put a glass under the dispenser.

"Do you have any idea where Kera might have gone? Like did she hang out with anyone much, someone I could talk to who might know. I'm at a loss as to where to even start." Deidre put her elbows on the bar and rested her chin on her fisted hands.

"Let me think." Ally rubbed her forehead. "The only person I know of was Mandy…what's her last—"

"Bakker?"

"Yeah, Mandy Bakker—shouldn't forget her last name. She's a big activist around here. I'm so bad with names. Oh, and Vinny. They sometimes call him Maryland. Anyway, Vinny is the guy she played pool with the other night. Oh, yeah, and Kevin, the real estate dude." Ally called to a waiter who was wiping down tables, "Hey, Dave, what's Kevin's—you know, the real estate guy—what's his last name?"

"Do you mean, Kevin McNeil? He's the only Kevin in real estate I know."

Ally thought a second. "Yeah, that's him. Thanks, Dave. I'm sure that's who it is, Kevin McNeil." Ally poured nuts in a dish and placed it on the bar.

"Anyone else?" Deidre asked.

Ally set a glass of Diet Pepsi on the bar in front of her. "I know Kera talked to people she was playing against in the pool tournament, but during those games—as far as I could tell—it's pretty much just kibitzing. They get pretty serious about their games when it's a tournament. Not much in the way of socialization, you might say."

"Well, Mandy doesn't know where Kera is." Deidre sighed. "Tell me about Vinny and Kevin. Do you know where I could find either of them?"

"Vinny owns that gun and knife shop out on the Blue Star Highway. Don't know where he lives, though. You could probably find him at his shop. He does come in here quite regularly on Thursday nights. He likes to play in the pool tournaments. He's here on other nights too, but it's random."

Deidre opened her purse and took out a small tablet and a pen. "What about Kevin? What's his last name again?"

"McNeil." Ally waited for her to write down the name. "He comes in here now and again. Let me think…he works with that real estate company, uh, the Janssen Group. Yeah, that's the name."

"Oh, that Kevin. I know him. Sort of, anyway. He works with Harry Janssen. I didn't know his last name or that he's gay."

"He's a real closet case." Ally looked at the door, focusing on some guys coming in carrying clothes on hangers and small suitcases.

"Hey, gals, I opened the dressing rooms up. Let me know if you need anything." She gestured toward a door at the back of the bar.

"Thank you, dear." One of the guys blew Ally a kiss.

"Tonight's our drag show night, gets people out on Mondays," Ally explained, turning her attention back to Deidre. "You know, I think it would be okay to tell you this, given Kera's in trouble and all. When Kera was in here last, she asked me to keep an eye out for anything that might come up regarding Don's death. You know, like if anyone was overly excited or talking about Don, being killed that is. Oh, I'm sorry, Deidre, I don't mean to be insensitive to your loss, but Don was—as you can probably guess—no friend to the gay community."

"I understand, go on." These days, she didn't know how she felt about Don. Mostly she was numb when it came to him. Maybe because she had so much else to worry about, there wasn't room for her feelings about him.

"Well, if anyone was acting suspicious, or like if they were overly happy or bragging about doing anything to Don, she wanted me to tell her about it. So I told her I would keep an eye out."

"Did you hear anything?"

"Well…"

Deidre realized Ally was hesitant to say something to her. "What is it, Ally? Please, anything, anything that might help me find Kera or figure out who killed Don, please tell me."

Ally seemed to study her. "It's about Don. You don't know, do you? Fuck."

"Know what? What about Don?"

"Aw, shit, I don't want to be the one to tell you." Ally had a sick look on her face. She wiped the bar, a section she'd already done.

Deidre prodded on, "Ally, what is it?" She had a bad feeling she was knocking on a door she'd rather keep closed. A chill ran through her body, like the time when her father came to the school, pulled her and Kera out of class and took them to the school counselor's room to tell them their mother had died. And now, she knew she wasn't going to like what she was about to hear. Her body stiffened.

Ally opened her mouth but nothing came out. Finally, she said, "Kevin was in here one night really drunk and started bragging about beating Don up at the gay beach." She took a deep breath and went on. "It wasn't the night of Don's death, but sometime before then." She went back to wiping the already clean bar surface.

"So Don had been out there before?"

Ally glanced at her. "Apparently, yes."

Deidre shook her head. "When I found out where he was murdered, I couldn't believe it. The only thing I could come up with was that he was out there trying to do his converting thing on gays. But even when I thought that…well, I just couldn't believe he'd do something so stupid, but I guess he did."

"Shit. You really don't know, do you?"

Deidre, feeling confused, looked at Ally. "Know what?"

"Okay, maybe Kevin was just running his mouth, but converting gays is not what he claimed Don was doing. Deidre, I can't tell you how much I hate being the one telling you this, but he was out at the gay beach doing exactly what all the gay boys who go out there do."

Deidre felt her mouth drop open.

"I'm so sorry, I really am…"

"Oh, God, no. I don't believe that. He hated gays. Everybody knows that. Maybe Kevin lied, you know, to make himself…I don't know what." She slumped and cradled her head in her hands. Good God, how much more could she take? Too much to take in, to grasp. An overflow threatening to spill out of her.

Ally was quiet. The music in the bar grew louder with Liza Minnelli belting out the lyrics to a song from *Cabaret*.

Deidre held her head with one hand, and put her other hand over her mouth, as though she could hold back the horror fermenting in her head and in her stomach. She closed her eyes, trying to pull away from invading pictures playing, uninvited, in her head: pictures of Kera at Sam's, pictures of Don at the gay beach.

Somehow, she told herself, she needed to block these images threatening to consume and paralyze her. She had to move beyond it all. Get on the other side of her horror and shock so she could keep fighting for herself and her sister.

But first she needed to get to the restroom before she puked on the floor.

When she returned to the bar, she said to Ally, "Okay, tell me exactly what Kevin said."

Ally raised her eyebrows. "Are you sure?"

"Yes." She was as prepared as she'd ever be for whatever else Ally had to say.

Ally took deep breath. "Okay, he said he didn't recognize Don at first, something about his wearing a mustache and glasses, some kind of disguise. Well, he was at the park and Don, you know, looking for… shit, I don't want to—"

"All right, I got that part, go on." Deidre bit her lip.

"Some piece of his disguise came off and Kevin recognized Don, I guess from pictures he'd seen of him. I don't know, maybe in the newspaper or on TV. I'm not sure where. Anyway, Kevin knew who he was and it really pissed him off because here was this gay-bashing minister raising hell against gays, and then shows up at McFarland Park looking for...well, you know. Anyway, Kevin said he 'beat the shit out of Don.' He said more, but you don't want to hear it, trust me."

"Was that sometime on Friday, the day before Don was murdered?"

"Not sure, but probably. That seems about right from what Kevin said. Why?"

"Because Don was beaten up then, but he had an entirely different story about how he'd been hurt."

Deidre's mind flashed back to when Don stood on the porch of her dad's house, telling her about the gang of kids at the church who'd supposedly attacked him.

Then she thought about what Mandy had said to her when they were on the beach. Now she realized Mandy knew what Don had been doing there, but she must have wanted her to figure it out for herself. Mandy hadn't wanted to be put in the position of having to tell her either. But if Ally hadn't told her, she'd never have come to such a conclusion. Don hating gays didn't make sense to her if he really was one himself. How could Don be gay or even bisexual? If he were, wouldn't he feel compassion and understanding for homosexuality?

Her head felt like exploding. The pieces of her life seemed to have been thrown into the air, coming down in another world and creating a different picture than the one on the cover of her puzzle box.

"I'm so sorry, Deidre. Are you going to be okay?" Ally came out from behind the bar and put her arm around her.

"I just need some time." Deidre let out another big sigh and picked up her drink. "I'm going to move over to that table. I need to get myself together."

The noise level of the bar had gone up considerably since her arrival. She figured people were probably coming for the drag show.

She kept reminding herself she was going to be strong. The only way to do that was to keep focused on what she needed to do and put everything else on the on the back burner—she would deal with Don's betrayal later. Now was the time to focus on helping Kera. Where should she go next? What should she do?

But what she felt like doing was going home, curling up in a fetal position, and going to sleep, but that kind of passive response was no longer available to her. She had to try and think things through, come up with some kind of a plan, get herself and her sister out of this mess.

Thoughts of Don kept invading like pop-up ads on the Internet. She pushed them away, only to have them resurface. Maybe she was sleeping, having a nightmare. She wished.

She should feel angry, really angry, but she didn't. Events seemed so random, so unexpected, like an unseen attack from a snowball landing straight between her eyes. Stunned, then pain, but no anger, not yet.

She didn't want to picture Don with another man. She couldn't. Don gay? It was sort of like trying to imagine a hungry lion cuddling up with its prey. How could she have been so fooled, so gullible, so out of the loop of her own life?

She'd been angry with Don for a lot of things, but for being gay? She guessed she'd have to accept, in her gut, that what she'd heard was true before she could feel the anger that must be hiding under her disbelief.

Ally came over to her table. "I wanted to give you some space, but don't think I'm ignoring you. If there's something I could do, please let me help. You were so good to me when I got out of the hospital. Please let me be there for you and your sister. If you need to talk, I'm available. John is here now and could handle things." She pointed to the court jester behind the bar.

Deidre gestured for Ally to sit down. "I just keep swirling the same stuff over and over in my brain. I need to try and move off Don and on to what I need to do next. Maybe you could help me keep focused and be a sounding board for me."

"Sure, be glad to." Ally sat down. She'd brought a glass of water with her.

"I was thinking maybe my next step is to talk to Kevin, see if he's seen her. I don't know if it would be safe. I mean, what if he killed Don? What do you think?"

"It's hard to imagine Kevin would do that, but then he had no trouble beating Don up, did he? Hmm…" Ally considered the idea. "Hard to say." She scooted her chair closer to the table.

Deidre took a sip of her drink, then said, "I don't know what else to do. But let's say he did kill Don. Doesn't mean he'd want to kill me. If he didn't kill Don and since he knows Kera…let's say he's talked to her recently, maybe he'd know something about where she is or where she might go. I don't know, but I have to start somewhere. The only thing I can think to do is go to Kevin's office, see if he's there and if so, talk to him. Certainly he wouldn't try to kill me there."

"This late in the evening? Would he still be there?"

"I don't know, but I do know Harry works late some nights. Real estate people have crazy hours. I could call and see if Kevin's there. If not, I could go there tomorrow—"

"Just a minute, let me get his phone number for you." Ally got up, went behind the bar and returned with her cell phone. She looked up Kevin's number.

Deidre punched the numbers into her phone and waited. He didn't answer, but his answering service gave her his cell phone number. She made the call.

"This is Kevin," he answered, "how may I help you?"

"Hi, this is Deidre Bledsoe."

There was a brief silence, then his stiff reply. "Oh, yes, what can I do for you, Mrs. Bledsoe?"

"I would like to talk to you. I don't want to go into it here on the phone. I was wondering if there'd be a time we could meet."

"Uh…sure. I'm pretty booked up the next few days, but let me see…how about on Thursday? I really can't do it before. Say, sometime in the evening around nine? Hope that's not too late. I could meet you at your house or you could come to the office. Whatever works best for you."

"Your office would be fine." Deidre really wished she could see Kevin before then, but she didn't want to ask him about Kera on the phone. "I'll be there at nine."

"See you then. Oh, Mrs. Bledsoe—"

"Please call me Deidre."

"Okay, Deidre, I heard about…well, I'm sorry for your loss."

She couldn't think of anything to say. She just bet he was sorry. This was the guy who beat the shit out of Don and, who knows, maybe even murdered him.

The silence on the phone hung between them, until Kevin said, "Well, see you on Thursday at my office."

"Yes, thanks." Deidre threw her phone into her purse and looked at Ally. "He's sorry for my loss. You think?"

Ally shrugged. "I guess he could be sorry for your loss, but not sorry for Don's death."

"Maybe. Anyway, I'll see him Thursday night. He said he was pretty busy. I didn't want to ask him if he had any idea where Kera is. I'm afraid the police may be able to intercept my conversations, if they're doing that sort of thing. If they are, I'm hoping they'd just think I wanted to sell my house. I also considered someone could be with him and overhear his answer, especially if Kevin knew where she was."

Ally nodded. "Good thinking."

Deidre continued, "I'm trying to figure out where Kera would go. She might try contacting some old friends, but offhand, I can't think who she would trust enough. Even if I come up with somebody, I won't know where he or she is now. Hmm, the Internet could help me, but I don't want to use my computer or the one at the library. The police could track my searches. I wonder where I could—"

"You could use ours here. I doubt the cops would even consider you using the one here. And even if they did, they'd have a hard time getting to this one, or at least it would take them a while getting a court order to allow it, I think. I'm certainly no lawyer but I watch *Law and Order*." Ally snickered. "Anyway, our computer is in the back." She pointed to another door behind the bar.

"Thanks, Ally, I really appreciate your help. Are you sure your boss won't mind? I don't want to get you in trouble."

"Don't worry about it. Like I said earlier, our community is here to help you and Kera."

"You know what I am most worried about now, Ally? If I find Kera, I will be leading the police right to her. I know I'm being followed. When I leave here, that cop will be right behind me." Deidre looked out the window, toward the street where the man in the car waited. "I don't—"

"Mistress Ally...oh, Mistress Allison." A high-pitched voice melodically called, emanating from somewhere back near the stage. The voice was followed by a head peeking out from the drawn red velvet curtain. "We need you, darling. We are so out of hair spray. Do you have any more?"

"Yes, I do, I'll get you some in just a second, James." Ally turned back to Deidre. "You're right, you need to get rid of that cop on your tail. Let me think about that. Meanwhile, I'll get you set up on the computer. Then I'll go back there and take care of my showgirls."

* * *

"Don't you think I would draw a lot of unwanted attention with that dress?" Deidre couldn't believe the garment James had picked out for her to wear.

James rolled his eyes. "Cher looked ravishing in it and darling, you so have the body to pull it off."

"That was Cher's dress, really?"

"No, darling, not exactly, it's a knockoff." He rolled his eyes again and brushed a speck of lint off the fabric.

Ally poked her head into the dressing room. "James, she's not going to be on stage. She needs street clothes, a wig and makeup, especially around the bruising from her broken nose." She entered and took the dress from James, handing him a brown ponytail wig. "She came in here as Deidre and she needs to get out of here as someone else, but not a drag queen. That dress would hardly be a costume she could get around town in and not stand out like a sore thumb—or a hooker."

"Okay, but if you ask me, it won't do any good for her to go out looking like some random heterosexual woman when that's how she came into the bar." James patted Deidre's shoulder and said to her, "I'm sorry, honey, I meant no offense. You are far from 'random,' sweetie." He turned back to Ally. "My point is that by her merely changing into regular, everyday clothes with a boring wig—almost the same color as her natural hair—won't help her be disguised. Trust me, I highly doubt the cop out there could tell you what Deidre wore coming into the bar or how her hair was done. Am I wrong here?" He pulled off the pumpkin orange wig from Deidre's head, tossed it into a drawer, and stood looking at Ally with his hands on his hips.

A guy's voice from behind a rack of clothes yelled out. "I got a wig for her."

"Oh, God no, Sean," Ally exclaimed. "Dolly Parton isn't what we need either. Don't you guys have something a little less flamboyant?"

"I really appreciate your helping me, guys, really I do," Deidre said, "but I just want to look different than when I came in. Can't you make me unrecognizable in some other way? If not, I can always try to leave out the back door." She was sitting at a makeup table looking at herself in an ornate mirror that resembled something out of a Hollywood set with bright lightbulbs streaming down in a row on either side.

James looked at Sean. "Do we have anything—let's say, understated—back here?"

"Maybe in your wardrobe, honey, but you wouldn't find that kind of thing in mine." Sean rolled his eyes. "I suppose this mean she doesn't want big bazooms either."

James regarded Deidre. "You could use a little augmentation, my dear."

"Cut it, girls." Ally went over to the drag queen's costume closet. "There's got to be something in here that would work without turning Deidre into—"

"How about something out of the drag kings' collection?" James opened another closet containing male clothing.

"Good idea, James," Ally agreed.

"I'm going to be dressed as a king? How's that going to make me look, well, ordinary?" Deidre wrinkled her nose. "Ouch." She put her hand to her sore nose and made a mental note not to scrunch it again.

"You aren't going to look like a king, dear, you'll look like a guy. Kings are women who dress like guys for our shows—you know, the opposite of guys in drag. We'll keep it toned down. Don't worry." Ally watched Deidre's reflection in the mirror while she spoke. "The makeup will get rid of that discoloration around your nose. The good thing is, the swelling makes your nose look bigger, more the size for a man's nose, so it will work out great for making you up as a guy."

"I'm glad my swollen nose is useful for something." Deidre allowed herself a smile, one that didn't wiggle her nose too much.

"You'll make a cute guy." James winked at her. "How about these?" He held up a pair of baggy blue jeans, black suspenders, and a black T-shirt with a montage of white-outlined skeletons covering the front and back. "Now to find some Reeboks, a wig and a baseball cap."

Deidre stared. "Oh, my God…but you know, those might just be the ticket."

"Sean, how about giving her a little facial hair as well. It'll help draw people's eyes away from her nose." Ally bent and plowed through the supply of shoes in the bottom of the closet. "What size shoe do you wear, Deidre?"

"Eight and a half. Geez, Ally, all I'll need now is an iPod," Deidre kidded.

Ally chuckled. "Wouldn't let you leave here without one. And James, I think we're going to need to flatten her out a bit since she'll be wearing that T-shirt."

James went over to the drag kings' closet to find some binding material.

Sean stared at Deidre's breasts. "Making these beauties go away seems so counterintuitive to me."

"Sean!" Ally yelled. "I realize you usually discuss breasts while looking at fake ones sitting in a drawer, but you're looking at a real live woman and acting like she's not the proprietor of the body equipment you're discussing."

"Oh, darling, I'm so sorry. I—"

"It's okay, Sean. We're all learning here."

Ally turned to her. "I've been thinking, you'd better take my old Ford Mustang when you leave. It's a bit of a clunker, but she's reliable."

"I couldn't take your car, Ally."

James came back with binding material and the T-shirt. "Okay, now for the binding. It won't take long, be done in a jiff."

Deidre reluctantly raised her arms as James took off her polo shirt and bra, and started wrapping the material around her torso. She closed her eyes. She didn't want the mirror to record this moment in her brain for future playback.

"Don't worry, dear," James reassured her. "You're just one of us girls. Think of it as showbiz. Can you imagine all the costume changes stars have to go through, and I assure you, they don't do it all by themselves."

When he finished wrapping her, the bindings felt a bit snug, but she guessed she'd have to endure if she wanted to pass as a man. Really, what choice did she have?

Ally found a pair of shoes and handed them to James before turning to Deidre. "You can't take your car now. Even made up as a guy, the cop is going to be wondering about the identity of the dude getting in your car and driving off. Any way you look at it, you're going to get followed if you take your vehicle."

"Maybe I could get a rental." Deidre helped James pull down her T-shirt.

"It won't take the cops long to get on to the fact you have a loaner car and they've probably already contacted all the rental places. They'll be watching out for you." Ally hung up a dress that had fallen on the floor.

"I don't want to get you in trouble, Ally, and besides, if I take your Mustang, what will you drive?"

"You won't get me in trouble. All I will know—if the cops even ask me—is that you asked to borrow my car and I said yes. And it's not like you are wanted as an escaped prisoner."

"Well, not yet." She wondered how long before the police took her in again. On second thought, she figured they probably wouldn't take her into custody if they hoped she'd lead them to Kera.

"I can borrow my mom's car. She's lent me her car before when my Mustang needed work. No big deal. My parents have another vehicle they can use. Don't worry."

Deidre nodded. Maybe it would be okay to take Ally's Mustang. Actually it was the only good choice she had.

Sean finished her makeup. He'd spent extra time putting on another layer of foundation and powder around her bruises. She'd watched him in the mirror and could hardly believe how well he'd disguised her broken nose.

He scrutinized his work. "Let's see now…how about we add a sexy three-days' growth of facial hair." He began dabbing more makeup on her chin and cheeks, making it look amazingly like stubble, then stepping aside to view his handiwork and returning to add more touches here and there.

She was amazed by her transformation. If she hadn't been watching the process, she wouldn't have known whose face looked back at her. Staring at a stranger's reflection felt like an out-of-body sensation, or more like being transported into someone else's body, not knowing where hers had been stashed.

"I hope you've been watching what I have been doing so you can repair it if necessary. I'll give you the stuff I used." Sean gathered up the makeup, put it in plastic baggie, sealed the top, and handed the bag to her. "When you wash your face, do you think you can redo what I've done here?"

"I hope so, but still, I'll go as long as I can without washing. I watched you work and hopefully I can replicate the effect, but it won't be to your perfection. You're a real artist at this stuff."

Sean faked humility. "Oh, how sweet of you to say so, but I'm just a novice."

"Here's a wig and your cap." James put the wig and baseball cap on her head.

"That's a better wig for what I need, not that I have anything against Dolly Parton." Deidre adjusted strands of the fake hair sticking down from her cap.

"Don't bend the visor. Keep it flat like this and turn it to the side or around to the back, like so." James adjusted the cap and turned to Ally. "What do you think?"

"You two have outdone yourselves." Ally raised her hand and gave a thumbs-up. "Perfecto! If I didn't see the transformation myself, I wouldn't know Deidre was under there."

She got up and walked around to see how her shoes felt. They seemed to fit okay. Maybe a little too wide, but they'd work.

"Oh, no!" James and Sean chimed in unison, laughing.

"What's wrong?" Deidre looked at herself, wondering what was so funny.

Ally began laughing too. "Honey, you are going to need some walking lessons. I'd better take over from here." She grabbed Deidre's arm and they headed out of the dressing room.

Sean called out, "She doesn't need to get all butch. She could be a femme guy, a real flamer!"

Ally yelled back, "Jesus, Sean, she already has a broken nose."

CHAPTER TWENTY-TWO

Kera

Kera felt relieved to be paddling Sadie instead of swimming in the river, even though the cool night air against her wet clothes chilled her. But maybe the chill and the pain in her shoulder were good since they kept her awake.

She felt jittery, cold and fatigued—edgy, like in Iraq, not knowing what she might encounter around the next bend. At this point along the river, there were fewer homes and more wooded areas, making it less likely someone might see her, but she couldn't allow herself to become complacent. She didn't know what the cops had found out about her. Did they know where she might go or what she might do?

She checked her pocket for her cell phone. Luckily, it had stayed dry in the plastic bag Vinny gave her. She considered calling Dee or Mandy but decided that might be a bad idea. The police could be intercepting their calls or checking their phones to see if she'd made contact with them. Maybe she should check to see if Mandy or Dee had tried to call her. Better not do that either. If anyone happened to be watching the river, the light from her phone might be seen.

She worked to keep Sadie hugging the bank, periodically stopping, listening, watching—not that she could see much—then moving on. She knew Mandy and Dee must be worried about her, maybe even be thinking she had killed Sam. No, Dee wouldn't believe she'd do such a thing, but Mandy?

Her canoe smacked into something...

A boulder.

After Sadie hit the high part of the protruding rock, the canoe twisted and bucked with the front half scraping onto the flat part of the boulder, or maybe another boulder, next to it, she couldn't tell. She took her paddle and pushed and pried until Sadie slipped free. Given the darkness, it was hard to tell if her canoe suffered any damage. She'd have to keep an eye on it to make sure Sadie wasn't taking on water.

The clouds returned, taking away most of the moon and starlight and making it even more difficult for her to see obstructions in the river. She'd have to move along more slowly. She knew her fatigue would make her prone to mistakes. She rubbed her eyes, begging them to stay open.

She slapped her forehead. Damn, now the mosquitoes were biting her. Why hadn't she picked up some repellent at her dad's house when she'd been there? As it was, she suspected she'd be eaten alive before she reached Moran's.

Kera began to wonder whether it had been a good idea to let Vinny take off out of town, but then, she couldn't have stopped him. Hopefully, Vinny would find his way back to Lakeside City after a few days. She would have a hell of a time trying to clear her name in Sam's death if he upped and disappeared for good. The authorities were already convinced her sister killed Don and thought she might have a part in his murder. Without any further investigation, they'd be more than willing to pin Sam's death on her. No questions asked.

A scary thought popped into her head. If Vinny killed Don, he'd most likely not return. Even if he believed she'd stand up for him, Vinny might worry the cops wouldn't believe her, given Vinny used a knife on Sam, slit his throat—as was done in Don's murder—and they'd consider the two murders related. Lakeside City's police were known more for their rush to judgment than for their thoroughness or discernment.

Famished and depleted, Kera remembered the box of Zone bars she'd thrown into the bottom of the canoe. She laid her paddle over her lap, balancing it on either side of the canoe's frame, and let Sadie drift while she fumbled around, found the box, grabbed a bar and tore off the wrapper. These bars would have to do until she could get to Moran's place for some real food.

What she believed she needed even more than food was sleep, then maybe she'd be rested enough to figure out what to do next.

She was way too tired to sort things out right now. Hell, she hadn't been sleeping well before all this happened, so she'd already gone past exhausted and was dangerously close to debilitated. The way she felt now, she probably could sleep for days, given the chance to—

Sadie crash into something again. She couldn't see what the canoe hit. Too damned dark. Was it another boulder? A tree limb?

Fucking bad luck is what it was!

She'd shifted her balance in time to keep the canoe from capsizing, but her paddle, jarred by the impact, fell overboard.

The canoe was being pulled downriver by the current.

"Shit!"

She felt stupid for having lost her paddle—an idiotic mistake. She considered jumping out and pushing the canoe to shore, but realized Sadie had turned and the current was pulling her into the river's bank. Hopefully, her paddle had been pulled off in that direction too. She decided to let the current pull her ashore.

Something smacked her in the head.

* * *

Kera rubbed her head and neck. God, it hurt. Whatever hit her—probably a tree branch—had knocked her out, but for how long? Seconds, minutes, hours? She realized the blow had caused her to fall backward. Luckily she landed squarely in the middle of the canoe, allowing her vessel to remain upright.

She rubbed her eyes and tried to pull herself up by bringing her elbows beneath her. Pain in her neck and head quickly put her back down.

She glanced up. Though her vision was blurred and it was still dark, she could make out the tree branch that must have been the culprit that'd taken her out. As far as she could tell, the canoe wasn't going anywhere. Sadie must be trapped in weeds and branches near the water's edge.

She tried to pull herself up again, but the pain was intense and accompanied by a rush of nausea. Maybe it would be okay to stay there until she felt a little better. Sadie seemed to be pretty well locked into the spot and she needed to rest, just for a little while. She closed her eyes.

Sometime later, how long, Kera had no idea. She heard the sound of Moran's voice. The canoe was rocking and moving. She hurt, but her eyelids refused to stay open. From the glimpses of pale gray light, it seemed near dawn. She thought Moran said something, but the words made no sense to her. Maybe she'd been dreaming. She couldn't keep her eyes open and felt herself sinking back into sleep.

Suddenly, she was jarred awake. The canoe was still moving. Looking up at the overhanging branches of the trees going by, she could tell Sadie was gliding through the water near the riverbank. She heard splashing, like someone plodding through water. The back of Moran's head bobbed in front of the canoe. She realized her old friend was towing Sadie.

* * *

A horrible headache greeted Kera as she regained consciousness. She opened her eyes. She reached behind her head, feeling the spot where the tree branch had hit her, "Damn that hurts."

"It's no wonder, you've got quite a lump there." Moran hovered over her, helping her adjust the pillow.

"What day is this?" Kera knew she'd been in and out of consciousness but didn't know for how long.

"This is Monday," Moran said. "Yesterday morning, I dragged you back here in your canoe. You've been sleeping on and off ever since." She opened the curtains near the bed. "Let's get a little light in here." She turned and asked, "Does the brightness bother your eyes now? It did earlier. I'll close them again if—"

"A little, but it's okay. Keep the curtains open. It'll help me stay awake. I feel like I could fall back asleep so easily." She carefully moved her body, adjusting her position, trying to get more comfortable. "Wow, this is Monday? I've been here that long?"

"Yes, dear, I've been feeding you a little soup and tea—when you'd wake up, that is. I've also been putting a cold cloth on your head where you've got that lump. What happened, did you get hit by a tree branch?"

"Wow, I don't remember much after losing my paddle and feeling something smack my head, probably a tree branch ambushing me, like you said. But I do vaguely recall you pulling the canoe."

"You've been pretty much out of it and got quite a wound on your shoulder. I cleaned it out, put on an antibiotic gel and bandaged it. I've been keeping an eye on it, though I should check it again soon."

"The wound wasn't part of my canoe accident. That's where this guy's gun went off and the bullet hit me, pretty much just grazed my shoulder, I think. I'll tell you about all it later. I'm feeling too foggy right now."

Moran opened Kera's shirt to examine the wound. "Your shirt was all bloody, so I took it off and put one of my old shirts on you." She pulled the bandage off. "The graze still doesn't appear infected, but with your head injury, you probably should have gone to the emergency room. Would have taken you, but I happened to have the radio on the other day, checking the weather forecast, and heard the news and about the trouble you're in. You're being described as a dangerous murderer on the loose." She shook her head and sat down in a wooden rocking chair next to the bed. "I had no idea."

"I want you to know I didn't kill Don. I didn't kill Sam either."

Moran bent over and patted her arm. "You didn't have to tell me, honey. I would never believe such a thing."

"But I need to be able to prove it." Kera painfully rolled over on her side to face Moran. "The police think Dee and/or I killed Don. Now they believe I killed Sam too."

"Yes, that's pretty much what they were saying on the NPR station."

Kera knew the local news would be following the killings of Don and Sam, coming to conclusions before all the facts were known. The local media loved a juicy murder, and even better, two killings. But NPR? She'd thought the national public radio station was more dignified, less prone to sensationalizing, more likely to be sure about their facts. Either she was wrong about NPR, or she was really screwed.

"It seems like the town has made up its mind about me, huh?" she rolled onto her back, again.

"They'll find the right person who killed those men. People in this community know neither you nor your sister would do such a thing. Here, you need to get water into your system, I've not been able to get you to drink much." Moran took the glass of water sitting on the nightstand and supported her head so she could drink.

Kera took a sip. "Oh, I don't know about that. When the cops think you've done something and let everyone know about it, what are people supposed to think?" Her head throbbed. "Do you have any pain pills?"

Moran nodded, left the room, then returned with some pills, and helped her hold her head up while she swallowed them.

"I don't know who I am anymore, or what's happened to my life," Kera said. "It's like I was on this train and a malevolent remote controller switched me onto another rail, fast-tracking me into this nightmare."

Moran scooted the rocker closer to the bed and took Kera's hand in hers. "As I told you the other day when you came to see me, you have a lot of invasions in your body. I worked on some, but there's so much more work to do. Those invasions are causing ruptures in your soul. That's why you've lost a sense of who you are, and you're right, this really isn't your world anymore, and you will have to fight your way out of it." She closed her eyes and began chanting.

Soon, Kera felt like her body was floating. When Moran went into a trance, she took Kera's spirit along for the ride, leaving her body and mind to rest.

After a while, she watched as Moran's arms rose in the air and she pulled an unseen force into her lap. She stood, bent over, and blew through her cupped hands, sending something into Kera's chest.

Kera felt a fluttering inside her.

Moran spoke. "My spirit guide told me to give you 'Wolf.' Wolf is strong, discerning, smart, quick, and she cares about her family, like you do. Wolf can take care of herself and those she protects. Wolf is now a part of you. Another power animal to help you."

"Thank you for Wolf."

"Don't thank me. She was a gift from my spirit guide." Moran smiled.

"Okay, thank your spirit guide. You know, I think Owl has been with me. When I was in Iraq, and just the other night when I was on the river, I felt the presence of Owl. I couldn't see Owl, but I felt her. And when I was in Iraq, I—"

"Oh, yes." Moran leaned forward. "I sent you Owl, after you left for Iraq. I got worried about you, so I took the liberty of sending her to you long distance." She winked. "I'm glad she made her presence known."

"She sure did. I'll tell you about it sometime."

Moran nodded.

"Speaking of feeling Owl's presence the other night on the river, and you bringing me back here, how did you manage to get me out of the canoe by yourself?"

"Orin Brinkley helped me."

"Damn, somebody knows I'm here? I'll have to get out of here fast." She felt a surge of panic run through her body.

"Don't worry, he would never say anything. You remember him, don't you? He's the old, militia-type guy who lives down the road. He's harmless these days and, besides, he has no love for the authorities. He's the last one who'd inform on you."

"Oh, yeah, I remember him. I'm surprised he's still around. He's got to be in his nineties, right?"

"Ninety-five to be exact. You wouldn't know it, though. He's in good health and still tough as old shoe leather. I have to say, Miss In-Your-Thirties, the two of us old folks got you out of the canoe and into this bed with little help from you." Moran's face sported a prideful smile.

"And I thank you both for it, but I've got to get out of here soon, anyway. I'm putting you in jeopardy being here, especially now that you know what's going on."

"What do you mean, 'now I that I know what's going on?'"

"I figured if you didn't know, you couldn't be blamed for harboring a fugitive, but you know now."

"I'm old, Kera. I seldom turn on my radio. Anyone who knows me can tell them that. And as I recollect, I haven't had the radio on in months, maybe longer." Moran's eyes twinkled. "Now, fill me in," she continued. "I won't remember what you have to say. In fact, I'll be lucky if I can hold your story in my mind for more than a few minutes. We old folks have horrible memories." She bent forward in her rocker. "I need to know how I can help you, dear. You are, as they say, in a shit load of trouble."

CHAPTER TWENTY-THREE

Deidre

Deidre opened her eyes to yellow and purple flowered wallpaper. Sepia pictures of flapper girls from the twenties hung around the spacious bedroom.

The sun shone through white café curtains billowing in the morning breeze. A twisting crystal dangling from the rod caught a sunbeam and gave off a dancing rainbow of color on the opposite wall.

The smell of fresh-baked cinnamon rolls and coffee wafted into the bedroom. Her stomach growled.

She didn't know what she would have done if not for Ally. She lay in bed thinking about Ally and the boys—or girls, as the bartender called them—making her into a guy and sending her to a lesbian B&B. She'd questioned Ally about the wisdom of hiding in a lesbian place dressed as a guy, but she was assured gay men were welcome there too, so she wouldn't look out of place. Ally had called ahead and made the arrangements. The owners, Joan and Marty, were told who she really was and why she was there, and had welcomed her with open arms.

Yesterday, she'd found Kera's high school best friend, Janet Cooley, via the Internet. She'd tried to call, but no one answered. At the time, she hadn't wanted to leave Janet a message. She decided she'd try again this morning. If she didn't get hold of Janet, she'd drive to her place, which was quite a ways out in the country.

Deidre's bladder nudged her. She got up, went to the adjoining bathroom and looked in the mirror. Although she expected to see a strange reflection, her gender transformation to a male still jolted her. She gently touched her nose, thinking maybe it wouldn't hurt as much today. She was wrong, but the bruised discoloration remained well covered by the makeup.

The outfit she'd worn to the B & B was in good shape and could easily be worn again. Yesterday, Ally had found an old suitcase in the props area and filled it with several changes of clothes. James had even run out and gotten her toiletries. She wondered what she would have done without their help.

Joan and Marty had absolutely refused to take any money from her. Marty had told her the city's tight-knit gay community watched out for each other. She'd also said Kera taught them self-defense, a few years back, which was how she and Joan knew her sister.

Deidre hadn't realized Kera was so well known in the local LGBT world. Of course, being the mayor's daughter—

A soft tap on the door.

In a low voice, "Deidre, are you awake?"

"Just a minute." Deidre pulled her suspenders over her shoulders and opened the bedroom door.

"Just giving you a wakeup call. Marty said you wanted to be up by nine, right?"

"Yes, thanks, Joan."

"Your breakfast awaits you."

"I'll be right down. I'm just finishing up."

Deidre sat down at the table in the kitchenette. The other guests were eating breakfast in the dining room, but Marty and Joan had invited her to stay in the kitchen with them. The couple rightly believed she'd be more comfortable not having to deal with other guests. She knew she should practice passing herself off as a guy, but she was glad not to have to start the act so early in the morning.

"Thank you so much for letting me stay here. It really is the perfect place. Certainly no one would ever expect me to be here." Deidre bit into a cinnamon roll, followed by a sip of her coffee.

"Would you like some eggs? I'm scrambling up some more. I got a hungry bunch out there this morning." Joan pointed toward the dining room with her spatula.

"To tell you the truth, I'm not that hungry, but this roll is absolutely wonderful." Deidre wiped her lips with her napkin. "I need to get going, but I'll be back this evening. Hopefully, I won't need to stay longer than a couple of nights. I don't want to wear out my welcome."

"Don't you be worrying about that, now. You stay as long as you need. Consider this your home." Joan scraped the scrambled eggs into a green serving bowl, placed some bacon on top of the eggs, grabbed the coffeepot and pushed through the louvered café doors leading into the dining room. "Wait, don't let me forget." Her head popped back through the doors. "I have a key for you, so you can come and go as you please."

* * *

It wasn't easy for Deidre to read the house numbers on the mailboxes as she drove along the country road. Some didn't even have numbers. Janet lived even further out in the boonies than she'd thought. Finally, she found what she thought was Janet's driveway.

She couldn't see the house when she first turned her car into the driveway because of so many evergreens obscuring the view, along with huge oaks, maples, hemlocks and an assortment of large green bushes. The gravel driveway wound back from the road to a red brick, Victorian-style house with a wraparound porch. Alongside the house and back a little, she could see a barn with a tractor nearby, and what looked like a chicken coop.

She'd made the decision to pay a visit instead of even trying to call because she wanted to be able to talk to Janet face-to-face, if possible, and pick her brain as to where Kera might go. And she thought it was good to get away from the city where she felt she could let down her guard a little.

She pulled her car up to the farmhouse and parked. Out of habit, she adjusted the rearview mirror so she could check her appearance. Momentarily forgetting her transformation, she startled herself once again with the male face peering back at her.

Janet came around the corner of the house, toting a baby on her hip.

Deidre rolled down her window. The after-rain smell of rich earth rushed into the car. The whole pastoral, mother-and-child scene was something out of a dream for herself. That hope had been snuffed out. Her baby came too early, landing in the toilet with the rest of her life. Tears flooded her eyes. She wiped them away.

Janet looked bewildered as she approached the car.

Of course, Deidre thought, Janet was wondering who the guy was who'd just driven up to her house. Actually, it was a good thing Janet didn't recognize her. Hopefully, that meant others wouldn't see through her disguise either.

She yelled out the car's window, "Janet, it's me, Deidre."

No sign Janet recognized her, but she continued walking up to the Mustang.

"Deidre Bledsoe…ah, Van Brocklin." Deidre took off her cap and her wig, along with the net that held her hair snugly to her head, allowing her hair to tumble down. "I'm going around as a guy these days." She managed a small smile.

Frowning and looking confused, Janet took a step back from the car. "You're doing what?"

"Okay, let me start over. I'm Deidre Van Brocklin."

"Oh, I can see that now." Janet's expression seemed to warm a bit. "But you say you're now a guy? Wow, I guess I never figured you for a what-do-you-call-them…a transsexual or a transvestite, not sure which. It's okay, I'm just, well, kind of surprised. I mean I've known for years Kera was gay, so why not—"

Deidre shook her head. "I'm not really any one of those—not that that wouldn't be okay," she hastily added. "I'm just in disguise today."

Janet appeared more bewildered than enlightened. "In disguise?" She shifted the baby to the other hip. "I'm sorry, but I'm feeling a bit confused."

"Janet, can we go in and talk? I've got a lot to fill you in on."

* * *

During their chat, Deidre had found Janet caring and concerned, but not helpful. She and her baby daughter had been visiting her sick mother at Henry Ford Hospital in Detroit. Janet had returned home last night and hadn't heard all the news in Lakeside City yet. Thankfully, she'd said she wanted to help Kera in any way she could.

Deidre drove back toward town, not knowing where to go or what to do next. Maybe she should go back and talk to Joan and Marty. Perhaps they'd have some ideas.

She saw a sign for Hoffmaster State Park which got her thinking about how Kera loved to camp. She wondered if Kera had somehow gotten to her camping gear and was hiding out there.

She figured the state park was a good hiding place since Kera probably wouldn't be spotted among the crowds of tourists who flocked there this time of year. Locals generally didn't visit Hoffmaster. If they wanted to go camping, they'd usually head up to Sleeping Bear, or Wilderness, or to the Upper Peninsula somewhere.

Deidre reconsidered that possibility. Kera didn't have a vehicle. At least, she didn't think so. Kera had left their dad's car at Sam's house.

Unless she found another vehicle...or rented one. No, in that case, she'd have to use her credit card and she wouldn't want to leave a paper trail. Besides, Kera would certainly suspect that the police had alerted the car rental places.

Maybe she stole a car. Hopefully not. Deidre cringed. Good God, Kera was in enough trouble already. But, she concluded, why not steal a car? How much more trouble could her sister be in?

Trying to figure this whole thing out made her feel like an ill-prepared criminology student taking her final exams. How was she supposed to find out where her sister was, who killed Don, and what happened with Sam?

Oh God, how did this whole mess come down on her anyway? Where had she gone wrong? Her mind flipped back through the pages of her life and came up with her big mistake: marrying Don.

The cinnamon roll rumbled in discontent, then made it clear it had to leave her body. Deidre pulled over to the side of the road, opened the car door, and dumped her breakfast.

As she was wiping off her mouth, her cell phone rang. She looked at the incoming call and answered, "Hi Janet, what's up?"

"I've been thinking about Kera. It's just a shot in the dark, but who knows?"

"What?"

"Do you remember the woman Kera used to visit? She lived a ways down the river from your place—your parents' house. She's a shaman. I met her once. Nice, but sort of a strange old woman. She and Kera were really close. And you know, Kera really got into that shamanic stuff."

"Yeah, I know. It worried my dad."

"I bet. But Kera loved that woman and spent a lot of time with her. The shaman kind of took your mother's place for Kera. I don't mean she really took her place," Janet quickly added, "but she filled—"

"It's okay, Janet, I know what you're saying."

"I don't know if she's still alive or if she even lives around these parts anymore. Jack and I just moved back here last year. I'm not up on everyone, plus having a baby, I don't get around much."

"I know who you mean, Janet. Her name...her name...it's a funny name...starts with M, I think. In fact, I've seen her around town on occasions. She rides an old bike with baskets on the front and back. Don't know how she does it wearing those long dresses. Let's see, her name is, uh, Margaret...Massey...Moray. Damn it, I know I know it. I hate when I can't remember names."

Janet jumped in, "Moran!"

"Yeah, that's right, Moran. She lived on the river, too, hopefully still does. Kera used to go to her place by way of her canoe. Oh, my God, that could be it! Kera doesn't have a vehicle, but if she made it home, somehow...not sure how she'd do that, but if she did, she could have taken her canoe and gone to Moran's place. It's a possibility. Thanks so much, Janet. That sounds promising and gives me someplace to start, something to go on."

"I hope it works out."

* * *

Deidre drove down the road that followed the river to her dad's house and eventually led to Moran's. As she came to her dad's place, she slowed, noticing a parked vehicle a little ways back and across the road from her father's driveway. A man sat in the driver's seat, seemingly busy reading a newspaper he'd propped up on his steering wheel.

Who sits and reads a newspaper in his car on this road, unless he's waiting for someone, like maybe her or Kera. She should've realized the police would be watching their house to see who might show up there. If Kera had shown up, the police must not have seen her, or the plainclothes cop wouldn't be sitting there now. Or maybe he would, if he happened to be looking for her too. Now that she knew the house was being watched, she definitely wouldn't stop to check if Kera had taken out her canoe.

Deidre continued on toward Moran's, constantly looking in the rearview mirror. She traveled about a half mile, continuing to watch for the unmarked cop car. So far, so good, no one behind her. She came to a four-way stop about a mile from Moran's house. She slowed down and cruised through the intersection.

"Damn!" Deidre saw the red blinking lights flashing in her mirror. Where had that cruiser been hiding? It must have been concealed by the trees near the Parkers' house, otherwise she'd have seen it. Was the cop car coming for her because she had just made a roll-through at the stop sign, or because they had somehow identified the car and figured out who was driving it?

Deidre pulled over to the side of the road. What now? She had a woman's driver's license and was presenting herself as a male. She looked at the driver's side mirror. The male cop was sitting in the car, not getting out. Probably checking the license plate. But what else might he be checking?

The fact that the car belonged to Ally shouldn't matter, unless the cop harassed people driving rolling billboards and/or gays. Kera had told her about that sort of thing. Among the many controversial messages on the car—several of which she didn't understand—she had seen a couple rainbow decals on the back window, an equal rights sticker, and a sign that read: We're here, We're QUEER, Get Used To It.

Deidre's heart rate doubled.

The cop got out of the car and strutted up to the red Mustang. "I need to see your registration and proof of insurance." He bent down and stared at her through the opened window, his face just inches from hers. He finished his request. "And driver's license, sir?" Saccharine sarcasm oozed from the word sir.

Was it because he knew she wasn't male, or because of the kind of male he perceived her to be? Or maybe just because he was an asshole kind of a cop? Deidre hoped he couldn't see her hands shake as she stretched over to the glove compartment and fumbled through the papers to find the requested paperwork. That's all she needed, for him to see her nervousness and speculate why.

She found what looked like a folder that might contain the registration, but ended up leafing through the car's repair receipts. "This is my—" She cleared her throat and started over in a deeper voice. "This is my friend's car, not sure where the registration stuff is."

The cop said nothing, just kept watching her.

She found a large envelope that looked like a possibility. It contained old registration and insurance cards, but nothing current. Damn, she knew Ally was barely making it financially. Hopefully she wasn't skimping on car insurance.

The cop tapped his fingers on the window jamb like an irritated school principal waiting for a wayward student to confess her guilt.

Deidre put the folder and large envelope on the passenger seat as she shuffled through the rest of the contents in the glove compartment. She grabbed the car's maintenance manual and opened it. The sought after cards fell out and onto the floor. Good grief, why would Ally put them in there? She picked the cards up and handed them to the cop.

"And now, if it isn't too much trouble, your driver's license please." The cop's voice took on a mocking tone.

Deidre felt like she'd been caught, snared, and he was playing with her, like a cat with a mouse.

"Yes, sir, I'm looking for it." Damn, what a stupid thing to say, like she didn't know where she ordinarily kept her driver's license. She knew how her fumbling, flailing, totally rattled behavior must look to him.

She searched for her purse and remembered she—disguised as a "he"—wasn't carrying one. She was making do with a wallet. She quickly ran her hands through her front pockets. Where was that damned thing?

She dreaded the scene that was about to happen when she handed the cop her female driver's license—if she could even find her wallet. One look at her picture and he'd be yanking her out of the car and hauling her off to jail.

The cop peered through the open window with a condescending grin on his face. "Weren't you taught to stop at stop signs? Slowing down and rolling through them isn't considered stopping."

"Yes, sir." Deidre checked her back pockets, thinking he must hear her heart pound. *He's enjoying this, damn him.* She felt like lashing out. She had confronted authority as a social worker. She knew how, but she was in no position to do it now.

"Do you even have a driver's license, sir?" The cop snickered and wiped away the spittle collecting in the corners of his mouth.

"Yes, I do, officer."

Her wallet wasn't in either of her back pockets. James had told her to put it in one of them, since that's where guys kept their wallets. But she'd been uncomfortable having the wallet there. It was like sitting on a stone. She checked her front pockets again, thinking maybe she'd missed it the first time. No, just her comb, some change and a small pack of tissues. Damn, where had she put her wallet after she took it out of her back pocket? She checked the floor to see if it had fallen out. No.

The cop's face was so close to her she could smell garlic on his breath. Made her stomach feel queasy. Didn't he know what breath mints were for?

Suddenly, a thought came to her. She'd probably set the wallet on the passenger's seat. It had to be under her jacket.

The cop said, "Are you sure you have one?" His smile was filled with sarcasm.

She pulled up the jacket to look for the wallet. It wasn't under there either.

"Maybe you should get out of the car." The cop's cynicism turned harsh. He adjusted the holster on his belt.

She was hot, sweating, but a chill ran through her, like her spine had suddenly been replaced with an icicle. Getting out of the car could only be worse for her. He would see through her disguise and know she was a woman—and didn't some cops react violently to that kind of thing? Didn't that happen to that guy—woman—in California? A cop ordered him out of his car and beat him to death when he found out that he was female, in the transgendering process.

"Oh, here it is, officer." She pulled the wallet from her jacket pocket. Damn, her voice was too high again, but what did it matter? The jig was up now anyway.

She opened her wallet and pulled out her license. The cop reached for it. She couldn't muster up enough moisture to swallow. Her heart felt lodged in her throat, but she managed to say, "Okay, I know—"

An engine's roar came from behind her car.

She looked into her rearview mirror. A motorcycle flew across the intersection she'd just rolled through. The rider not only hadn't stopped, but he flew through as though he were the terrified prey of a cheetah.

The cop's head whipped around. He yelled, "Jesus, Mary and Joseph!"

He pushed her cards and driver's license back through her car window, dropping them on her lap. He tore to his cruiser, got in, turned on the flashing lights and siren, and took off after the motorcycle.

She expelled the stale air she'd been holding in her lungs and sucked in fresh.

CHAPTER TWENTY-FOUR

Kera

Kera heard a car turn into the driveway as she and Moran were eating breakfast. Her heart started beating faster.

Moran reached over from her chair, pulled aside the yellow café curtain and peered outside. "Do you know anyone who drives a red...I don't know, I couldn't tell you one kind of car from another. You take a peek."

Kera took a quick look and backed away from the window. "It's a Mustang, an older model."

Moran let go of the curtain. "I wonder who that is. Wasn't expecting anyone. Do you know who it might be?"

"Haven't a clue, but doesn't look like anything a cop would drive unless, of course, a cop is trying not to look like a cop."

"Oh, dear, Kera, maybe you should hide just in case. You can go to the attic. It's pretty stuffy up there, but—"

"Moran, if I hide in this house and they find me, they'll charge you with harboring a fugitive. I'm not going to put you in that kind of a situation."

"I'm an old lady. They're not going to put me in jail. Don't worry about that. For all I know, you snuck up there when I wasn't looking."

"No. I'm getting out of here. I'll go out the riverside door and over into the woods. I can watch the house from there. If it isn't a cop, signal me by opening the curtains in the dining room." Kera looked around. "Then put that blue candle on the windowsill." She pointed to a large candle on the dining room table.

She wanted to make sure that if the visitor were a cop, he wouldn't open the curtains to look around and inadvertently give her the signal to come back inside. A second signal—moving the blue candle to the windowsill—should keep her from walking into the hands of the cops.

Moran peeked out the curtain again. "Okay, dear, but you'd better hurry. A young man just got out of the car and is coming up this way. He doesn't look like a cop, but, as you say, who knows."

Kera darted for the door leading out to the river, stopped and called over her shoulder, "Moran, get rid of our breakfast dishes on the table. Mine, at least. There should only be one person in this house." She opened the door and left.

She found a hiding spot in a clump of trees where she could view the roadside driveway, front door and dining room window. She watched the young man coming up the homemade slate walk that she and Moran had put in the summer of her junior year in high school. For all the backbreaking work, it had been a wonderful time. Being with Moran always felt like living in a stress-free zone. However, it wasn't exactly a peaceful experience, now, with the cops looking for her.

Something seemed strange. Was it the guy's size, or the way he walked and carried himself? Kera leaned forward, trying to get a better look. Perhaps her perception was distorted. She still felt a little woozy from the tree branch smacking her in the head. Moran told her she probably had a concussion.

She had slept most of the last two days. This morning, she'd woken up with a full-blown lump on her skull and the same old headache she'd been toting around since she woke up Monday morning with Moran hovering over her. Unfortunately, Moran didn't have anything strong enough to do much more than put a dent in the pain coming from both her head and shoulder.

Even though she wasn't feeling that great, she knew she needed to move on. She'd hoped to spend a day or two grabbing more rest, getting her head clear and her shoulder feeling better before trying to face the world again. Actually, facing the world wasn't exactly her plan. More like sneaking around in it. If this man happened to be a cop, there'd be no more time for pampering from Moran. She would have to leave and continue trying to figure out who killed Don, whether or not she was ready.

Moran let the guy into the house.

Kera watched the dining room window. It seemed like the guy had been in the house a long time, but she checked her cell phone and found only a few minutes had passed. She wondered if Moran was showing him around the house, letting him see no one else was there. The man hadn't shown Moran any identification before he went in. A cop would have to do that, well, he certainly should have identified himself. And a cop would need a search warrant, but Moran might not know that, and if she volunteered to let him in, he was within his rights to check around.

The curtains opened. The blue candle appeared in the window.

Kera was still not convinced it was safe. Who in the hell was this guy? Did Moran fully understand no one should know she was there? She carefully looked around, moved out of the woods and slipped up onto Moran's porch to an opened window. She ducked down underneath it and listened.

She heard Deidre's voice.

* * *

Later that day, Kera and Dee walked up to Moran's house. The old woman stood in the doorway, "Oh, my god, I wouldn't have known you, Kera." Moran was muffling a chuckle.

She and her sister were returning from their trip to the Out-and-About, and she was feeling miserably uncomfortable wearing her new attire. "Damned shoes," she yelled out, not finding the high heels funny.

The queens—who'd dressed her in her new disguise—had been amused too. The guys had cracked up watching her stumble around in the ridiculous things. The footwear was just another source of pain—mental and physical—she didn't need. The shoes seemed to fit okay, that wasn't the problem. The trouble was, she'd never learned to walk in high heels.

Deidre said to Moran, "I knew if I took her to the bar, the drag queens would do a great job on her. After all, they morphed me into a guy who fooled both of you."

"Yeah," Kera injected, "but when you were walking up to the door, I thought there was something familiar about you. I just couldn't figure out what it was."

She thought she'd better sit down before she fell down. These shoes were going to be the death of her.

Deidre fiddled with one of Kera's curls. "Didn't you always wonder, sis, what you'd look like as a blond? Not bad, I say."

"Not good. Blond and curly is not my look. I look like one of those damned poodles." Kera grimaced at her reflection in the mirror on the wall. Besides having a hairdo befitting a small, cuddly dog, she wore a dress—something she hadn't done since she'd been under her mother's wing. She felt like a guy in drag.

It was one thing to see Deidre turned into a male and quite another thing to allow herself to be femmed-up. But she had to admit, Ally had a great idea, using the talents of the guys at the bar to disguise them. Now she and Dee could travel around Lakeside City undetected. Hopefully.

Moran ran her fingers through Kera's hair. "Being a blond, you'll blend in around this town. You've taken on that Dutch look, though your skin is a bit too dark. Maybe they'll just think you've been in the sun too long. These curls are quite something. Did they give you a perm?" Moran was touring around her, checking her out.

"I won't blend in anywhere if I don't learn to walk in these heels. And yes, they bleached, permed, and—"

"My dear sister, those wedges are hardly heels."

"To you, maybe, but to me, I feel like I'm walking with wobbly, wooden blocks stuck to the bottom of my feet." Kera tramped across the room to demonstrate.

Deidre turned to Moran and rolled her eyes. "I'm going to have to work with her on walking in wedges."

Moran gently touched Kera's head. "How does that lump feel, dear?"

"Sore, especially with all the messing around the guys did with my hair. I still have a headache, but it's a bit better."

Moran sat on her sofa and looked at her. "The makeup job is something else. Those glasses help too. But I hope those aren't somebody's prescription lenses. Won't help your stability on those shoes."

"No, they're just frames with clear glass." Kera adjusted her glasses.

Deidre looked at her face. "They did a good job on you. I don't think I would have known you. They're talented guys. They sure did a great job on me. My broken nose and black eyes really did go down and fade a bit, but still, they had to do a lot of work to make it look as good as it does. Ally said the swelling actually helps distort my face and makes me look more masculine."

"I have to say, my dears, I'm impressed with those folks. You two look like a young heterosexual couple." Moran smiled.

Kera scoffed. "One problem—we're playing the wrong roles. I should get the pants and Dee should have the dress." She wondered how she'd ever function in the damned dress.

"Well, I conquered a male swagger, Kera, so you can certainly work on your feminine side." Deidre joined Moran on the sofa.

Both of them watched her practice walking in the white wedges. She could tell they tried to hold back their laughter. "I'm not sure the word 'conquer' quite fits, Dee, but I am impressed you've found your inner male." She laughed. To her, Dee's walk resembled a gay guy trying not to be femme.

Deidre turned to Moran. "I'm so grateful to Ally. She got everyone together to pull off Kera's new look. Ally found us the hairdresser and makeup guy, someone else went out and found the dress, shoes and matching handbag."

"Hopefully, we both can get around town without being noticed." Kera took off the shoes and rubbed her feet. "But these damned shoes could be my downfall."

"Oh, Moran, look, I have to show you this." Deidre pulled out a nun's black habit from a duffel bag she and Kera had brought back from the makeover session at the bar. "There's another one just like it in the bag. The guys thought if we needed a change of costume, we could use these. Can you imagine, they had these things in their wardrobe room." She held the habit next to her body. "The costumes come with crosses, a Bible and the most horrific shoes."

"You mean sensible shoes." Kera continued to massage her feet.

Deidre seemed to ignore her comment as she slipped the habit over her head and adjusted the top. "It's polyester. Look, no wrinkles."

Moran fingered the cross hanging from Deidre's waist. "It strikes me you might stand out more in those things. Not that many Catholics in this city, but I guess we do have the convent up the road, not that you see the nuns around that often. They must be fairly cloistered."

"I used to think when I was in junior high that I wanted to be a nun." Kera plucked the other habit from the duffel bag, shook it out, and held it against her front. "The outfits are a bit...well, cumbersome and drab, but the shoes won't hurt my feet." She looked at Deidre, certain her second shoe remark would get a rise out of her sister.

"You would like those hot black oxfords, Kera." Deidre smirked. "And I remember you talking about the convent, but I never could figure how you planned on becoming a nun when you weren't even Catholic. Did that little snag never occur to you?" Deidre tossed her a questioning glance.

"A small, solvable problem, Dee. I wasn't a soldier either until I signed on the army's dotted line."

"Did you think you could become Catholic? You never were much for participating in Christianity of any sort. Mom and Dad had a hard time getting you to Sunday school—or staying there, for that matter." Deidre backed over to Moran, gesturing for help with a zipper. "You always found your way to the playground next door to our church."

"I didn't believe in killing either, Dee, but that didn't stop me from going into the army. Sometimes you do what you have to do, but luckily, for the Catholics and me, I figured out I was gay—and didn't have to marry a man—before I made a commitment to celibacy, the Roman Catholic Church, and some mighty fine shoes."

Deidre threw her a rope tie with a cross attached. "Your self-discovery was a blessing, for sure, especially in regard to shoes."

Kera put the tie around her waist and slipped on the shoes. "Now these fit fine. They're actually wonderful after those horrid heels. Say, Moran, how do we look as the...uh...Sisters of We-Get-No-Mercy?"

Moran started to laugh, but quickly reacted to the last four words. "I'm hoping you won't need mercy. You and Deidre are good young women who have done nothing wrong, but unfortunately, it looks like you're going to have to prove it."

Deidre started taking off the nun's costume. "Playing dress-up was fun, took my mind off things for a while. But suddenly I'm back to feeling really scared, Kera."

"I know, I'm scared, too."

Deidre looked over at her. "I thought you were never scared of anything."

"You were wrong."

CHAPTER TWENTY-FIVE

Mandy

Mandy's dream of making love to Kera was following her into waking moments. She tried to crawl back, stay with the pleasure, but the sensations let loose of her, sending her toward the day. She held on to the lusciousness of her dream as long as she could, until the last images faded and blew away, leaving her with reality.

Shit!

She threw off her blanket, got up, went into the bathroom and turned on the shower. She still hadn't heard from Kera. Now she didn't know where Deidre had gone. She'd found out from her sources that the police had been tailing Deidre, hoping she'd lead them to Kera, but they'd lost her when she'd gone into the gay bar. So now, there was an all-out search for both of them.

Mandy adjusted the water temperature and slipped into the shower. She couldn't get Kera out of her head. It wasn't just about sex. Her feelings were becoming far more serious. She realized she was falling for Kera. No, not falling—to be honest with herself, it was a done deal. She'd already fallen in love with Kera. And falling for Kera should not have happened on so many levels. She shouldn't be involved with—in love with—a client's sister, a person with PTSD, or a woman who still pined for her dead lover.

Then there were the what-ifs. What if Kera killed Sam? What if she killed Don? The situation was getting too complicated and almost certainly would end in disaster.

What if both Kera and Deidre were involved in Don's death? Her gut told her neither of them was capable of murder, but what if her feelings were in cahoots with her desires? Were her desires covering her eyes, keeping her from seeing the truth?

What if Kera's mental stability never got better? She thought she could probably be okay with the PTSD, which she hoped would lessen in time, but Kera being a killer? Even if Kera murdering someone had to do with her PTSD—making her not totally responsible for her actions, at least a legally mitigating factor—she'd personally have a hard time accepting it. And, would Kera be likely to kill again?

She realized a PTSD excuse wouldn't keep Kera out of jail, so worrying about an intimate relationship was a moot point.

Her mind returned to the starting block of her list of fears, hitting the same worrying points. She plowed through her list over and over again, trying to find a fallacy in her thinking, anything that might bring her to a more favorable ending—something she could live with, something she could survive.

Mandy stepped out of the shower and toweled herself dry, continuing to ruminate.

Could Deidre and Kera have found each other? It wouldn't surprise her. The twin sisters floated on the same wavelength. Not that they were all that much alike, personality wise, but they were so in tune, so emotionally inseparable, so in rhythm with each other, like the tide to the sea. Somehow, someway, she had to believe they'd find each other, sooner or later.

Once she dressed, she went into the kitchen and filled the coffeepot. She opened a can of cat food and scraped the contents into Mr. Moxin's bowl. At the sound of the can popping open, the cat came running into the kitchen.

"Well, Mr. Moxin, how are you this morning?" Mandy put down his dish on the black and yellow paw print mat and brushed his fur with her hand.

She walked to the door leading to the outside and retrieved the *Lakeside City Journal* from the porch. She sat down at the table and opened the paper.

VAN BROCKLIN DAUGHTER SOUGHT IN DEATH OF LOCAL MAN
Lakeside City police are looking for Kera Van Brocklin, 33, a suspect in the

death of Sam Zander, 51. Zander was found on July 25 stabbed to death in his home.

A Buick Le Sabre, registered to the former mayor of Lakeside City, Willem Van Brocklin, was found in the driveway. The vehicle was known to be last driven by Kera Van Brocklin. The police have asked if anyone has any information as to Van Brocklin's whereabouts, they should call the Lakeside City police immediately.

Though not confirmed by the police, it is rumored that Kera's twin sister, Deidre Bledsoe née Van Brocklin is wanted for questioning.

Sam Zander was recently laid off from...

The coffeepot stopped perking. Mandy stood and poured a cup for herself. Reading about Kera's problems took her breath away. How could this be happening to her friend? The word "friend" wasn't quite right. She guessed the correct term was lover, but she didn't want to think about her feelings again. She went back to the table and sat down. She skimmed the article and stopped at a particular section that caught her eye.

Pastor Don Bledsoe was stabbed to death a week prior to Sam Zander's murder. Police had no comment regarding the possibility of a relationship between the two deaths...

She was certain the police would try to tie the two murder cases together. They know Kera was at the scenes of both murders. Good God, she'd started to sweat. Maybe she'd have to take another shower. She picked up her napkin and wiped her brow. The article made the threat of linking the two murders far too real. She continued reading.

...Our investigation has uncovered that many members of the late Pastor Bledsoe's church have been active in opposing the inclusion of the LGBT community into the city's Civil Rights Ordinance. However, no official spokesperson for the church would confirm a Citizens Against Perversion (CAP) connection.

"It figures!" she blurted.

Of course the members wouldn't admit a connection to CAP, the bastards. She figured the church's denial should say something to the people of the city. Hiding behind anonymity only highlighted their hypocrisy. Then again, she realized she was being overly optimistic. People would believe what people wanted to believe. She went back to reading.

The proposed inclusion of LGBT people into the ordinance passed the council by one vote. However, CAP is sponsoring a petition drive to rescind that decision by having the question of LGBT inclusion in the ordinance put to a vote of the electorate in the upcoming November election.

"Goddamn them!" She glanced up and saw Mr. Moxin had stopped eating. The cat stared at her. He was used to her talking to him, but not in that tone of voice. She reassured him. "It's okay, Moxin. Your mommy's upset, but not at you, sweetie."

He went back to his food. She went back to the newspaper article.

According to Harry Janssen, 43, a city council member and owner of a local real estate company, Kera Van Brocklin is a member of LEAP, an organization that opposes the idea of putting gay rights to a vote.

Now that was an out-and-out lie if she ever heard one. She tried to keep her thoughts from bursting out loud and scaring poor dear Mr. Moxin, again, who'd abandoned his food in favor of curling up on her feet.

Janssen had no idea whether Kera was or wasn't part of the group. Kera's only involvement was losing her temper and going after the damned demonstrators at the bar—and that hadn't been a LEAP activity, more like spontaneous combustion. Janssen was just trying to throw gasoline on the fire, fueling the right-wingers. She knew his opinions on gay rights.

She read through to the end of the article.

Janssen denied knowing much about CAP. He said he doesn't "get involved in local political activities of any sort..." However, it is on record that Janssen was against adding the LGBT community to the Civil Rights Ordinance...
(See Editorial: page 3, Section A: "And the Beat Goes On" for more.)

Mandy got up and poured another cup of coffee. Mr. Moxin stood at the door, ready for his morning rounds. She opened the door and let him out before taking her hot coffee and sitting down to her newspaper. She turned to the editorial page.

And the Beat Goes On
By Daniel Williams
This spring a proposal was being considered by the Lakeside City Council to include LGBT people in the city's Civil Rights Ordinance. Since this proposal was introduced—and now passed—there has been considerable opposition to

it, spawning a petition drive (spearheaded by a group called CAP) to rescind the council's decision by a vote of the people. The objection has come mostly from fundamentalist Christian churches in our community, but the debate has spread to almost every man and woman on the street.

The recent ordinance change is supported by LEAP.

The lines have been drawn.

Those opposed to the inclusion of the LGBT people, hide behind fortified institutions, and throw poison word darts...

A chill ran through Mandy. In the last few days, she'd gotten antigay hate letters, harassing emails and messages—two of them threatening her life—on her voice mail at her work. Her boss at Legal Aid had notified the police, but other than a perfunctory visit from an officer who'd filed a report, nothing seemed to come of it. Luckily, the public didn't know her home address or her cell phone number—at least she hoped not. She was determined not to focus on the hate and threats in those messages. Their purpose was to scare her off. *Not going to happen!*

But fear began to rise up and push through her bravado like a deadly gas. Fear constantly stood by, trying to shoot a hole in her determination. She quickly stuffed her anxiety down, took a deep breath and went back to reading the editorial.

But it appears that it may be more than just a feud of beliefs, ideas and way of life—more than just words.

We have had two murders; both victims were part of the group against the inclusion of LGBT people into the ordinance and from the same church.

What does this mean?

We do know our city has become divided over this ordinance. We don't have any solid proof that the ordinance issue is the motive behind either murder, but it certainly causes a thinking person to pause and wonder.

If you go into almost any café, the mall or any other place where people gather and talk, you'll hear the rancor that has been generated from this issue. I have yet to find a citizen who is neutral on this matter, but I have interviewed many red-faced, angry people who have turned against a neighbor, a friend and even a spouse, because of this debate—

Bam!

It sounded to her like a gunshot. Her heart beat hard and fast, like it was about to break loose and fly out of her chest.

Someone was out there, making good on the death threat against her. She ducked down, crawled to a corner in the kitchen where she couldn't be seen from a window. She didn't have her cell phone nearby, so couldn't call the police.

She had never been so scared. She waited, shaking, not knowing what to do next, feeling paralyzed.

Finally, she checked her watch. She calculated about five minutes had gone by, and no one was trying to break in. No more gunshots, no noise at all.

She slowly moved over under a window facing out on the street, and carefully moved up and peered out.

Nothing. It just looked like a quiet suburban neighborhood, not any strange vehicles around. She noticed Mr. Moxin ambling across the street to the neighbor's house.

She took a deep breath. It must have been a car backfiring.

She wished she didn't have to go in to work today. Her nerves were frayed already. Besides, she found it hard to focus on her other clients' problems when she was so worried about Kera and Deidre. She wished they would call, but she understood why they wouldn't.

She sat back down at the table. Life felt heavy. She needed to calm herself and refocus so she could go on with her day, with her life. She closed her eyes, took a deep breath and tried to bring down her anxiety level. She wasn't back to normal—whatever that was these days—but her heart had slowed, and she did feel a little calmer. She'd give herself a few more minutes before getting ready for work.

She picked up the newspaper and read about the dedication of the city's new Willem Van Brocklin Water Adventures Park this coming Saturday.

Then, she got up and went into the bathroom to fix her hair. She wondered how Kera and Deidre felt at not being able to attend the ceremony honoring their father. They should be at the dedication, but wouldn't dare show up, not even to watch. Given the situation, perhaps not taking part in the ceremony was the least of their concerns.

Actually, she decided, Kera's and Deidre's absence was probably a good thing because of the faceoff that would happen between CAP and LEAP at the dedication. CAP was planning to use the event to get enough signatures on their petition, while LEAP would be there to prevent that outcome.

At the last LEAP meeting, Mandy had directed the group to come up with a strategy for countering CAP's petition signing on Saturday. She'd thought they'd done a great job, devising a plan to ask the LGBT community and their allies to come out—those who felt comfortable doing so—and be a presence at the dedication of the new water park.

They would try to convince people not to sign the petition and explain why having the LGBT community protected in the ordinance was important. They'd give out balloons with the words: "Decline to Sign" on them.

Since the city council had voted to name the park after Mayor Van Brocklin, Mandy didn't like the potential confrontation at the honoring of the twins' dad, but what could she do? CAP needed to be stopped. She figured Kera and Deidre would agree with her on that. And, if CAP didn't show, she'd pull LEAP out as well. She made a mental note to talk to her LEAP co-chair, but she was convinced CAP would be there. She glanced at the time. It was getting late. She needed to get to work.

* * *

Mandy was exhausted. She hadn't taken a break all day, except to run out for fast food and bring it back to her desk. She glanced out the window. It was starting to get dark. Legal Aid was in a pretty seedy side of town. She didn't like staying late, but she'd been getting so much done, she'd lost track of time. Being alone in the office felt spooky. She checked the clock: nine twenty. This time of year didn't get really dark until almost ten o'clock since Michigan was on the tail end of the Eastern Time Zone.

She had hoped to get a call from Kera or Deidre today, but she'd heard nothing, like they had been sucked into a black hole. Earlier, she'd called her ex-girlfriend at the prosecutor's office. She didn't learn anything new, but was informed the police hadn't found Kera or Deidre yet. She didn't know whether that was good news or not.

Mandy had been spending so much time with LEAP activities and dealing with Kera and Deidre's problems, she'd gotten behind in Legal Aid work. She had a few other things she wanted to finish up, which would only take about a half hour more, then she would go home.

She'd been holding down the fort all day at Legal Aid. Though the agency was officially closed today, she still had a few people come by to pick up papers and a few others wanting appointments. The rest of the staff was attending a citywide symposium of all the agencies in Lakeside City serving the poor.

The late Mayor Van Brocklin had been a great supporter of these agencies. When federal and state funds started drying up, he'd worked to find funds from the city's coffers. And when the City funds dried up, he'd planned and held fundraisers, along with twisting the arms of Lakeside City's affluent. With his death, funding had become uncertain and the agencies were huddling together, hoping to come up with some solutions, or—as Carolyn Rogers, her boss, told her last week—there could be layoffs.

About a week ago, Carolyn had asked her to go over some papers and give feedback about a few cases. There was one case Mandy knew needed her immediate attention and had promised Carolyn she'd get it done tonight, because Carolyn needed it tomorrow.

Mandy searched her desk for the case file, but couldn't find it. She recalled her boss telling her the relevant file was in her file cabinet.

She got up and went into Carolyn's messy office. She thought Carolyn took advantage of the fact that her office was in the back, out of the public's sight. Anyone working on the main floor—like her—had to make sure everything was cleared off their desks and locked up at the end of the day.

From the window, she saw a flash of light. A moment later, she heard a crack of thunder. She hadn't heard a storm was coming in tonight. The wind started to hurl rain against the west window in Carolyn's office, pounding so hard, she feared it would break through the glass. Crap. She'd left her umbrella in her car.

She opened the desk's lap drawer and found the key to the file cabinet.

A sound came from the front of the building, like someone had opened the main door. She was sure—almost sure—she had locked that door at around five o'clock, after the last person wanting an appointment left the building.

She listened, but didn't hear anything else. Must be the wind from the storm jiggling the door, she decided. This was an old creaky building. The noises weren't as apparent to her in the daytime when the place was humming with activity. She figured she must be still edgy from what she'd thought was a gunshot this morning and had turned out to be nothing.

Now she heard water dripping from somewhere close by. She looked around and up toward the ceiling and spotted a leak. Water dripped onto an empty potato chip bag in a trashcan. She imagined Carolyn had strategically placed the trashcan in that very place because of previous rain showers.

Mandy returned to her work and fingered through the files. The material she sought should be under S, but damn it, Carolyn needed a personal filer. There seemed to be no rhyme nor reason for what was filed under any particular letter, leaving her to wonder how Carolyn ever found anything. She found a package of Planter's Peanuts under S—two P words, for God's sake. She giggled out loud.

She heard another noise.

This time, she thought she heard the floor creaking. She stopped and listened, but heard nothing more. Still, her body reacted with a prickle of fear rushing up her spine. What if someone was out there…

Finally, it occurred to her that it was probably another lawyer coming in to do some catching up like she was doing, or someone picking up something for tomorrow due to an early morning court case. Yeah, that had to be the explanation.

But if that were the case, why wasn't she also hearing other kinds of noises, like desk chairs being pulled out and drawers or file cabinets being opened?

She froze, holding her breath, hoping at any moment to hear a fellow worker calling out to her.

Silence.

Footsteps moved slowly toward Carolyn's office, then stopped, but she could hear breathing.

This was no friendly visitor.

She looked for an escape and realized she was trapped. There was only one door out of Carolyn's office and if she tried to go out that way, she'd face whoever was out there. She looked around. Maybe she could get out the window. She could probably break the glass with a chair and use it to step on and climb out.

Could she do it in time?

She flicked off the lights, hoping to buy herself some escape time. It would be harder to see her in the dark, especially now, since very little light came in from the outside. She grabbed the chair, ran over to the window and smashed the panes. Glass flew out and blew back at her along with the wind and rain.

Hands grabbed her from behind.

CHAPTER TWENTY-SIX

Kera

Kera couldn't sleep. She felt like a snagged fish flopping around in the bottom of a boat. She couldn't stop thinking about the conversations she'd been having with her sister since her arrival at Moran's. Dee found out from Ally that Kevin had bragged about beating up Don at McFarland Park, which would have been sometime on Friday. Kera figured the incident certainly fit into the time frame and sequence of events around Don's death since she'd seen Kevin's bleeding knuckles at the Out-and-About Saturday night, just before their fray with the demonstrators.

She agreed with what Mandy had told her about Kevin—he had a lot of rage in him. She'd seen that bottled-up anger before in other soldiers. And to be honest, in herself as well. She knew how a guy like Don could easily ignite that anger. She believed Kevin was capable of beating the shit out of him, maybe even murdering him, but that begged the question why hadn't he murdered Don on Friday? What was the difference on Saturday night? What happened? What made him decide to kill Don then?

Well, she surmised, maybe after beating up Don on Friday, Kevin thought about it and wished he'd eradicated Don, shut him up permanently. Kevin could have gone back to McFarland Park on

Saturday night, revved up from the fight outside the bar, and hung out there, hoping Don would show up again so he could finish the job. Or maybe Kevin just happened to be at McFarland when Don showed up and he took his anger to the next level.

God, what was Don thinking? What had possessed him to go back there after being beaten the day before…how crazy was that?

As far as she was concerned, Don was a slimeball. Worse, he was a blight on society. She had to admit she was pissed enough at what Don did to others—especially to her sister—that given the right circumstances, she might have murdered him herself. That was a scary thought…

Or maybe a frightening revelation.

When she'd told Dee she hadn't killed Sam, her sister had seemed relieved. Did Dee see a killer lurking in her? She wondered. Maybe Iraq had changed her. She'd killed there. She'd had to kill in Iraq—kill or be killed. Was blaming Iraq a convenient excuse? Or had the war unleashed something already inside her?

In civilian life—not in war, not in self-defense, not in the defense of someone else—could she kill someone because she was pissed at them? She'd like to think not, but could she guarantee she wouldn't lose control? No.

She turned her thoughts away from the question that scared her, made her cringe, and she couldn't answer anyway. She focused on something she could do. Thursday was Dee's scheduled meeting with Kevin. She was glad she would be going with Dee, instead of her sister going to see Kevin alone. She'd be there to hear what he had to say and be able to protect Dee if needed.

She was amazed and pleased at her sister's newfound strength. Maybe the strength had always been there, but hadn't come out in the past because Dee had always counted on her to be the strong one, and she'd always accommodated her twin. She really liked what she saw in Dee. Now, she had a partner she could count on.

Meeting with Kevin could prove dicey, so she needed to be ready. She couldn't count on taking Kevin in a fight—if it came to that. Her sister had no experience fighting—at least none she knew of. Dee wouldn't be much help in a physical confrontation, new courage or not.

Even though Kera was trained in hand-to-hand combat and had earned a black belt, Kevin was trained in combat and martial arts too. She had seen him fight at the Out-and-About that night. He was good, but thinking back to the brawl, maybe she could take him. However, in this situation, she definitely needed to be sure she would come out on top. That's why she needed a gun and would have to get one tomorrow.

Vinny's Gun and Knife Shop would be her supplier. No place else to go, given her unfortunate life circumstances, notoriety and piss-ass bad luck.

She was quite certain Vinny wouldn't be back in town yet, but perhaps she could break into his shop and take a gun. God, crazy how the idea of breaking the law came to her so quickly and seemed normal—that couldn't be good thing.

Her life in Iraq had put her into a different world with different rules. A time when she'd had "U.S.A. Army Approved" stamped on her head and a time when dealing with the enemy often required breaking in, busting down doors, and sometimes taking things. Now, she felt stuck somewhere in an in-between land—and she was desperate. She acted as a civilian in the United States, but she'd have to function under hostile, wartime conditions if she was going to find Don's killer and keep her sister and herself out of jail.

She remembered Vinny had bars on his shop windows, except for one in the back storage area that he'd recently installed for ventilation. He'd told her he hadn't gotten the bars put in that window yet. When did he say the bars would be installed? Oh, yeah, now she recalled. He'd said the installers couldn't get there to mount them until mid-August sometime. He'd been worried about waiting that long, fearing a break-in.

Well, his fears would turn out to be well-grounded, because she was about to make a trip out to his shop to do just that. Of course, she intended to give his gun back when she was done with it. Maybe she'd even leave him a note, letting him know…no, that would be dumb, really dumb.

Kera yawned and closed her eyes.

* * *

Kera heard her name. Now, someone was tapping on her shoulder. She jerked awake to see Moran standing by the bed. She took a deep breath, working to calm herself and not react like she had when her sister woke her. The expression on Moran's face was saturated in concern. In spite of her body's hyperalert response, she could barely think. She felt so groggy, out of it, like her mind was slugging uphill in mud.

"Kera…Kera, you need to wake up. Mandy's been hurt."

When she heard Mandy's name, she yanked herself into the day. "Mandy hurt? How? Where?" She sat up.

"Deidre had the radio on. It was on the news this morning. Mandy was in her office last night and someone attacked her. They don't know who."

"Is she okay?" Rubbing her eyes, Kera swung her legs around and put her feet on the floor.

"They said she's in critical condition."

"I've got to get to her and find out—" Kera stood.

Moran put a hand on her shoulder. "Do you think that's wise, dear?"

* * *

"Is this going to work, Kera?"

"I'm planning on it." Kera was determined to get in to see Mandy, and she'd come up with the best plan she could think of, and she didn't need her sister's doubts or fears. She'd decided to make use of the nun costumes in order to get into the hospital. She figured it would not only be a great disguise for them, but might make it more likely they'd be allowed to see Mandy.

"You can wait in the car, Dee. You don't have to come into the hospital with me. But I need to find out how Mandy's doing and if she knows who attacked her. I can handle it myself. I'm just hoping she's in good enough condition to talk to me."

"Are you sure no one will know me? I mean, I work with these people—or at least I did. This is going to be so weird." Deidre angled the rearview mirror so she could take a quick look at her face. She'd wiped off the stubble, given she was now playing a nun. Her facial features were still distorted and she didn't think she'd be easily recognized, but she couldn't be sure. She returned the mirror to its original position.

Kera glanced at her. "Believe me, they won't know you. You can keep your face down, if you want, like you're contemplating deep thoughts or praying." Kera reached over and patted her sister's cheek. "You've always been the deep thinker in the family." She grinned. "But like I said, you don't have to come in. You can wait here and—"

"I didn't put on this outfit for nothing and besides, haven't you heard nuns always travel in pairs? I'm coming in with you." Dee pulled the red Mustang into the hospital parking lot.

"Do they travel in red Mustangs with gay and Wiccan stickers on them?" Kera flashed a quick smile before reaching down to retie her shoelace.

"Wiccan? What's Wiccan?" Deidre frowned.

"You don't know?"

"I wouldn't be asking if I knew, Kera. Don't be a smart-ass."

"Witchcraft. Ally's into paganism, witches, that kind of thing."

"Oh, God!" Deidre slammed on the brakes.

"Close your mouth, Dee. It doesn't make her a wicked person. There's such a thing as good witches. It's just a form of paganism. But these stickers on the car makes us, as nuns, stand out like a pimple on a beauty contestant's nose."

"I'm lucky that cop didn't kill me." Dee stared ahead, motionless.

Kera looked at her sister. She didn't seem to be functioning. "Dee, move this car. There are people coming in behind us."

Hearing her name seemed to activate Dee. Her foot found the accelerator.

"Park over there." Kera pointed to the empty far side of the parking lot.

"You haven't exactly told me your plan." Dee turned off the engine, took a breath, and looked at her.

"We'll have to play it by ear—"

Dee raised her eyebrows. "That means you really don't have a plan. Am I right?"

"Don't worry, Dee, with your large nose and the fact that people don't expect to see you as a nun, you'll get by. Besides, I'll do the talking. You keep looking down at the floor like you're praying or something." Kera reached for her fake glasses on the dashboard and put them on. She checked herself in the mirror. She made sure she had some of her curly blond hair sticking out. Being identical to her sister in looks, she had to be careful that she wasn't taken for Dee. She thought her disguise was good enough and who in hell would expect either one of them in nun's attire, even so, she decided to avoid direct eye contact as much as possible.

Deidre took the Bible and hesitantly got out of the car. Kera walked over to Dee's side of the vehicle and grabbed her arm, "Come on Dee, it's showtime."

Deidre rolled her eyes.

Kera talked to one of the two women at the reception desk. She didn't want to give them Mandy's room number, explaining Mandy couldn't have any visitors other than close family.

Kera insisted Mandy's family lived out-of-state—she didn't have to lie—and they'd specifically requested to have someone from her parish come and pray with her. She figured Mandy most likely hadn't been in any condition to specify a religious preference when she was brought into the hospital emergency room, so making Mandy a Catholic for the day would probably fly.

She glanced down, fiddled with the cross hanging around her neck while she went on to explain how "Father Norm" from their parish would be very upset if they didn't get in to pray with Mandy.

The other receptionist, who been filling out some forms and overhearing Kera's request, stopped her work and made a call, explaining the situation—several times—then finally put down the phone and told them they had permission to go to Mandy's room to pray with her.

Kera and Deidre got into the elevator.

"I'm shaking all over." Dee pulled the Bible closer to her chest.

"It's a good thing you have on that bulky habit to cover up your shaking. Don't worry, all you have to do is keep your head down. Remember, you're the praying nun and I'm the talking nun." Kera grinned.

The elevator opened. She saw a tall, balding man dressed in gray pants and a matching shirt pushing a mop over the corridor's floor, leaving a strong scent of cleaning solution. A uniformed cop was stationed in an open sitting area. Kera kept her head slanted down, focusing mostly on the floor as she walked. From out of the corner of her eye, she saw the cop looking their way, then he turned his attention to a woman who approached him.

Another cop sat on a chair outside Mandy's room.

She and Dee approached the door.

The gray-haired cop struggled to rise as they neared. He looked like someone who had held mostly desk jobs throughout his career. His potbelly stuck out and muffin-topped over his belt. He put down the magazine he'd been reading and said, "Sisters, the lady at the desk called up to tell us you were coming, but Ms. Bakker hasn't been conscious since she was brought here, so she can't really pray—"

"But," Kera glanced up, "we came to pray for her, officer." She quickly looked back down.

"So I heard. The doctor gives you ten minutes with her, but I'm giving you just five 'cause I'm not supposed to let anyone in here except the doctors and nurses. Those were strict orders from the chief and that's who I take orders from, not the hospital staff. But I'm a devout

Christian myself and I believe in prayer. So pray the short ones—if you Catholics got short ones." He opened the door and ushered them inside, then pulled the door closed, all except for a crack.

Dee stood at the bottom of the bed, her head down.

Kera went over to the side, bent over Mandy and whispered, "Mandy, can you hear me?"

Mandy's eyes were closed and sunken in their sockets. Her face appeared covered in white onionskin. Her hair was matted and sticky looking. Kera saw some clotted blood still stuck in her hair. She was wired to tubes, machines and monitors that pumped and beeped.

She leaned in closer to Mandy's ear. "Mandy…Mandy." She gently touched her on the shoulder and kissed her cheek. "It's Kera, can you hear me? Please talk to me." She felt tears coming into her eyes. "Mandy, I need to know who did this to you."

Mandy slowly opened her eyelids partway and looked up. Her eyes were glazed over, like she wasn't quite there. She didn't speak.

"Mandy, can you hear me? Do you know who I am?"

Nothing.

"Mandy, it's me, Kera. I'm in nun drag." Kera managed a slight smile and pointed at her sister. "That's Dee under the sister's habit. We disguised ourselves to get in here. We don't have much time and need to talk to you."

Mandy's gaze seemed to reflect comprehension. Her lips turned up slightly at the corners.

Kera glanced at Dee in relief, but her sister wasn't watching. Looked like Dee took the praying thing seriously. She whispered "Come on over here Dee, so Mandy can see you."

She looked back down at Mandy. "You are going to be okay. You just need to rest." She didn't know if that was true, but she wanted to reassure Mandy and give her something positive to help her fight for her life.

She felt like she should tell Mandy she loved her—a good thing, a comforting thing to say. She did have love for Mandy, but what if Mandy heard it as "in love?" Telling Mandy she loved her could put her in a position she couldn't handle. How could she later say I meant, I love you, but I'm not in love with you. And if she didn't have the courage to hurt Mandy by telling her the truth, she could propel herself into a future she wasn't ready for. After quickly swirling those thoughts around in her brain, she decided not to say anything about love—as it was, she had enough life-choice consequences haunting her.

"Mandy, do you know who did this to you?" She gently rubbed Mandy's cheek with the backs of her fingers.

Mandy seemed to try to speak, but her voice was faint and strained.

"I can barely hear you." She put her ear right up to Mandy's lips. "Say it again, Mandy."

Mandy repeated what she'd said.

Kera pulled up, turned to Dee and said, "You listen, she didn't make much sense to me."

Dee put her head down close to Mandy. "Tell me who did this to you."

Kera saw Mandy moving her lips, saying something to Dee.

The door opened.

Dee straightened as the cop stuck his head inside and said, "Time's up, sisters."

Kera put up her hand and made the sign of the cross over Mandy, like she'd seen the Catholic army chaplains do. Mandy's eyes closed. She thought Mandy had slipped back into sleep.

* * *

"Let's get the hell out of here and back to Moran's house. Driving around dressed as nuns in this bright red car with police-attracting stickers slapped all over it is not exactly keeping us out of the spotlight." Kera felt hot and sweaty. Wearing the nun outfit over her regular clothes was part of the problem, but pulling off her impersonation of a nun, dealing with her sister's jumpiness, and having the cop—on the way out—eyeballing them like he could see through their costumes and through their intent might have added to her discomfort. Then again, she might be misinterpreting the cop's suspicion. Maybe the nun outfit came with Catholic guilt attached.

Dee pulled the car out of the hospital parking lot. "What's that half-ass grin on your face about? That was one hell of a nerve-wracking experience…and you're sitting there grinning."

"Nothing, really. Just thinking about Catholic guilt." Kera worked to unzip her costume.

Deidre let go of the steering wheel to pull off the top of her habit. "Really? Sometimes I just don't get you. How can you—"

Kera reached over and grabbed the wheel, "Jesus, Dee, watch where you're going. You almost hit that car. Why don't you pull over and stop a minute if you want to get out of those clothes."

"It's okay now, I just needed to get the headpiece off. I'll finish changing when we get back to Moran's."

"I know you were nervous in there, sis, but you played your part very well." She felt she needed to encourage Dee's bravery. For the most part, she was impressed. Not that long ago, Dee would never have done anything like that.

"Well, I have to say, I'm sure glad to get out of there. I could just see us getting caught and ending up in jail."

"The thought crossed my mind as well."

"Really? You looked so calm and cool in there. I don't get it, you seem calmer when you're putting yourself at risk than when you're supposedly relaxing." Dee gave her a quizzical look.

She'd noticed that about herself as well, but didn't have an answer for it.

"Before I forget," Dee continued, "I want to compliment you on your priestly—or should I say, nun-ly—blessing of Mandy."

"Just one of my many survival skills I learned in the army." Kera gave her sister a smug grin.

"Well, before you become too self-satisfied, I think you might have done it backward. I mean, the sign of the cross thing."

"Look, I was the one who was almost a nun, not you. I should know." Kera snickered. "Besides, the cop wasn't Catholic. He probably wouldn't know one way or the other."

"You always have to have the last word, don't you?"

"Uh-huh." Kera thought a moment and said, "Don't forget, 'uh-huh' is a word."

Dee pursed her lips and shook her head.

Kera started thinking about what she should do next. She needed to get out to Vinny's shop and "borrow" a gun. She wondered how a little burglary would go over with her sister. Not well, she figured, but she was—

Deidre broke her train of thought, "When I tried to listen to Mandy, I didn't really understand what she'd said, either."

"Yeah, it sounded garbled. What did it sound like to you?"

"It sounded like 'eerie lands end.' That doesn't make any sense to me. Does it to you?" Deidre held the steering wheel with one hand and combed her hair with her fingers.

Kera thought for a moment. "No, and it also doesn't sound at all like what she said to me."

"What did you hear her say?"

"Geez, Dee, I thought she said something about a person named 'Carolyn.' I don't know anyone named Carolyn." She shook her head. "But I'm not sure if that's what I heard or not. And I doubt that anyone named Carolyn could beat the shit out of her like that…unless, of course, she was some kind of Amazon woman."

"Wow, we each heard something really different, but neither of her utterances seem to mean anything…to us, anyway." Deidre kicked off one of her nun shoes and pushed it away from the gas pedal. "We can't even be sure she knew who we were, or even how alert she was. I've dealt with a lot people in the hospital in that kind of condition and fifty percent of the time their responses are pretty much gibberish. "

"I think she knew me. I really do."

"That may be true, but whether or not she could understand what you were asking or even able to give back an intelligible response is questionable."

"If that's true, we've accomplished nothing as far as finding out who did this to her, or who may have killed Don." Kera stuffed her habit into the duffel bag and threw it on the backseat of the car.

"Another thing." Dee glanced at her. "It doesn't make sense to me that Don and Mandy were attacked by the same person. What on earth do they have in common?"

"I hate to put it this way, but how about homosexuality?" Kera winced at the sick look coming over her sister's face. Well, she figured, it was the truth. They couldn't pussyfoot around it for the rest of their lives. She moved on. "Even so, I'm not sure the gay thing is meaningful. Don was a closeted, self-hating gay and an active gay-basher; and Mandy has been so out there, proud and fighting for gay rights."

"Yes, you're right, they're on different sides of the fence, politically speaking."

"It's puzzling. The reason I'm suspicious of Kevin is that he found out about Don's sexuality and was pissed that Don was fighting against the gay community. That's why he beat the shit out of him and certainly could have gone a step further and killed him. But Kevin doesn't fit as a suspect when it comes to Mandy's attack. Kevin wouldn't have a reason to hurt Mandy. Hell, they're on the same side. Besides, I could tell Kevin really liked Mandy. There's no motive for him to hurt her."

Deidre added, "Unless there's a motive we don't know about."

"Maybe. I haven't been part of the gay community that long, or should I say, it's been sporadic at best. There could be something I'm not aware of. But then again, maybe we're talking about two different attackers. Two different, completely unrelated cases, although there might be a connection or thread linking them. Like, let's say, Kevin killed Don, but someone else, someone who didn't like Mandy's work fighting CAP's efforts, attacked her."

"That could be."

"You weren't there the other night, but I have to say, any one of those nuts who spoke at the city council or those antigay demonstrators at the Out-and-About bar might have been out to get her. She's been in the newspapers and on TV. She's really put herself out there."

"Maybe it's like a revenge killing. Someone killed Don, so now someone else thinks he should kill the leader on the other side."

"Could be, but who is it, or who are they?" Kera scratched her head. Ever since she'd had her hair bleached, her scalp itched.

"When you were telling me about Vinny killing Sam, I began wondering if he could have killed Don too. After all, he used a knife on Sam. Didn't you say it was done in the same way Don was killed— coming from behind and slitting his throat? Good God, it makes me sick thinking about it all."

She glanced over and saw Dee's face had turned pale. "Dee, I'm sorry. We don't have to talk about it." She reached over and rubbed her sister's shoulder.

"No, no, I have to talk about this stuff. It's just what it is, and I have to deal with all the shit that's come down. I've got to be strong and I will be." Deidre gave her an unconvincing smile.

"Well, okay, then, let's get back to Sam's death. At the time, he had his back to Vinny. It was natural Vinny would come at him from behind, but using a knife, slitting his throat, yeah, that piece could link both murders. And frankly, I'm not sure Vinny had to kill Sam at all. I think he could have disarmed Sam, and I was there to help if he needed it. At the time, he wasn't aware I'd taken a bullet to my shoulder. The only thing I can come up with is that Vinny really hated Sam because of his encounter with him on the night of the demonstration at the gay bar."

"Oh, yes, you told me, but that hardly seems like reason enough—"

"It's not easy, Deidre, for gay people to be referred to as abominations and made scapegoats for the ills of society. It's fucking wearing." Kera glared. "It's not an excuse for killing Sam, but it is a reason things like that might happen."

Dee didn't speak for a moment. "Okay, I get what you're saying.... and speaking of gay bashing, I'm so sorry, Kera. I had no idea how involved Don's church became in all the antigay stuff. I should have figured it out at Dad's funeral, but I guess I was blinded by my own desire not to see. And to think how Sam acted to both you and Vinny..." She shook her head. "I just never saw Sam in that way. I'm horrified. With Don, I hope someday you will forgive me for burying my head in the sand when it came to his hatefulness and his behavior against gay people, and you in particular."

Kera couldn't look into Dee's eyes and didn't respond to her sister's need for forgiveness. The memories were too fresh, the wound still open, still stinging. But, of course, she would forgive her sister—just not right now.

She cleared her throat and moved the subject back to possible suspects. "Speaking of Sam, we can't discount the idea that he might have killed Don. After all, he was desperate, had big financial problems and owed lots of money to the kind of people who play rough. Don wouldn't return his donation. He threatened Don."

"I know. I couldn't believe he wouldn't return Sam's money. Don was so holier-than-thou about it. How could he act that way to Sam, then turn around and do the kinds of things he did—" Deidre's voice lowered, "—with men. Then go after them the way he did. How could he do that?"

"I guess you could do those kinds of things by denying who you are and reinforcing your denial by persecuting others for the thing you most hate in yourself."

"But Kera, you didn't rail against homosexuality when you were closeted. You weren't hurtful to others."

"No, but for too long, I put my sexuality in a shoebox, closed the lid and put it in the back of my closet—and stood guard twenty-four hours a day, seven days a week, three hundred sixty-five days a year. It's suffocating, debilitating and spirit robbing. I put up a barrier between me and everyone else. Even you, Dee."

"Will you talk to me more about that someday?"

"Maybe."

* * *

On the way home from seeing Mandy at the hospital, she tried to reason with Dee about the need for a gun, but her sister didn't budge on her insistence that a gun wasn't necessary or a good idea. When they got to Moran's place, Moran joined in with Dee, but Kera was adamant. She was not about to show up at Kevin's office without a weapon. Why couldn't either of them understand the possible danger they would be in if Kevin had murdered Don? What were they thinking? Did they really believe she could somehow sweet-talk Kevin to the police station?

Dee and Moran were the most important people in her life and undoubtedly the people she loved most, but as far as she was concerned, they were too naïve about some things. Mostly, she found their innocence charming, but not when it came to the harsh reality of people doing bad things. She had to trust her own more reality-based sensibilities.

As much as Dee didn't want her to steal the gun, her sister had insisted on coming with her to get it. She supposed Dee had a need to stay physically close to her, probably more like she was hanging in there with her to keep trying to change her mind—a futile mission. Nevertheless, Dee hadn't given up and they were still having the same argument while driving the car to Vinny's shop.

"I really hate guns, Kera. You know that."

The headlights caught a pothole. Kera swerved the car to avoid it. She was annoyed, though not terribly surprised, that Dee couldn't understand. "In this case, it's not about hating or not hating guns, it's about needing one. Right now, I think we need a gun. Doesn't mean we'll—I'll—use it. I'll just have it if I should need it. Got it? Let's not talk about this anymore. We've beaten this topic to death."

"Until you've done something, there's always time to rethink things. And we haven't gotten a gun yet."

Kera decided she would ignore that last comment. Keeping quiet wasn't easy for her. Her sister always blabbed on about her needing the last word. Well, this time, her last word would be silence. Not responding could put a period to a conversation.

She pulled into the parking lot of Vinny's Gun and Knife Shop. Earlier, she'd called to find out if Vinny happened to be at his shop, not that she expected him to be there, but if by chance he were, she'd buy the gun from him. However, when she called, she got his business voice mail letting her know he would be "on vacation," not specifying a return date. That left her with no choice. She had to break in.

She drove the Mustang around to the back of the shop and looked for a place to park out of sight. There was no perfect spot. If someone drove behind the shop, they were going to see the car, but at least it wouldn't be noticeable from the highway.

On the way home from seeing Mandy at the hospital, she'd stopped at a hardware store and picked up a bolt cutter and a few other tools, a flashlight and a padlock. The door to the storage room in the back of the building had an exterior padlock on it. If she decided to cut off the lock instead of going in through the window, she wanted to be able to secure it again, keeping anyone else from taking advantage of an unsecured knife and gun shop, as well as discouraging someone from reporting the break-in. She knew the shop didn't have an alarm system because Vinny had told her he didn't have one, but that a security system was on his list of must-haves in the next year.

"Okay, so what do we do next?" Dee was wringing her hands.

"Since you insisted on coming, you can watch out for anyone who might show up here. I have no reason to believe the cops are keeping an eye on this place, since no one knows Vinny was involved with Sam's death. But I would guess there are extra cops out these days, especially at night, checking out a lot of places because two people have been killed and another victim… She stopped. She felt a pain in her gut just thinking about Mandy lying in the hospital, so pale she could almost see through her skin. The lingering image needed to go. She pushed it out of her mind and focused on the sound of Dee's voice.

"Oh, like a lookout."

"Dee, you've been watching too many cops and robber shows on TV, but yeah, you're the lookout."

"Well, maybe I have, but we are the robbers. I don't like this side of it. I'd rather be the good guys, the cops."

Kera looked over at her sister, wondering why she had given in and allowed her to come on this mission. She was used to dealing with military people. Good guys, bad guys weren't an issue up for discussion. You gave orders and they had to deal with it. "The fact is, we are the good guys. We're trying to find Don's killer and escape our own imprisonment, I might add. Sometimes good guys have to do things that are against the rules or things they'd rather not have to do, and this is one of those times."

Except for the wringing of her hands, Dee's entire body looked like it'd been frozen in time, like the still picture on the television where the action stopped.

Shit, she was mad at herself. There she was again, doing the last word thing. She was sure that was what Dee was thinking under all that fear. Old patterns hang on tight. But what was she supposed to do? She'd told Dee she didn't want her to come. Dee shouldn't be here. But, damn it, it was her choice. Now she needed to suck it up and be helpful.

"This is what we're going to do." Kera pointed to a clump of trees. "You go over there and hang out behind those spruce trees. There are hardly any clouds tonight and lots of stars, so you'll be able to see pretty well. If you see anyone coming in here, you signal me. Got it?"

Her words seemed to push the resume button on her sister. Dee turned to her and asked, "What kind of signal?"

"Hmm…why don't you do your bird call, you know, the one you used to do, sounded a lot to me like 'purdy-purdy-purdy.' I don't remember what kind of bird that was supposed to be."

"Okay, you mean my cardinal call."

"Yeah, that's it."

"Hopefully, there aren't any cardinals out tonight."

"I hope there aren't any cops out tonight." Kera got out of the car, opened the trunk to get her tools out, then decided to first check the door going into the shop.

Deidre headed for the trees.

"Hey, Dee, when you get over there, give me your bird call. I want to make sure I can hear it."

Dee raised her thumb up in the air and kept walking. She disappeared behind the spruces. "Purdy, purdy, purdy."

Kera returned a thumbs-up and hurried over to the back door.

She hadn't noticed the dead bolt on the door when she left Vinny's after he'd bandaged her up. She'd thought it was just padlocked. To get in, she'd have to cut off the lock and bust in the doorframe to break the bolt's hold. She knew how to do that, but the place would end up looking like a crime scene. If anyone ventured behind the store, they'd call the police. Not a good idea to take the door out.

She decided to take a look at the new side window—the one without bars—to see if that might be an easier entry. She'd be visually vulnerable from the highway if she broke in through the window, but she had little choice.

When she'd been considering the various ways she might be able to break into Vinny's, she'd estimated the window was about four and a half feet off the ground, so she'd thrown in Moran's kitchen stepstool with her tools. She ran back to the car to get the stool and a pair of gloves.

She climbed up onto the stool, popped out the screen and was about to smash the glass when she noticed the window wasn't closed tightly. She pushed open the sliding window. Vinny had forgotten to close it. Thinking about it, she wasn't really surprised. Hell, Vinny had just killed someone and they were on the run. She tossed the screen inside and climbed through the window.

She was glad she'd been firm with Moran and Dee about not wearing the dress and stupid heels, wedges, whatever. They'd been afraid if the cops stopped her, she might be recognized without her complete disguise. She'd argued that it would be dark when they left and dark when they came back. If the cops saw her in the car, they'd really just see her blond hair, makeup and glasses, and most likely not see her that clearly anyway. God, she wouldn't know how to climb through a window in a dress and heels. Probably rip her damned dress and break an ankle in the process.

Once in, she was met with stale air, mildew and the smell of old boxes permeating the storage room. She glanced around but didn't see any guns or boxes that might contain firearms.

She tried to open the door to the salesroom in the front of the shop where she knew there were guns, but the door was locked. She pushed her weight against the door, trying to pop it open, but the bolt lock on the hardcore door didn't budge. She was going to have to go out to the car and get her equipment. With her tools, she'd have no problem breaking through the lock and it wouldn't be noticeable to anyone who might check on the shop because the damage wouldn't be seen from the outside.

She glanced over by a coat hook and saw a pair of handcuffs hanging with the key attached. That was weird. What would Vinny be doing with handcuffs? Maybe Vinny aspired to or fantasized being a cop. Maybe he had a little kink going in his love life. *Hmm, wonder if he prefers to be the cop or—*

"Purdy, purdy, purdy…purdy, purdy, purdy…purdy, purdy, purdy."

Kera saw headlights flicker on the wall. She bent down, made her way to the window and peeked over the sill. A cop car was turning into the shop's parking lot. The vehicle cruised through the front parking area and into the back where she'd parked the Mustang. Hopefully he'd drive through, see the empty car and think it was parked there for the night and drive on.

She closed the window and locked it.

She heard a car door close and guessed he must have parked and gotten out. Probably checking the Mustang. Damn, now she had dragged Ally into this mess via her car. She heard voices on the cop's radio but couldn't hear or see him coming toward the shop. He was probably checking Ally's license plate.

What's he doing now? She figured he'd had plenty of time to see who the car belonged to.

"Purdy, purdy, purdy…purdy, purdy, purdy."

She moved away from the window. Dee must be signaling that the cop was coming up to the shop. She heard footsteps on the wooden stoop outside the back door. The doorknob twisted and wiggled, but held tight. Probably the window was next. She moved out of sight, crawling around and hiding behind two five-foot high stacks of boxes pushed together.

Something moved and caught her eye. She looked over and saw a spider dangling from the ceiling, making its way down to a smaller stack of boxes just to the right of her. She followed the spider's path downward to its landing pad on the box.

What was on that box? Damn, she couldn't believe it—a small pistol, right there. She reached over and snatched the gun, a Glock 28, a nice little gun and easily concealed. She pulled out the magazine. Fully loaded. She shoved the magazine back in. She considered maybe there was a god…no, she wouldn't go that far, but she'd take her discovery as a good sign. Hopefully, she didn't need any more ammo. If she did, she knew she would be in even more trouble than she already was, and she didn't want to go there in her head.

The gravel-crunching, weighty footsteps moved around to the side of the shop. A picture of the kitchen stepstool sitting under the window flashed in her head.

Why hadn't she thought of that? But she knew why—she wasn't at her best, not even close to it. Shit, she might just as well have left a trail of colored pebbles and fluorscent spray-painted arrows pointing the way to her place of entry.

Kera saw the flickering of a flashlight outside the window.

She questioned whether or not she would dare resort to using the gun in this situation. The last thing she wanted to do was shoot a cop. The gun was for self-defense only, like in the case of Kevin threatening her. She assured herself she could physically take down any cop on the Lakeside City Police Department, if needed.

She tucked the gun in the back of her waistband and waited, peering out from a crack between the two stacks of boxes. She had the advantage of being able to see the window, but the cop wouldn't be able to see her.

The barrel of a gun, followed by the cop's head, emerged in the left side of the window frame and slowly moved until both the gun and the cop's face were fully exposed.

"That's dumb," she said under her breath. Didn't he consider he could get his fool head blown off doing that?

He tried to open the locked window. A beam from his flashlight moved from one end of the room to the other, up and down.

Kera barely took in any air as the light flicked by her boxes.

Finally, his face, gun and flashlight moved away from the window. The gravel footsteps lumbered away, probably returning to his car.

She heard police radio noises again, then the sound of a car door slamming shut. The cop was probably back in his vehicle.

Kera got up, went to the window and peeked out. She heard the cop's car coming around toward the window and yanked her head back. The car slowed and rolled by. No doubt giving the window one last look. Then she heard the cruiser peel out, spitting gravel as it left the parking lot.

She slid open the window and looked down. The stepstool was gone. Had he taken it? But why would he?

She climbed out, dropped to the ground, reached up and slid the window shut. She started for the Mustang and saw her sister coming over from the trees. She squinted, trying to see what Dee was carrying.

It was the stepstool.

CHAPTER TWENTY-SEVEN

Deidre

Deidre removed the rubber band from the *Lakeside City Journal* that had been rolled into the shape of a cylinder, then laid the paper down beside her cereal bowl. Moran had gone over to her neighbor, Orin Brinkley, and borrowed the paper for her to read.

"I'll have to thank Mr. Brinkley," she told Moran, "for the use of his paper. I'll take it back right after my coffee, since he's obviously not read it yet."

"Oh, you don't have worry about it. Orin doesn't want it back." Moran chuckled. "He told me the paper wasn't any good yesterday, so it probably won't hold anything of interest today. In fact, he said we could use it to start fires if we wanted to. With Orin, you're never quite sure what he might mean, being an old militia man." She laughed again. "Mostly he's pretty mellow these days—age can do that to you—but there's still spunk in him, that's for sure." She handed Deidre a napkin.

"Apparently so. Kera told me how he helped you get her from the canoe into the house."

"Speaking of your sister, she's still isn't up. Do you think I should check in on her?" Moran warmed up her coffee.

"I think she's all right, just exhausted. It was a long day yesterday and by the end of it, I could see how drained she was. And I'm sure you've seen or at least heard what happens to her when she's suffering from stress and fatigue."

Moran nodded. "Yes, it sets her up for an anxiety attack or a flashback. All she needs then is something to trigger it."

"Right, I get worried about her. She's been through so much in Iraq and now to come home to all this mess. I thought it would be good if she could get some extra rest today." Deidre took a sip of her coffee.

"I'm concerned about you both and how you're going to get through this dreadful situation." Moran put the coffeepot back on the stove.

Deidre bit her lip. She thought about yesterday's trip to the hospital and then their escapade acquiring the gun. She and Kera had told Moran about seeing Mandy and how they got into the hospital, then about getting the gun at Vinny's shop, but left out the "breaking into" part. Moran had found the hospital adventure—as she called it—funny, but she would have no doubt been horrified if she knew she and Kera had broken in and stolen the gun, and almost got caught.

Well, technically, Kera did the breaking in, but she was part of it. They both could have easily landed in jail. She didn't know where she'd rounded up the courage to get that stepstool before the cop got there. Come to think of it, it wasn't courage so much as desperation and cold fear of the consequences if she hadn't. She shuddered, tried to block the pictures of their exploits bombarding her.

She opened the newspaper to find something else to concentrate on, wondering if it carried anything on Mandy's attack and any update on how she might be doing.

On the first page above the fold she saw the headlines:

LOCAL GAY ACTIVIST BEATEN, IN CRITICAL CONDITION
Local gay activist, Mandy Bakker, was attacked by an unknown assailant late Tuesday night at the offices of the Lakeside City Legal Aid. She is in critical condition...

Deidre looked up from the paper, a chill going through her. She couldn't stop her mind from bringing up yesterday's events.

She hated that she hadn't been able to stop shaking while she was in the hospital, worrying one of her co-workers might recognize her, or Kera. She'd thought that Jeanne, one of the two women at the front desk, might have recognized her under her nun's outfit and makeup. Luckily, Jeanne wasn't the woman Kera was directly talking to, but she'd glanced Dee's way when she'd taken over by making the phone call to see if they could get permission to visit Mandy. My God, she'd gone to lunch with Jeanne just last week.

When they finally got into Mandy's room, she'd waited for the police to come barging in, exposing them, and hauling them off to jail because Jeanne had finally figured out her real identity.

Deidre browsed down the story to the last paragraph.

The police declined to give any further information about why Bakker might have been targeted or by whom, stating the investigation is in its early stages. Bakker remains heavily guarded and is not allowed visitors.

(See page 4, Section A for related article: Is This Civil War?)

Deidre had to giggle when she read "heavily guarded." *Yes, unless you're a nun—or dressed like one.* Hopefully Mandy's attacker wouldn't come up with a good way of getting to her.

She turned to page four.

Is This Civil War?
By Daniel Williams
Lakeside City has now seen the deaths of two opponents to the inclusion of LGBT people into the city's Civil Rights Ordinance: Pastor Don Bledsoe and one of his parishioners, Sam Zander. Now on the other side of the issue, Mandy Bakker, co-leader of LEAP, has been brutally beaten, and according to reports, is struggling for her life…

Deidre thought about seeing Mandy in the hospital. The woman hadn't looked good to her and she worried Mandy might not make it. She didn't want to tell Kera, but when she'd followed her out of the hospital, she'd overheard two nurses talking about Mandy's condition at the nurse's station. She didn't really hear that much, more their tone and body language that concerned her. She sighed, moved down through the editorial, and stopped at a paragraph.

The tension has grown hour by hour, and now the lines are drawn in the city's dirt.

Actually, it is far more than merely lines in the dirt of the city—it's more like trenches. I've gotten emails, telephone calls, and personally interviewed many of Lakeside City's citizens regarding this issue. The scope and intensity of the discord in the hearts and minds of our citizens astounded me. The friction has reached the grounds of our schools. Personnel at both the high school and the middle school have reported to me there is fighting over the issue in hallways and on their campuses. Students who are out as gay—or perceived to be gay—are targets for emotional or physical abuse...

Deidre felt grateful Kera hadn't come out in high school other than to her and Janet. It would have been horrible for Kera and probably her as well.

She remembered how scared she'd been when Kera told her she was gay. She'd worried if Kera came out, she'd be assumed to be gay too, and she'd feared it could be true because they were not just twins, they were identical twins. When Kera kept telling her that she was gay but too scared to accept it and therefore living a lie, she'd been terrified Kera might be right. Looking back, she realized that fear had driven her to acting and dressing ultra feminine—her way of trying to tell Kera they weren't gay and Kera was the one living the lie.

She took a deep breath and read on.

When I contacted several agencies dealing with domestic violence, they all reported a forty to fifty percent increase in caseloads. Although bad economic times is a factor, the issue of gay rights has been dividing families as well, according to the director of Family Aid Services: "families in stress often seek a reason for their problems, often outside themselves—a scapegoat. When they blame the economy, both parents are usually in accord, but when you add the gay issue, mom, dad and kids don't necessarily see it the same, causing a rift within the family. Violence often ensues. It's like father against son, brother against brother, wife against husband..."

Deidre felt sick. She couldn't escape the fact that she was part of what the writer was talking about: the effects of prejudice on families. The problem wasn't just about Kera and her longstanding issue with their sexuality. Intolerance was like a fast-spreading disease that affected lots of relationships.

She thought of it as like a kind of virus hanging below the surface, able to rise up and flourish when conditions were ripe. She'd noticed things had been getting increasingly tense between Harry and Sylvia over the gay rights issue. Sylvia was losing her patience with Harry's antigay sentiments.

Most of all, she was concerned about her relationship with Kera. She'd apologized to her about not giving her support. Well, that wasn't exactly true. She'd always supported Kera, personally, but not when it came to standing up for her sister against Don and his church people. With Don, she'd fought against his attitude—well, most of the time. But when she heard a gay slur by members of the church, she'd remained silent or pretended not to hear.

That was pretty much true at her work in the hospital, too. When she came across people she perceived or knew to be gay, she did go out of her way for them. Though in retrospect, her attitude was more like doing penance for everything she hadn't done for her sister.

She would like to think she would've been more actively supportive of Kera if Kera hadn't been constantly telling her she was the twin "lying" about her sexuality… Damn, she knew she was making excuses for herself, and there were no excuses for what she'd done or not done—at least not valid ones.

Deidre shifted in her chair. She didn't feel very good about herself. For her, it wasn't just a matter of wanting or having Kera forgive her, she needed to forgive herself.

She returned her attention to the article.

Even the cops on the beat report more hate crimes, specifically targeting people thought to be gay. According to the police, three bars last night reported fights, two of them directly attributed to the issue of gay rights.

With the beating of Mandy Bakker and the added violence in the city, the police have put more officers out in the community.

The words of the director of FAS, "brother against brother and father against son" reverberated in the back of my head. The last time I heard that expression used was when I read about our country's Civil War. When you walk around this city, you see buttons with slogans indicating either they're for or against the ordinance.

Are those slogans and buttons representing our version of the gray and the blue? What kind of price will we pay for our fear and hatred? So far it appears to have cost us civil and family strife along with two lives and possibly a third.

Is Lakeside City having its own civil war?

Deidre closed the paper and turned to Moran. "Didn't find out anything more about Mandy, but the paper points out how horrible things are getting in this city around all the ordinance stuff. Hope it will do some good, get people to think about what's happening. It sure made me think." She got up from the table. "Do you mind if I use your phone?"

"Certainly, it's in the other room there." Moran pointed to the living room.

Deidre wanted to call Sylvia, but didn't want to risk using her cell phone. She knew Sylvia would be worried about her since she'd been vague about her whereabouts in the goodbye note when she'd left.

"Hi, Sylvia, thought I better check in." She sat on the sofa and pulled her legs under her.

"Oh, I'm glad you did. I've been so worried about you and your sister."

The "and your sister" sounded sincere to her, but Sylvia had always been supportive of Kera. Just not always in front of Harry. "We're okay for the time being, anyway." She grabbed a throw blanket and covered her legs. The chill from the night lingered in the house.

"Do you know where your sister is?"

"I'm not going to answer that question, Sylvia. Not because I don't trust you. It will be best if you don't know some things right now."

"I understand."

"Other than checking in to let you know I'm okay, I wanted to know about you. I was reading that column by Daniel Williams in the paper this morning and among other things, I started worrying about you and Harry. I know my staying with you and Harry caused problems."

"Really, it had nothing to do with you, Deidre."

"But it did, in the sense that my presence in your house was hard on Harry because of his—"

"There's more to it, believe me." Sylvia hesitated. "It had more to do with Harry always defending Don."

"What do you mean?" Deidre knew Harry defended Don, but that had always been true.

"Don physically abusing you, causing you to lose the baby and then breaking your nose. Harry just won't own up to Don's abusiveness, even after seeing your face. You know how he was the other night when you were here, totally in denial."

"Yes, I know he doesn't believe me, so of course he doesn't believe you either."

"He believes Don's story and that's it. I told him I couldn't stomach his believing Don over me. It makes me physically ill...it really does. Harry told me on Saturday night, the very night Don was killed, that shortly after he talked to Don that night—"

"Yeah, Harry told me he was probably the last person to speak to Don Saturday night and—"

"That's true, but what I was trying to tell you was Don told Harry that you had...what was it? Oh, yes, you'd run into a door or something.

So I informed Harry that Don told him an out-and-out lie because I had called you when you and Kera were in the emergency medical facility, so I knew the real story. Well, Harry didn't believe me at all. Can you fathom it? He believed Don over me." Sylvia's voice boomed, causing Deidre to pull the receiver back from her ear. Sylvia's words resounded through the room. "I got so mad, I went to bed and told him he wasn't welcome in the bedroom—and I've not invited him back."

Deidre glanced up to see Kera in an old T-shirt and underpants with a pillow under her arm. Kera flopped on the other end of the sofa, threw up her feet and plopped them on her lap.

"I knew Harry didn't believe me about Don hitting me," Deidre said to Sylvia while rubbing her sister's foot, "and I could see the stress between you both. I guess I was so wound up in my own troubles, I didn't think about what you were going through. But I did realize I was a burr in your relationship and I needed to leave your house." She hesitated and then added, "So that's why Harry was sleeping in the guest bedroom. Harry told me that—"

Sylvia interrupted, "It's not your fault, dear, really. Harry loves... loved Don, and he wouldn't believe anything ill of Don ever—even, I swear, if Don had broken 'his' nose in anger. He'd make up an excuse for him. But I can't live with my husband believing someone over me. I really can't take that. Good grief, I'm his wife! What kind of relationship do I have, anyway? I can't deal with being married to someone who won't believe me."

Deidre heard the hurt in Sylvia's voice.

"Well," Sylvia went on, now beginning to cry as she talked, "he said that right to my face and more than once." She stopped a moment, seemed to get a hold of herself and said, "And get this, Deidre, he said you and I were making that stuff up. And he didn't appreciate our lies, our attempts at disgracing Don."

"You're kidding!" Deidre understood Harry sticking by Don, but to go that far, not be able to face the truth, or even entertain the possibility, felt crazy to her.

"He claims you and I were trying to make Don look bad. I couldn't believe what came out of his mouth. I asked him, 'Why on earth would we do something like that?' He just looked at me, like...like I was evil or something."

"Oh, my God, Sylvia, that sounds so bizarre." Deidre could hardly believe what she was hearing.

"Yes, it has felt crazy to me. I know Harry has been working too hard at all the church and city council stuff and all his business dealings. He's way overextended himself. And you know with the housing market down, he's had to let some people go, cut back on stuff. But even though I understand all these things are weighing heavily on him, I'm tired of making excuses for him. He's gone too far this time."

"So what are you going to do?" Deidre handed her cup of coffee to Kera and mouthed, "Have some."

Kera grabbed it and took a sip.

Sylvia was quiet for a second, then said, "I've been thinking I might go back and spend some time with my grandmother. I need to check in on her anyway. And frankly, I need to have time away to think about all that's been going on around here with Harry and me. I love him and he's a good man in so many ways, but I can't stand being around him right now. Maybe this is the end. I don't know."

"I understand and I'm so sorry. It's confusing for me too. He's been so good to me, supporting me, believing in my innocence. He stood up for me with the DA and let me stay at your place. But then saying I'm a liar...And now, how he's been treating you, and thinking we're making up stories to make Don look bad. I just don't know what to think anymore."

"Yes, I think I need to give him space as well as needing it for myself. He's been through a lot. Maybe he needs time away too. Perhaps if I'm not around, he'll get some perspective and be able to see things better. As you see, I just go back and forth in my feelings about him. I'm so confused."

"Understandable. In fact, I know the feeling all too well. That's what I did. I was the champ at making excuses for Don." Deidre pulled her throw blanket over Kera's cold bare toes.

Sylvia continued, "And besides, this town is crazy right now. Getting away will help, but I don't want to leave you if you need me here."

"I think it is a good idea for you to get away for a while. I have a place to stay and am doing okay. If you think about it, you're only a phone call away if either of us needs to talk."

"That's true. Oh, I think I hear Harry coming in. I'd better go now. Goodbye."

"Okay, love you, dear, I'll stay in touch." Deidre hung up the phone. She thought about Daniel Williams' article on the civil war in the city. He certainly had nailed it—husband against wife. She sighed and looked at Kera. "Things are really bad for Sylvia."

Kera yawned and rubbed her eyes, "Yeah, I could hear Sylvia from here."

"Yes, she's very upset."

"Sounds like good old Harry is banished from his marital bed, not getting any sex these days. Serves him right, I'd say." Kera handed the coffee cup back to her.

CHAPTER TWENTY-EIGHT

Kera

Kera was pissed. Really pissed.

Ally had called and told her Vinny was at the Out-and-About bar trying to find a partner for tonight's pool tournament. In the process the bastard was letting people believe he'd left town on the Friday before Sam's death, saying he'd just gotten back in town this morning. She could see how the son-of-a-bitch was setting her up. He wasn't planning on admitting he was at Sam's house on Saturday—when Sam was murdered—let alone admit he was the one who killed the man.

She needed to put a stop to his attempt to kick dirt over his own shit. She and Dee were on their way to the bar to confront Vinny.

She realized Vinny must have been thinking everything through, imagining how the police would view the death. Sam had been killed pretty much the same as Don—both attacked from behind and their throats cut. Vinny didn't want to be the guy who filled in the blanks for the cops because Sam's death might link him to Don's. She understood his concern. However, his fabricated alibi left her holding the bag, and he knew exactly what he was doing.

She also wondered if Vinny worried she might think killing Sam wasn't necessary. After all, he could have overcome Sam physically and she'd been right there to help secure him. Still, she hadn't planned on feeding Vinny to the cops, like he was attempting do to her. Even with her misgivings, she'd give Vinny the benefit of the doubt.

She wasn't sure what she'd do when she saw him, but she was certain she and Vinny would be having a "conversation" about him supposedly not being around town during the time of Sam's death.

But where did Kevin fit in this picture? She and Deidre had put together all they thought they knew about Kevin when it came to Don's death. He'd bragged about beating up Don at McFarland Park sometime on Friday. Did Kevin go back again to the gay beach on Saturday night after the brawl at the gay bar? He sure hadn't stayed long enough at the fray to get arrested like her. Where had he gone and what had he done later Saturday night?

She and Dee had spent hours last night going over and over the facts, trying to figure out who could have killed Don—Kevin or Vinny—and why.

After considering Kevin, they'd decided Sam was the "wild card" suspect. Maybe Sam killed Don, so neither Vinny nor Kevin had anything to do with the murder. Sam certainly had threatened Don and had reason to hate him, though he'd vehemently denied killing Don when she'd made the accusation. But why would he confess to her? And as far as she knew, he had no alibi.

She and Dee had decided to focus on Vinny and Kevin. They would meet Kevin later tonight at his office, but first, they'd deal with Vinny. Hopefully, nothing would spook him away from his Thursday night tournament.

She was jarred out of her thoughts when Dee put her hands out in front of her like she was patting the air. "Slow down, slow down Kera, or we're going to get stopped by the police for going too fast."

Kera looked at the speedometer. She was going fifteen miles an hour over the limit. She lifted her foot from the gas pedal. "Guess I'm too anxious to get my hands on that asshole."

"Besides not wanting to get stopped, Kera, neither of us is fully decked out in our disguises. You're wearing those slacks instead of a dress and—"

In exasperation, Kera lifted her hands off the steering wheel as if in surrender, looked at her sister and said, "Dee, how am I supposed to function in this world with a dress and those stupid shoes? Why not just tie my hands behind my back? And since when didn't het women wear pants?"

"Kera, watch the road!"

"I am." Kera put her hand back on the wheel.

"You could have bought a more girly blouse. And those new slacks and loafers aren't exactly—"

"Well, may I ask where your five o'clock shadow is today?" Kera reached over and tweaked her sister's chin.

"I planned on getting it put back on, but I was thinking Ally or one of the boys could do a better job. We'll be at the bar soon. Anyway, you know from my attempts that I'm not very good at it. I'll never be a makeup artist, that's for sure. But at least I've kept my same outfit."

"Well, without your stubble, you look like a boy version of yourself."

"Okay, I said I'm going to get it fixed. But it would really be better if you had worn a dress. What if someone recognizes you? God knows, they wouldn't recognize you in a dress."

"Got that covered. When we get there, I'll go in the back door and find another cute little dress." Kera tossed Dee a sarcastic smirk. "Put it on before I go out into the bar. Come to think of it, it would be a good idea if you could hang in the bar while I'm changing my clothes—it won't take me long—and you could keep an eye out for Vinny. If he's there, make sure he stays there. Okay?"

"And how do you think I'm going to keep him there? Work my feminine charms?" Dee returned the smirk.

"Look at what you're wearing, Dee, and consider your audience and where you will be tonight: at a gay bar, impersonating a guy—maybe a too-young guy, but nevertheless, a guy—make that a gay guy. Now, my dear, think about it. You can flirt. Maybe Vinny is into teenage boys with baby-butt faces." She glanced at her sister. "You did do pretty well covering the bruising on your face, though." She reached over and pinched Dee's hairless cheek.

"Don't you think I should get my facial hair on first?"

"Well, that would be best, but I need to get into the bar ASAP, so I need to go and get my girly clothes on first, then you can go to the makeup area and get fixed up. I wouldn't worry too much. It's pretty dark in the bar, so I think you'll get by okay. Just don't sit under a light, not that there are any bright lights in that place anyway."

"How will I know Vinny?"

"He's a short, dark, stocky Italian guy with tattoos on his arm. Oh, yeah, he and I have our pictures up over by the pool table area, off to the right—take a look. We won the last Thursday night tournament, so we're celebrities for a week."

Kera drove the Mustang into the staff parking area behind the bar and parked. She and Dee jumped out and headed to the back door of the bar.

CHAPTER TWENTY-NINE

Deidre

Deidre entered from the employee's entrance to the Out-and-About and made her way to the main part of the bar. She glanced around looking for a short, Italian-looking man. The place was packed for a Thursday, a weeknight, but then it occurred to her the crowd was probably due to the pool tournament.

Loud music mixed with clanking dishes, laughter and the good-natured kidding around the pool tables felt at odds with what was going on in her life. Certainly not a happy time for her and her sister. She glanced around the room a second time, but couldn't find anyone who fit Vinny's description.

She looked at the bar and saw Ally mixing drinks.

Ally looked up, saw her and waved her over. "Looking for Vinny?"

"Yes, it's kind of dark in here. My eyes haven't adjusted yet." Deidre blinked several times, trying to speed up the process.

Ally pointed. "He's over there by the pool tables, looking at those cue stick racks on the wall. He said his stick got stolen in some out-of-town bar, so he's trying to find one for tonight's tournament."

"Kera's in the back changing her clothes. She should be out here in a few minutes." Deidre stepped up to the bar. "I'm supposed to keep my eye on Vinny until my sister can get out here. Then I'll go back there to get the rest of my makeup and facial hair on." She patted her cheek.

"Got ya. Why don't you sit up here? I can keep an eye on him and let you know what he's doing?"

"Sounds good to me." She sat down on a stool at the end of the bar.

"Want something to drink?"

"Just some water for now." Deidre knew she was a lightweight when it came to alcohol and needed to keep her wits about her.

"Coming up." Ally returned with a glass of water, set it in front of her, and said, "Don't look around, Vinny's heading this way."

Deidre put her elbow on the bar and her head in her hand, staring down at her water, waiting, wishing she were invisible. She hoped he wouldn't get too close to where she was sitting, but there were only three empty seats at the bar, which were all next to her.

"What's up, Vinny?" Ally moved over to him.

"Well, this little baby will have to do, though it will be a miracle if I win tonight. Would you mind holding it behind the bar for me?" Vinny handed over his cue stick.

"No problem." Ally grabbed the stick, brought it over the bar and set it in a corner. "It will be here for you when you're ready."

"I need to find me a new one soon. Maybe if I got time, I'll go looking for one tomorrow."

Vinny was standing close by, only two empty seats separating them. She kept staring down into her glass of water, carefully glancing his way now and then. She noticed a drinks menu on the bar, grabbed it and feigned interest.

Ally continued talking to Vinny about the night's tournament, obviously trying to help by distracting him from paying any attention to her.

Deidre heard a barstool pull out. Vinny said, "I think I'll grab a bite. Didn't have any dinner, don't want to drink beer on an empty stomach."

"What can I get you?" Ally asked.

"How about a burger and fries, and a Bud, on tap."

Deidre felt too close to Vinny. Only one barstool separated them now. She didn't come out here to engage him, just keep track of him until Kera got out. She felt anxious and scared. Good God, how long did it take for Kera to put on a damned dress? It seemed like hours had passed already, though it could only have been a matter of minutes.

She had no idea what she'd say to Vinny if he started a conversation with her. What if he came on to her? Kera thought her disguise was funny when she'd pinched her cheek and teased, saying he might like young boys. Well, it wasn't funny to her, especially at this very moment. Here she was, dressed as a man—but without stubble, more like a boy a year or two from being legal in a bar.

She had never been comfortable with the "come on" thing, never knew what to say, but she was really out of her league posing as a male with another male coming on to her. Good God, how did that work? She decided she'd be better off if she went over to a nearby table. She grabbed her water and started to leave.

A hand touched her shoulder, followed by, "Hey, I haven't seen you around here, have I?"

Shit! She put down the water and slowly turned toward Vinny.

"I'm Vinny." He extended his hand.

"Glad to meet you, Vinny. I'm…I'm David." Better not shake his hand. Her hand was not a man's hand. He'd figure that one out fast enough. "What's up?"

Vinny seemed to take no offense. "Gettin' some grub."

Deidre looked at Ally for help, or some clue as to what to do next, but Ally was looking past her toward the door. She looked concerned.

Deidre turned slightly to see a casually dressed guy coming into the bar.

Ally glanced at Deidre and mouthed the word, "Cop." Then she walked out from behind the bar and headed for the back rooms.

Deidre figured Ally was going to warn Kera. She looked at the man, wondering how Ally knew he was a cop since he wasn't wearing a uniform—maybe he'd been in here looking for her after her makeup session when she hadn't returned to her car.

The cop sat down at a table near the window. A waiter went over to him. She didn't know whether or not she should get out of there. What would Kera do if she were sitting here in this situation? Leave out the back? Try to stay cool and see?

"Where are you from? Not around here, right?" Vinny slurped his beer.

"That's right, just passing through." Deidre picked up the drinks menu again and looked at it to avoid more eye contact.

"Where to?"

"Up north. Going to do some fishing." She hoped he wasn't a fisherman and wanted to talk about it, since she knew precious little about the sport.

"You even old enough to have a beer?" Vinny reached over and tapped the liquor menu.

She suddenly felt hot, like she could faint. She took off her Windbreaker and tossed it over on the table behind her. She wished she could move over to a table—or better yet, run out the door. "Yeah, man, I'm old enough, just trying to decide what I want to drink."

"Well, you sure look young. You been in a fight or something? Looks like ya got a shiner. Trying to cover it up, huh?" Vinny laughed.

"Yeah, you know how it goes."

"Yup, someone popped you good. You sure remind me of someone I know, and your voice sounds sort of familiar too." Vinny cocked his head, looking puzzled. "Where did you say you were from?"

"I didn't." Deidre lowered her voice. "But I'm from Chicago."

"Boystown?" Vinny smiled.

"Look, I said I was old enough to drink." Now she figured he was making fun of her and it wouldn't be long before he saw right through her act.

Damn, where was Kera? Her sister needed to get out here and save her. She turned and saw Ally coming back to the bar area. She called out to Ally, "Give me a Killian's Red, would ya?"

"Coming right up." Ally grabbed a mug and put it under the tap.

Deidre glanced at Vinny and looked down again. He was staring at her really hard. She could have kicked herself for coming here without her false beard redone—at least she should have tried to do it herself.

"Kera! It's you, isn't it?" Vinny stood up, eyes wide, and declared, "I thought you looked familiar. Why are you—?"

She looked at him straight on and put her finger to her lips. "Shhh, there's a cop over there." She gestured with her head. "At the table near the window."

Vinny slowly twisted his head around and looked, then turned back to her again and said in a low voice, "What's going on with you, Kera?" He said her name louder than the rest of the words he spoke.

Deidre looked around and saw the cop watching them intently. He was a cop, all right. Had he heard Vinny say Kera's name? Probably not. She was just being paranoid. Vinny hadn't said it that loud, had he?

Ally grabbed her tray and walked behind Vinny and Deidre. She picked up Deidre's discarded jacket from the table. "Let me hang this up for you." She turned to Vinny. "I just went back to check on your burger. It'll be right up." She picked up dishes from a nearby table and placed them on her tray. Then she went over to a coat tree and hung up Deidre's jacket and went into the kitchen.

Deidre decided not to deny being Kera to Vinny. Thinking she was Kera, maybe Vinny would tell her something useful. With the cop in the place, Vinny might not hang around long. Who knew where he'd go? She'd try and get something out of him. She hoped Ally had warned Kera about the cop in the bar. It was no time for Kera to come out here, in disguise or not.

Ally returned and put Vinny's food on the bar. He picked up his burger and took a big bite out of it, then washed it down with a couple of gulps of beer.

Deidre kept her voice low. "As you might imagine, Vinny, I'm here trying to look for Don's killer."

Vinny wiped mustard off his mouth with the back of his hand, stopped chewing and asked, "In here?"

"Who knows?" Deidre looked at him hard and straight in the eyes and said, "But speaking about people getting killed, I do have to ask why you're running off your mouth about being out of town during the time Sam got killed?" She was pleased by her words. "Running off your mouth" was how Kera would have put it. She went on, "That makes me believe you're trying to set me up as Sam's killer."

Vinny's gaze dropped. He didn't say anything.

"Look, I know you killed Sam to save me and I appreciate that, but why are you trying to throw me under the bus?"

Vinny put his hands on the bar and tipped his barstool back. "That's insane. You've got to be kidding, Kera!" This time, he shouted out Kera's name.

Vinny meant to draw attention to her. Deidre saw the cop at the table by the window get up and walk toward her and Vinny. He didn't take his eyes off either of them. When he reached the bar, he had his suit jacket pulled back, exposing his gun. He had an intense look on his face, probably seeing through what was left of her disguise. He held out his badge for her to see and commanded, "Get off that stool and put your hands on the bar."

Deidre did as he demanded.

"Are you Kera Van Brocklin?" The cop frisked her, not seeming to need her answer.

"No, I am not." Deidre's heart throbbed and felt like it would pop out of her chest. Was this really happening to her again?

The cop looked at Vinny. "What's your name?"

"Vinny Belsito, sir."

"Do you know this person?"

Vinny looked at Deidre, nodded and said, "Yes, sir, she's Kera Van Brocklin."

"I'm not Kera, I'm Deidre Van Brocklin. I'm sure you know we are twins and you have the wrong twin."

"Can you show me proof?" The cop's lip curled up on one side in a smirk.

"Can I get my jacket over there?" Deidre pointed to where Ally had hung it. "My wallet is in the pocket." She was grateful Kera hadn't come out. Soon, the cop would see that he had her, not her sister. By that time Kera would know what was happening, hopefully, and get the hell out of the bar.

"Just stay where you are, I'll get it for you." The cop backed up, never taking his eyes off her. He grabbed her jacket off the hook, searched and found her wallet, and then handed it to her. "Now I need to see some ID."

Deidre opened the wallet, flipped through to her driver's license, and gave it to him.

The cop stared at her license, looked at her, then back at the license. "It says here Kera Van Brocklin, not Deidre Van Brocklin. It appears I do have the right twin."

"It says what?" This felt like an *Alice in Wonderland* nightmare. Out of the corner of her eye, Deidre saw Vinny slip away and head for the door.

The cop handed her the driver's license. She looked down at it. God, it was Kera's. How had Kera's license gotten into her wallet? She glanced up in time to see a pair of handcuffs coming at her.

"You have the right to remain silent…"

CHAPTER THIRTY

Kera

"I'll kill that little weasel. I swear it." Kera snarled to no one in particular as she got into the old Mustang, slammed the door shut, put the key in the ignition and got the engine going—on the third try—and backed out of the parking space. The gears ground as she shifted into first, then flew out of the parking lot, leaving a rooster tail of gravel and dirt in her wake.

The loud noises from the car sounded more like she was driving a tractor in a race at the county fair. She figured the muffler must have sprung a hole, because the Mustang hadn't roared like that when she and Dee drove into the employee's parking lot earlier—at least not this bad. She slowed down, trying to cut the rumble.

At the bar, Ally had come back to the dressing room—thankfully before she'd changed her clothes—and told her how Vinny was feeding Deidre to the cops. If something hadn't been done, she knew she'd be in jail right now. She couldn't help feeling bad, though. She'd just betrayed her sister by allowing Ally to switch their driver's licenses when she hung up Dee's jacket.

She'd peeked out to watch as the cop took Dee away in handcuffs. It'd killed her to see them taking her away, especially since she'd been part of setting up her sister. But she had to let the cop take Dee instead of her. Dee couldn't do what she needed to do right now. The cops would find out soon enough they had the wrong Van Brocklin twin. She had to be free to go after Vinny and keep the appointment with Kevin tonight. Her sister would just have to understand.

Kera turned off the radio, which for some unknown reason to her had popped on with loud rap thumping along with the rest of the clatter. She needed to be able to think, figure things out, and plan while she drove.

She decided to head over to Vinny's house first, and if he wasn't there, he'd probably be at his shop...that would be her two best guesses as to where he had gone. If he wasn't at either of those places, she believed he would be on his way out of town...then what would she do?

Her anxiety bounced back to her sister. Before she'd left the bar, Kera had asked Ally to call someone at Legal Aid to get down to the police station as soon as possible since Mandy was in no condition to help Dee. She imagined that Dee must be an emotional mess right now, having her second trip to the police station. Hopefully, her sister had learned not to open her mouth or say anything without a lawyer present.

Nevertheless, she feared Dee was such an open book, she was liable to say things she shouldn't. Her sister always thought a question required an answer.

Thoughts circled and spun in her head. She wondered about Mandy—seeing how bad she'd looked and sounded in the hospital. Her skin had felt hot when she'd touched her. She couldn't be there to support Mandy and she didn't like it.

She could call the hospital and maybe find out how Mandy was doing. The hospital number was in her cell phone. She considered the possibility that her calls might be traced, but decided she'd just have to take a chance. She pulled over to the curb and shut off the engine, getting rid of the rumble, before dialing the number.

"Room 412, please," she said when the switchboard answered. She waited, listening to music she'd never choose to hear.

"Hello." A female voiced answered—not Mandy's.

"I'm calling to find out how Mandy is doing."

"I'm just a student nurse here. And I'm sorry but I'm not supposed to give out information about any of our patients."

"Oh, I'm so sorry I understand, but I'm Sister Mary Margaret. Sister Sheila and I were up there praying for Mandy the other day and we've been so worried about her. We wanted to check on her."

"Uh-huh, but as I said—"

"Oh, I know, I know." Kera hoped if she kept talking, the student nurse might gain more confidence in her—the supposed nun—and decide to bend a rule. "We've been continuing to pray for her recovery. In fact, we had a special Mass for her today. I'm sure you can understand our concern." She held her breath.

"Well, I shouldn't really…but I did hear you were here to visit and pray for her. I'm Catholic, too, Sister. Not many of us around here, so we need to stick together, right?" The student nurse giggled. "Let me just say she seems a little better. Her vitals are stronger, but she hasn't opened her eyes or talked to anyone yet. That's about all I know."

"Well, you have been such a dear to talk to me. I'll pass your information on to Sister Sheila and we'll keep praying."

"And I will too, Sister. Oh, dear, I have to go now, my supervising nurse is coming in the—"

"God bless you and take good care of her." She heard the phone on the nurse's end click off.

Kera smiled to herself. So her alter ego must be Sister Mary Margaret. That name had just spilled out when she needed it.

Her attention went back to Vinny. She thought about Mandy, lying in the bed and hooked to machines, and how helpless she'd felt seeing her there, not being able to stay with her. Then Mandy's mumbled nebulous words, ending in what sounded like the name "Carolyn" came back to her. She didn't know a "Carolyn," certainly no one on her radar, away. And she still couldn't believe the kind of beating Mandy took could be dished out by most women. She must have gotten the name wrong. Maybe something that sounded like "Carolyn." She kept repeating the name over and over in her head until…

Shit, that's it!

Mandy wasn't saying Carolyn. She was saying, "Maryland." She meant Vinny!

That fucker beat up Mandy!

But why? It didn't make sense to her.

Come to think of it, she'd been out of communication with Mandy for a while before her attack. Maybe, in the meantime, she'd discovered something about Vinny, something that would implicate him in Don's death. If Vinny had learned, somehow, that Mandy had evidence that would incriminate him, he would want to shut her up—so maybe he'd tried to kill her too.

She really needed to find him tonight before he took off again—if she wasn't already too late. Ally had told her the creep slunk out the door right after the cop cuffed Dee. He'd done his job handing Kera—so he'd thought—over to the cops, then he'd beat it out of the bar.

Fucker!

She estimated Vinny had about a fifteen-minute lead on her. Even if he decided to head out of town again, he'd probably go home to pack some things and/or head over to his shop, maybe to get a weapon. She decided to try his house first, and if he wasn't there, she would go to his shop.

Before she left the bar, she'd asked Ally if the cops had contacted her about her car being parked at Vinny's shop last night, purposely leaving out the part about her stealing the gun. Luckily, Ally reported to her there'd been no visits from the police and, thankfully, she didn't ask her why she was inquiring. She imagined Ally hadn't been curious because so much else was going on that the thought didn't occur to her. She also guessed the cop hadn't suspected anything after looking around the shop. So traveling around in the Mustang might still be okay except for the loud noise, but it wasn't like she had an alternative. Unless she decided to purloin a car, she had no choice except to use Ally's clunker.

She slowed down when she got to Vinny's house. His pickup truck wasn't parked in the driveway or on the street. She sped up and headed toward his shop.

She glanced in the rearview mirror. Fuck! There was a police cruiser behind her. She assumed it must be the damned loud muffler that had grabbed his attention. If he stopped her now, she'd be the prize, not the loud muffler. In that case, she'd have to make a run for it. She could see no alternative.

She looked down to check her car's speed—only two miles over the limit. She kept her pace steady, came to a stop sign, stopped dead, put on her blinkers and turned right. The cop turned with her. She kept driving, heading out of the residential area. She turned left, checking the rearview mirror.

The police car hung tight to her, so close it was like she was pulling a trailer. She muttered about the damned Mustang being a cop magnet, bad muffler or not. She understood why Dee had been terrified when the cop stopped her in this moving counter-culture billboard. Any minute now, she knew he'd turn on his flashing lights. Her eyes darted around, searching for an escape route.

The cruiser seemed even closer to her. The bubble top lights came on. The siren blared.

Kera decided she wouldn't speed up and try to outrun the cop, but instead, she'd abandon the car and take off on foot. Her chances were better that way. She slowed the car and pulled it to the side of the road, put her hand on the door handle and pushed it down slowly. Through the side-mirror, she watched the cop approach.

She pulled her key out of the ignition, reached over for her purse, and positioned her feet for escape. Just as the cop got to her door, she jumped out, smashing the car door into him. He fell onto the street, then tried to get up, but before he got far, she put a foot in his solar plexus. He lay on the street, gasping for air.

Kera looked at him, figuring he'd be okay. He just needed to get his air back. Before he did, she planned to be long gone. She was less than a half mile from Vinny's shop. Only a few minutes more...she took off at a run.

Reaching the gun and knife shop, she made her way through the brush. The bastard's truck was in the parking lot. She moved close to the building, climbed up onto the back stoop and grabbed the door handle, hoping he hadn't locked it. She stood beside the door, held her gun up and slowly twisted the knob. It turned.

She cracked open the door and slipped inside. Vinny wasn't in the stuffy storage room, so he had to be out in the sales area. She gently opened the door into the front part of the building. Sounded like he was moving the sliding door of one of his glass showcases, probably getting himself a weapon. She peeked around the corner. His back was to her, but she could see a gun in his hand, down by his side.

"Drop that gun and put your hands over your head, Vinny, or I'll blow your fucking head off."

Vinny let the gun drop to the floor, then lifted his hands over his head.

"Turn around, you bastard." Kera pointed her gun square at Vinny's back and moved her aim to his head as he slowly turned around to face her.

Vinny seemed confused. "Are you..." He squinted. "Are you Kera's sister?"

"No, you worm, I'm Kera—the blond version. You managed to send Deidre to jail, not me. Now kick your gun over in my direction."

He booted the gun toward her. "Hey, Ker, I had nothing to do with what happened at—"

"Don't lie to me, you asshole. You sold me out. I know what you've been saying at the bar and what you did when that cop was in there, so you'd better not hand me another lie. Don't give me an additional reason to pull this trigger. I'm already so pissed, I have all I can do to control myself." She picked up his gun from the floor and tossed it aside.

Vinny stood with his arms raised. "Ker…Kera, I got scared. I figured you'd tell the cops that I didn't really need to kill Sam, and maybe I did go too far, but I just lost it, Kera. Sam was no good. A fuckin' bastard. You know that. He deserved—"

"Where were you the night Don was killed? After the cops showed up at the bar, and I ended up in jail. Where did you go, Vinny?"

"I went to Grand Rapids, honest. Geez, if you think I—"

"What'd you do there and did anyone see you? In other words, you'd better have an alibi for me." Kera kept the gun firmly aimed at his head.

"Damn, Kera, I went to one of those places where my dick would be more likely recognized than my face. After that I visited a guy. He sells me weed, but he's not going to cop to selling me that stuff." Vinny brought his hands in to his chest, the palms turned inward. "No one else saw me."

Kera watched Vinny's hands drop further down, almost to his hips. "Put those hands back up behind your head!"

"Okay, okay."

"You don't have an alibi for the night Don was killed, do you?"

"I guess not, Kera, but I didn't kill Don, I swear."

"Your word means nothing to me, Vinny, not after what you pulled at the bar."

Kera couldn't decide if she believed him or not. She understood Vinny's fear that she might not back him up, because they both knew he hadn't needed to kill Sam. And he was a worm for telling people he wasn't around during the time of Sam's death and having no trouble fingering her sister, thinking it was her sitting at the bar with him. But all that didn't make him Don's killer.

The knife thing popped into her head. Vinny seemed to like knives, at least have them on him, and that's how Don was killed, too. He—

"Please, Kera, I know why you would have a hard time believing me, but I didn't kill Don. I'm not saying he didn't deserve to be killed, but I didn't do it. I swear I didn't."

"What about Mandy Bakker? I suppose you didn't beat her and leave her for dead, either."

"I didn't have anything to do with that. I'd never hurt Mandy. I like Mandy. Shit, she works hard for our community. I wouldn't do something like that to her. Kera, please believe me!" Vinny's usual tough-guy façade completely abandoned him, replaced by a helpless man begging for life with sweat dripping from his forehead.

In Iraq, she'd seen people begging for their lives, like that, just before they were peppered with bullets, eliminated, wiped out. She blinked, trying to get rid of the images flipping by like an old movie projector speeding out of control. Her legs felt like cooked noodles.

She told herself to breathe…breathe…breathe. She sucked in air slowly, deliberately, dragging herself back to the present. She registered Vinny's arms slowly coming down again. "Put you goddamned hands behind your head and leave them there. The next time I won't ask. I'll just start shooting."

Vinny snapped his hands back up, interlocking his fingers together against the back of his head. "Calm down, Kera, I'm not trying to—"

"Don't tell me to calm down! You see, I'm having this problem believing you didn't hurt Mandy. I visited her in the hospital. She was barely conscious, but when I asked her who did this to her, she said, 'Maryland.' That's your nickname, you fuckin' asshole. You did it to her."

Vinny took a step backward and held out his hands as if trying to push back her conclusion. "Man, I don't know why she'd say such a thing. I would never hurt her. Never!"

Kera jerked the barrel of her gun upward. "Goddamn it, put your hands where they belong!"

If she didn't think otherwise, she would have believed Vinny. He either didn't hurt Mandy or he was an incredible actor. But Mandy had said, "Maryland." Well, she'd heard it at the time as "Carolyn," but that name didn't make any sense, she had to have been muttering the name, "Maryland."

But what if, "Maryland" wasn't what she trying to say?

She didn't know what to believe or what to do. She wanted clarity—no, more like certainty. She knew asking for that was ridiculous because she'd never been certain about anything else before. Why should she have it now? Her mind thrashed around. Maybe she was crazy. *Here comes that roulette wheel again.* Why did she keep seeing a roulette wheel with a ball dancing on it? The ball landed on "truth." Oh, fuck, not "truth."

A sham, an illusion, a fucking shape shifter.

Her finger tightened on the trigger, wanting to squeeze. She craved spraying bullets everywhere, at the windows, at the gun case… at Vinny.

Her mind reached out, looking for a rope to pull herself out of the mental chaos, something to help her climb back into reality, anybody's reality. *There didn't seem to be a rope, only corded gray matter morphing into a pile of fabric electric cords, frayed, ready to catch fire and blaze through eternity.*

Her finger begged to pull the trigger and extinguish life. Vinny's or her own, it didn't matter to her. Suddenly—

A huge wolf appeared in front of her. His eyes locked onto hers, connecting to her like a lightning strike to a tree. A loud crack sounded as a streak of fire split her open. Balled up rage discharged from her as though from a cannon. The wolf snapped up the rage and swallowed it, then backed up and lay down, resting his head on his paws.

Kera blinked hard. The wolf was gone.

"Kera…Kera?" Vinny's eyes were wide. Sweat soaked his shirt.

She took a few deep breaths, let them out, as she refocused her eyes. Okay, maybe he didn't kill Don or hurt Mandy. Maybe. Her finger loosened on the trigger. She lowered the gun. "Vinny I'm going to give you the benefit of the doubt, but at any moment I could change my mind. Do you get that?"

Vinny's head bobbled. His mouth opened like he was trying to say something, but nothing came out.

"Move on out of here into the back room." Kera waved her gun to emphasize her directions. She moved over to the side, giving Vinny a path to the storeroom. She followed him in and said, "Get that rope over there in the corner."

Vinny went over to a shelf, where a coiled rope lay.

Kera remembered the handcuffs. She took the cuffs and key off the hook. "Grab the rope, put it on the floor, and kick it over to me."

Vinny carefully followed her instructions.

"Now turn around and put your hands behind you." Kera handcuffed him. She grabbed an old wooden chair and pushed him down on the seat, then tied him to the chair, hooking his feet so he wouldn't be able to scoot around. She looked around, found a red oil-stained rag and tied it in and around his mouth as a gag.

Vinny stared at her, a pleading look in his eyes.

"I suppose that doesn't taste too good, but that's the breaks. I'll be back when I figure things out."

She needed to go. It was getting late. Time to meet with Kevin and find out what he had to say. She grabbed the keys to Vinny's truck and left.

* * *

Kevin's office was located in the old red brick First National Bank Building. Kera hoped he remembered his late night appointment with

Dee. She looked at the clock embedded in the building's tower—ten to twelve—which must have been when the gears stopped long ago.

She checked the time on her cell phone. It was actually, sixteen minutes after nine. Hopefully, Kevin hadn't left for the night when her sister hadn't shown up at nine. She saw a light in the upper right corner of the building, maybe—she hoped—it was Kevin's office.

She'd laid her fake glasses on the passenger's seat. She decided she should wear them just in case someone spotted her going into the building.

She tried the front door. Locked. She went around to the side of the building and found a door that opened. She stepped inside and saw an office directory on the wall. Kevin's office was on the second floor.

The dimly lit building was quiet, except for her footsteps as she started climbing up the creaking oak staircase. It smelled musty, stuffy and thin, like confined air circulating from one person to another, depleting itself of oxygen.

A male voice called, "Deidre?"

Kera glanced up to see Kevin standing at the top of the stairs. The lights clicked on, but they barely brightened the staircase.

"Sorry, I just realized how late it was and that you were coming tonight," he said. "I was on my way down to check and make sure the door didn't get locked, and the stair lights were on. These dim old lights need to be changed out for new brighter ones—sorry about that. Watch your step coming up."

Kera reached the top of the stairs. "I'm Kera, not Deidre. I'm keeping Dee's appointment for her. She wasn't able to make it tonight, so I'm filling in for her."

"Wow, is that really you, Kera? I wouldn't have recognized you. I haven't seen Deidre in quite a while, but I just thought she'd changed her hair color."

"Well, it was me who changed the color of my hair, along with adding some curls."

He kept staring at her hair. "Interesting."

She figured that meant ugly. She'd have to agree with him.

"Come on in, but I have to warn you, the place is a mess." He stood back while she entered his office.

Kevin's desk faced the door. She sat down in one of the two identical leather chairs positioned across from his desk. She chose the one closest to the door, since it would put her in better position to get out of there, if need be.

Kevin's eyes narrowed. "So beside changing your hair to curly blond, you now wear glasses and makeup. Makes you look, well, real girly." He smiled, he was obviously amused by her transformation.

"Yes, indeed, I've altered my looks a bit." Kera took off the glasses. "To get around town, I had to go through a costume change, you might call it. I'm sure you've heard about Sam's death, and that the police are looking for me."

"Yes, I heard that."

"Just for the record, I didn't do it."

"O-o-okay." Kevin leaned forward, resting his elbows on the desk and clasping his hands together. "What can I do for you? Or Deidre? She's the one who made the appointment, so I'm assuming it's her mission you're on."

"Well, it's really in both our interests. As you can imagine, Dee and I want to find out who killed Don, because both Dee and I are presently suspects in the case. By the way, neither one of us killed Don, but the police don't seem inclined to look beyond us. Then there's Sam's death. I didn't kill him either—as I said—but I know who did. So I'm back to Don's death. I came here to talk to you about his murder."

Kevin raised his eyebrows but didn't say anything.

Kera continued, "Let me get right to the point. The night I met you at the Out-and-About, your knuckles were bleeding. You'd obviously been in a fight. Later, I find out you were wasted and bragging about having beaten up Don at McFarland Park on Friday night."

She watched Kevin closely as she talked. She needed to be prepared for his reaction. She didn't know how he might respond, given what she'd said. She had her gun in her purse, her purse on her lap, and her hand ready to reach in and grab it.

Kevin didn't move or even look like he was about to. He had a pained look on his face. She was nonplused by his reaction. Maybe it was time to stop talking and see what silence would bring from him.

Finally, Kevin looked her and sighed. "Yeah, I sure was wasted that night, shot my mouth off like a fool. I've been waiting for it to come back and bite me."

"Did you go back to McFarland Saturday night, wait for Don and kill him?" She decided she might just as well put her cards on the table.

"No, I didn't, Kera." Kevin looked straight into her eyes. "I hated that bastard for what he was doing, but I didn't kill him."

"Okay. Where did you go Saturday night after the fight at the Out-and-About?"

"I came back here, to my office." Kevin patted his desk. "To pick up the flyers I had forgotten. I needed them for the open house I was having on Sunday morning. When I was here, I saw some papers I had to finish up by Sunday, so I worked on them."

"How long were you here?"

"Not sure. Maybe an hour or two, but I went right home afterward."

"Did anyone see you at your house?"

Kevin leaned back in his chair. "Hell, Kera, I live alone, so nobody saw me. It was late and I don't suppose anyone saw me driving into my garage."

"How about here at the office. Did anyone see you?"

Kevin shook his head. "Don't think so."

Kera felt like she learned more from people by watching their body language than by what they said. Kevin wasn't looking or reacting like a guilty guy, but she was messed up these days and didn't know how much she should trust her own perceptions. And he couldn't back up his whereabouts during the time of Don's death.

This wasn't what she'd expected. It didn't seem like Vinny was lying, and now she had a hard time believing Kevin was lying. But if they were both telling the truth, then—

"Just a minute." Kevin sat up straight. "How could I have forgotten? That was the night Harry and I got into it. Harry was here at the office when I came back that night. He'd been in his office in the back, but I didn't know he was there until a little later. He and I talked about a closing we had coming up. I don't know how I forgot that. Well, more like I forgot it happened on Saturday night."

"Oh? So Harry was here and can validate that you were here?"

"Yeah, he stays late here at the office a lot."

"What do you mean you guys 'got into it?'" Kera picked up a business brochure from his desk. She glanced at it and put it to use as a fan, apparently the air conditioning wasn't working or had been turned off for the night.

"Well, you know Harry knows I'm gay. I told you that, remember?"

She nodded. She recalled him talking about it.

"Well, when I got back to the office that night, I had a few bruises myself, plus I was messed up from fighting. You know, my shirt was dirty and had a tear in it. Looked like I was in a fight, I'm sure." Kevin ran his fingers through his hair. "Harry said I shouldn't be at the office looking like that. I told him I didn't expect any customers at that time of night and I was just dropping by to pick up stuff for my open house. He asked me how I got to be such a mess. I told him about the right-wing idiots at the bar and how they instigated a fight. I was still so riled up I didn't give a damn what Harry thought." Kevin got out of his chair and walked over by a window, turned around and continued, "Well, Harry starts in about 'queers,' of course, knowing I am one—

something he usually tries to forget." He came over and sat next to Kera, turning the chair toward her. "Look, Kera, I could have been canned for what I told Harry. In fact, I don't know why I still have this job. It's really so strange he didn't fire me right then and there." He shook his head. "Anyway, I told Harry his good friend, Don Bledsoe— his bigoted minister—was a queer. That's exactly what I said."

"You're kidding!"

Kevin went on, "Harry's face turned beet-red when I said that. He was livid. The man yelled at me and said I was an out-and-out liar. That pissed me off, so I told him I'd seen Don at the gay beach at McFarland Park, and in fact, I'd almost fucked him. That is, until I saw who he was when his fake mustache fell off. Anyway, all the anger I'd stored up at Harry came out that night. I was so mad by then, I told Harry I'd beaten the shit out of his 'queer little friend.'"

"Oh, my god…what did he say to that?"

"He didn't say anything. He just stood there a second, looking at me as though I was the Devil incarnate, then he stormed out of here. Like I said, Kera, I don't know why he hasn't fired me. Maybe it's like I told you at the bar." Kevin held up his forefinger and his thumb and rubbed them together. "He can't afford to get rid of me. He needs the gay real estate market business, especially in this horrid economy. That's all I can figure."

Like Kevin, she couldn't come up with a reason for Harry not to fire him on the spot. She remembered how enraged he'd gotten at her when she'd said something against Don. Other than threatening to sue her for saying Don was an abuser, he had no power over her. But with Kevin?

She needed more time to think.

CHAPTER THIRTY-ONE

Kera

Kera picked up a cheeseburger, fries and water at the Wendy's drive-through. She parked Vinny's truck to eat and think about what Kevin had just told her at his office.

Harry had found out about Don's trips to McFarland Park's gay beach just hours before Don was killed and he'd gotten really angry at Kevin for telling him Don was gay. Had he actually believed Kevin? Or was the man angry over Kevin "slandering" his friend, as he'd put it?

Harry was as much of a gay hater as Don. If he'd believed Kevin, would he have been so upset he'd go after Don, and end up killing him? Harry had called Don that very night. He'd even told Deidre he was probably the last person to speak to Don.

The question she asked herself was, would he be that crazy, that irate, feel that betrayed to go after Don, his best friend?

Maybe.

She reached over, took the fries out of the take-out bag and began munching. She spotted the brochure she'd picked up in Kevin's office and used as a makeshift fan. She slumped in her seat, smoothed out the surface and stared at Kevin's picture on the front of the brochure. She thought it was a good picture of him, actually helped cover his look of "Ichabod-ness."

She'd told Kevin before she left his office she was heading out to Harry's house. He'd warned her to be careful, because bringing up anything negative about Don would probably send Harry off on another tirade.

She was starved, couldn't remember her last meal. She grabbed her burger, unwrapped it and took a bite.

She opened the brochure and saw a picture of Harry and Kevin standing together by a house with a For Sale sign reading, "The Harry Janssen Group," with the word, "Sold," slapped diagonally across it. She hadn't been aware Harry used to use his first name as part of his business name: The Harry Janssen Group. She'd seen his signs around town. The company name, now, was just The Janssen Group. She vaguely wondered when he'd dropped his first name from his business name.

She noticed Harry and Kevin looked friendly toward each other in the picture. Maybe that was before Harry knew Kevin was gay or maybe it was a just-for-pictures smile. She took a sip of her water.

The Harry Janssen Group. Harry Janssen. Hmm? She repeated the name. Har-ry Jans-sen. That sort of sounds like…maybe. She said his name aloud, over and over, dragging out the sounds and repeating his name quickly, blurring, slurring, amalgamating the syllables until she heard—well not what she'd heard, but what Dee thought she'd heard: "eerie lands end…airy landsend…arry lansen…Harry Janssen." Shit, had Mandy been trying to say Harry Janssen's name to Dee? Mumbling in a coma-like state, "Harry Janssen" might come out as "eerie lands end."

But why would Harry want to hurt Mandy. What would Mandy have to do with anything? She could see how Harry might be so mad at Don's betrayal—by being gay—that he'd lost it and gone after Don.

But Mandy too?

She certainly hadn't seen a violent side of Harry. Then again, she knew people worked hard to hide their bad sides. But Dee had never mentioned to her that Harry was physically abusive with Sylvia…

Come to think of it, she remembered when Dee stayed with the Janssens, she'd seen bits and pieces of Harry's temper, but it'd seemed contained. Maybe Harry's temper was like a grenade that needed someone to pull the pin and set off the explosion. Is that what Don did, pull Harry's pin?

Okay, maybe he went after Don, but for the life of her, she still couldn't figure out why he'd go after Mandy. So, for now, she needed to focus on Don's death. She searched her memory. Dee had told her Harry said he was at home that night playing cards with his wife, and he'd called to talk to Don about his parishioners being in the hospital due to the fight at the gay bar. Since Sylvia was home that night, he couldn't have left without her knowing, could he?

Nevertheless, she needed to find out. She would have to ask Harry what he was doing the night of Don's death.

She took the last bite of her cheeseburger, balled up the wrapper and tossed it into the sack. Time to pay Harry a visit.

It'd only taken her five minutes to get to the beach. She'd driven too fast, would have gotten stopped if a cop had been near, but she couldn't seem to lighten her foot on the gas pedal. She parked the pickup on a little used access road leading down to the beach, about an eighth of a mile from Harry's house. She planned to walk up the beach to his home so she wouldn't need to leave the truck in his driveway for anyone to see. If he wasn't home, she would break in.

Well, she didn't exactly need to break in—she had a key—so it was more like she'd let herself in. Good thing she'd grabbed the keys out of Ally's car before abandoning it. Harry's house key was on Dee's key ring along with the key to the Mustang. Her mind flipped back to assaulting the cop. Damn, she wished she hadn't had to do that to the guy—a cop—but she'd worry about all that later. Not now.

The sparkle of the night sky glittered on the lake as she walked on the beach toward Harry's house. She sat down, set her purse in the sand, took off her sandals and linked them together—she never could traverse loose sand with those damned things on. She'd have to carry them.

As she got closer to Harry's, she glanced off to the west. Dark clouds were coming in from the lake. Soon the little remaining light in the night sky would be completely gone and the waves would kick up. The breeze was already intensifying, blowing up sand against her face and in her hair.

Kera smelled a dead fish, then felt the slimy carcass under her foot as she slipped, twisting her ankle. Shit! She hopped on her other foot, sat down in the sand and tried to rub out the pain. She stood and gingerly took a few steps. Her ankle hurt like hell. She was going to have to deal with it, work through the pain. Hopefully, she wouldn't have need to run tonight.

As she got closer to Harry's house, she couldn't see any lights on inside. Sylvia didn't appear to be there. The woman had probably already left to visit her grandmother.

Kera put her shoes on and limped up the wooden stairs to the house. She ducked around the house to see if any cars were parked in the driveway. None. She peeked in the garage window. No cars in there either. She decided to go back around to the lakeside of the house by the sunroom to try to get in. She figured she'd be less likely spotted entering there than through the front door. With any luck, all the doors would be keyed alike.

The awnings on the sunroom creaked and moaned from being beaten by the wind. She searched Dee's key ring for the Janssen house key. She got the right key on the second try and crept inside.

A blue lava lamp was on, white globs rising to the top like stuffed, malformed bubbles. Near the lamp, she saw a large candle that looked well used, but still had a lot of burn left in it. She picked it up and sniffed it. Smelled fruity. A tube of fireplace matches lay next to it. She lit the wick, deciding the candle would have to do for lighting since she didn't want to risk turning on lights while she wandered through rooms investigating the house.

She heard a noise. Sounded like it came from outside. She went over to the windows overlooking the lake. Nothing. She decided it must be the wind rattling things.

Glancing around the sunroom, she wasn't sure what she was looking for or what she might find that would further point the finger at Harry. She moved into the living room.

The phone rang. She stopped. If anyone happened to be up in the bedroom area, they'd answer the phone, but it kept ringing until the call transferred to an answering machine.

Sylvia's voice boomed, "Harry, I was just calling to remind you that you have a dental appointment tomorrow morning. I'm not sure if I put it on your calendar. Also, Bob called me—because he couldn't get you—about the hunting cabin you and Don were going to rent this year. He said he'd heard about Don's death, but he didn't know if you were still planning to go up there. Grandma seems to be doing okay, given her age and all she's gone through…I guess that's all."

Click.

Kera noted the curtness of the message, not particularly loving or even friendly. Didn't sound like Sylvia and Harry's relationship had gotten any better.

She search through the lower part of the house, but didn't find anything other than a kitchen with two days' worth of dishes on the counters, and a mounted deer head hanging over the fireplace in the living room with a tie hung over its antlers.

Even though she figured no one was home, she tiptoed up the stairs, pain shooting through her ankle with each step. She knew she should be icing her ankle, but that wasn't going to happen soon.

Kera moved in and out of the bedrooms, nothing significant other than realizing Harry was messy. He'd left clothes all over the floor of the guest bedroom. Apparently, he hadn't returned to sleeping with his wife after Sylvia kicked him out because the master bedroom was spotless.

She went into the bathroom. Towels and washcloths balanced precariously on the racks. Toothpaste, deodorant and every product known to mankind to save him from the ravages of time sat out on the counter. The smell of aftershave lingered.

She set down the candle and looked in the medicine cabinet. Maybe there'd be something to help relieve the pain in her ankle. She found a bottle of extra strength Tylenol and popped two into her mouth, bent over and washed them down with water from the faucet.

The next room she entered was Harry's den, paneled in a dark cherry wood. He had mounted fish on the walls, as well as a bearskin with its head still attached. The defeated, skinned bear hung feet up, head toward the floor next to an oak desk. The bear's mouth was open, baring its yellowed sharp teeth, looking as though he dared anyone to walk too close.

She sat down at the desk. As far as she could tell, there were mostly real estate and church papers strewn over the top. She kept flipping through the papers and found a handwritten note from Sylvia to Harry dated Sunday, July 20. She held up the note to the candle so she could read it.

Harry,

As usual, I can't get my point across to you. You don't let me. You think your opinion is fact. Well, it's not. You also think Don is God's Chosen One and he walks on water, and that is so wrong too. I know what happened to Deidre and how she got her broken nose and I know she didn't get it from walking into a door in the night. This wouldn't be the first time Don has hit Deidre, as I said last night. I know you don't want to believe this, but it's true.

Yesterday I asked you to sleep in the guest bedroom. That was done in anger, but today, I've been thinking about things and I make this decision not in anger, but after much prayer. For now at least, I'm asking you to continue to sleep in the guest room. I need time to think about "us."

Sylvia

"Marriage on the rocks," Kera murmured to herself.

She looked at several pictures of a silver Mercedes on the desk. The first one showed Harry sitting in the Mercedes, a big smile on his face. She flipped the snapshot over. Written on the back was "Harry's first Mercedes. Isn't he proud!" The notation appeared to be in Sylvia's handwriting.

She looked through the other three photos picturing Harry's car from all angles. She'd never seen Harry's car before. Apparently, real estate had been good to him.

Hmm, a Mercedes. Hadn't she seen a Mercedes parked about half a block down from the gay beach when she was driving back to Mandy's—in the early dawn following the night Don was killed there. She couldn't swear it was silver, but if she had to guess, that's the color she'd come up with. When she'd seen it, she'd figured it was some gay guy's car, since she'd seen several Mercedes at the gay bar and, of course, didn't know what kind of car Harry drove. But come to think of it, none of the Mercedes at the bar had been a silver color. Quite possibly, more than likely, she'd seen Harry's car just outside the parking lot.

She heard a noise. She couldn't figure out what it could be, then decided it was most likely the wind knocking something around. She listened for a while, but heard nothing more.

She searched his desk for a calendar, pawing around, picking up papers, and finally finding a calendar desk mat under the pile. She wanted to check the date of Sylvia's note banishing Harry from her bed. She used her finger to follow back to July twentieth, the Sunday Sylvia wrote the note, the Sunday the cops found Don's body in the early morning hours. So Sylvia had made it known sometime the day before Don's death, on Saturday, that Harry was no longer welcome in their bedroom. That was the night, probably around ten or so, that Kevin told Harry about Don being at McFarland Park and Harry had stormed out of Kevin's office and left the building.

She knew Harry had talked to Don late that night. He'd said Don was at the church preparing his sermon when he talked to him. Maybe after Harry left Kevin's office, he went looking for Don at his home or tried to call him there, but Don wasn't at his house. Dee wouldn't have been there either because she'd been staying with her at their dad's place. Anyway, not finding Don at home, he'd eventually called the church and found Don there, and later followed or found Don at McFarland Park.

As she was scrambling facts around, putting events in an order that made sense, she was opening desk drawers, finding pretty much the normal run-of-the-mill desk items: paper clips, stapler, stamps, envelopes. In the last drawer, the candlelight flickered on a small marble container with a lid. She opened it. Inside, she saw a black onyx ring with diamonds in the shape of a cross.

Don's ring.

It didn't make sense to her. What would Harry be doing with Don's ring? Don had been wearing the ring the last time she'd seen him. In fact, she remembered Dee telling her he loved that ring, never took it off, not only because he thought it was beautiful, but also because Harry had given it to him and it was some kind of inspiration thing for Don. She wondered if Harry had taken the ring back...say, after he'd found out from Kevin about Don's trysts to McFarland Park, he followed Don out there, killed him, then took the ring off—

Kera heard a noise again—the sound of a door creaking.

The ceiling light flashed on and a male voice said, "It seems I have a prowler."

She whipped around.

Harry stood in the doorway. He held a hunting rifle pointed at her, his finger on the trigger. "What are you doing in my house and at my desk, may I ask?"

"I didn't hear you come in." She realized that was a dumb thing to say. Of course she hadn't heard him, otherwise—

"I'm sure you didn't. I saw a light darting around from the window when I was driving in. I thought someone might be robbing me. Then when I opened the door and came in, I smelled that candle Sylvia likes to burn, and then I thought, she's not at home, but you're here." Harry looked at the lit candle she held. "And guess what, it's the 'wanted woman' of Lakeside City. Again, I'm asking you, what in the hell are you doing here?" He moved into the room, stopped and glared at her.

"Actually, I'm finding some pretty interesting things here." She kept her voice level, though her heart pounded and her insides shook like her nerves had a few loose bolts. She was angry for letting herself get sneaked-up on. She put the candle on the desk.

Feeling even more vulnerable in a sitting position, she stood up. He already had the advantage with his rifle pointed at her and his body blocking her way out of the room. She evaluated her chances of taking him off guard and disarming him. He was taller and much heavier, and a wrestler to boot. Not good, but possible.

She thought about the purse she'd tossed on the sofa when she came into the den, but didn't allow her eyes to look over at it, as it could cause him to get suspicious of its contents. Damn, why hadn't she taken the gun out of that stupid purse? Her answer came flying back to her like a boomerang: ever since she had gotten home from Iraq, her brain had been functioning on only one or two cylinders.

"I doubt you can find too much interesting in my desk, but I do know the police are going to be happy when I call them and let them know I've caught a killer. And not only that, but we can add burglary, or at least breaking-and-entering to the charges against you." Harry balanced his rifle against his body with his arm, holding his finger on the trigger. With his right hand, he took out his cell phone.

"I wouldn't do that so fast, Harry." At some point she would welcome the police, but not until she made sure the pieces of her puzzle were firmly in place.

"And why is that?" Harry started to punch in a number with a finger on his left hand.

"Because, the cops might prefer to take you instead of me."

"What do you mean?" He was having a hard time making his call while holding the gun.

She inched closer to him and momentarily saw an opportunity to attack. His gun lowered and his attention was on his phone while he tried to make his call. Suddenly, Harry looked up, probably hearing her move. He raised his rifle. "Don't come any closer or I'll have to pull this trigger." He put the phone down on a small nearby table, apparently scrapping the idea of making the call right then, and said, "Now, didn't I ask you a question?"

"First, let me ask you one. Where were you the night of Don's death?"

"What does that matter?" The muzzle of Harry's rifle was now aimed at her heart.

"Believe me, Harry, it matters." Kera watched his eyes, looking for a clue as to what he might do next.

"Not that it matters, but I was here in the house. My wife will attest to that."

"Oh, will she? How would she know you were in the house all night?"

Harry's voice rose. "Because we were playing cards—she can tell you that—then we went to bed."

Dee had told her that Harry and Sylvia played cards some evenings, but she doubted they'd played cards that night, but she knew for a fact that they were not sharing a bed. "But you haven't been sleeping with her lately, have you? And you weren't sleeping with her the night of Don's murder. You could have easily slipped out of this house and back inside without her ever knowing."

Harry didn't deny what she'd said. He just kept staring at her, apparently trying to figure out what he'd do or say next.

She looked at his hand on the rifle. His finger moved nervously on the trigger. "Let me show you something, Harry. I'm going to put my hand in here." She patted her pocket. "See, there's no weapon."

Harry's eyes followed her hand. She believed he wouldn't shoot her, not right then, anyway. He'd want to see what she had to show him, because it would be important to him to know what evidence she might have on him. She slowly put her hand in the pocket, pulled out the note written by Sylvia and held it up for him to see.

"It says," she went on, "you're not sleeping with her. Right here in Sylvia's own handwriting and signed by her—even dated. My guess is that she won't be able to give you an alibi, at least not airtight." Kera shoved the note back in her pocket. "Is there anyone else that can prove you didn't leave this house that night? Like, leave it to kill Don?"

Kera realized the closer she came to showing all the evidence implicating Harry in Don's murder, the closer he came to pulling the trigger. She was going to have to find or create an opening to get the rifle from him.

Harry looked shaken having seen Sylvia's note, but he pushed on. "Why would I kill my best friend? Nobody would believe that for a minute. Everyone knows I loved Don. He was my spiritual leader. How could I kill him? Maybe Sylvia and I had a marital spat, but that hardly means I killed my best friend. That note from Sylvia proves nothing, nothing at all." Harry's eyes were glued on the pocket where she'd returned Sylvia's note.

"No, but it does mean you don't have a solid alibi for that night."

"You still haven't explained why I would want to kill Don. You see, I have every reason why I wouldn't kill him and absolutely no reason why I would. I think they call that motive, or lack of motive in my case," he sneered.

"Well, you know, Harry, I've been thinking about your possible motive, and this is what I've come up with. Let me know what you think. I talked to Kevin and he informed me that on the night of Don's death, he'd met you earlier in the evening in his office. Kevin told you Don had been at the gay beach soliciting for sex and he'd almost had sex with Don himself. That is, until he realized it was Don, then Kevin beat the shit out of him. Kevin said you were—what was the word he used?—'livid,' I believe. After he told you, you stormed out of the building."

"So?" He was staring at her, hard.

"I know you called and talked to Don later that night at the church. You've admitted that yourself." She didn't think it wise to mention she'd seen his Mercedes at McFarland Park. Not yet, anyway.

"Well, Kera, you've been busy trying to figure this thing out, haven't you? But I won't allow you to pin Don's murder on me. Besides, everyone knows you killed Sam Zander and—"

Kera looked beyond Harry, who had his back to the door, and saw Kevin slide into view from the hallway. She couldn't believe her eyes. What in the hell was Kevin doing here? Goddamn, there she was again, someone holding a gun on her and another person sneaking in from behind. Was this going to be a recurring nightmare where someone got killed and she was blamed? It seemed death followed her like a bloodhound.

Sweat oozed from her pores. There wasn't enough air in the room. She tried to suck in a deep breath, but it didn't feel like the extra oxygen did her any good. She was light-headed. Her head began spinning or was it the room? She couldn't tell, then:

Harry's face blurred and was floating, detached from his neck. His lips moving, sneering. She was fading away, or maybe Harry was, or maybe they both were. She couldn't tell. Gravity let go of the contents of the room, causing things to drift around. She tried to make her way through the chaos, to get hold of something, anything. She reached out for the rifle gliding through space.

Her foot moved forward to keep her from toppling over, igniting pain from her ankle that shot up to her brain like an electric current snapping her back.

Kera sat down on the desk chair, tried to steady herself and get her bearings. The objects had settled down, gone back to their original places. The floating rifle was now firmly in Harry's grip, pointing at her.

She willed herself to sort through her clouded thinking and try to figure out what was going on. Kevin had been concerned when she'd told him she was coming to Harry's house. Did he come there to help her? She'd believed Kevin at the time, but Kevin could have been setting up Harry to throw suspicion away from himself.

Her mind swirled, trying to land on something solid, something certain, like who was the good guy here? She had to make a decision, a determination, a likely guess. She decided to cast her lot with Kevin. Her reasoning and gut—for whatever they were worth—told her Harry had killed Don.

She sure as hell hoped so.

"Kera, do you have any other supposed evidence you would like to tell me about?" Harry's voice seemed unnaturally calm. He sounded like someone who was sure of what he was about to do. "That is," he continued, "before I get rid of you, the burglar I've caught trespassing in my house, going through my things, threatening me. You see, I'll tell the police you went for my rifle, we struggled, and I accidently shot you. I'll make it good." He appeared totally unaware of Kevin's presence.

Kera knew she needed to keep him talking just a little bit longer, hoping to hell Kevin was the good guy. "I figure it went this way, Harry. Some way or another, you had reason to believe Don was going to the gay beach that night. You went out to McFarland Park and found him there. Or maybe you followed him, doesn't really matter. Anyway, you saw it all with your own eyes. Here was your goddamned best friend and spiritual guide, as you put it, out fucking men, the very kind of men you and your church were waging war against. It must have thrown you over the edge. So you killed him. How'd I do, Harry?"

He didn't say anything, didn't move, and kept the rifle pointed at her. She knew his finger could pull the trigger at any moment. She had to divert Harry for a little longer. She'd lay out her last piece of evidence.

"Just one more thing." She stood slowly and patted her hand on her other pocket. "As you see, I don't have a gun in here either. But I have something else to show you." She pulled out Don's ring. As she stretched out her hand toward Harry, the ring in her palm, she moved a few small steps closer to him.

His gaze was fixed on the ring, as she'd hoped. He didn't seem to notice her forward movement.

"After you killed him," she continued, "you took back the ring you'd given him. I imagine you didn't feel he deserved it anymore. Am I right about all that?"

Harry's eye's narrowed and his face turned red. His lips tightened and released just enough to let out words. "Well, Ms. Queer Detective, you got it right. God appointed Don Bledsoe to wipe out gays from this city, but the Devil got hold of him."

Kera could barely breathe. She knew the slightest movement from her at this moment could send a bullet into her body.

"Don't you see," Harry calmly explained, "he had to die. And now, so do you." Harry's low voice morphed into a growl, "But no one else is going to know, are they? It is just you and me here and you won't be getting a chance to talk."

Kera glanced behind Harry, watching Kevin edge closer. She still needed to keep providing a distraction, buy more time, keep Harry engaged so Kevin could get within range to strike. She didn't think it would be smart to bring up that she saw his car out by McFarland. Since she was probably the only witness to that, he'd surely feel it was time to pull the trigger. She had to come up with something else… "Well, there is something I didn't figure out."

"Oh?" His voice turned calm again.

"Yeah, why did you go after Mandy and leave her for dead?"

"I guess there is no harm in telling you but it should be obvious." Harry's finger eased off the trigger but hovered close by. "Mandy is a troublemaker, a leader, the queen of the queers, so to speak. By getting rid of her, I figured it would take the wind out of LEAP's sails. But enough of this." He put his finger back on the trigger, ready to fire.

Kera jumped in. "But you may have failed at that, Harry. Mandy isn't dead."

Kevin was close, about two more steps to be in striking range.

Harry's face tightened. "I'm not going to fail with you and I'll get Mandy finished off too." He snickered. "If she ever comes out of her coma. When they brought her in, I heard the docs didn't have much hope for her." He sneered. "God's army will get stronger because Don will now serve as Our Martyr, our rallying cry." He mocked, "You see, Don will serve God's cause, after all. Just in a different way than we'd all envisioned. As they say, God works in mysterious ways."

Kera swallowed hard. This guy was crazier than she'd thought, maybe a bigger fanatic than Don. Hate mixed with religious extremism—a venomous cocktail.

"But now, Kera, it's time for you to go to the Hell you deserve."

"I don't think so, Harry."

The voice behind Harry startled him. He jerked and turned toward Kevin, his rifle not making it around quite as fast as the rest of his body, but clearly not pointed directly at her anymore.

Kera took advantage, moved in and kicked the rifle out of Harry's grip.

Kevin grabbed Harry and threw him down. Harry landed on his back, hitting his head against the floor.

Kera moved in and smashed her foot into Harry's groin, causing the man's knees to pull up as he rolled to his side, groaning. She glanced up and saw Kevin grimacing.

Kevin shook his head. "Shit, Kera, remind me never to piss you off."

"Crushing his balls might have felt good, if my damned sprained ankle didn't hurt so bad." She smirked. "Nevertheless, I have to say it was rewarding."

Kevin winced. "From a guy's perspective, that last move was hard to watch. But I understand why you went for the crotch, the bastard deserved it." He picked up the rifle and put the end of the barrel to Harry's head.

"Don't kill him! Don't, please." Her nightmare was returning.

"Hmm, Harry, what do you think? Should I spare you, turn you over to the cops, or take you out of your misery? I'm just saying, Kera's stomp on your balls had to hurt you bad, man, way more than it hurt her. Maybe a shot to the head would help alleviate your pain."

Harry was doubled-up, groaning, nonresponsive to Kevin's threat, but Kera could see the terror in his eyes.

"Really, Kevin, we don't need another death."

"You're right. I don't really want to kill him. I'd so much rather see a public trial to expose what's been going on in this community." Kevin looked down at Harry. "So Harry, if you start feeling better any time soon and decide to try anything before the police get here, I'll just blow your fucking arm or a leg off. Maim you, but try not to kill you."

"I think he's not feeling like putting up much of a fight." Kera got her cell phone out of the purse ready to call the police, then thought better of it. "Kevin, I need you to call to the police because I'm going to have to get out of here, fast."

"You're going to what! Leave me with this mess?"

"Just for a bit. If I'm here, the cops are going to arrest me for Sam's death, along with assaulting a police officer, resisting arrest, and who knows what else they could come up with." Kera tossed Kevin a sick smile. "I need to get some things straightened up before I let them at me. And I've got to get to Vinny so he can talk to the cops about how Sam died, but he's sort of tied up right now. I need to check in on him. He's probably already peed his pants."

"Peed his pants?"

"It's a long story. Tell you about it at another time."

Kevin stared at her, his jaw dropped and his eyebrows elevated. "Well, what am I supposed to tell the cops?"

Kera picked up her purse. "After the cops get here, tell them what happened, then let them know I went over at Vinny's shop. But give me about a half hour start before you call them. Okay? I need a little time."

"Ah, well, okay."

"When the police get to Vinny's place, they can hear what Vinny has to say about Sam's death. I need to make sure I'm there when Vinny talks to the cops, so the little worm will be inclined to tell the truth."

She left Harry's house feeling depleted, like she'd hit the wall in the last mile of a marathon. She desperately wanted to find a bed and fall into a Rip Van Winkle sleep. But the police would be at Vinny's soon and she needed to be there so they could hear Vinny tell them how Sam died.

To save time, she hurried down the road that paralleled the beach to get where she'd left the truck. She wondered if Ally had heard anything about Dee since she'd asked her to call Legal Aid and get her sister an attorney. She took out her cell phone and punched in Ally's number. "Hey, Ally, this is Kera. Were you able to get a lawyer for my sister?"

"Sure did. I talked to the secretary of the woman who's the head of the agency. She told me she'd get someone over there right away."

"Have you heard anything more?"

"Yup, the attorney called me back when she was leaving the jail, said they'd arrested Dee because she had no way to prove that she wasn't you. But the lawyer—forgot her name—told me she'd made sure to tell Dee not to answer any of their questions other than to say she wasn't you. Oh yeah, the woman said she'd done all she could for Dee for the time being and was leaving, but would be back tomorrow, hopefully being able to prove Dee was who she said she was."

Kera heard music and people laughing in the background. Life felt crazy to her. People partied while others fought for their lives. She thought it was definitely her and Dee's turn for some party time.

Ally said, "Hey, I haven't seen hide or hair of Vinny. He never returned to the bar. Have—"

"That's because he's currently tied up. I mean, I literally tied him up." Kera laughed. She suddenly felt giddy.

"You sound like you've been a busy girl." Ally chuckled.

"Oh, I have, Ally. But I have one more important thing to do, I'm hoping to get the circumstances of Sam's death cleared up tonight." Kera had reached the truck and got in and pulled out onto the road. It would only take her a few minutes to get to Vinny's shop from there.

Kera decided not to speak further about Vinny or Harry. She didn't want to count on anything until the police were convinced about who killed Don and Sam. She knew her evidence and Harry's confession should certainly be enough and, hopefully, Vinny would cooperate in clearing her name in Sam's death. But she'd better be careful, not be too buoyant, too sure of the outcome or too optimistic, because she believed she should never let the fickle gods know what she wanted or was hoping for.

"You take care, Kera," Ally said.

"Hey, thanks so much for helping us, Ally, I'm making progress and need to keep moving, so I better go, and let you get back to your job." She put her phone in her pocket.

Kera drove into the parking lot of Vinny's shop, got out, went to the door of the storage area and opened it. She glanced at Vinny, sitting there, looking pathetic. "I take it you've been okay while I was gone?" She couldn't contain her smile as she entered the room.

Vinny's pleading brown eyes stared up at her.

She reached down, pulled out the oily red rag from his mouth and sat down on a box across from him. Vinny coughed and worked his tongue around, then spit out a fragment of red cloth.

"Well, Vinny, I've had quite a productive night, but I'm really tired so I need you to listen very carefully. I'm in no mood for fabrication. Do you hear what I'm saying?"

"Yeah, Kera. I won't lie to you, honest." Vinny's eyes were locked on the gun she was flipping from one hand to the other, like playing catch with a baseball.

"First, let me tell you I know now you didn't kill Don or hurt Mandy."

Vinny's facial muscles loosened. He sucked in a deep breath.

Kera continued, staring hard into his eyes. "All I'm asking of you is when I call the cops to come here, you will tell them exactly what happened at Sam's house. Can I count on you for that?"

She wouldn't have to call the cops because Kevin would send them over, but she didn't want Vinny to know that or to know she was in a time crunch trying to get him to cooperate.

Vinny nodded, his face flushed. "Yes, I promise I will, Kera. I'll tell them exactly what happened. Believe me."

"See, here's the problem. It's the 'believe me' thing that's worrisome to me. We need to work it out because, when the cops come, I won't have a gun on you. They might frown on me pointing a firearm at you while you admit to having killed Sam." Kera smirked. "So how am I to be sure you'll tell the truth to them? Do you see my problem here?"

"Yeah, I do…uh, well, for one thing, now you know I didn't kill Don—or hurt Mandy—so it's not like I'm worried you're trying to pin all that shit on me. Now, it's just down to the Sam thing." Vinny frowned, thought for a moment, then asked, "Who do you think did kill Don and hurt Mandy?"

"I know who did it—Harry Janssen. You know, the guy on the city council and Don's so-called friend."

"Son-of-a-bitch. Did he beat up Mandy too?" Vinny grimaced as he tried to move. His skin was red where the rope pressed into his flesh.

"Yup."

"How did you find out?"

"I'm not inclined to go into that right now, Vinny. I'm too damned tired and I want to solve my problem: getting a guarantee you'll tell the truth to the cops when they get here."

Vinny shrugged. "Hell, I don't know if I can give you anything that will guarantee I'll tell the truth, but like I said, since Don's killer is caught and you know Mandy was beaten by Janssen, not me..." His voice trailed off.

Kera hoped everything went well with Kevin handing Harry over to the police. She had to trust the man. But what about her life would allow her to believe things would turn out, as they should? She tried to shake off the last thought. She had to move on and hope. Life wouldn't be worth living without hope, would it? But needing hope didn't make hope happen for her. Needing to keep loved ones from vanishing from her life didn't make it happen. Needing anything, for that matter, was sort of irrelevant, as far as she could tell. She felt her mind swirling around and around like an eddy.

"Kera, I know we have a, uh, situation here, but—"

She shook her head and focused on Vinny. "What do you mean by 'situation?'"

"Look, Kera, I know I was wrong in what I was doing at the Out-and-About, telling everyone I was out of town at the time. Like I said before, I was worried you wouldn't back me up. And I know I used more force than I probably should have on Sam, killing him. But I just kept seeing that bastard—all arrogant—out there on the street with his sign, trying to make me feel like a piece of shit." Vinny cleared his throat and went on. "Anyway, I figured you'd have time to think about me killing Sam, how it went down, and one way or another, I'd end up going to jail. Shit, I was scared, Kera, really scared." He broke eye contact with her and looked down toward his lap.

Kera didn't like Vinny's fluid morality—lying to save his own ass while putting hers up as bait—but she understood his train of thought, his logic, and his fear.

Vinny looked back at her and continued, "You know, Kera, you say you have a problem believing me, like you're concerned I won't tell the truth. But do you understand I have a problem being sure you'll back me up and not say I went too far once I've already told the cops I killed Sam. Like, I need to believe you'll convince them I had to kill Sam to keep you and maybe me alive. You know, self-defense." His tongue found another fragment left by the oily gag and spit it out.

"Yes, that's where the rub is, isn't it." Kera took a deep breath and let it out.

Vinny nodded. "Yup."

"Well, Vinny, I don't like that you got, let's say, carried away, but I understand how it could happen." She appreciated having problems with control. She had all she could handle keeping herself contained, especially when things felt crazy. Who knew, maybe Vinny did save her life by killing Sam. She might not even be having this conversation if he hadn't shown up. But lying, bending the perception of actions to fit outcomes? Had she just opened another trap door into the murky pit of truth?

She considered Vinny's pain, made to feel like shit because he was gay—she understood. He was a needy, insecure bastard, trying to get people to like him. Who knows why? What had life done to Vinny? She'd never know what he'd gone through in his life. Maybe, life was all about individual truths, no an all-encompassing one.

And, maybe she was merely justifying everything.

There she was again, her brain twisting, grinding, groaning with no clear answers. She needed to move on, get an exit for them both, a way out of the dilemma. She couldn't wait for a moral decision to be handed down from some sage or guru, or somebody's idea of a god. She'd needed to make a decision right now, then live with it.

"Okay, Vinny, I'm going to be backing you up about you struggling with Sam, and our lives depended on you killing him. For the second part of our dilemma—that is, trusting each other—I have a solution. It can be handled by timing, the sequence of telling the police what happened. Here's how we do it. When the cops come, I tell them what happened between Sam, you and me. How Sam had a gun and was about to shoot me. You showed up, jumped him from behind and saved my ass—like what happened. Then Sam started getting the better of you, being he was such a big bastard. You saw that I couldn't be of any help because of the bullet hitting me in the shoulder. So you had no other choice and in self-defense you stabbed him. That way, you'll have your assurance right off the bat that I'm backing you up all the way, before you even have to admit to the cops that you stabbed him. What do you think of that?"

Vinny beamed. "Yeah, that'll work, Kera."

She moved behind him, reached up to a shelf, got the key to the handcuffs, took them off, and untied him.

Vinny got up from the chair, rubbing his wrists where the handcuffs had dug into his flesh. He walked around, stretching his arms and legs.

Just then, several cars pulled into the parking lot, reds lights flashing through the window of the shop and dancing on the walls.

"Is that the police, already?" Vinny asked.

Kera peered out the window. "Yup, the cops are here, Vinny. It's showtime."

Vinny's eyes grew large. "How could they be here so fast? I thought you needed to call. We haven't coordinated the fight scene. I want to make sure we get it right."

She heard the doors of the police cars slamming shut. The sound of feet moving through gravel let her know they had no time to plan. "When they get in here, I'll start by telling them what happened. You listen well and don't change a hair of my story. After I give my side, you tell them that that's how it went down and you don't have anything to add. Later, if you don't know something or can't recall what I said, just tell them you don't remember. In situations like this, that's not uncommon."

"Yeah, okay, I can do that." Vinny took the handcuffs and hung them up near the key, then seemed to think better of it, grabbed them, tossing them on shelf behind some boxes.

"Oh, another thing," Kera said. "They'll take us in, separate us and have us tell our stories again. That's standard procedure. They'll try to poke a hole in what we've said, or get one of us to recant what we've already told them, maybe get one of us to blame the other one, or they might say to you that I ratted on you so I'd get a lesser sentence. Shit like that. I won't do that to you, and don't you do that to me." She gave him a stern look, hoping he felt confident about their plan, and would want to redeem himself with her.

Vinny nodded. "I promise I won't do that. I promise."

Kera added, "If they start to badger you or go on too long with it, ask for a lawyer and don't say another word. Got it?"

"Got it." Vinny nodded.

The door pushed open.

* * *

"Will Vinny be released, too?" Deidre opened the back door of the taxi and climbed inside.

"Yeah, the cops believed what we had to say. Really, when you think about it, there was no one else there to contradict us. Vinny's not out yet, but I saw him working to finish signing his papers about what happened at Sam's, like I had to do." Kera got into the cab after her sister.

She and Dee had gone to a café and eaten breakfast, where Dee told her everything that had happened after she'd been taken to jail from the bar, and Kera had filled her sister in on her end of the night.

After the cops hauled her and Vinny in for questioning, Kera had called Mandy's boss to ask her to act as her lawyer. She hadn't previously known Mandy's boss's name was Carolyn Rodgers. But when she found out, a light went on for her. In the short break from her coma, Mandy wasn't saying "Maryland," Vinny's nickname. She was probably trying to say something about Carolyn, her boss.

Also, Kera wanted Carolyn there to make sure Dee was released as well. She wouldn't have put it past the cops to neglect releasing her sister.

She'd endured hours of questioning at the police station that night, extending into the early hours of the morning. They'd separated her from Vinny, as she'd predicted, and made her go over and over how Sam's death went down. She was sure they'd done the same thing to Vinny. He had to have hung in tight with their story or they wouldn't be leaving right now.

When she'd seen him briefly on her way out, he'd given her a smile and a quick thumbs-up. Luckily, the cop walking beside him hadn't seen him do it, or they might have yanked them both back into their respective interrogation rooms.

Surprisingly, she wasn't ready for bed, though she'd been up for hours on end. She was extremely fatigued, but floating in blissful triumph, propelled by fumes of success causing her to feel high. She'd gotten herself and her sister out of the mess they'd fallen into.

When Dee had asked her how she could have so much energy, she'd told her she was on a drug called Escape from Disaster. But she knew she would crash and fall at any moment and needed a bed nearby to catch her. That's when Dee called the taxi.

Deidre moved over on the backseat of the cab to make room for her. "Wow, so much happened, it's hard to absorb all you've told me.

I feel so bad for Sylvia. I just don't know what she'll do now. I can't believe it about Harry, you know—"

"Oh, here, the cop at the desk said he forgot to give this to you." Kera held out the cap Dee had been wearing with the rest of her disguise. "Maybe you ought to keep it, kind of looks cute on you, not to speak of the baggy pants, suspenders and T-shirt. And have I told you how cute you look in a skeleton motif?"

"Shut up, Kera. You're in enough trouble with me, having Ally switch our driver's licenses and sending me, once again, to jail—this time to a cell." Dee's words were tough, but Kera saw the smile and love on her face. "It doesn't matter to me that you had your reasons for doing it, I—"

Kera slapped the cap on Dee's head and yanked the visor down over her face, curtailing the flow of their mother's tone coming out of her sister's mouth. "There's just no appreciation going on here, Dee. I keep us from a lifetime in prison, clear our names and—"

The driver turned to look at them. "Excuse me, but where do ya want to go?"

She and Dee glanced at each other, then at the driver, and in almost-perfect unison chimed, "We're going home."

EPILOGUE

Almost A Year Later

Kera bent over, took off her sandals and rolled up her jeans. She wanted to feel the cool, hard-packed sand on her feet as she walked along the beach with her dog, Lakota.

Mandy ran up behind them. She'd stopped to pick up a shell. "What did your therapist say?" Mandy reached down and plucked out a gull's feather sticking straight up in the sand. She rubbed it on the side of her face and reached over with it, tickling Kera on her neck.

"She says it will take time, that's what she always says. Mostly right now, I'm into short-term goals, like not being so jumpy or worrying about what or who is around every corner. That's what I like about walking on the beach. I can see all around me and far away, no surprises around corners, or wondering who or what is in a room or building."

Kera enjoyed cool water on her feet as she splashed along the water's edge. She'd walked the beach all winter, no matter how cold or snowy. The walks calmed her. Now with summer almost here, the temperature was warm enough to take off her shoes and feel the connection with the earth.

"I get jealous of her." Mandy watched the tan and black German shepherd-rottweiler mix running toward them with the tennis ball Kera had thrown out for her. "Lakota's got the place in your heart that I want, or at least be able to share a piece of."

Kera took the slobbery wet fuzzy ball out of Lakota's mouth and threw it back down the beach. "Can you fetch a ball or pop a corner for me?" She gave Mandy a serious look, then cracked a smile and said, "It's a requirement for conquering my heart." She knew her last statement really wasn't much of a joke. She was doing better these days, having Lakota with her all the time. Plus, the dog was her love.

"So that's what it takes." Mandy laughed. "I think I'd have no problem fetching a ball, but popping a corner? I'd try if I knew what it was."

"It's going in a place ahead of me, making sure there's nothing lurking or threatening."

Mandy squeezed her lips shut, twisting them up on one side. "Hmm, I could be taught like Lakota. That is, if I have the right handler." She gave Kera a wry smile. "By the way, how did Vinny learn how to teach Lakota to do all those things?"

"He's trained dogs in the past. He worked with some famous trainer years ago—at least, famous in the dog-training world. Actually, after working with Lakota, he's decided to get back into it. Said he missed it. He figures he could do both dog training and run his shop without a problem. Who would have guessed it? The dog that came barging in and sent me under that table at the Pink Door is now a calm and protective part of my life." Kera took the ball Lakota offered her, then gave her a quick scratch behind her ear.

Mandy stopped, sat down on a large rock, took off her shoes and socks and rolled up her pant legs. She looked at Kera. "I think I could block people from getting near you, like Lakota does."

"She's never done that to you, has she?"

"Yes, she did. Don't you remember when I got in your car at the airport? She insisted on sitting in the passenger's seat until you made her get in the back. But I have to say, since you've let her know I am okay, she's been...well, more tolerant of me." Mandy patted Lakota on the head.

The dog now pranced between them, the ball secure in her mouth.

Kera had missed Mandy these past months while she was gone. Shortly after Mandy got out of the hospital, she'd taken a leave of absence from Legal Aid and gone to Arizona, staying the winter with a cousin to give herself time to fully recuperate.

While Mandy was away, Kera had realized how valuable Mandy had been to the LGBT community because LEAP fell apart after her departure. No one had been strong enough or had the will to step up and fill in for Mandy, allowing Citizens Against Perversion to manage a successful petition drive and vote, resulting in LGBT people being excluded from Lakeside City's Civil Rights Ordinance, cementing in prejudice and keeping itself one of the most backward cities in the state.

Mandy had been back in town only a week. Kera was happy to see her return, but she wasn't sure what she could give to Mandy or what Mandy expected of her, emotionally or otherwise.

Kera had spent the winter at her dad's house sorting through things and trying to settle his estate. She'd found the task arduous and depressing, but her sister wasn't up to it, so the job fell to her. During that time, Dee was pretty much the only person she saw except for her therapist, support group and good ol' repentant Vinny.

One Thursday night, when she and Vinny had teamed up for the pool tournament, Vinny asked her about adopting Lakota.

Vinny had caught the stray mutt who'd knocked him off the ladder and was looking for a home for her. He thought maybe Kera would like the dog, but she hadn't been sure she wanted the responsibility of trying to take care of something other than herself. One day, Vinny told her about a program where dogs were being trained to help people with PTSD. He'd looked into it and was sure he could teach Lakota the way those dogs were being trained. She'd thought about it, but continued to be skeptical about the whole thing. However, on Christmas, Vinny brought her the dog with a big red bow around her neck. Lakota had walked right up to her, carrying a leash in her mouth and proffering a paw.

Looking in those big brown eyes had melted her heart. Now she and Lakota were inseparable. Just running her hands through the dog's fur calmed her. Vinny was convinced Lakota's soothing properties had improved her pool game as well.

She took Lakota everywhere. The Out-and-About bar, the Pink Door and other public places around town let Lakota come in with her, the same as they would any service dog.

Today, she was giving Lakota off-duty playtime. She tossed the ball down the beach. The dog took off, but before she reached it, another dog, a white Labradoodle, raced over, got it and stood with the ball in its mouth, tail wagging and watching excitedly as Lakota came up.

A woman yelled, "Sakari, that's not your ball, drop it, please."

Kera yelled back, "That's okay, my dog's friendly and would love to share her ball and play with your dog."

The woman smiled, sat down on a beach blanket next to another woman and picked up a book, while the two dogs ran on the beach together, jumping in and out of the water.

Mandy asked, "How's Deidre doing? I saw her at the mall yesterday. She mentioned she liked being full-time at the hospital these days. And she introduced me to a woman…uh, Cheryl, can't remember her last name. I think I caught a vibe between the two of them. Is there anything going on there?"

"Who knows? Dee needs to come around, sooner or later. Hopefully, in this lifetime. If there is anything going on between them, Dee will take her sweet time telling me. She'll hate it that I'm right about 'our' sexuality."

The dogs came running back to her. She took the ball out of Lakota's mouth and threw it for her and the Labradoodle friend. They tore off, chasing it down the beach.

"We can just hope the best for her, can't we?" Mandy chuckled. "And it wouldn't be the first time an in-denial lesbian married a closeted gay man."

"Yeah, Don tried so hard to keep his sexuality down by preaching against it. That's my therapist's take, anyway. For me, I couldn't keep it down like that. It would be like trying to hold a beach ball under the water. It'd keep popping up on me."

"Well, it did for Don too. His religion didn't save him, did it?"

Kera shook her head. "Sure didn't."

"But the outcome kind of begs the question about Deidre, don't you think? If she's gay, how's she kept it down all these years?" Mandy took out sunglasses from her pocket and put them on.

"I'd say, by marrying a guy who probably wasn't that interested in sex—at least not with her. Besides, she's always had more control than I've had. Probably because she needed to be the good girl, for the sake of our parents. Maybe she figured having two of us like me would've been pretty hard on our mom and dad. I don't know, but maybe with all that's happened and with our parents gone, she'll be able to rid herself of being the 'good child.'"

Kera felt the dog's nose nudge her hand with the wet, sandy tennis ball. She reached for the ball and saw Sakari, not Lakota. She laughed, grabbed the ball and tossed it in the water. Lakota and Sakari bounded into the lake. "Say, I forgot, when did you tell me you were starting back at Legal Aid?"

"Next Monday." Mandy picked up a small piece of driftwood and examined it. "I think this would look good on my mantel, don't you?"

Kera nodded.

"Speaking of working, what are your plans for supporting yourself for the rest of your life? You haven't talked about that, at least not to me." Mandy put the driftwood in her jacket pocket.

"In a month or two, I should be finishing up Dad's estate. After that, I'm thinking I'll just fish off that dock up there." Kera pointed to the city pier. "That'd take care of me for this summer. Then for the winter, I could find myself a woman to live off—a sugar mama. That's my first year's plan." She laughed. "Actually for now, I don't have to worry about it. I have funds and my therapist says I should give myself time to heal."

Lakota came back with the ball, handed it over and shook herself, scattering droplets of lake water. "Lakota, why do you always have to do that right next to me? Go shake somewhere else." Kera shooed her dog away.

"The economy is horrid right now, just as well you're not in the job market." Mandy had gotten some of Lakota's shower as well. She wiped her wet arm on her pants.

"I really have been thinking about my future. I don't want to turn into some of the soldiers I see coming back from the war. Some have been back for years and still not gotten it together. It's not pretty."

Mandy raised her eyebrows. "So what are you coming up with?"

"I don't think I want to work for anyone if I can help it. I'd be better off self-employed. I've been thinking about my background in college—journalism and criminology—and my work as an MP in the army. Maybe, I'll look into becoming a private investigator. I will be getting money from Dad's estate. That should carry me for a while, until I can establish myself and start making money at it." She turned to Mandy. "What do you think of that?"

"I say it's a good thing the District Attorney dropped the charges against you for assaulting an officer, because that kind of a rap would definitely keep you from getting licensed."

"Yeah, I guess the DA figured they'd made lots of mistakes on their part of the investigation, so it was sort of a tit for tat thing."

"Really, Kera, I think you'd be very good at that kind of work. Hell, you solved Don's case for the police—"

"Well, I had personal interest in the case, like trying to keep me and Dee from going to prison. But thanks for the vote of confidence. I told my plans to Dee the other day. She shuddered and said I was trying to make her life miserable." Kera picked up a stone and skipped it on the water's surface.

"What did she mean by that?"

"By choosing 'another dangerous career,' according to her. She's always worried about me. Ever since she turned around and saw I was following her out of the womb, she's been fretting about me for what I am doing or what I might do. When I went to Iraq, she was distraught. You'd have thought I was already sent home in a body bag."

"I'm not sure I would have felt much differently." Mandy looked at her.

Kera ignored Mandy's comment and went on. "But back to doing detective work, I think it would suit me, at least after a while, when I'm feeling like my emotional feet are squarely under me. I've also thought about journalism, a reporter maybe, but I'm not sure where that field is headed given all the newspapers shutting down. Private investigative work might be best. There'll always be a demand. I'm glad you think I'd be good at it, because I'll need the encouragement, and even more so, the prodding. Right now, I don't feel like doing much. The only reason I even thought about what I might do in the future was because my therapist asked me to. It was one of her homework assignments she likes to give me. But frankly, I feel like I could spend the rest of my life sitting on a dock with a fishing pole."

"I didn't know you liked to fish."

"I didn't say anything about fishing, just sitting with a pole in my hand." Kera gave Mandy a smile, but she knew that wasn't far from the truth of it. She really had no ambition to do much else, other than hang out with her dog.

"It'll get better for you." Mandy took her hand and squeezed it.

She liked the feel of Mandy's hand holding hers, but the feeling scared her too. "I'm not ready…I mean, I'm not relationship material. You know that, right?"

"You will be someday and you don't have to be perfect to have a relationship. Not with me, anyway. Besides, you're okay just as you are. But I respect your needing space and healing right now. I'm not going anywhere. I'll be around when the time comes, if that's what you want. Until then, how about us being friends and maybe get some lovin' now and then?" Mandy tossed her a seductive glance.

Kera smiled. "I think I could handle that."

Bella Books, Inc.

Women. Books. Even Better Together.

P.O. Box 10543
Tallahassee, FL 32302

Phone: 800-729-4992
www.bellabooks.com